As ife, with the life she'd carved out for herself, she wanted Will.

Maybe it was just lust.

She sighed and then realized that he'd been staring at her.

"Sorry. I guess I'm getting tired. What did you say?"

"I didn't say anything. I was only watching you, regretting that I didn't kiss you when we were on our ride," he said.

Kiss her? "I thought we'd both decided that was a bad idea."

"I like bad ideas," he said.

* * *

Billionaire's Baby Bind
is part of the series Texas Cattleman's Club:
Blackmail—No secret—or heart—
is safe in Royal, Texas…

BILLIONAIRE'S BABY BIND

BY
KATHERINE GARBERA

First Published in Great Britain 2017
By Mills & Boon, an imprint of HarperCollins*Publishers*
1 London Bridge Street, London, SE1 9GF

Special thanks and acknowledgement are given to Katherine Garbera for her contribution to the Texas Cattleman's Club: Blackmail series.

ISBN: 978-0-263-92839-6

51-1017

Our policy is to use papers that are natural, renewable and recyclable products and made from wood grown in sustainable forests. The logging and manufacturing processes conform to the legal environmental regulations of the country of origin.

Printed and bound in Spain
by CPI, Barcelona

USA TODAY bestselling author **Katherine Garbera** writes heartwarming and sensual novels that deal with romance, family and friendship. She's written more than seventy-five novels and is a featured speaker at events all over the world.

She lives in the UK with her husband and Godiva (a very spoiled miniature dachshund), and she's frequently visited by her college-age children, who need home-cooked meals and laundry service. Visit her online at www.katherinegarbera.com.

Thank you to all of the Harlequin Desire authors,
editors and readers who have welcomed me
as part of this wonderful reading family.

One

Amberley Holbrook wasn't too keen on meeting new people; she preferred the company of her horses and keeping an eye on the stables where she worked. Normally her boss, Clay Everett of the Flying E, was happy to let her do what she wanted. But they had a guest on the property who had told Clay that he liked to ride. So as a courtesy Clay had suggested she stop by and introduce herself and offer to take the guest for a ride.

This held little appeal for Amberley. First of all, the dude was from Seattle, and the last time she checked there weren't any real cowboys from there, so that meant he was some kind of city slicker. Second...she and city slickers didn't get along. She would be the first to admit that was all down to her and her lousy attitude, which was something her father had advised her to keep in check if she wanted to keep this job.

Third…well, there wasn't any third. Digging in her heels and refusing to do as Clay had asked certainly wasn't an option. Amberley had packed more into her twenty-four years than most of her peers. She knew she needed to keep her job because she loved the horses she took care of and she certainly didn't want to go back to her family's ranch in Tyler, Texas.

That was something her daddy had been sure to remind her of when she'd called him earlier and told him about Clay's guest. She and her father were close. Her mom had died when Amberley was thirteen and she'd had four younger siblings to watch over. She and her dad had worked as a team to make sure everything on the ranch got done and her younger siblings, ranging in ages from four to ten, were taken care of. Sometimes her dad would say he cheated her out of a childhood, but Amberley never felt that way. She had her horse, Montgomery, and her family, and until she'd turned eighteen, that was all that had mattered.

Amberley understood why she was nervous about this new guest. The city guy had rented a danged Ford Mustang to drive around in this rugged Texas landscape. She could see the sports car parked next to the guest house that Clay had assigned him.

The Flying E was a sprawling ranch built in the heyday of Clay Everett's Professional Bull Riding career. He'd been at the top of his game until a bull named Iron Heart had thrown him. Clay had had a few ups and downs, but landed back on his feet and started a new career as CEO of Everest, a company that provided ironclad cloud infrastructure to companies. Amberley was the first to admit she had no idea what that really was, but it made Clay a nice fortune and enabled him to employ her as his full-time horse master.

She took care of the stables on the Flying E, provided lessons to locals from Royal and the surrounding county and made sure any guest of the Everetts had access to horses. The ranch itself was sprawling, with a large mansion for the main house and several smaller guest houses. Amberley lived in a cottage that suited her to a T. She'd always wanted her own place and lots of ranch land, something that was beyond the budget of a simple barrel racer like herself. So living on the Flying E and working for Clay gave her the best of both worlds.

She took another look at the sports car.

City guy.

As a teen, she'd watched shows like *Gossip Girl* and longed to be in Manhattan, though she'd have stuck out like…well, a sore thumb, but she had liked the fantasy of it.

So perhaps it wasn't quite so surprising that this man was making her curious before she'd even met him.

"Are you going to knock or just stand here all day?" Cara asked as she stood in front of the guest cabin that had been assigned to Will. The cabin itself was really a sprawling three-bedroom cottage that was all natural wood and glass.

Cara was seventeen and also worked on the ranch with Amberley, as her apprentice. She'd brought the teenager with her to meet Clay's new guest to be sure Amberley didn't do anything…well, stupid.

"Yeah. I was just waiting for the music to die down a little."

"I don't think it's going to," Cara said. "I thought he had a baby. You'd think the old dude would put on some headphones."

"You think he's old?"

Cara raised both eyebrows at Amberley. "Most def. He's got a kid, right? So, I'm guessing he must be old—"

"Geez, kid, back in my day we had to boot up a big old DOS machine and wait half a day for our computers to start working."

The voice was deep and rich, like the faux bass line in White Stripes' "Seven Nation Army," and Amberley felt a blush starting at her chest and working up over her cheeks as she turned to look at him. Their eyes met. His were forest green and made her think of the meadow she rode past each morning on her dawn ride on Montgomery.

There was a sardonic note in his voice that she totally got.

He wasn't old.

He wasn't old at all.

He wore a faded MIT T-shirt that clung to his shoulders and lean stomach. He had on a pair of faded jeans that hung low on his hips, and as she glanced down at his feet she noticed he had on Converse sneakers.

He was exactly what she'd been fearing and, if she was honest, secretly hoping he would be.

"You don't look too bad for your age," Amberley said. "I'm Amberley Holbrook, horse master, and this is my apprentice, Cara. Clay asked me to introduce myself and let you know that the stables are available for your use."

"Thanks," he said, holding out his hand to Cara. "Will Brady. Ancient one."

"Geez, dude, I'm sorry. I was just being mouthy. My mom has been warning me about that forever," Cara said.

"It's all right. I probably do seem ancient to a high schooler."

Cara shook his hand. Amberley wiped her hands on the sides of her jeans and took a deep breath and then their hands met. His skin wasn't dry and rough, the way so many of the hands of the men on the ranch were. They were soft, and as she looked down she noticed that his nails were neat and intact, not split from accidentally smashing one with a hammer.

She rubbed her thumb over his knuckles and then realized what she was doing and dropped his hand.

"Anyway… Come over to the stables anytime. I'll have to observe you riding before I can clear you to ride alone."

"No problem. I'll probably stop by this afternoon," he said. "I have a conference call with the sheriff this morning."

"Is this about Maverick?" Cara asked. "I heard you were in town to stop him."

Will shrugged and gave her a self-deprecating smile. "Just going to see what I can find on the internet to track that SOB down."

"I know we will all be glad for that," Amberley said. "I'm pretty much always at the stables, so stop by anytime."

Cara arched one eyebrow at Amberley but kept

her mouth shut, and they turned and walked back toward the stables. She tried to tell herself that he was just a guy…but she knew that he was so much more than that.

Amberley wasn't the kind of woman who had time for gossip or staring at hot guys. Yet she'd found herself riding by his place for the last two mornings hoping for a glimpse of him. Instead she'd had a conversation with Erin Sinclair, Will's nanny, and she'd even cuddled his cute daughter, eleven-month-old Faye.

Will had called down to the stables earlier to say he was going to come by for a ride, but he wasn't sure when the computer program he'd been running would be done. So it could be anytime between now and sunset. She was trying to focus on the work she had to do. There were horses to tame to the saddle, and she liked it that way. She'd always preferred animals over people. They were easy to predict, she thought. She'd grown up in a very large family, and the thought of having her own, well… She liked kids and men, but having to take care of her own brood made her break out in hives.

"You have to admit he's hot," Cara said. "Not old at all."

"He's a city slicker who probably can't tell a horse from steer. Who has time for that?" Amberley asked.

She and Cara were both grooming horses for the newcomers so they'd be able to take a ride around Clay Everett's ranch and get the lay of the land. When Cara had asked Amberley if she could help her out at the ranch, her gut instinct had been to say no. After all, what exactly did she have to teach the high school girl, but Cara had been insistent and one thing had led to another, and now she was in the barn grooming horses with a chatty seventeen-year-old.

"I'm just saying if a guy like that looked at me—"

"Your boyfriend would be jealous," Amberley said. Cara was dating one of the varsity football players.

"Yeah, he would be. For now. Next year he'll be gone and I'll be…I don't know where I'll be. Did you ever wish you'd gone to college?" Cara asked.

Amberley thought about it. At seventeen she'd wanted to get as far away from Texas, her siblings and the ranching life as she could. She'd wanted a chance to be on her own. But her family hadn't had the money for college and, to be honest, Amberley had only been an okay student. No one had been offering her any money for school and this job with Clay had come along at the right time. She'd met his foreman when she'd been rodeoing during her early teens and he'd offered the job.

It hadn't been her dream, but it had meant she'd be out of her dad's house and away from the siblings she'd had to babysit, and that had seemed like a dream.

At times, it was easy to forget she'd once wanted something else from life. She wasn't a whiner and didn't have time to listen to herself think of things that might have been. It was what it was.

"Not really. I have my horses and Clay pretty much lets me have the freedom to run the barn the way I want to. What more could a gal ask for?" Amberley said, hoping that some of her ennui wasn't obvious to Cara.

"I hope I feel like that someday."

"You will. You're seventeen, you're not supposed to have it all figured out," she said.

"I hope so," Cara said. Her phone pinged.

"Go on and chat with your friends. I can finish up the other horse. You know he mentioned he didn't know when he'd be down here."

"Here I am," a masculine voice said. "I hope I'm not interrupting."

Amberley felt the heat on her face and knew she was blushing. She could blame it on her redhead complexion, but she knew it was embarrassment. She could only be glad he hadn't arrived any earlier.

"Not disappointed at all," she said, reaching for her straw cowboy hat before stepping out of the stall and into the main aisle of the barn.

She'd sort of hoped that he wouldn't be as good-looking as she remembered. But that wasn't the case. In fact, his thick blond-brown hair looked even thicker today and his jaw was strong and clean-shaven. His green eyes were intense and she couldn't look away from him.

She told herself her interest in him was just because he was so different than the other men around the ranch.

If he had a pair of Wrangler jeans and some worn ranch boots she wouldn't be interested in him at all. But the fact that he had a Pearl Jam T-shirt on and a pair of faded jeans that clung to all the right spots was the only reason she was even vaguely attracted to him.

She noticed his mouth was moving and she thought she wouldn't mind it moving against hers. But then she realized he was speaking when Cara, who'd come out of her stall as well, looked at her oddly.

"Sorry about that. What did you say?"

"I was just saying that I'm sorry if just showing up messed up your schedule. I do appreciate you being available on my timetable," he said. "If you need more time to get ready I can wait over there."

She shook her head. He was being so reasonable. But she just had a bee in her bonnet when it came to this guy. Well, to all men who came from the city. She wished he wasn't so darn appealing. That maybe his voice would be soft or odd, but of course, he didn't have some silly city voice. Instead, his words were like a deep timbre brushing over her ears and her senses like a warm breeze on a summer's day. Since it was Texas, October wasn't too cool, but it was fall and she missed summer.

But with him… Dammit. She had to stop this.

"I'm ready. Cara, will you show Mr. Brady to his horse?" she asked her apprentice, who was watching her with one of those smirks only a teenager could manage.

"Sure thing, Ms. Holbrook," Cara said sarcastically.

"You can call me Will," he told Cara.

"Ms. Holbrook, can Will call you Amberley?"

That girl. She was pushing Amberley because she knew she could. "Of course."

"Thanks, Amberley," he said.

She told herself that there was nothing special about the way he said her name, but it sent shivers—the good kind—down her spine. She had to nip this attraction in the bud. Will was going to be here for a while helping Max St. Cloud investigate the cyberbully and blackmailer Maverick, who'd been wreaking havoc on the local residents, particularly the members of the Texas Cattleman's Club, releasing videos and other damning stories on the internet. Will was the CTO of the company, so he was more of a partner to Max than an employee, and rumor had it they were old friends.

"No prob," she said. "How'd you end up here in Royal?" Amberley asked Will while Cara went to get his horse.

"Chelsea Hunt and Max go way back. So she asked for our help to try to find the identity of Maverick."

Maverick had been doing his best to make life hell for the members of the Texas Cattleman's Club. He'd been revealing secrets gleaned from hacking into smartphones and other internet connected devices. He'd made things uncomfortable for everyone in Royal.

"I like Chelsea. She's smart as a whip," Amberley said. And she seemed to really have her stuff together. No shrinking violet, Chelsea was one of the women that Amberley looked up to in Royal. She lived her life on her own terms, and Amberley was pretty sure that if Chelsea liked a guy she didn't have to come up with reasons to avoid him…the way that Amberley herself had been doing.

Cara came back with Will's mount and Amberley went back into the stall and saw her faithful horse, Montgomery, waiting for her. She went to the animal and rested her forehead against the horse's neck. Montgomery curved her head around Amberley's and she felt a little bit better. She had always been better with horses than people.

And normally that wouldn't bother her. But it would be nice not to screw up around men as much as she just had with Will. She didn't enjoy feeling like an awkward country bumpkin.

Will hadn't expected to feel so out of place in Texas. He'd been to Dallas before and thought that the stereotype of boots, cowboy hats and horses was something from the past or in the imagination of television producers. But being here on the Flying E had shown him otherwise.

Amberley was cute and a distraction. Something—hell, someone—to take his mind off Seattle and all that he'd left behind there. All that he'd lost. To be honest, coming out here might have been what he needed. His baby girl was sleeping with her nanny watching over her, and he was someplace new.

Max hadn't batted an eye when Will had told him he needed to bring his daughter and her nanny along with him to Royal. His friend had known that Will was a dedicated single dad.

He had work to do, of course, but he'd ridden a long time ago and thought getting back on a horse might be the first step to moving on. From his wife's death.

It was funny, but after Lucy's death everyone had been comforting and left him to process his grief. But now that so many months had gone by and he was still in the same routine, they were starting to talk, and his mom and Lucy's mom weren't as subtle as they both liked to think they were, with their encouragement to "live again" and reminders that he still had a long life ahead of him.

Lucy had had a brain hemorrhage a few weeks before she was due. The doctors had kept her alive until she gave birth to Faye. Then they took her off the machines that had been keeping her alive and she'd faded away. He'd asked them to wait a week after Faye's birth because he hadn't wanted his daughter's birthday to also be the day she'd lost her mom.

"You okay?"

"Yeah. Sorry. Just distracted," he said.

"It happens," she said. She spoke with a distinctive Texan drawl. It was so different from Lucy's Northwestern accent that he… Hell, he needed to stop thinking about her. He was getting away for a while, helping out a friend and having a ride to clear his head. He knew he should let that be enough.

"It does. Sorry, I'm really bad company right now. I thought…"

"Hey. You don't have to entertain me. Whenever I'm in a bad place mentally—not saying you are—but when I am, I love to get out of the barn, take Montgomery here for a run. There's no time to think about anything except the terrain and my horse—it clears away the cobwebs in my mind."

He had just noticed how pretty her lips were. A shell-pink color. And when she smiled at him her entire face seemed to light up. "Just what I need. Let's do this."

"Well, before we get started I need to know what your horsemanship level is," she said. "We'll pick our route based on that."

"Summer camp and college polo team," he said.

"I stopped playing about three years ago. I'm a pretty decent rider and keep a horse at a stable near my home. But haven't been riding much since my daughter was born."

"Sounds like you might be a bit rusty but you've got some skills," she said. "I'll start ya out easy and see how it goes."

"I'm yours to command," he said.

"Mine to command? Not sure I've ever had anything with two legs under my command."

He threw his head back and laughed. She was funny, this one. He wasn't sure if she'd meant that to be a come-on, but there was something sort of innocent about her so he guessed not. She was very different from Lucy, his late wife. That twinge he always experienced at the thought of her colored the moment.

"Let's start with a ride," he said.

She nodded. "There's a mounting block over there if you need a leg up. I'll let you go first."

"Thanks," he said, leading his horse to the block and mounting easily. He shifted around in the saddle until he was comfortable. The horse she had him on was easily controlled and led and seemed comfortable with him as a rider.

"So why are you here?" she asked as she mounted her own horse.

He told himself to look away but didn't. Her jeans hugged the curve of her butt and as she climbed on the horse there was something very natural about how she moved. As she put both feet in the stirrups and sat up, he realized she looked more at home on horseback than she had talking to him.

"Ah, I'm here to investigate all the trouble that Maverick is causing. I'm really good at tracking someone's cyber footprint."

She shook her head and then gently brushed her heels against her horse and made a clicking sound. "I don't even know what a cyber footprint is."

He laughed a little at her comment. "Most people don't think about it, but with smartphones and social media apps, we all are leaving a trail that can be followed."

"That makes sense," she said. "You ready for a run or do you just want to take it slow and steady?" she asked as they left the barn area and reached the open plains.

The land stretched out as far as he could see. It was October, so in Seattle it was rainy and growing colder, but the sun was shining down on them today in Texas and the weather was warm. He lifted his face to the sun, taking a deep breath. It was a good day to be alive.

As the thought crossed his mind, he remembered Lucy again and shook his head. He wasn't going to cry for the wife he'd lost or the family that had been broken. Not now and not in front of this strong, sunny cowgirl.

"Run," he said.

"Just the answer I was hoping for. Follow me. I'm going to start slow and then build. This part of the ranch is safe enough for a run."

She took off and he sat there for a moment stuck in the past until she glanced over her shoulder, her long braid flying out to the side, and smiled at him.

"You coming?"

This ride was just the thing he needed to draw him out of the gloom of the past.

"Hell, yes."

Riding had always been Amberley's escape. But with Will riding by her side, she felt more fenced-in than free. Clay had asked everyone at the Flying E to make Will feel welcome and she tried to tell herself that was all she was doing now. He was just another guest, a city boy, at that. He was here temporarily. She didn't like to think about her past or about the guy she'd fallen too hard and too quickly for. But there was something about Will that brought that all up.

Mostly, she realized it was superficial. They were both outsiders to her way of life. But where Sam Pascal had been looking for some sort of Western fantasy, it seemed to her that Will was looking…well, for a cyberbully but also for some sort of escape. There was a sadness that lingered in his eyes and when he thought no one was looking she could see that he was battling with his own demons.

Something she battled herself.

She heard him thundering along behind her and glanced over her shoulder. He sat in the saddle well and moved like he'd been born to ride. It was hard to keep him shoved in the city-slicker box when she saw him on horseback. She turned to face the field in front of them, taking a moment just to be glad for this sunny October day.

It was good to be alive.

The air had the nip of fall to it and the sky was so

big it seemed to stretch forever. She slowed her horse and waited for Will to catch up to her.

He did in a moment and she glanced over to see a big smile on his face.

"I needed this."

Two

"Not bad for a city boy," Amberley told him as they allowed their horses to walk and cool down after their run. "I'm sorry I was judgmental about your skills."

Will couldn't help but like his riding guide. She was blunt and honest and it was refreshing. At work everyone treated him like he was the walking wounded and, of course, at home his nanny only discussed Faye. Rightly so. But Amberley didn't. She'd been treating him like a regular guy.

He hadn't realized how much he needed to get away and be with people who didn't know the personal details of his life. There was something freeing about being with Amberley on this sunny October afternoon. He felt for a moment like his old self. Before Lucy.

He felt a pang. Shook his head to shove the feeling from his mind.

"I didn't realize you were judging me," he said.

She tipped her cowboy hat back on her head and turned to gaze at him with a sardonic look. Her face was in shadows beneath the straw cowboy hat, but he could read her body language. She was sassy and funny, this cowgirl.

Distracting.

"I was judging you and it wasn't fair. It's just the last time I was around city folk was when I worked on this dude ranch in Tyler and a lot of them were… well, not very good riders. So I lumped you in with them. I should have known Clay wouldn't have told me to give you free rein if you didn't know what you were doing," she said. She held the reins loosely in one hand, and pushed the brim of her hat back on her forehead with the other.

Her eyes were a deep brown that reminded him of the color of his mocha in the morning. They were pretty and direct and he was almost certain when she was angry they'd show her temper. Will wondered how they'd look when she made love.

Then he shook his head.

This was the first time lust had come on so strongly since Lucy's death. And it took him by surprise.

He shook his head again. "To be fair, I'm not sure he knew my skill level. I think Max asked him to make sure I get the full Texas experience."

"The full Texas? That's funny. Well, this might be about it," she said, gesturing to the pastures.

He skimmed his gaze over the landscape and then settled back in the saddle. It reminded him of some of the places he'd visited growing up. His family had some property in Montana and there was a similar feeling of freedom from the real world here.

"I'm sure riding across the open plain isn't the only thing that's unique to Texas," he said. "You mentioned Tyler—did you just visit that dude ranch?"

"Nah," she said, looking away from him. But before she did he noticed a hint of sadness in her eyes. "I worked there when I was in high school in the summers. Clay offered me this job after…well, when I was ready to leave my family's ranch. My daddy said I was losing myself by mothering my brothers and sisters and he wanted me to have a chance to have my own life. I'm pretty good with horses. My daddy has a nice-sized ranch in Tyler. What about you? Where are you from? The Northwest, right?"

"Yes. Seattle area. Bellevue, actually. It's a suburb," he said. He'd never wanted to live anywhere else growing up. He loved the mountains and his waterfront property, but after Lucy…well, he'd been struggling to make Bellevue feel like home again.

"I've heard of it. I think Bill Gates lives there."

"We're not neighbors," Will said with a laugh.

She shook her head and laughed. "I'll jot that down. You ready for a ride back or you want to see some more?"

"What's left to see?"

She rocked back in her saddle, shifting to extend her arm. "Out that way is the south pasture—there's a creek that runs through it. Down that way is the—"

"Let me guess—north pasture."

"Ha. I was going to say castration shed. We do that in the spring," she said.

He shook his head. "I'll skip that."

"Guys always say that."

She was teasing him and he observed that her entire countenance had changed. Her relaxed smile made him realize how full and lush her mouth was, and the way she tipped her head to the side, waiting for his response, made him want to do something impulsive.

Like lean over and kiss her.

He slammed the door on that idea and sat back in his saddle to be a little farther away from her. There was just something about her easy smile and the wind stirring around them. And he was on horseback in Texas, so far away from his normal world, that he wanted to pretend he was someone different. A man who wasn't so tired from not sleeping and hoping he was making the right choices all the time.

He knew that nothing would come of kissing Amberley. He wasn't here to hook up. He was here to do a job. Besides that, he wasn't ready for anything else. He knew that. But for a moment, he wished he were.

"Back to the ranch."

She didn't move, but just stared at him—there was a closed expression on her face now. "Sorry, sir, didn't mean to be inappropriate. Follow me. You want to run back or walk?"

"Amberley—"

"I was out of line. I guess I forgot you were a guest for a second."

"Who did you think I was?" he asked.

"Just a guy," she said, turning her horse and making a clicking sound. Then she took off back the way they'd come.

* * *

He galloped after her and reached over to take her reins, drawing both of their rides to a stop.

She took back her reins and gave him a good hard glare. “Don’t do that again.”

“Well, I couldn’t figure out another way to stop you,” he yelled. He wasn’t sure what he’d stepped into, but he could tell something had changed and he was pretty damn sure he was the cause.

“Why would you want to?” she asked. “I’m pretty sure you want to get back to the ranch and I’m taking you there.”

“Don’t act that way,” he said. “I’m sorry. My life is complicated.”

She nodded and then looked away. “Everyone’s life is complicated. We’re not simple hicks out here on the ranch.”

He hadn’t meant to hurt or offend her.

And all of a sudden he felt ancient. Not twenty-eight. Not like a new father should feel, but like Methuselah. And he hated that. He’d always been…a different man. His father had said he was lucky and someday his luck would wear thin. But he knew his father wouldn’t rejoice in the way his luck had run out. Losing Lucy had changed him, and some people would say not for the better.

“I’m sorry,” he said. The words sounded rusty and forced but they weren’t. She didn’t deserve to be treated the way he’d treated her, because he wanted her and he knew he wasn’t going to do anything about it. He wasn’t about to invite another person into the chaos that his life was right now.

“What for?”

"That sounded…jerky, didn't it? Like I'm trying to imply that your life isn't complicated," he said. "That's not at all what I meant. I just meant I'm a mess and this ride was nice and you are wonderful…"

He trailed off. What else could he say? He thought she was cute. Maybe he'd like to kiss her, if he wasn't so stuck in that morass of guilt and grief. And then more guilt because his grief was starting to wane. And it's not like Lucy would have expected him to grieve forever, but moving on was like saying goodbye again.

"I wouldn't go that far," she said.

"What?"

"Saying I'm wonderful. I mean, I have faults like everyone else," she said. Her words were light and obviously meant to give him a way back from the dark place he'd wondered into. But in her eyes he saw weariness and he knew that she wasn't as…well, undamaged as he had believed she was.

"You seem like it from here," he said at last.

"Then I better keep up the illusion."

But now that she'd brought it up he was trying to see what there was to the young horsewoman. She seemed uncomplicated. He thought about how when he was her age, life had been pretty damned sweet.

"Tell me," he prompted.

"Tell you what?" she asked.

"Something that isn't wonderful about you," he said.

"Ah, well, I think that would be easy enough. I have a short temper. I believe I gave you a glimpse of that a moment ago."

"You sure did," he said with a laugh. "But that could also be called spunk. I like feisty women."

"You do?" she asked, then shook her head. "What about you? What's one of your faults?"

"Hell, I'm not even sure where to begin," he said. And he knew that he didn't want to open that can of worms. His life was littered with regrets lately. Only spending time with Faye or sitting in the dark working on the computer tracking down code seemed to get him out of his own head space.

"I'm not as clever as I once believed I was."

She started laughing. "Well, I think that's the same for all of us. Race you back to the barn?"

"Sure, but since I haven't ridden in a while I think I deserve a handicap."

"Really?" she asked. "That is such a load of crap. If I hadn't seen you ride out here I might have fallen for it."

"It was worth a try," he said.

The fall breeze blew, stirring the air, and a strand of her red hair slipped from her braid and brushed against her cheek. He leaned forward in his saddle and gripped the reins to keep from reaching out and touching her.

He'd just shoved a big wedge between them. A smart man would leave it in place. A smart man would remember that Amberley wasn't a woman to mess with and he had never been the kind of man who screwed around with anyone.

But he didn't feel smart.

He felt lonely and like it had been too long since he'd been able to breathe and not catch the faint scent of hospital disinfectant. He wanted to sit here until night fell and then maybe he'd think about heading back to the life he had. He wanted…

Something he wasn't in a position to take.

He knew that.

"Hey, Will?"

He looked up, realizing that she'd been staring at him the entire time.

"Yeah?"

"Don't sweat it. I've got a beef with city dudes and it's clear that you have something with your baby's mama to deal with. You're hot and the way you ride a horse makes me feel things I'd rather not admit to, but that's it. You're on the Flying E to work and as a guest and I'm going to treat you like that. So don't think…"

"What do you feel?" he asked.

Will knew he felt reckless and dangerous and he wasn't going to stop now. He wanted to kiss her. He wanted to pull her off the horse and into his arms and see where that led.

"Like I said, I'm not going there."

He shifted in the saddle and dismounted his horse, dropping the reins on the ground to check that the horse would stay, and it did.

Will walked over to her and stood there next to her horse, looking up at her. He was closer now, and he could see her eyes, and he wasn't sure what he read in her expression. He was going to tell himself it was desire and need. The same things he was feeling, but he was afraid he might be projecting.

"Come on down here," he said. "Just for this afternoon let's pretend we aren't those people. I'm not a guest and you're not a ranch hand. We're just a guy and his girl and we've got this beautiful afternoon to spend together."

* * *

Never in her life had Amberley wanted to get off a horse more. But her gut said no. That this wasn't going to be sweet or uncomplicated. And the last time she'd been sweet-talked by a guy it hadn't ended well. It didn't matter that she was older and wiser now. She didn't feel as if she was either.

Riding hadn't helped to chase away her demons back then, when she'd found herself pregnant and alone at eighteen, and it wasn't helping now. He stood there in his clothes, not fake-cowboy duded up the way some city guys dressed when they came to Texas, and to be fair he looked like he fit in. He wasn't chasing a Wild West fantasy, he was here to do a job.

And her job was to make him feel comfortable.

What could be more comfortable than hanging out together?

Dumb.

Stupid.

His hair was thick and wavy and he wasn't wearing a hat, so she could see the way he'd tousled it when he'd run his fingers through it. She wasn't getting off her horse. She was going to be sensible.

Please, Amberley, be sensible.

But she never had been.

She suspected it was because she'd had to be so responsible so young. She'd always had to take care of her younger brothers and sisters. But that was in Tyler, and she was away from there now, with no one to worry about but herself.

And this was safe. He just wanted to spend the afternoon together.

One afternoon.

Surely even she could manage that without having it go to hell.

She shifted and started to turn to swing her leg over the saddle and dismount, then she saw the smile on his face and the look of relief.

He was unsure.

Just like her.

Except he wasn't like her. He had ties. And she hadn't asked about them earlier. There was so much she didn't know. Where was his baby's mother? That baby was pretty damn young to be living with a nanny and her father. Was there any way this could be just an afternoon?

If it was…then the mom didn't matter… Unless they were still together. That would be—

"Hey, before we do this. Where is your baby's mother? I don't want to pry but you're not still with her, right?" she asked.

He stepped back—stumbled was more like it—and she suddenly wished she'd kept her mouth shut.

There was no denying the way all the color left his face, or how he turned away from her and cursed under his breath.

"No," he said, walking back over to his horse and taking his saddle with much skill and finesse.

"We're not still together. She's dead." He made a clicking sound and took off across the field as if the hounds of hell were chasing him, and Amberley guessed maybe they were.

She stood there, a wave of sadness rolling over her. A part of her had died when she'd miscarried. Seeing Will…had made her realize that they were two sides of the same coin. She had no baby and no family and he had a baby and no wife or mother for the child. He was trying to deal with the loss the same way she had been.

She knew that riding helped at times but she'd never been able to outrun the pain. Those memories and the truth of her life were always waiting when she'd gotten off the horse.

She clicked her mare and followed Will close enough to call out if he took a path that wasn't safe, but he had watched their trail on the way out and he made no mistakes on the way back.

She slowed her own horse to a walk as Will entered the stable area and decided that maybe she should just let him go. Give him some space to dismount and leave before she entered the barn again.

She saw the ring that she'd set up earlier to practice barrel racing and rode over that way. Montgomery and she had been partners for the last year or so. And when the Flying E could spare her she took the horse and went and competed in rodeos.

Three

Will had just spent the last ten minutes in the barn trying to avoid a confrontation with Amberley—the woman he'd practically run away from. But he had no doubt she would be avoiding him after his foolish reaction to her harmless question about Faye's mother.

It was hard to think that at twenty-eight he was turning into his father, but it seemed that way more and more. And it wasn't Faye who was forcing the change. It was him. It was as if he'd lost that spark that had always driven him. And the therapist he'd seen for two sessions at his mom's insistence had said that grief took time.

But as he left the barn and spotted Amberley exercising her horse in the ring, he felt that stirring again.

It was lust, because even though he was grieving he wasn't dead, and the feeling was laced with something more. Something much more. She was one with the horse as she raced around the barrels, her braid flying out behind her as she leaned into the curves and got low over the horse's neck, whispering encouragement, he imagined.

He watched her and wanted her.

She stopped at the end of her run and looked over toward the barn. Their eyes met and he felt stupid just standing there.

He clapped.

But that felt dumb, too.

It seemed that he'd left his smarts behind in Seattle, he thought. Everything was different here. He tried to justify his feelings—like he needed an excuse to find a woman pretty or be turned on by her. Yet in a way he felt he did.

But that was his issue, not Amberley's. And it wasn't fair to her to bring her into the swirling whirlpool that his emotions were at this moment.

She nodded and then turned away from him.

Dismissing him.

He'd had his chance and he'd ruined it.

Maybe it was for the best. He had Faye to take care of and a criminal to catch. In fact, he needed to get back to work. Without another glance at her he turned and walked to the golf cart that had been allocated for his use during his stay on the Flying E. He put it in gear and drove to the house that Clay Everett had been generous enough to provide. To be honest, he knew that Clay had a stake in Will finding Maverick, as did most of Royal.

He shifted gears as he drove farther and farther away from the barn and the cowgirl that he'd left there, but a part of his mind was still fantasizing about the way his afternoon could have gone.

His nanny, Erin Sinclair, was waiting for him at the door when he got back.

"Faye's asleep and I need to run to town to pick up some more baby food and formula. Are you okay if I go now?" she asked.

He had hired Erin to help with the baby even before Lucy's untimely death. His late wife had been a product rep for a large pharmaceutical company and traveled a lot for work. Though Will spent a lot of time in his home office, he tended to have a single-minded focus, so he knew that by the time Faye was born, both he and Lucy would have needed help with the baby.

"Yes, go," he said.

He went into the bedroom they used as a nursery and looked down at Faye's sleeping face. He tried to see Lucy in her features but he was starting to forget what she looked like. Of course he had pictures of her but he was starting to lose that feeling of what she'd looked like as she smiled at him. The different feeling she'd stirred in him with one of her expressions that a mere photo couldn't capture.

Dammit.

He turned away from the crib and walked out of the room. He had a monitor app on his phone and had a window that he could keep open on one of the many monitors in his office so he could keep an eye on her.

He walked into the darkened large bedroom that he'd turned into his office for the duration of his stay in Royal. He had four large computer monitors that were hooked up to different hard drives and were all running multiple programs that would determine where Maverick was basing himself online.

Almost all of the attacks had been cyber-based, so Chelsea was working on the theory that he was very internet savvy. In a way that worked in their favor because there weren't many top computer experts in Royal. But then hackers wouldn't be known to many.

One of Will's skills was the ability to look at code and see a digital fingerprint in it. Maverick had habits just like everyone and Will was searching for those, looking for a trail back to the creep's identity.

He opened his laptop after he checked the progress on the different computers and made sure all of his scripts were still running.

He launched his internet browser and searched for information on Amberley Holbrook. He wasn't surprised to see her listed in a bunch of small-town rodeos, stretching from Texas to Oklahoma to Arkansas, as a winner or a top-three finisher in barrel-racing competitions. There was a photo of her winning run in a recent event and he clicked to open it larger in his photo application so he could zoom in on her face. There was concentration but also the biggest damn grin he'd ever seen.

That girl was happiest on the back of a horse.

Why?

He noticed how she was when she was off her horse. On her guard and waiting to see how everyone around her reacted. Given that he was starting to behave that way, he wondered what had happened to force her to build those kinds of walls. She definitely had them.

Why?

And why the hell did he care?

Because she intrigued him. She was different. Funny, sexy, sassy. She made him think of things he hadn't in a really long time.

And he'd just walked away from her. He'd decided he had too much baggage to dally with a woman who was tied to Texas and this ranch. He wasn't here for longer than it took to find the cyber coward Maverick, then he was out of here. And back in the Pacific Northwest, where he could slowly rot from guilt and grief.

That sounded damn pitiful. He had never been that kind of man and he wasn't too sure that Faye was going to want a father who was like that.

He knew he had to move on.

Will had come here in part because Max had asked and also because he knew he had to get away from the memories, get away from the guilt and the grief. But he was in no position to move on. He had to keep moving forward until he figured out what he wanted next. Amberley had been a distraction but also something more. She was honest and forthright. He liked that.

He liked her.

If he were in a different place in his life then the zing of attraction that had arced between them…well, he would feel better about acting on it.

But he wasn't.

And that wasn't fair to her.

Who said life was fair… The words of his therapist drifted through his mind. He'd been lamenting the fact that Faye would never know Lucy and that it wasn't fair.

Well, life might not be, but he knew he couldn't just use Amberley for himself and then leave. That wasn't right.

And he hadn't changed at his core.

But she intrigued him…

Amberley blasted My Chemical Romance as she got ready to go out. It was Friday night and two days had passed since…whatever the hell that had been with Will. She tried to remind herself he was a city dude and she should have known better than to be attracted to him, but that hadn't kept him out of her dreams for the last two nights.

So when her cousin from Midland had called and said she'd be driving through Royal on Friday and did Amberley want to go out, she'd said yes. Normally she was all for comfy jammies and binge-watching one of her favorite TV shows on Netflix, but tonight she needed to get out of her own head.

She was ready to dance to some rowdy country music, drink too much tequila and flirt with some small-town boys who wouldn't walk away from her without a word. It had been a long time since she had blown off steam and it was the weekend. Even though she sometimes acted like she was ready for the retirement home, she was still young.

But she didn't feel it.

There was a weight in her heart that made her feel older than her years. And when Will had said his life was complicated she'd…well, she'd ached because she knew complicated.

She knew what it was like to be a big, fat, red-hot mess masquerading as normal. She'd done that for a year after she'd lost the baby and then gotten the devastating news that she'd never be able to have a child. A part of her should have rejoiced that he'd only seen what she had wanted him to—a cowgirl who was damn good with horses.

But that connection she'd felt with him had made her want him to see more.

And he hadn't.

He hadn't.

She was wearing her good jeans—a dark wash that fit like a second skin—and a pair of hand-tooled boots that her brothers and sisters had given her for Christmas. They had a fancy design featuring turquoise and she'd completed her outfit with a flirty peasant top. She'd taken the time to blow-dry her hair and not just pull it back in a braid, so it fell around her shoulders.

She finished her makeup and put a dash of lip gloss on before grabbing her purse and heading out. She was halfway to her truck when she realized someone was in her yard. Not that it was really her yard, since Clay owned all the property, but that little area in front of her place.

Amberley glanced over and realized the someone was a dog. A ragged stray that was making mewling sounds that she couldn't ignore. He was a rather sad-looking animal with a matted coat. She tossed her purse on the hood of her truck and turned toward the dog, careful not to spook it as she walked toward it. She crouched low and held out her hand for it to sniff once she was close enough.

The animal whimpered and then slowly moved closer to her. She held her ground, noticing that it limped. One of his legs was injured. Just the distraction she needed. Animals were the one thing on this planet that she was actually good with.

She waited until the dog came closer and noticed that there were some briars wrapped around his hind leg, and when she reached for the leg he moaned and moved away from her.

"All right, boy. I'll let it be. But we are going to have to take you to get that looked at," she said. She stood up, pulled her phone from her back pocket and texted her cousin that she'd be a little late. Then she went back into her place, got a blanket, a bowl and bottle of water. Then she grabbed a carrot from the fridge and went back outside.

The dog was exactly where she'd left him. Waiting for her.

"Good boy. You're a boy, right?" she asked.

The dog didn't answer—not that she expected him to. She put the bowl down in front of him and gave him some water and stood to watch him as he drank, then texted the small animal vet that Clay used to let him know she'd be bringing in an injured dog. Though it was after hours, Clay had an agreement for the ranch that included 24/7 coverage.

She spent the next hour getting the dog settled at the vet. He had a chip and the vet contacted his owners, who were very glad to find him. Amberley waited until they arrived before leaving to meet her cousin. But the truth was she no longer wanted to go out.

The dog—Barney—reminded her of how alone she was. Even the stray had someone to go home to. His owners had been really nice and so happy she'd found him and Amberley was gracious to them, but a part of her had wanted the stray to be a loner. To maybe need her.

She hated that she was feeling down about her life. She'd finally gotten past everything that had happened when she was eighteen and now some dude was making her question her situation. She'd never been this knocked on her butt for some guy. Yet there was something about him that had made her want to be more. Want to be someone she hadn't thought about being in a long time.

But there it was.

She wanted to see him again.

Her cousin was waiting in the parking lot of the Wild Boar, a roadhouse that served food and drinks and had a small dance floor with live music on the weekends. There were pool tables in the back and a mechanical bull. If you weren't in the upper echelon of Royal and weren't a member of the Texas Cattleman's Club, then this was the place to hang out.

"Hey, girl. You ready to blow off some steam?"

She nodded. Maybe a night out with Royal's rowdy crowd was what she needed to remind her of where she belonged and whom she belonged with…and it wasn't a hot guy from Seattle.

Midnight was his favorite time of night and when he found the most clarity when he was working—tonight wasn't any different. Faye was a little night owl like he was, so the baby was playing on the floor at his feet while he watched the scripts that were running and tracking down Maverick on the monitor nearest to him.

She'd woken up crying. Erin was worn out from

a long day of dealing with Faye teething, and since Will was up at night working anyway, they'd established that he would take the night shift.

Maverick wasn't the cleverest hacker, but whoever he was, the man was running his internet through a few connections. It would have fooled someone who didn't have Will's experience, but he'd been a pirate hunter in high school for a large software company that his dad had helped found and he'd spent a lot of years learning how to follow and find people who didn't want to be found.

"Dada."

"Yes?" He looked down at Faye. Her face was so sweet and she was holding a large round plastic toy up to him.

He took it from her.

She immediately reached for one a size smaller and held it up to him. This was one of her favorite new games. She gave him all the toys around her and then he had to sit still while she took them back and put them in a seemingly random order in front of him.

But this time she was done handing them all to him, so she crawled over to where he sat on the floor next to her and crawled onto his lap. He scooped her up and hugged her close.

His heart was so full when he held his daughter. She smelled of baby powder and sweetness. He knew sweetness wasn't a scent, but when he held Faye it was what he always felt.

He stood up and walked around the house with her while she babbled at him. He set a notification on the computers to alert his phone when the scripts were finished running and then put Faye's jacket on her so they could go for a walk. He'd grown up in Bellevue, near the water, and some of his earliest memories were of being outside with his mom at night looking at the sky.

He knew that many people would expect Faye to be in bed at midnight, but she wasn't looking sleepy at all. It was probably his fault for having a long nap with her in the afternoon. He'd been keeping odd hours since they had arrived in Royal.

He walked toward the barn, telling Faye the stories his mom had told him. Will's mom's people had been sailors and the sky and the water were a big part of their history.

He heard the rumble of a truck engine and turned as a large pickup rounded the corner. He stepped off the dirt track to make sure he wasn't in the path of the vehicle.

The truck slowed and the passenger-side window rolled down. He walked over and was pretty sure it was Clay Everett. But Will knew if he had a woman like Sophie waiting for him at home, he'd have a better way to spend his night than patrolling his ranch.

"Hey, Will. You okay?" Amberley asked.

He was surprised to see her. She had obviously been out, as she smelled faintly of smoke. Her hair was thick and fell around her shoulders. The tousled tresses, so different from her neat braid, made his fingers tingle with the need to touch her hair.

He regretted leaving her the other afternoon. One kiss. Would that have been so bad? Even Lucy wouldn't begrudge him that. But he hadn't taken it.

So instead a need was growing in him fast and large. Each day it seemed to expand and he knew he was losing control.

"Yeah. Faye's a night owl like me so I thought I'd take her for a walk."

Faye heard her name and started babbling again.

"Want some company?" Amberley asked.

"Sure," he said.

She turned off the engine of her truck and climbed out, coming around by him. Her perfume hit him then—it was sweet like spring flowers. There was a slight breeze tonight and Amberley tipped her head back and looked up at the sky.

"When I was little, my dad told us that if we were really good we'd see a special angel in the sky."

"Did you ever see one?"

"Yeah," Amberley said. She stretched out her arm and pointed to Venus. "There she is."

"That's Venus."

"Show some imagination, Brady. That's my special angel. She watches over me at night."

"Does she?"

Amberley nodded. But she wasn't looking up anymore—she was staring at Faye. "She'll watch over you, too, little lady."

Faye answered with one of her babbles. And Amberley listened until Faye was done and then she nodded. "I know. It's hard to believe that someone up there is looking out for you, but she is."

Faye babbled some more.

"Your mama?" Amberley asked when she was done.

Faye babbled and then ended with "Mamamam."

"Mine, too. They are probably friends," Amberley said.

Faye shifted toward Amberley and Amberley looked over at him for permission before reaching for the baby. Will let Faye go to Amberley and watched the two of them talking to each other. She was good with the baby. He was surprised that Faye had wanted to go to her. She was usually pretty shy with strangers.

He noticed that both of the girls were looking at him.

"She's usually not so eager to go to strangers."

"Well, we're not strangers," Amberley said. "We chatted up a storm while you were holding her."

"You sure did," Will said.

Something shifted and settled inside of him. It was a tightness he wasn't even aware of until that moment. And then he realized that he wanted Faye to like Amberley because it didn't matter how guilty he may feel afterward, he wanted to get to know her better.

Four

The night sky was clear, filled with stars and the waning moon. Amberley tipped her head back, feeling the emotions of the week fall away. The baby in her arms was sweet and soft. She had been cooing and pointing to things as they walked and Amberley fought against the pain in her heart she'd thought she'd finally gotten over.

She loved babies. Loved their smiles and their laughter. The way that they communicated if you just took the time to listen to them.

Her dad had told her that she shouldn't give up on a family, but the hysterectomy she'd had at eighteen had pretty much put paid to that. She couldn't have a baby of her own. So she tended to spoil any kiddos she met.

"You're awfully quiet over there," she said, realizing that Will hadn't said much in the last few minutes. She'd suggested they lie in the bed of her pickup truck and watch the night sky. Will had agreed but only, he'd said, until Faye got sleepy.

"Just trying to get this app to work," he said.

He'd mentioned having an app that could show meteor and comet activity in the night sky and was trying to get it to work. Amberley had spread a blanket she kept for picnics on the bed of the truck and she and Faye had been playing together while he tried.

"If it doesn't work we can just make up stories," she said.

"Like what?" he asked.

"That star over there is Lucky."

"As in it brings luck?" he asked.

"No, its name is Lucky. Sometimes the star falls to earth and takes on the persona of a rock superstar during the day, and at dusk it's drawn back up into the night sky, where she stays steady and true so that little cowgirls and cowboys who are out late on the range can find their way home," Amberley said.

She'd been a huge Britney Spears fan when she'd been about ten and her dad had made up that story about one of the pop star's songs.

"Okay, let me give it a try," Will said. He shifted his shoulders and leaned back against the cab of her truck. Faye crawled over to him and he lifted her onto his lap. The baby shifted around and settled with her back against his chest.

They were so cute together, Amberley thought. She ached for little Faye because even though she had her daddy's love and attention, Amberley knew that one day Faye was going to need her momma.

She just felt close to them because she saw herself in the two of them.

"See that constellation?" he asked, pointing to Sirius.

"Yes."

"That's Lobo and he is really good at catching the people who skunk around in the shadows. Every night he looks down on the earth for clues and then during the day he turns into computer code and helps track down the bad guys."

She smiled. "Like you."

"Yeah. Like me."

"How's that going? Is it okay to ask?"

Faye turned in his arms and he rubbed his hand over her back. He lifted her higher on his chest and she settled into the crook of his neck.

"It's going pretty well," he said, his voice pitched low so as not to disturb his daughter.

"I'm glad. Will you be here for long?" she asked.

"Probably a month."

A month…not enough time for anything serious.

"I'd love to know more about what you do," she said. Sometime between the dancing and talking with her cousin tonight she'd realized that no cowboy or Royal guy could make her stop thinking about Will. Probably not her wisest idea, but she had decided she wasn't going to just walk away unless he pushed her to.

"Stop by anytime and I'll show you. It sounds more exciting than it is. Usually it's me in a dark room with my computers running programs or tracking scripts."

"That is so foreign to me. I spend all my time outside and with animals. I mean, I have my phone, which keeps me connected, but I don't even own a computer."

"I don't see why you should need one," Will said. "Smartphones can do just about everything you'd need a computer for."

"Want me to drive you guys back home?" she asked.

"I don't have a car seat so we probably shouldn't," he said.

She felt silly because she'd been used to riding in the back of the truck from the time she'd been a child. She guessed it wasn't that safe, but there wasn't much out here to cause an accident. It underscored to her the many ways they were different.

But he was only here for a month.

Why was she trying to make it acceptable to get involved with him?

She knew why.

She was lonely. It had been a year since her last boyfriend and she was using that term loosely. She and Pete had hooked up at a rodeo and then gone their separate ways. But she felt something stirring inside of her.

Maybe it was just lust.

She sighed and then realized that he'd been staring at her.

Crap.

"Sorry. I guess I'm getting tired. What did you say?"

He shook his head and shifted around, setting Faye on the blanket next to him. The little girl curled onto her side and cooed contentedly as she drifted to sleep.

"I didn't say anything. I was only watching you,

regretting that I didn't kiss you when we were on our ride," he said.

Kiss her.

"Uh..."

Great. He'd rendered her speechless.

No. He hadn't. She wouldn't let him.

"I thought we both decided that was a bad idea."

"I like bad ideas," he said, leaning in closer. He wasn't touching her at all, but he'd tipped his head and she knew he was going to kiss her.

She licked her lips, tilted her head to the side and met him halfway. His lips were firm but soft and he tasted...good. There was something right in the way he tasted as his tongue brushed over hers. She closed her eyes and forgot about everything except this moment.

Will had tried avoiding kissing her, but with the certainty that the moon would rise every night, he knew he really couldn't keep from falling for Amberley. Tonight, sitting in the back of her pickup truck with Faye, had been one of the first times he'd been able to just enjoy being with his daughter and not think of all she'd lost.

He hadn't felt that gnawing guilt-and-grief combination. And now, when his lips met Amberley's, he'd stopped thinking altogether.

God, he'd needed this.

Just to feel and not think of anything but the way her lips had softened under his.

He lifted his head and looked down at her. By the light of the moon he could tell that her lips were wet from their kiss and her eyes were heavy-lidded. She lifted her hand and rubbed her finger over her mouth.

"Damn. I wish you didn't kiss like that," she said.

Surprised, he tilted his head to the side.

She shrugged. "Just would have been easier to write you off as a city slicker if you didn't know what you were doing."

He threw his head back and laughed at that statement. "Glad to know I didn't disappoint."

Faye stirred at the sound of his laughter and he realized it was getting late, even for two night owls.

"You didn't disappoint… Did I?"

The woman who'd fiercely ridden her horse around the barrels and who walked with a confidence that made him think she could conquer mountains was asking him if he liked her kiss. He patted Faye on the back and she settled down before he looked back over at Amberley.

Her hair was tousled, her lips swollen from his kiss, and he knew that later tonight, when he was alone in his bed, he was probably going to fantasize about doing much more with her.

"You were fantastic," he said. "If we were alone one kiss wouldn't be enough."

She nodded.

"For me, either."

"Good," he said. "Now I hate to do this but I really should be getting Faye back home. But maybe I can see you tomorrow?"

She nibbled her lower lip and he moaned.

"What?" she asked.

"You are making it damn hard for me to resist kissing you again," he said, but Faye had begun to wake up. He needed to get her back and into her comfortable crib.

"Sorry. It's just I like the taste of you."

He groaned.

"I could do with a little less honesty from you, cowgirl," he said.

"I'm not made that way," she admitted.

"I'm glad. I'll see you tomorrow afternoon."

"Okay. I'm giving a riding lesson from one until three, so after that, okay?"

"Perfect," he said. He leaned over and stole a quick kiss because he liked the way she tasted, too, and then he stood up with Faye in his arms and hopped down from the bed of the truck. He glanced back over his shoulder and noticed that Amberley had moved to the tailgate and sat there watching him walk away. It was pretty dark, but he was using the flashlight on his phone. And the moon was full, a big harvest moon that lit up the land around them.

He waved at her and she waved back.

"Good night, Will," she said, and there was a smile in her voice.

"'Night," he returned and then cuddled his daughter closer as he walked back to the guest house.

He kept the image of Amberley watching him walk away until he entered the house and saw the photo of Lucy on the hall table.

He took Faye to her room. He removed her coat and then changed her diaper before laying her in the bed. He turned on the mobile that Lucy had picked out for her and that guilt that he'd thought he'd shaken free of was back.

When Will first came to the guest house on the

Flying E, he'd asked if Clay would allow him to set up Faye's room as it had been in Seattle. He wanted her to feel at home and little things like the mobile and her crib and her toys were important. Clay hadn't minded at all and told Will to make the guest house into his home, which he had. And Erin had been instrumental in making sure everything was set up the way they liked it.

Lucy had been so excited when she'd seen it in a magazine. It was a version of the cow jumping over the moon, similar to one that Lucy remembered from her own childhood. They'd had to search all over to find it. Will had scoured the internet—exhausting every avenue—to find it. He remembered how thrilled Lucy had been when she'd opened the package.

He touched the cow as it spun and instead of thinking of Lucy he remembered Amberley and the way she'd played with Faye while he'd been on his phone trying to get technology to work in the middle of the night.

She hadn't gotten impatient with him the way the nanny sometimes did. He liked how easily Amberley got along with his daughter, but a part of him also knew that Lucy should have been the one holding her daughter.

But she was gone.

This job out here in Texas was supposed to give him perspective and help him finally realize that Faye needed him. It was easier here in Texas to shake off the gloom of the last year. And he was moving forward. Slowly. He hadn't realized how isolated he'd let himself become. His world had shrunk to just his work, and then Faye and Erin.

It had been a while since he'd just had a normal conversation. He and Erin mainly just talked about the baby and her eating habits or how teething was going.

He'd never felt like he would be raising his daughter alone.

He had no idea how to do it.

As much as he enjoyed being with Amberley, she wasn't his forever woman. Will had had that. Faye drifted off to sleep and Will went to his own room to shower away the scent of Amberley and then he brushed his teeth and used mouthwash to try to forget the way her kiss had tasted.

But he remembered.

And he still wanted her. His arms felt empty through the night and when he dreamed he was making love to a woman and he looked at her face, it was Amberley's and not Lucy's.

And the dream left him wide-awake, tortured with lust and need and the kind of guilt that felt like he was never going to be normal again.

When Will had been a no-show for their afternoon ride, Amberley chalked it up to him needing to do his job. Clay had told her that Maverick had struck again. Clay had even been a victim of Maverick. The hacker had made it seem as if Everest's cloud encryption software had been compromised, causing clients to panic. But luckily that had all been cleared up.

So Will was probably deep into his investigation. At least that's what she told herself.

Except he hadn't come around the next day, or the day after. A week later she was beginning to believe he might be more like Sam, the guy she'd hooked up with nearly six years ago, than she'd wanted to believe.

Amberley finally went by Will's place one afternoon only to be met at the door by Erin, holding Faye on her hip.

"Hi, there, Amberley," Will's nanny said.

"Hey. Sorry to bother you. I was stopping by to see if Will wanted to go for a ride," she said.

Erin stepped out onto the porch. "He's not here. He had to go into town to meet with Max and Chelsea. Something about Maverick."

"Clay told me he might have struck again," Amberley said. "I've never really had much patience for bullies. Especially ones like Maverick. If I have beef with someone I take it to them. I don't attack from a hiding place in the bushes, you know?"

Erin laughed. "I do know."

Erin's phone beeped. "That's my timer. I was making some teething biscuits for little Miss Faye here. Want to come in and chat? It's kind of lonely out here."

"It is. I'm used to it, though," Amberley said as she stood up. She glanced at her watch, that old battered Timex she'd been wearing for as long as she could remember. "I could stay for about thirty minutes."

"Good. Come on in," Erin said.

As soon as they stepped into the kitchen, Erin put Faye in her bouncy chair on the counter and went to the oven to check on her biscuits. Amberley went over to play with the baby, who was making her nonsensical sounds again.

She looked into the little girl's eyes and wondered what had happened to her mother. Without really thinking about what she was doing, she turned to Erin, who was putting the biscuits on a wire rack.

"What happened to Will's wife?" she asked.

Erin finished moving all the biscuits to the rack before she took off her pot holder and turned to face Amberley. "She had a brain hemorrhage before Faye was born. They kept her alive until about a week after Faye was delivered. It was heartbreaking."

"I can imagine. Is that when he hired you?" she asked.

"No. Lucy was planning to go back to work so I'd already been hired. They wanted the baby to be familiar with the nanny so the thought was Lucy, Will and I would all be in place from the moment Faye was born," Erin said.

That just broke her heart a little bit more. It sounded like Lucy had been ready for motherhood. That their family was getting settled and then bam, the unexpected. Her daddy had always said that change was inevitable, but Amberley thought it would be nice once in a while if things just stayed on course. Like they should have for Faye's family.

Erin offered her a glass of iced tea. She accepted and stayed to chat with her about the Fall Festival, but she felt uncomfortable in the house now that she knew a little bit more about Will's wife. Lucy. She had a name now, and when Amberley left a few minutes later, she saw the photo on the hall table. Lucy had been beautiful.

It was the kind of classic beauty that Amberley, with her tomboyish looks, could never pull off. She wasn't down on herself; it was simply that Lucy was really different from her. And Amberley wondered if she'd been fooling herself to think the man she'd sat under the stars with could see her as anything other than a distraction from his real life.

She wasn't sure she could see herself as anything other than that.

Determined to remember what she was good at and how great her life was, she spent the next few days with the horses and deliberately tried to shove Will Brady out of her mind.

The following weekend, Amberley went into town for the Fall Festival at the Royal elementary school. It was way past time for her to start decorating for the season. She pulled into the parking lot at the elementary school and realized the mistake she'd made.

There were families everywhere. Why wouldn't there be? This was a family event. Perfect for a Saturday.

She'd come after she'd finished her morning routine with the horses and now she wished she'd stayed on the Flying E with her animals. Instead she was watching everything that she would never have and she hated that.

She'd been devastated when she'd had the hysterectomy. But as her father had pointed out in his sanguine way it was better than the alternative, which in her case would have been death.

But she'd never expected to feel this alone.

She'd always thought when she'd been growing up that she'd one day have a family of her own. And holding Faye a week ago had just reminded her of all that she was missing.

She was twenty-four—too young to feel like this.

She got out of the truck because she felt silly just sitting there. She needed pumpkins. Some to carve, some for making pies and muffins, and some just to use as decorations that she'd keep out until Thanksgiving.

She walked through the playground, which had been turned into the Fall Festival, and tried to make a beeline to the pumpkin patch, but Cara was working at the caramel-apple booth and waved her over.

"Hey, Amberley! I'm glad you showed up."

"You know I need a pumpkin," Amberley said. The booth Cara was using was staffed by high school kids from the Future Farmers of America. They still wore the same jackets they had when Amberley had been a member in high school. She'd also done 4-H. She bought a couple of caramel apples and met Cara's boyfriend, who was clearly smitten. They were cute. It seemed easy for them to be together.

Unlike Amberley, who always seemed to find the rockiest path to happiness with a man. Whatever that was about.

"See you on Monday, Cara," Amberley said leaving the booth and carrying her bag of goodies with her.

The pumpkin patch had an area at the front set up for pictures and she saw the kids lined up for photos. She walked past them, head down and focused on getting what she needed and getting home. She was going to give herself the rest of the day off. Maybe stop at the diner in town and grab some junk food and then go home, sit on the couch and binge-watch something on Netflix. Anything that would take her mind off the place where she kept going back to.

The missing family that she craved.

Will.

Screw Will.

He was clearly messed up from his wife's death. She got that. She could even understand what he must be going through. She was pretty damn sure he hadn't married a woman and had a kid with her if he didn't love her. That just didn't strike her as the kind of man he was. It was going to take him time to get over it. Obviously more than a year and she didn't begrudge him that.

She was angry at herself. She'd spent way too much time thinking about him. She should be thinking about one of the guys she'd met at the Wild Boar, or maybe one of the guys she'd met at the rodeo. Or no guy.

Maybe she'd just start collecting cats and build herself a nice life surrounded by animals and friends. Sure she'd miss having a man in her bed, but she could deal with that. Eventually.

She picked out five pumpkins to decorate her porch and two for the house—she had two windows that would look good with jack-o'-lanterns in them. And then she paid for a large bag of mini gourds and accepted the help of a pumpkin-patch employee to carry them all to her truck.

She carried the last pumpkin herself after three trips to the truck and was feeling much better about her day as she pulled into the diner. She'd phoned in her order so all she had to do was go in and grab it. She hopped out of her truck and walked straight to the counter to pick up her order when she heard someone call her name.

Will.

She turned to see him sitting at a corner table with Max St. Cloud. Though she'd only seen him in town, she knew Max on sight. And she tried to smile and wave, but she was just still so pissed.

She hadn't realized how much she'd been counting on him to be different from every other city guy she'd ever met. She settled for a little wave as the girl at the register called her name. She walked over and paid for her patty melt, fries and onion rings and then turned to walk out of the diner without looking over at Will.

One of them had to be smart and no matter how country she was, she knew it was up to her.

Five

"What was that about?" Max asked Will as they watched Amberley walk out of the diner.

"Nothing."

"Will, talk to me," Max said. "Did I make a mistake when I asked you to come to Royal?"

"No. It is not affecting my work. In fact, I think I am getting close to finding the hub that Maverick is using to run most of the cyberbullying he's doing. He uses a bunch of different accounts, but they are all fed from the same source…or at least that's what I'm starting to suspect."

Max sat back in the bench and nodded. "Good. But I wasn't referring to your work. You have been sending me reports at all hours of the day with updates."

"Then what are you asking?" Will was trying to focus on the conversation with his boss, but he couldn't keep his mind from wandering to Amberley.

"We're friends, right?" Max asked.

"Yeah. But unless you want to hear about what a sad mess I've become you should lay off this questioning right now," Will warned his friend. Max had known him before he'd married Lucy. He was one of the few people who really knew him well enough to understand what he'd gone through when he'd lost Lucy. How marriage had changed him and how her death had sent him to a darker place.

"What's up?"

"Nothing. Just the mix of pretty girl, messed-up guy and trying to do the right thing," Will said.

He took a sip of his coffee and leaned forward because he didn't need everyone in the diner to hear his business. "For the love of me, Max, every damn time I try to do what I know is right it backfires."

"Then stop trying," Max said.

"If it was that easy," Will said.

"It is. You said that you tried to do the right thing and it backfired. Maybe it was the wrong action," Max said. "All I know is that life isn't like a program. You fix the code and make it work, but there is always something unexpected. You know?"

Will leaned back. Like Lucy dying in the hospital after Faye's birth. "Yeah. I do know. Thanks, Max."

Max nodded. "People are getting more tense as this Maverick remains at large. I know you are doing all you can, but right now, because no one knows who Maverick is, everyone suspects each other. If you can get me something…well, the sooner the better."

"I will. Like I mentioned I think I have a lead on something that should lead to Maverick. I just needed to understand the server set up at the Texas Cattleman's Club."

"I put you on the guest list so you can go check it out."

"Thanks. I want to add the access tracking to the main terminal and the server. I'm pretty sure it's got to be an inside job."

"I think there is a connection there, too," Max said. "So you don't want anyone to know why you are there."

"Yeah."

"A date would be good camouflage."

"Of course it would," Will said.

"Just trying to help a buddy out. You look like you need a nudge toward her."

"Thanks… Not a nudge. I need to get out of my own way. Every time I'm around her I forget things… Lucy. And then when I'm alone I'm not sure that's what I should have done."

"Only you can answer that for yourself, but you can't keep punishing yourself for living," Max said. "I'm going to ask Chelsea to make you a dinner reservation at the club for tonight. Get a date or not—it's up to you."

They discussed how Will would deploy the tracker physically on the server. They didn't want to do it remotely, in case Maverick was able to see the code in the program. Max and he parted company and instead of heading back to the Flying E, Will went to one of the boutiques in town and bought a gauzy dress in a small flower print for Amberley. The dress had a skirt that he suspected would end just above her knee and a scooped neckline. He also purchased a pretty necklace that had a large amber gemstone pendant in the center that would rest nicely above the neckline of the dress.

He had it wrapped and then wrote a note of apology on the card and asked for it to be delivered to her.

He checked his watch and then went to the Fall Festival to meet Erin and Faye. Faye looked cute as could be in her denim overalls and brown undershirt. He held his daughter and knew that he'd be mad as hell if he'd been the one to die and Lucy was hesitating to get on with her life.

But it was harder on the heart than it was on the head. And as much as he knew what he needed to do, it was like Max had said—this wasn't code that he could correct with a few strokes of the keyboard. It was so much easier and conversely more complicated than that. He had no idea what he was really going to do about Amberley, but he'd made a move today. No more backing away.

If Amberley gave him this third chance, he wasn't going to waste it.

When he got back to the ranch, he dropped off Erin and Faye at the guest house since it was Faye's nap time and then he got in the golf cart and drove over to the stables to look for Amberley.

She was running the barrels when he got there and he watched her move with the horse and knew that she was worth the risk he was taking. He had spent a lot of time pretending that he could walk away from her, but the truth was he knew he couldn't.

He wanted her.

Not just physically, though that was a big part of

it. He also wanted that joie de vivre that she seemed to bring to him when he was around her.

He liked the man he could be when he thought of spending time with her.

She noticed him and drew her horse to a stop. She dismounted and walked over to the fence around the barrels, and he went to meet her.

"What's your deal?"

She hadn't meant to sound so confrontational. She'd gone back to the ranch and intended to waste away the rest of the day in front of the television. But instead she'd felt trapped in her house. She'd felt restless and edgy and just as she was about to leave, that package from Will had arrived.

With a handwritten apology note and a gorgeous dress and necklace. Who did something like that?

It was safe to say that no man she'd dated before had made such a gesture. But Will was different. And they had never dated. What had possessed him to do such a thing?

She was tired of playing games. It didn't suit her.

"My deal?"

"Yeah. We shared a great kiss and I started to think I could really like this guy and then you just up and disappear, not even a word about not showing up for our scheduled ride. You must think all country girls are just looking for a big-city man to marry them and take them away from all this, but you're wrong. I like this life. I like it just the way it is, and when I kissed you it was because I thought we had a real connection," she said, opening the gate and stepping out of the ring. "And it's clear to me that we have absolutely no connection at all by the way you keep backing out of stuff, but then you send me that dress and necklace and that apology. It sounds heartfelt, Will. And I'm tired of feeling stupid because I think one thing and your actions say something else. So what's your deal?"

He rocked back on his heels, as if he was trying to absorb the force of her aggression. She knew she was being hostile right now but she was tired of feeling the fool. The way he had treated her, the way she'd interpreted his actions…well, she wasn't having it anymore. She'd been nice and if he went to Clay and complained, she knew Clay well enough that she'd be honest with him and she was pretty sure he'd side with her.

"I am sorry. The note was meant to be heartfelt," he said, holding his hands up to his shoulders. "I like you, Amberley. When we are together I forget about the emptiness that I usually feel when I step away from my computer. But then I hold Faye and it comes back. I'm trying to get out of the swamp that I've been trapped in since Lucy died. And I can't figure it out. I'm not playing a game with you. I promise. I was going to invite you to dinner, but on second thought—"

"Do you really want to have dinner with me?" she asked, cutting him off. His explanation made her sad for him. She could feel his pain when he spoke. She, of all people, understood how hard it was to move on after a tragic loss. She could be his friend. Just his friend. That was something she could handle.

"Yes. I do."

"Okay, then let's have dinner. But as friends. We

can be friends, right?" she asked. "You can tell me about Lucy and maybe we can figure out a way to get you free of your swamp. It doesn't have to be anything more than that."

She could be his friend. Sure, she had wanted more, but the last few days had convinced her that wasn't wise. The anger and the despair from his rejection hadn't been what she'd expected. She had uncovered something buried deep inside her that she didn't like.

She wanted to celebrate being young and alive. Not feel old and bitter. She'd never been bitter about the hand that life had dealt her and she hated that this thing she felt for Will was eliciting that response in her.

"Friends?"

"Yes. Seems like a good place to start."

"Okay. Friends. Then I should tell you that I need a date for cover. I want to install a program on the server at the Texas Cattleman's Club, and in case it's an inside job, I don't really want anyone to know what I'm doing."

"So I'm your cover?"

"That's the plan, but I would also like it to be a date," he said. "I am tired of where I am and would like to get to a better place."

Sure, he would. As friends, she reminded herself. "I can do that. And I can provide some cover for you. What time is dinner?"

"Eight. That gives me time to spend with Faye before she goes to bed," he said.

"That works for me. How is she? I really enjoyed playing with her the other night."

"She's good. A little cranky earlier today, but that's just from teething. She's already got one tooth so this is another new one. She bit me last night when we were playing. She's been drooling a lot, so I was letting her chew on my finger and then *ouch*."

Amberley smiled at him like she would if he was a friend. She could do this. Keep her feelings on neutral terms. If only he wasn't so darn cute when he talked about his daughter.

He walked away and she turned her attention to her horse, brushing Montgomery and talking to the animal. He listened to her the way she suspected she'd listened to Faye. Montgomery lowered his head and butted her in the chest when she was done and she hugged him back, wishing she could understand men half as well as she understood horses.

Will took his time getting dressed for dinner after Erin and he had put Faye to bed. Erin was video chatting with her boyfriend back in Seattle, so he knew that she was set for the evening. He went into his office to check his computers again and took the small USB flash drive that he'd loaded his tracker program onto and put it in his pocket.

He was nervous.

He wasn't sure if that was a good thing or a bad thing. Faye always made him feel pretty okay...well, a little sad and bad that she didn't have her mom, but she had that sweet smile, which kind of helped to center him at times.

This was different. He went to the mirror in the guest bathroom and checked his tie again. He favored skinny ties no matter if they were in fashion or not.

He didn't think of himself as a slave to trends and preferred a look he thought worked for him. He'd spiked up his hair on the top and traded his Converse for some loafers his mom had sent him after her last trip to Italy.

He went in to check on Faye and kissed her on the top of her head before letting Erin know he was leaving for the evening.

He walked out of the house, took a deep breath of the fall evening air and realized how much he liked Texas. To be fair, October was a far cry from July, when he knew the temperature would be unbearable. But right now, this cool, dry night was exactly what he wanted.

He drove over to Amberley's house, having texted her earlier to tell her he'd pick her up. There was a bunch of pumpkins on her front step and a bale of hay with a scarecrow holding a sign that said Happy Fall, Y'all on it. He smiled as he saw it. He leaped up the stairs to her front porch and knocked on the door.

"It's open. Come in."

He did as she asked and stepped into the hallway of her place. The house smelled like apples and cinnamon, which reminded him of his parents' place. There was a thick carpeted runner in the foyer that led to the living room.

"I'll be right there. Sorry, I'm trying to curl my hair but it's being stubborn," she called out from the back of the house. "I am almost done."

"No problem," he said, following the sound of her voice. He found her standing in front of a mirror at the end of the hallway off the living room. He stopped when he saw her as his breath caught in his throat.

She was beautiful.

She'd looked pretty the other week after she'd been out, but this was different. Her hair had been pulled up into a chignon and that tendril she was messing with was curling against her cheek.

"Sorry. But in magazines this always looks so perfect and, of course, the reality is my stubborn hair won't curl the right way."

"I don't think it's a problem," he said.

She turned to face him and he had to swallow. The dress he'd picked out was fitted on the top and then flared out from her waist ending just above her knees. And she'd paired the dress with a pair of strappy sandals. The amber pendant fell on her chest, drawing his eyes to the V-neck of the dress.

"You are gorgeous," he said.

She blushed.

"Don't be embarrassed, it's just the truth," he said.

"Thanks for saying that. I don't get dressed up often, which is why I was trying this new updo. I figured I should at least make the effort. Plus, the folks of Royal aren't used to seeing me in anything but jeans and a straw cowboy hat. Do you think Maverick is working in the club or even a member…? Oh, that would really stink if he was a member, wouldn't it?"

"It would. I'm not a member, as you know, but I am aware of how close-knit the members are," Will said. "Are you ready to go?"

"Yes. Let me grab my purse and shawl. I figured that would be nicer than my jean jacket."

He smiled at the way she said it. She looked sophisticated and polished, almost out of his league, but she was still Amberley.

She disappeared into the doorway next to the hall mirror and reappeared a minute later. "Let's go."

He followed her through her home. It was small and neat, but very much Amberley. Not like the guest house, which was almost too perfectly decorated—this place had a more lived-in quality. It was her home. "How long have you lived here?"

"I got the job when I was nineteen…so that's five years."

"Wow, you were young. Were you worried about moving away from home?" he asked.

"Not really. Dad and Clay have known each other for a while. And it's not like it's that far if I want to go home for a visit," she said. "Plus Clay has an excellent stable and he lets me have time off to rodeo when I want to—it's the best place for me."

She was animated when she spoke of her father and her job and her life, and he realized he wanted to see her like this always.

She'd suggested they be friends and he knew now that was the only route for the two of them. Because he wanted her to stay the way she was just now. With her skin glowing, her eyes animated as she talked about the things in her life she loved. Getting involved with him could only bring her down. And even though he knew he felt like he was missing out on something special, her smile and her happiness was worth it.

Six

The Texas Cattleman's Club dining room was busy when they arrived. Since Maverick had started his assault on members of the club, and on Royal, some of the friendliness that Amberley had always associated with the town was gone. Everyone was a little bit on edge. She wasn't going to pretend she understood what Will was doing with the computer, but she'd Googled him and read up on him.

They were dining as guests of Chelsea Hunt and she'd met them early at the bar.

If anyone could unearth Maverick it was Will Brady. He was a whiz at tracking down cyber criminals and had made millions selling the code he had designed to the US government. He was gaining a reputation for keeping secrets safe as well, having successfully blocked an all-out assault on one government database by a foreign entity intent on doing harm to the US. Obviously, Will was a well-respected expert in his field.

One of the articles had been accompanied by a picture of him and his late wife dressed up to go to the White House, where Will had been given a commendation.

Seeing that picture of Will's late wife had made the woman very real to Amberley. And she was even more glad she'd decided just to be friends with Will. She liked him. She wasn't going to pretend otherwise. As she went to the bar while he excused himself to go do whatever he had to do in the computer room, she thought more about all Will had lost.

She wanted to be a good friend to Will. He needed a friend.

She remembered how he'd made up a story for her while they'd sat under the stars. No one had done that for her since she was a girl. The men she had dated…they saw the tough cowgirl and they didn't always realize she was vulnerable. But Will treated her differently.

"What'll it be?" the bartender asked her.

"Strawberry margarita, frozen, please," she said.

"Should I open a tab?" the bartender asked.

"No. I'll pay for this. I'm having dinner with someone," she said.

She settled up with the bartender, took her drink to one of the high tables and sat down to wait. She saw a few people she knew from town, but they glanced over her as if they didn't recognize her and she shook her head. She didn't think she looked so different with her hair up.

Finally, one of the parents of her horse-riding students recognized her and came over to chat with her for a few moments. It was nice to have someone to talk to while she was waiting for Will. She felt a little bit out of place here at the club. She didn't come from money. Her father made a good living and the ranch was worth a fair amount, but they weren't wealthy. They were ranchers.

Will walked in a few minutes later and scanned the room before spotting her. He smiled, buttoning his coat as he strode over to her. He looked good in his thin tie and his slim-fitting suit. His hair was slicked back, making him look like he'd just stepped out of one those television shows she loved to binge-watch.

She sighed.

Friends, she reminded herself.

"I didn't order you a drink," she said, wishing now she had.

"That's okay. I'll get one and join you," he said.

He was back in a moment, sitting across from her with a whiskey in one hand. "Sorry to keep you waiting."

"I don't mind. Did you get everything straightened out?"

"I did," he said. "How has it been for you?"

"Funny," she said. "I've seen a few people from town but most didn't recognize me."

"Really?"

"Yup. I'm a woman of mystery," she said. "I like it."

"Me, too. It's nice to be anonymous," he said.

"Are you usually recognized?" she asked. "I read a few articles about you online."

"Did you?" he asked. "That's interesting. But to answer your question, I'm only recognized at home. Mainly it's because I don't live that far from where I grew up. One subdivision over, actually, so I just know everyone when I go to the gym or the grocery store. And most people know about Lucy so it makes things awkward..."

She put her hand over his.

"Do you want to talk about her?" Amberley asked. "When my mom died everyone stopped mentioning her name. It was like she'd never existed and I wanted to talk about her. Finally, one night I lit into my daddy about it. And he said he missed her so much just hearing her name hurt and I told him for me, too, but ignoring her was making her disappear," Amberley said, feeling the sting of tears as she remembered her mom. She'd been gone for years now, but there were times like this when she still missed her and it felt fresh.

"I...I'm a little bit of both. I don't know if I want to talk about her," Will admitted. He took his hand from under hers and swallowed his drink in one long gulp.

"If you want to, I'm here for you," she said.

He nodded. "I'm going to go and check on our table."

She watched him walk away and she wondered if she'd said too much. But she knew that she couldn't have kept silent. He had admitted to her that he was stuck in a swamp and there was no clear path out of it. She suspected it was because he didn't know how to move on and still hold on to the past. And while Amberley knew she was no expert, she'd done her best to keep her mom alive while accepting the woman her dad had started dating when she'd turned eighteen.

So maybe she'd be able to help him.

Dinner started out a little stiff but soon they relaxed into a good conversation, mostly centering on music and books. They differed in that everything he owned was digital—both books and music—while Amberley had inherited her mother's record collection when she'd moved out and had a turntable in her house, where she listened to old country and rock from the '80s.

"What about scratches?"

"Well, that does make for some awkward moments when I'm singing along to a song that I've learned with all the skips in it. Records do that," she said with a wink. "And then I realize there's an entire phrase I've missed."

"You know I could show you how to download all the albums you already own on your phone so you could listen to them when you are riding," he said.

"I know how to do that, Will," she said. "I just prefer to listen to the albums at home. It reminds me of when I was growing up. Like Mom loved Michael Bolton and when I listen to his album I can remember Dad coming and the two of them dancing around. And I have a lot of CDs, too. Between the two of them I think they owned every album they loved on cassette, CD and vinyl. It's crazy," she said. "Dad stopped listening to it all after Mom died, but I wanted my brothers and sisters to have those memories, so Randy and I would put the albums on when Dad was out of the house."

"How many siblings do you have?"

"Four. Two brothers and two sisters. Randy is three years younger than me, then Janie, Michael and Tawny."

"Sounds like a houseful," he said. He'd always sort of wished for a bigger family but he'd been the only child and had gotten used to it.

"What about you?" she asked.

"Only child."

"Spoiled," she said, winking at him.

"Probably," he admitted. "Lucy and I had planned to have at least two kids. She said we should have an even number—she had two sisters and said one of them was always left out."

"It was that way at home a bit when Mom was still alive, but once she died and I became the boss when Dad wasn't home the dynamic changed."

"How old were you?" he asked.

"Thirteen," she said. "You know you could always have more kids if you remarry."

"Uh, I'm barely able to think about going on a date, I'm not sure more kids are in the cards for me," he said. "What about you? Do you hate the idea of being a mom since you kind of had to be one to your siblings?"

She sat back in her chair and tucked that tendril she'd spent so much time trying to curl behind her ear. She shook her head. "No. I sort of always wanted to have a family of my own."

There was something in the way she was talking that made him think she thought she wouldn't have a family of her own. "You're young. You can have a family someday."

She chewed her lower lip for a minute and then shook her head. "I can't. I physically can't have kids."

He was surprised and wanted to ask her more about it, but it seemed obvious to him that she didn't want to discuss it further. She started eating her dinner again and this time didn't look up.

He reached over and put his hand on top of hers, stopping her from taking another bite, and she looked up. There was pain in her eyes and it echoed the loss he felt in his soul when he thought about Lucy being gone.

"I'm sorry."

She nodded. "Thanks. Wow, I bet you're glad this isn't a real date."

"It is a real date," he said. Because he knew now that there was no way he could walk away from her. Yes, he had been hesitating, but when he'd bought the dress for her things had changed and he wasn't going to let it go back to where he'd been when he'd first come to Texas.

"No, we said friends."

"Friends can go on dates. How else do you think friends become lovers?"

She flushed. He loved her creamy complexion and the fact that her face easily broadcast her emotions. He guessed it went hand-in-hand with her bluntness. Amberley didn't hide any part of who she was.

"I can't deal if you are going to blow hot and cold again," she said. "I wasn't kidding around this afternoon. I mean, I understand where you are coming from—"

"Amberley? I told Chris that was you," Macy Richardson said, coming over to her. Macy's family had been members of the Texas Cattleman's Club forever. Chris had grown up here in Royal on the wrong sides of the tracks. But he'd gone away and made his fortune, only to come back to claim Macy and a membership at the club. Their daughter took riding lessons from Amberley.

"It is me," she said. "Probably didn't recognize me without my cowboy hat on. Macy and Chris, this is Will Brady. He's a guest of Chelsea Hunt's."

Will stood up and shook Macy's and Chris's hands. "I hear you're in town to help catch Maverick."

"I am," Will said.

"Good. I'm sure you're going to get the job done. Chelsea has a lot of good things to say about you," Macy said. "We will leave you to your dinner."

A few other members stopped by to chat with them, including Clay and Sophia, who seemed to be enjoying their night out.

When the interruptions were over, Will picked up the thread of their conversation. Amberley's accusations about his behavior were fair, and he owed her a response.

"You're right. I'm not going to do that to you again. I said friends to lovers. We can take this slow," he said.

But a part of him knew that slow was going to be hard with her. It almost felt like if it happened in a rush it would be easier for him to move past the memory of Lucy, but as he watched Amberley he knew that he was always moving forward. He was excited about the prospect of something fresh and new with her. He wasn't about to give up now that he had her. He could do slow, but he wouldn't do never.

"So books… Do you have a bunch of dog-eared paperbacks instead of ebooks?" he asked, changing the subject and trying to pretend like everything was normal.

"Dog-eared? I love my books—I don't treat them poorly. In fact, sometimes I buy the paperback and then read it on my tablet because I want to keep it in good shape," she admitted.

He had to laugh at the way she said it and then he noticed how she smiled when he laughed. Something shifted and settled inside of him and he realized that he wasn't going to let her ride out of his life until he knew her much better.

Will drove her home at the end of the night, playing a new track he'd downloaded of Childish Gambino. It had a funky sound that reminded her of some of the jazzy music her dad liked from the '80s.

"This is really interesting. I love it," she said.

"I thought you might like it," he said.

"Why?"

"Because I do and we seem to have similar taste in music," he said.

"You think so?"

He nodded. "Tonight I have learned we are more alike than either of us would have guessed."

She swallowed hard—he meant the loss. It was funny that grief should unite them, but then her grandmother always said her mom was up there watching out for her, so maybe that was the reason behind this.

"Were you surprised?" she asked.

"Yes, and shame on me for that. Because from

the moment you showed up on my front porch with Cara, I knew you weren't like any other woman I'd met before. A part of me put it down to you being a Texan, but I knew there was something about you that was just different from every other woman," he said.

"Well, not everyone can be born in the great state of Texas," she said with a wink. "You can't really hold that against other women."

He laughed, as she hoped he would. She noticed that he got her sometimes odd sense of humor and it made her feel good. As much as she'd sort of always crushed out city guys that she'd met, he was different. Maybe that was why she kept giving him a second chance.

"I wouldn't," he said solemnly.

"So do you have any country music on your device?"

"Big and Rich," he said.

"They're okay but I think you need to listen to some old-school country. I'll give you some of Dad's old cassettes," she said, again teasing him because she knew he would just download the songs. And he was right that some songs sounded better digitally remastered, but for the sake of not agreeing with him she was going to stick by her guns.

He groaned. "Just give me a list. Actually, give me a name and I'll put it on right now."

"How?"

"Verbal commands," he said.

"Does that work for you?" she asked.

"All the time. Why?"

"Well, Siri hates me. Whatever I say she changes

it to something crazy. I mean, it's not like I'm not speaking English," she said.

"Siri can't hate you, she's a computer program," Will said.

"Well, she does. One time I texted my cousin Eve and told her where to meet me and do you know what that phone sent her?"

"What?" he asked.

"'Meet me where we once flew the summer wind,'" Amberley said.

He burst out laughing. "You do have a bit of an accent."

"No crap," she said. "But that is crazy."

"When we get to your place I'll fix it so your phone can understand you," he said.

"You can do that?"

"Hell, yes," he said. "I might not be any good with people but I'm excellent with tech."

She looked over at him, his features illuminated whenever they passed under a streetlamp as they drove through Royal. "You're good with people."

"Some of them. I tend to lose my patience. But with tech I'm always good."

She hadn't seen that impatient side of him. She wondered if that was because he was only letting her see what he wanted. Maybe the grieving widower was all he wanted her to know about him. But then why would he be talking to her now? She was making herself a little crazy.

They had both been beat up by life and were doing their best to survive. And she didn't doubt that he liked her. She'd seen the way he watched her and she knew when a man wanted her.

The truth was she didn't want to be hurt again and her mind might have been saying that friends was enough for her, but she knew in her heart that she'd already started liking him.

She liked that he cared about Royal even though it wasn't his town. She liked the way he was with his daughter, even though raising her without his mother was obviously hurting him. She just plain liked him and that wasn't how she wanted to be feeling about him.

Friends.

That was easy. She was supposed to be keeping things friendly. Instead she was falling for him.

It would have been easier if she knew that he would stay, but he was a flight risk. She knew he was just tiptoeing through an emotional minefield, trying to figure out how to move on. And of course once Maverick was found there was no reason for Will to stay in Texas. And then she shifted things in her mind. What if he was a mustang stallion that just took a little longer to gentle to the saddle? What if she just approached him with stealth, could she win him that way?

And was she really going to try to win him over?

She twisted her head and looked out at the dark landscape as they left Royal and headed toward the Flying E. She saw the moon up there following her and then she spotted Venus and thought of her own special angel, and not for the first time in her adult life, she wished her mom was here to talk to. She needed some advice on what to do next. She wasn't someone to hedge her bets and she wanted to be all in with Will. But a part of her was afraid that it was just wishful thinking on her part.

He turned onto the Flying E property and slowed the car, as they were on the dirt road and not paved highway. When he stopped in front of her house she turned to face him.

He shut off the car and sat there for a long moment and she felt a tingle go through her entire body that wasn't unlike what she felt when she was sitting on the back of Montgomery waiting for a barrel run to start.

"So, you want to come in?"

Seven

The dinner hadn't gone as Will had expected and this end to the evening was no different. He'd told himself he wouldn't kiss her good-night. They'd said they'd go slow. Maybe if he repeated it enough times it would stick and he'd get the taste of her off his tongue.

Unfortunately, he was never going to get the vision of her wearing the gauzy, long-sleeved dress he'd bought for her out of his mind. And it didn't help matters that the hem of her dress had ridden up her legs. In the light of the moon and the illumination of the dashboard lights he could see the tops of her thighs.

He clenched his hands around the steering wheel to keep from reaching over and touching her. Lust was strong and sharp and it was burning out all the cells in his brain, making it impossible for him to think. He wanted to be suave and smooth, all the things he liked to think he usually was around a woman, but tonight he wasn't.

He'd told her things he'd never said to anyone else. Like making up stories under the stars and just talking about stuff. Not business or his baby, but stuff that he'd locked away when Lucy died. And all the sophistication he'd thought he'd cultivated over the years was gone. He wanted her and really there wasn't room for anything else. Maybe it was the way she'd watched him as he'd driven back to the ranch.

Hell, he didn't know.

Frankly, he didn't care.

"You really want me to come in?" he asked, his voice sounding rough. He cleared it but he knew short of burying himself hilt-deep between her legs there was nothing he could do about it.

"Do you want to come in?" she asked.

"Hell."

She turned in her seat and the fabric of the dress was pulled taut against the curves of her breasts and he could only stare at her body as she leaned in close. A wave of her perfume surrounded him and now he knew he wasn't leaving.

He reached across the gearbox in the middle of the two bucket seats and wrapped his hand around the back of her head. He slid his fingers along the back of her neck, and his hand brushed against the part where she'd twisted up her hair—he wanted it free and flowing around her shoulders but right now he wanted her mouth more.

He needed to feel her lips under his. To prove to himself that lust had addled his thinking. That there was no way she tasted as good as he remembered. She couldn't.

No woman could taste like sin and heaven at the same time.

He tried to justify this kiss just to prove to himself that it had been the absence of kissing in the past year that had made hers unforgettable.

But as he leaned in closer, watching as her lips parted and her tongue darted out to wet her lips, he knew that was a lie. There was a jolt of pure sexual need that went through him and his erection stirred, pressing tight against his pants. He wanted to shift to relieve some of the pressure but he needed the pain to keep him grounded. To remind himself this wasn't a fantasy but something that was truly happening.

Now.

He brushed his lips over hers and her hand came up to rest against his chest. Her fingers moved under his tie to the buttons of his shirt and slipped through. She brushed the tip of one finger over his skin just as he thrust his tongue deep into her mouth. She moaned, shifting on the seat to scoot closer to him. He felt her arms wrap around his neck and shoulders as she drew herself closer to him. He grabbed her waist, squeezing her as he caressed his way around to her back. She felt like a ball of fire in his arms. Like a mustang that was wild and would take him on the ride of his life if he could hold on long enough.

He had a feeling deep in his soul that he could never tame her.

Amberley was going to be the ride of his life, he knew that. And for a second the grief he'd shoved into a box before he'd gone out with her tonight tried to rear its ugly head, and in response he lifted his head and looked down into her face.

Her hair was starting to come loose from the chignon, thanks to his hands in her hair, and there was a flush on her face, her lips were parted. And her pretty brown eyes were watching him. A little bit with patience and a lot with need.

She needed this as much as he did.

Tonight had shown him that they were both broken in ways that the world would never see. He felt honored that she'd let him see the truth that was the real Amberley.

He put his forehead against hers, their breathing comingled as he wrapped both arms around her and lifted her from the seat. It took a little maneuvering and it wasn't comfortable at all, but he managed to move into the passenger seat and get her settled on his lap.

"That was…I didn't realize you were so strong," she said, softly.

"I'm not."

"You are. I'm not a lightweight," she said.

"Yes, you are. You are perfect," he said.

She put her fingers over his mouth. "Don't. I'm not perfect and you really don't think I am. No lies. This is…what we've both wanted since that moment in the field when you got off your horse. And I don't want to ruin it, but honesty…that has to be where this comes from."

He wanted that, too. Wanted this sweet Southern girl who was blunt and real and made him want things he wasn't sure he was ready for. But walking away wasn't going to happen.

He needed her.

But he didn't want to talk and if he was being honest with himself he didn't want to think at all.

Instead, he reached for the seat release and pushed it all the way back. She shifted around until she straddled him. He reached up and pulled the pins from her hair, then gently brought it forward until it hung in thick waves around her shoulders.

Carefully, slowly, he drew the fabric of the skirt part of her dress up to her waist until he could touch her thighs. They were smooth and soft but there was the underlying muscled hardness of her legs. She shifted against him, her hands framing his jaw as she tilted her head to the left. Her hair brushed against his neck as she lowered her mouth and sucked on his lower lip. She thrust her tongue deep into his mouth as she lowered her body against him.

And his pants were too tight. He reached between their bodies, his knuckles brushing against the crotch of her panties, and he felt the warmth of her there. But he focused on undoing his pants and sighed when he was free of the restriction of cloth.

He took her thigh in one hand and then squeezed, sliding his hand under the fabric of her panties and taking her butt in his hand. He drew her forward until she was rubbing over him.

He groaned and tore his mouth from hers.

He wanted to feel her naked against him.

"Shift up," he said.

"What?"

"I want to take your panties off."

She nodded, bracing herself on the seat behind him. She moved until he was able to draw her underwear down her legs and off. He tossed it on the driver's seat and then turned his attention to her breasts, which were in his face. He buried his head in her cleavage, turning his head to the left and dropping sweet kisses against her exposed flesh. She shivered and shifted her shoulders as she settled back on his lap, moving over him, and suddenly he didn't know how long he could last with her on top of him.

She was hot and wet and wanted him.

He found the zipper at the back of her dress and drew it down, and the bodice gaped enough for him to nudge the fabric aside until her breast was visible. She wore a demi bra that bared part of the full globe of her breast. He reached up and pulled the lacy fabric down until her nipple was visible and then leaned forward to suck it into his mouth. With his other hand, he caressed her back, drew his nail down the line of her spine to the small of her back, then cupped her butt and drew her forward again.

He encouraged her to move against him. She started to rock, rubbing her center over his shaft, and he felt a jolt at the base of his spine as his erection grew again.

He suckled harder on her nipple and she put her hands on his shoulders, rubbing against him with more urgency. He reached between their bodies, parting her until he could rub her clit with his finger. She groaned his name and put her hands in his hair, forcing his head back until her mouth fell on his. She thrust her tongue deep into his mouth, her tongue mimicking the movements of her hips.

He felt like he was about to explode and started dropping little nips all over the curves of both of her breasts and her neck. He tangled one hand in her hair as he traced the opening of her body, then pushed his finger slowly up into her.

She made a wild sound that just drove him higher and he thrust his finger up inside her, feeling her body tighten around it. Then he added a second finger and she shifted, until she had her hands braced on his shoulders. She rode him as fiercely as she'd ridden her horse as she chased the barrels in the ring.

He rubbed her with his thumb while continuing to thrust his fingers inside her and then she threw her head back and called his name in a loud voice as she shuddered in his arms before collapsing against him.

He kept his fingers in her body and wrapped his arm around her back, holding her to him. He was on the edge and wanted to come but a part of him wouldn't allow it. Giving her pleasure was one thing but taking it for himself was something he wasn't ready to do.

She shifted and he moved his fingers from her body. He was tempted to bring them to his mouth and lick them clean. Taste her in that intimate way. But he didn't. He felt her shift her hips and the tip of him was right there, poised at the entrance of her body.

He tightened his buttocks and shifted his hips without thinking, entering her without meaning to.

She felt so damn good. Her body wrapped tightly around his length. It was almost as if she was made for him.

She was tight and it was only as she shifted and he felt himself moving deeper into her that he realized what he was doing. He was in the front seat of his car, hooking up with Amberley.

Amberley.

He'd promised himself that he wasn't going to hurt her and he knew if he let this go any further…

He couldn't do it. He couldn't have sex with her and then lie in bed with her. He couldn't just take her on the front seat of his car. Their first time should be special.

He wanted to be better than he knew he was.

She tightened her inner muscles around him and he knew he was going to lose it right then. So he lifted her up and off him. Turned her on his lap so that she was seated facing to the side. Gingerly he reached for his underwear and tucked himself back into it. He was so on edge it would only take one or two strokes for him to come, but he wasn't going to do that.

Not now.

She deserved better than this. Bold and brash Amberley, who had always given him a kind of honesty that made him want to meet her more than halfway.

Now that his mind was back in the game and he wasn't being ruled by his hormones he realized that a part of him had chosen the front of the car because it wasn't the bedroom.

Like the bedroom was only for…

Lucy.

"Uh, what's going on here?" Amberley asked.

He couldn't talk right now. The only thing he was capable of saying would be a long string of her curse words. And she certainly didn't need to hear that.

"Will? It's okay. Whatever it is you're thinking, it's okay."

"It's not okay," he said.

She put her hands on his face and forced him to

look up at her. She leaned down and kissed him so softly and gently that he knew he didn't deserve to have her in his life.

"Yes, it is. Am I the first…since Lucy?"

He nodded. "It's not that I don't—"

"You don't have to explain," she said. "I am going to go into my house now."

He couldn't stop her even though a part of him wanted to. He wasn't ready to make love to a woman who wasn't his wife. It didn't matter that he knew Lucy was gone and that Amberley was sitting here looking more tempting that a woman had a right to.

He wasn't ready.

Damn.

He had a half-naked woman in his lap and he was about to let her walk away.

"I'm sorry," he said abruptly. There had been a lot of firsts since Lucy had died and he'd never thought about this situation. It had felt natural and right…and then it hadn't.

"Don't be. We're friends."

"Friends don't do what we just did," he said.

"Some of them do," she returned. "'Night, Will."

She opened the door and got out of the car, straightening the top of her dress. He reached out and caught her hand. Brought it to his lips and kissed the back of it. He wished he had words to tell her what this night meant to him. How she was changing him and the way he looked at life and himself, but he could only gaze up at her. She tugged her hand free and touched his lips before turning and walking away.

He watched her leave, knowing he should go after her. But he didn't. He just sat there for a few more minutes until he saw her door close and then he got out and walked around to the driver's side of the car and got in. He was breathing like he'd run a fifty-yard dash, then he put his head on the steering wheel, unable to move.

He was torn. His conscience said to go back home and sleep in his empty bed. Let the frustration he felt make sleep impossible because he deserved to suffer.

He was moving on when Lucy couldn't. But he knew that was survivor's guilt talking. He took a deep breath. But all he could smell was sex and Amberley, and he wanted her again. His mind might be preaching patience but his groin was saying to hell with that and to take what he needed. But he couldn't.

It wouldn't be right for Amberley.

He knew this was a first.

The therapist he'd seen after Lucy's death said each first was going to be like a milestone and everything would continue to get easier. Hell, it couldn't get any harder than this. But damn, when was that going to happen? He felt like Don Quixote tilting at windmills and not getting anywhere. He was chasing something that was always just out of reach. But for tonight—tonight he'd almost touched it.

He'd almost given himself permission to move on. But he wasn't ready. What if he never was? What if by the time he was, Amberley had given up on him? Was she the one?

She'd certainly felt like someone important as he'd held her in his arms. He wanted more from her. Wanted more for himself than he'd taken tonight. He just wasn't sure what kind of sign he was waiting for.

It wasn't like Lucy was going to tell him it was

okay to move on. She couldn't. He knew he was the only one who could decide when it was time.

Was it time?

Maybe it wasn't time that was the important thing, it was the person. And it had felt very right with Amberley.

He finally felt like he'd settled down enough to drive back to the guest house he was staying in. As he got out of the car, he fastened his pants and then looked down and saw her panties on his seat.

He lifted them up, tucked them into his pocket and walked into the house feeling like a man torn in two. A man with both the past and the future pulling at him.

He didn't know what he was going to have with Amberley, but as he walked into the house and locked up behind him, he realized that Erin had left a light on for him and he went down the hall to Faye's bedroom.

He looked down on his sleeping little girl and felt that punch in the heart, as he knew he had to make sure that she didn't lose both her mom and her dad that day that Lucy had died. He knew that she deserved to have a father who was participating in life, not one who was locked away in his office and spending his days and nights in the cyberworld because he was afraid to live in the real one.

He leaned over the side of the crib and kissed her forehead.

And he could only hope that Amberley had meant it when she said she forgave him for tonight because he wasn't done with that cowgirl yet.

Eight

Amberley didn't sleep well that night. She wasn't a heartless monster—she understood where Will was coming from. And when they were at dinner at the club she'd realized that he was going to take some extra time if they were going to be more than friends. And being friends…well, how could she not be his friend.

She was hurt. She didn't hook up and sleep around, not anymore. She had found a place for herself where she'd started to adjust to her life. She'd begun to feel like she'd found a peace that had always been just out of reach. Then Will Brady showed up, arousing feelings from her past and reawakening the passion she'd thought she'd buried a long time ago.

But as she stared down at her breakfast cereal she knew she had wanted some kind of romantic fantasy.

That was the problem with watching as much television as she did and reading as many books. There were times when she just wanted her life to have a little more romance than it did.

Last night in his car, Will had made her feel things that she hadn't ever felt before. It had been more intense than the other times she'd had sex.

She wasn't really eating her cereal so she carried the bowl to the sink, and even though she knew she should clean it out right now, she just dumped the bowl in the sink, rinsed the cereal down the drain and then left it.

She had told Clay that she'd break in one of the newer horses and she intended to use Sunday morning to do it. She had a lesson this afternoon and then she needed to keep practicing her barrel riding, as she was signed up for a rodeo at the beginning of November.

But this morning all she had to do was get Squire ready for riding and lessons. The hands mostly had their own horses or used some of the saddle horses that Clay kept on the ranch. And Amberley's job was to make sure they were all in good shape and exercised if they weren't being used.

She heard some sounds coming from the stall set away from the other animals at the end of the stables and turned in that direction. She saw Sophie, Clay's pregnant wife, standing outside the stall talking to the bull inside of it.

"Sophie? Everything okay?" Amberley asked as she walked down toward her.

The stall held Iron Heart...the very same bull that had ended Clay's bull-riding career. Clay had saved the animal from being euthanized and brought him to the Flying E ranch.

"Yeah, just talking about stubbornness with someone who understands it."

Amberley had to laugh. "Clay."

Sophie nodded. "You'd think I was the first woman to ever be pregnant."

Babies again. It seemed that no matter how hard she tried she couldn't get away from pregnancy or babies. "I think it's sweet how protective he is."

"Well, that's probably because you're not the one being smothered," Sophie said with a small smile.

"I was once the one being ignored and told not to have a baby," Amberley said. She hadn't meant to. She was pretty sure that no one here knew about her past except her doctor in town.

"Oh, Amberley, I'm so sorry. Did you—"

"No. I had a miscarriage," Amberley said. "Gosh, I don't know why I'm telling you all this. I guess just to say that having Clay dote on you is a very good thing."

"I agree. Just wish he wasn't so stubborn all the time."

Amberley knew exactly how Sophie felt. "Aren't all men?"

"They are," Sophie said and then waved goodbye as she left the barn.

Amberley went back to Squire's stall, brushed and saddled the horse and then took him out for a ride. But she wasn't alone. Not in her mind. She remembered the way that Will had ridden when she'd taken him out here. She remembered how he'd looked when he'd gotten off his horse and looked up at her. Asked her for something she hadn't wanted to give him at the time.

Now she was wondering if that had been a mistake.

She was trying not to feel cheap and used. She'd meant it last night when she'd said she understood him calling things off. She had. She couldn't imagine the emotions he was going through as he tried to process his grief and move on from losing his wife. She only could funnel it through her experiences of losing her mom and of losing…

She shook her head to shove that thought away and focused on the ride. Squire wasn't really in the mood to run and when Amberley tried to force the issue he bucked and she hung on the first time, but when he did it again, she was knocked off and fell to the ground, landing hard on her shoulder.

Angry at herself for being distracted, she got up and took Squire's reins and started walking back to the stables. But the horse nudged her shoulder and she looked into those eyes and decided he was ready for another chance. She got back in the saddle and they took a leisurely gallop across the field, and she suddenly stopped thinking as she leaned low over Squire and whispered to him. Told him how he was born to run and that she was only here to guide him.

She had one of those moments where everything shifted inside her. Maybe it had been being bucked off the back of the horse that had shaken her and made her see things differently.

But she knew she couldn't keep doing everything in the exact same way. Squire liked being talked to. It had been a long time since she'd had a horse that needed to hear her voice. Mostly she communicated with clicks of her tongue and the movement of her thighs.

She realized that Will was like Squire and last night…well, last night he'd bucked her off, but if she was careful she could find a way to get him back into the stable. She shook her head.

Did she want to work that hard for a man whose life was somewhere else?

She drew in a sharp breath and realized that it didn't matter where his life was, he was going to be one big ol' regret if she didn't do everything she could to claim him. That she wasn't going to be able to just walk away. But she'd known that.

That was the reason why she'd said just to be friends even knowing there was no way she'd ever be satisfied with less than everything he had to give.

Last night he'd taken the first step in moving out of the past. She was willing to give him a little breathing room, but she wasn't going to let him retreat again.

She got back to the barn and stabled Squire and then went to her place to shower and change. She found that there was a note taped to her front door. She opened it.

Amberley,

Thank you for an incredible evening. I'd like to take you out to dinner tonight. Please be ready at seven. Wear something glamorous.

Will

This was the romance she'd been wishing for. And as she opened her front door and went to her bedroom to try to find the right dress, she knew that he wasn't running this time. And her heart did that little fluttery thing when she thought about him.

Will had taken care of everything for his date with Amberley. In the meantime, he was busy at his computer. The program he'd loaded onto the server at the Texas Cattleman's Club was spitting out all kinds of data and Will focused on analyzing it.

Erin had gone to town to run an errand and Faye was sitting on his lap chewing on one of her teething toys and babbling to herself as she liked to do while he worked. He squeezed his little girl closer to him as he continued working. A few articles popped up that he hadn't read before.

One was about a recluse who seemed to have a beef with just about everyone in Royal. Adam Haskell.

The reason his name had come up in the database was that he had written several strongly worded letters to the members of the town commission as well as local business owners. He might not leave his house very often, but he was very active online using Yelp and other local forums to criticize most of Royal. Will used his smartpen to send the articles and the name to Max to get his feedback. Perhaps his friend would have more intel on Haskell.

Faye shifted around on his lap and he turned to set her on the floor. She crawled toward the big plastic keyboard he'd picked up for her in town recently and then shifted to her feet and took two wobbling steps.

She walked.

His baby girl…

She dropped back down and started crawling

again. Will forgot the computers and got down on the floor.

"Faye, come to Daddy," he said.

She looked at him and gave him that drooly grin of hers and then turned and crawled to him.

The doorbell rang and he scooped Faye into his arms and carried her with him as he went to answer it.

Amberley.

"Hi," she said. "I wasn't sure how I was supposed to let you know I was available for our date tonight."

"I thought you'd text."

"Oh, sorry," she said. "I was here so I thought I'd just stop by."

"It's okay. Want to come in?" he asked, stepping back so she could enter. Faye was already smiling and babbling at Amberley.

"If you're not busy," Amberley said.

"I'm not busy. But this one just took two wobbling steps. Want to see if you can help me get her to walk?" he asked.

"Did she?" Amberley asked. "I'd love to help."

He carried Faye into the living room and then he was kind of at a loss. He placed her on the ground and she crawled around and then sat up and looked at him.

"Let me help. You sit over there," Amberley said, scooping Faye up and moving a few feet from him. Then she set Faye down on her feet and held Faye's hands in each of hers.

Faye wobbled a bit and Will realized he wanted to get this on camera.

"Wait. Let me set up my camera. I don't want to miss this," he said.

"Go ahead. We are going to practice, aren't we?"

Amberley asked, squatting down next to Faye and talking to her.

She smiled at Faye and Will watched the two of them together. They were cute, his girls, but he didn't let himself dwell too much on that. Instead he got his camera set up so that he would be able to capture the entire walk from one side of the room to the other. Then he went back to sit down so his baby could walk to him.

"Okay, I'm ready," Will said.

"Are *you* ready?" Amberley asked Faye.

She wobbled and Amberley let Faye hold on to her fingers and she started moving slowly, taking one step and then another. Will hit the remote so that the camera would start recording. Amberley let go of one of Faye's hands, and then the other, and his daughter smiled at him as she started walking toward him.

He clapped his hands and called her and she came right to him. He felt tears stinging his eyes as he lifted her into his arms, hugging her and praising her for doing a good job.

"She's such a rock star," Amberley said.

"Sit down," Will said. "Let's see if she will walk back to you."

Amberley did. "Faye, come to me."

Will set her on her feet and steadied her, then she took off again in that unsteady gait, walking to Amberley, who kept talking to her the entire time.

She scooped Faye up when she got to her and kissed the top of her head and Will realized that he'd found someone special in Amberley. She had a big heart and she deserved a man who would cherish that heart and give her the family she'd always craved. He wanted to believe he could be that man but he still had his doubts.

They spent another half hour letting Faye walk back and forth between them until Erin got back home.

"Look what Faye has mastered," Will said. "Amberley, go over there."

She did and they got Faye set up to walk over to her and Will noticed a look on Erin's face that he'd never seen before. It was almost as if she was disappointed that she hadn't been here for Faye's first steps. And suddenly he realized this was the first milestone in Faye's life that he hadn't shared with Erin.

"Sorry you missed her first steps," Will said. "I recorded it, though. She's so eager to go."

"She is. She's growing up so fast," Erin said.

"Yes, she is," Will agreed.

"Well, I'll leave you two alone," Erin said. "Are you still going out tonight?"

"Yes, I'm going out with Amberley."

"Oh, that's nice," Erin said.

Amberley left a few minutes later because she still had a lot to do, but Will felt deep inside that something had changed between them and he couldn't help getting his hopes up.

Amberley wasn't sure what she'd expected but the limousine Will pulled up in wasn't it. Will wore a dinner jacket and formal shirt and bow tie. He had his hair spiked and there was excitement and anticipation in those forest green eyes of his. She'd twisted her hair up and tonight the style and her hair seemed to be on the same page.

The dress she'd picked was a fitted dress in a deep purple color with sheer sleeves and a tiny gold belt. She'd paired it with some strappy gold heels that matched the belt. She put on the amber pendant he'd given her and some pearl drop earrings that her dad had given her when she'd turned eighteen. She felt further from her cowgirl self than she ever had before, yet perfectly at home in her skin.

"Damn, you look good," he said.

"Ditto," she said with a wink. "Why do we have a limo?"

"In case things get heated in the car again," he said.

"I assumed when you said you were spending the night that you meant at my place," she said.

"I did," he said. "I just really wanted to shower you with luxury and a limo seemed the right choice. Are you ready to go?"

She nodded. She didn't bother locking her door since the only way on or off the ranch was through the main drive. Will put his hand on the small of her back as they walked to the car. The driver was waiting by the door and he held it open for her. She wasn't sure how to get into the car and still look ladylike.

"Well, you can dress the girl up but that's about it," she said. "How the heck am I supposed to get into the car?"

"You sit down, ma'am, then swing your legs inside," the driver said.

"Thanks," she said. She wasn't embarrassed at having to ask. The truth was if she didn't know how to do something, unless she asked about it, she was never going to learn. She sat down and looked up at

Will as she swung her legs into the car and then she scooted over on the seat and he just smiled at her and then climbed in the way she would have.

"Next time we rent one of these I'm going to insist you wear a kilt so you have to do the same crazy maneuver I had to do," she said.

"Deal," he said.

The driver closed the door and she realized the back of the limo was very intimate. The lighting was low and Will put his arm along the back of the seat and drew her into the curve of his body.

"Thank you for coming out with me tonight," he said.

"Thanks for asking me out. You are spoiling me."

"Figured I had to make up for it since you already know I'm spoiled," he said with a grin that was both cocky and sweet.

"I was just being a bit jealous because I'm one of five and we always had to share everything. You haven't ever really acted spoiled around me," she said.

"Thanks," he said sardonically. The car started moving.

"Where are we going?"

"It's a surprise," he said, taking a silk blindfold from his pocket. "In fact, I'm going to have to insist you put this on."

"Uh, I'm not into any of that kinky *Fifty Shades* stuff," she said. She'd read the books, and while it had been exciting on the page, it wasn't really her thing.

"Understood. This is just to preserve the surprise I have in store for you."

"Okay," she said, turning to allow him to put the blindfold on her.

As soon as he did it, she felt more vulnerable than she would have expected. She reached out to touch him, her hand falling to his thigh. She felt the brush of his breath against her neck and then the warmth of his lips against her skin. She turned her head and felt the line of his jaw against her lips and followed it until their lips met.

Will let her set the pace, which she liked. But then he sucked her lip into his mouth as he rubbed his thumb over the pulse beating at the spot where her neck met her collarbone. She closed her eyes.

The scent of his aftershave and the heat of his body surrounded her.

The limo stopped and Will stopped kissing her.

Damn. He had distracted her. She hadn't been paying attention to anything. Not even how long they'd been in the car.

She reached up to take off the blindfold. "Leave it," he said.

"Will."

"It's part of the surprise," he said. "Trust me?"

Trust him.

She wasn't sure…which was a complete lie. She did trust him or she wouldn't be here. Or maybe it didn't matter if she trusted him or not. She wanted to be here and she was going to do whatever he asked.

Except for the kinky stuff…maybe.

She nodded.

"Good. Now scoot this way," he said, drawing her across the seat. She felt a blast of cold air as the door of the limo was opened and then Will kept his hand on hers, drawing her forward until she was on the edge of the seat.

"Swing your legs around," he said.

She did.

The ground beneath her sandals felt like dirt, not pavement.

"Where are we?"

He didn't answer her question. Instead he lifted her into his arms. "Please come back for us in two hours."

"Yes, sir," the driver said, and Amberley wrapped her arms around Will's shoulders, listening to the sound of the limo driving away.

Then Will started walking and the breeze blew around them a bit chilly until she felt a blast of heat, but they hadn't gone inside. He set her on her feet and took off the blindfold and she saw that they were on a wooden platform with those large infrared heating things positioned around a table. There were twinkle lights strung over the top of the table set for two and covered chafing dishes on a buffet next to it.

The ranch land spread out as far as the eye could see. The sky had started to darken and as she glanced up she saw her angel star.

"Surprised?"

More than he would ever know. It was as if he'd glimpsed into her soul and saw every romantic notion she'd ever had and then amped it up to provide this evening for her. Which meant her heart was in for a whole heap of trouble.

Nine

After almost losing her life at eighteen, Amber had promised herself she was going to live in the moment. And it was something that she'd always strived to do. On the back of a horse it was easy—there was no time to worry about if she was behaving the right way or if someone could see her imperfections. She just hadn't always felt comfortable in her own skin. But tonight she did. In town running errands it was a struggle, which was why she usually had to brace herself before she left her truck and walked among everyone else.

It was easier in Royal because no one knew her history the way folks back in Tyler did. But tonight was one of the few times where she felt totally present and like nothing else mattered.

She faltered a little when she saw the dishes he'd

had made for them. Some of them looked so fancy she was tempted just to stare at them instead of eat them. But Will put her at ease. He was snapping photos and then telling her that he was posting the photos of them online. She figured it was something like the photo story app that Cara had shown her but she wasn't interested.

She didn't want to connect with a world that was bigger than the ranch or Royal and maybe a few folks back in Tyler. That was good enough for her.

Will looked like she imagined a prince would look. He was polished and he talked easily and kept the conversation moving along from topic to topic. He knew horses and led her onto the topic of polo ponies and where she saw the breeding changes leading that field. And it didn't matter that she was dressed like a woman and not a cowgirl—she felt at ease talking about the animals.

"I did read an article last month that talked about a breeding program that a Saudi prince was spearheading. I think it's interesting in that he is working on increasing agility while maintaining stamina."

"That makes sense. I knew a guy in college who had gone to Europe to learn a centuries-old custom of Spanish horse dancing. It is basically training the horse to do very practiced moves, not unlike the Olympic horse events but even more controlled. He used some of those practices when we were playing polo and they worked," Will said.

"There really is room for crossover in all types of training. I was recently trying a technique with Montgomery that I saw used in the Olympics. Barrel racing is speed and mastery not only over the horse, but also over yourself."

"How often do you practice?" he asked.

"I try to get a couple of hours in every day. I am only really participating now when I can get away from the ranch," she said.

"And I couldn't tell the pattern you were using, but is there one? Or do you just have to circle all of the barrels in the least amount of time."

She took a bite of her dinner. "You have to go in a cloverleaf pattern and the one who does it the quickest is named the winner. They use an electric eye to do the timing. The key is to get as close to the barrels as you can so that you are taking the shortest route around them all."

"I'd love to watch you compete sometime," he said.

"Sure. I'll let you know the next time I'm going to a rodeo. I try to stay local here in Texas."

"Cool," he said and she wondered what that meant. Was he going to be in Texas for a while?

It wasn't really a response but she was living in the now. So that meant not pointing out that he could be back in Seattle before her next rodeo. Or would he?

She didn't ask the question because, to be honest, that would make things more complicated. Give her another thing to worry about it and that wasn't what she wanted right now.

"I've never had a guy buy me clothes before. Not even my dad. He used to have my grandma buy us stuff or take us shopping," Amberley said.

"Was it odd? It just reminded me of you," he said.

"Well, you were right. I would never have picked it out. I was surprised when I put it on," she said.

"I'm not surprised, I could picture you in it as soon as I saw it."

"Well, aren't you clever?" she said, winking at him. He was too charming for his own good. She suspected he knew it, as well, because he kept moving through life like nothing could touch him.

She wondered if that was how he had dealt with losing his wife all along or if it was just with her that he ran. Because some of the time he'd seemed to be okay. But then she remembered the other night, when he'd stopped himself from making love to her.

And she wondered if he was pretending like she was. She had gotten pretty damn good at believing the lie she told herself that she was okay. She wanted it to stop being a lie. And she knew she wanted to help Will get to a place where he was okay, too.

She suspected that it would happen in its own time and she knew she had to be patient, but a big part of her was afraid that time was going to take him back to Seattle before she could witness him getting there.

"So there I was standing in the middle of the river in Montana with a client that Dad wanted to impress, and he's asking me where I learned my fly-fishing technique, and all I could think of was if I say the Wii, Dad's never going to forgive me," Will said to Amberley as they finished up their meal. They had been having the most carefree conversation, and Amberley loved how he was telling all these personal stories from his childhood.

"What'd you do? I would have straight up said a video game," she said.

"I said natural instinct," Will said as he took a

sip of his wine. "Then my dad came over and said, 'Yup, that boy has a natural instinct for bull.' The client started laughing and I did, too, and honestly it was one of the first times my dad and I connected."

"That's funny. So did the client do what your dad wanted?" Amberley asked.

"Yes. Dad offered me a job after that, but as much fun as the trip to Montana was I knew that I didn't want to have to work that hard to charm people. Computers are easier," he said. "So I turned down the job and that pissed the old man off but I already had the job offer from Max so he got it."

"What does Max do?" Amberley asked.

"He's an ex-hacker-turned-billionaire tech genius. He owns St. Cloud Security Solutions. I'm the CTO for the company…the Chief Technology Officer."

"Dad would have been happy for me to stay on our ranch," Amberley said. "But I knew if I did then I'd spend the rest of my life there. It would have been easy to hide out there and just keep doing what I'd been doing."

"You wanted more," he said.

"I did. I still do. I like working for Clay and Sophie now that they are a couple, but I really would like to have my own stables someday," she said. If she had one dream it was that. She'd let horses take over the parts that she'd thought she'd fill with kids and a husband.

"Why would you have been hiding out if you had stayed at home?" he asked. "You seem like you grab life by the—I mean, you're pretty gutsy."

She smiled at the way he said that. She had tried grabbing life by the balls, but it had grabbed back, and her father said that actions had consequences, which she'd never gotten until that summer.

She took a deep breath. She'd thought telling Will about the hysterectomy would be the hard part, but this was a big part of who she was and why she was here in Royal.

"Um, well, I… This is sort of a downer, maybe we should save it for another night," she said.

Will nodded. "If that's what you want. But I want to know more about you, Amberley. Not the stuff that everyone can find out. The real you. And I think whatever made you want to hide is probably important."

She pushed her plate forward and folded her arms over each other on the table as she leaned forward. It was cozy and intimate at the table. Will had created an oasis for them in the middle of the Texas night.

"I took a job working at a dude ranch the summer I graduated from high school. I was thinking about what I'd do next and I knew I wasn't going to college. It just wasn't for me."

"Makes sense. You have a lot of natural ability with horses and I read about your rodeo wins online."

"You did?" she asked. "I didn't realize you'd looked me up."

"Yeah. I wanted to know more about you even as I was running from you and pretending that you didn't fascinate me."

"That's corny and sweet," she said.

"Thanks, I think."

Will made her feel like she mattered. It was kind, and it wasn't that others hadn't done that but he made her feel like she mattered to him. That it was personal and intimate and she hadn't had that before.

"So, you're on a dude ranch…"

She sat back in the chair and the words were there in her mind and she practiced them before saying them. It was easy in her head to remember what had happened. The cheap wine they'd bought at the convenience store. The way he'd never driven a pickup truck, so he had convinced her to let him drive. And then when he'd parked it and moved over to make out with her in the front seat until it had gone much farther.

Then of course she'd gotten pregnant and had expected Sam to be, well, a better man than he was. Of course, he'd said he was back to his real life and he'd help her financially but wanted nothing to do with her or the baby. It had hurt and there were times when his rejection haunted her. It made it easier for her to isolate herself on the ranch. But she wasn't going to say any of that to Will.

"There had been a group of guys from back east staying as guests at the ranch. They'd decked themselves out in Western clothes and they were flirty and fun and I ended up hooking with one of them. It was my first time and not his, and I'm afraid that freaked him a little bit and then…" She paused. She wasn't sure she could say the next part.

She looked at Will. He'd stopped eating and was watching her carefully.

She took a deep breath and the words spilled out quickly. Like tearing off a bandage, she did it as fast as she could. "I got pregnant. But there were complications, I started hemorrhaging and I almost died. I did lose the baby, and the only way to save me was for me to have a hysterectomy."

She stopped talking and it felt too quiet. Like even the animals and insects that had been in the background before were surprised by her words. She blinked and realized how much she hated telling this story. She never wanted to do it again.

Will didn't say anything and she started to regret telling him, and then he got up and walked around the table. He pulled her to her feet and into his arms and hugged her close. He didn't say anything to her, just wrapped her in his body, and the panic and the pain that had always been buried with that story started to fade a little bit as he held her and made her feel like she was okay.

That she wasn't damaged and broken.

Will didn't know the words to make everything all right and he could tell by the rusty way the story had come out that she was still a little broken from everything that had happened. He knew because no matter how many firsts he had after Lucy's death there were still things that bothered him. And there was no way that he was ever going to be completely washed clean of the past.

And now he knew that Amberley wasn't going to be, either. She was deeply scarred, as he was.

Hell, he wanted to do something to fix this thing that he couldn't fix.

He thought about how caring about someone could suck sometimes. He'd loved Lucy but had been unable to save her and he was starting to care more deeply for Amberley than he wanted to admit and there was no way in hell he could ever fix what had happened to her. No matter how much he wanted to.

"Siri, play Amberley playlist."

The playlist started and it was Jack Johnson's "Better Together." It was the perfect song for how he felt at this moment. He pulled her into the curve of his body and took one hand in his and kept his other wrapped around her waist as he danced her around the table, singing underneath his breath in that off-key way of his.

"You have a playlist for me?" she asked, tipping her head to the side and resting her cheek against his shoulder.

"I do. It's a bunch of songs that you might not have on vinyl," he said, hoping for a smile. He'd made the playlist this afternoon after she'd left his house. He'd wanted to give her something.

She rewarded him with a little half smile. And then he kept dancing and singing to her. He knew there were some pains that words couldn't heal and that time could only scab over. He had been debating his own pain for a year, trying to figure out if he was going to scar or just have a scab that he kept scratching and refreshing the hurt.

"I like this one," she said.

"I do, too," he said.

He wanted them to be better together. They could bring out the best in each other. Tonight he felt they'd jumped over that first hurdle. But he knew each of them was going to have more obstacles that they would bring to the relationship.

"I think we are going to be more than friends," he said.

"Me, too. I want more than that from you," she said. "But I don't want to make another mistake. I picked a guy who had nothing in common with me before. A man who didn't look at the world the same way I do."

"I care about you, cowgirl," he admitted.

"Me, too, city boy," she said with a grin.

The song changed to "SexyBack" and she just arched one eyebrow at him.

"Oops. Not sure how this got on there," he said.

"Maybe you were thinking about the way our last date ended," she said with a sassy grin.

Music had done what he couldn't as there were sweet and fun songs in the playlist, and after about five songs he noticed she wasn't tense and the tightness around her mouth had faded. She was laughing and smiling and while he still ached for her and the pain she'd gone through, he felt better for having cheered her up.

"So what do you think? Is there a place for the twenty-first-century technology in your music life?" he asked.

"You're a complete goofball, Will. I told you I use the music app on my phone," she said.

"You did but you said it was just for stuff you already loved."

"Not all the songs you selected are newer," she pointed out. "I think you like my kind of music."

"I do like it. And I was trying to ease you into it. Keep the shock value low," he said, aware that they were both talking about something inconsequential to keep from talking about the real emotions that were lying there between them. The truth that was there in the silence under the music that just kept playing on.

"Thank you."

"You're welcome," he said. "How does dessert sound?"

"Sweet?"

Some of her spunk was coming back and that was exactly what he'd been hoping for. "Good, because I asked for pineapple upside-down cheesecake with a salted caramel sauce."

"That sounds interesting," she said.

"Exactly what I was aiming for." He held her chair out for her and she sat back down.

He cleared away the dinner dishes and then brought back dessert. Everything had been set up by a private chef he'd hired in Royal. The dishes had been labeled and set up so that he could easily find them.

"Coffee or an after-dinner drink?" he asked.

"Coffee would be nice," she said.

"Decaf?" he asked.

"God, no," she said.

Another thing they had in common. He poured them each a cup of coffee from the carafe that had been prepared and then took his seat across from her again. He ignored the questions that still rattled around in his head. Instead he looked around at the night sky.

"My app still isn't doing what I want it to, so I'm not sure we are going to see anything fabulous in the sky tonight," Will said. He was unsure how to get the conversation back on track now.

"That's okay. I'm pretty happy sitting here staring at you," she said.

"Yeah?"

"Yup," she said. "Did that thing you did at the club last night work?" she asked.

"I think it might have. Do you know Adam Haskell?"

"Know him personally? No," she said. "But I do know his reputation. He seems to have a gripe about everyone and everything in town. Do you know he gave my riding lessons a low score on Yelp even though he's never taken a class from me?"

"I'm not surprised. He showed up in a relay link that I was chasing and then when I searched on his name it seemed to make sense that he might be the one releasing everyone's secrets. Do you know if he has any computer knowledge?" Will asked. Being able to post a bad review on Yelp and trolling people on social networks didn't take any real knowledge of computers or hacking. And a part of him had thought that Maverick was more skilled than Haskell seemed to be.

Ten

Will was just about to ask Amberley more questions about Haskell when his phone pinged. He ignored it, after making sure it wasn't Erin. Then it pinged again and started ringing.

"Sorry about this but I think I need to take this," Will said.

"Go ahead," Amberley said.

"Brady," he said, answering his phone.

"St. Cloud," Max said. "Where the hell are you? It looks like Haskell might be our man. I need you to come to Royal now. He's leading the cops on a high-speed car chase and I'm with a judge, the sheriff and a lawyer right now getting a warrant to search his property. I need you to analyze what we find and tell me if he's our man."

Will wasn't ready to end his evening with Amberley but business had to come first. This business, anyway. Once Maverick was caught he would be free to focus on Amberley and see where this was leading.

"I'll be there as quickly as I can," he said.

"Good. I'm texting you Haskell's address. Meet me there."

He ended the call and then looked over at Amberley, who was watching him carefully. "Haskell is on the run and Max is getting permission for me to go through his computer. I'm sorry to cut our date short—"

"No, don't be. I want that bastard Maverick caught as much as everyone else in Royal does. What can I do?"

"I could probably use your help going through things at Haskell's if you want to come with me."

"Will the cops let me help?"

"I don't know," he said. "But I didn't want our night to end."

"Me, either. I think I would. I don't really want to go home yet."

"Okay. Let me get the limo and we will head out."

The limo driver was quick to retrieve them and Will had him take them to his car, tipped the driver to move a box from the trunk over to his car while he and Amberley went inside and then sent the driver home. He checked in on Faye and updated Erin on what was happening before he and Amberley drove into town.

"I never imagined your life would be like this. I figured you just did things on your computer and that was it."

Will laughed. "Usually it's not this exciting. In

a big city Haskell could have slipped away anonymously. And if he was smarter he'd be driving sensibly instead of leading the cops on a high-speed chase."

"I know. He's not the brightest bulb according to the gossip I've heard at the diner."

"Really?"

"Yes, why?" she asked.

"It's nothing," he said. But in his mind there was a new wrinkle to Haskell being Maverick. It would take someone really smart to set up the kind of cover that Will had encountered while trolling the web for Maverick's true identity. It seemed a bit far-fetched that someone people considered not so bright would be able to do something like this on his own.

Was he working with someone?

Will was confident he'd be able to find the answers on Haskell's computer.

"Catching cyber criminals isn't usually like this. Though one time I did have to chase a guy down an alleyway. He'd had a program running on the police scanner to alert him if cops were dispatched to his property. It was a clever bit of code," Will said. He'd tried to convince the hacker to give up breaking into secure systems and bring him over to work for him but the guy wasn't interested.

"That must have been… Was it scary? I mean, are hackers and cyber criminals usually armed?"

"Some of them are. But usually I find the evidence and I don't go with the cops to arrest a criminal unless they are on some sort of mobile relay, where I have to track them while the cops move in. One time I had to wear a bulletproof vest and was stationed in a SWAT truck. There were all these guys with guns and riot gear on and there I was with my laptop…I felt like the biggest nerd."

"You could never be a nerd," she said.

"Thanks. But I can be. I'm sorry our date has taken a crazy turn."

"I'm not. Honestly this is the most exciting thing I've ever done," Amberley said.

He shook his head. There was pure joy in her voice and he realized again how young she was. True, there were only four years between them and she'd had a very harrowing experience when she was eighteen, but the way she was almost clapping her hands together at the thought of being part of the investigation enchanted him. And turned him on.

"Why are you looking at me like that?" she asked.

"Like what?" he countered, trying to sound innocent, not like he'd been imagining her wrapped around him while he kissed her senseless.

"You know," she said.

"Uh, this is the place," Will said as he turned into the driveway of a run-down ranch-style house. The yard was overgrown and there was a big sign that said Keep Off the Grass and No Solicitors.

As they got out of the car, Will noticed there was also a sign in the front window that read Protected by Smith & Wesson.

"Not the friendliest of men," Amberley said. "So what do we do now?"

Max was waiting outside for them and a patrol car was parked at the curb with the lights flashing. Some of the neighbors poked their heads out of the front door but most weren't interested.

"Thanks for coming. The sheriff wants us to help go over the house with his team just to be an extra set of computer expert eyes. He thinks we might see something relevant that his officers would overlook since it's not the kind of crime they are used to dealing with," Max said. "Did I interrupt a date?"

"Yes."

"I'm sorry," Max said. "Dang, I wish this had happened another night."

"Me, too. But it didn't. So let's get this taken care of," Will said.

Max knew that this was the first real date that Will had been on since Lucy's death.

"Do you want to take his computer back to your place?" Max asked.

"Let me see the setup first," Will said. "Do you know Amberley Holbrook? She's the horse master at Clay's ranch."

"Nice to meet you Amberley," Max said.

"Same."

They went into Haskell's house and the cops were gathering other evidence while Max, Will and Amberley found his computer. "This doesn't look very sophisticated."

"No," Will agreed. "It looks like it's about ten years old."

Not that you needed a new or sophisticated machine to hack. Most of the time if he ran from a DOS prompt he could get into over-the-counter software and some social media sites.

Will hit the mouse to see if there had been a program running or if there was a security login.

And then he sat down in the dirty chair to get

to work. He lost himself in the computer programming…or tried to. But the smell of Amberley's perfume lingered in the room and he couldn't help but think this was one time when he didn't want work distracting him from his real life.

Tonight he'd come closer than ever to finding something with Amberley that he hadn't wanted to admit had been missing in his life.

Max and Will talked quietly while the computer ran some program. Everyone had something to do and she was just standing in the corner trying not to get in anyone's way.

She hadn't seen Will work before. She stood there watching him when she thought no one was looking. He was intense as his fingers moved over the keyboard. He took a small dongle from his key ring and plugged it into the USB drive and first lines of text started scrolling on the screen, which meant nothing to her, but Will nodded and then started typing on the keyboard.

"He's one of the best in the world."

She glanced over her shoulder at Max St. Cloud, who stood next to her. She didn't know much about the man except he was Will's partner at St. Cloud Security Systems. She also knew he was engaged to Natalie Valentine, a local wedding dress designer.

"He's awesome," she said, then realized how lame that sounded. "Sorry, I'm really better with horses than people."

Max laughed in a kind way. "It's okay. I should probably leave you alone but I was curious about you."

That didn't sound very reassuring.

"Why?"

"Will hasn't done anything but work since... Faye's birth. I think you're the first woman he's been out with," Max said.

"I know," she said. She was the first. That's why she should be cautious about falling for Will. He was a city guy who'd lost his spouse, so in her mind there were danger signs all around him. But he was also the guy who'd made her a special playlist and could ride like he'd been born in the saddle.

"Good," Max said. "Want to help me look for USB drives, other storage devices, a tablet, maybe an external hard drive?"

"Sure," Amberley said. "I know what some of those things are but what's an external hard drive?"

Max smiled. "Should be a rectangle shape and thin. Follow me, the lead detective needs to give us some gloves and tell us how to search."

Amberley followed him into the other room and after a brief explanation of what they were to do and orders to track down an officer and let him know if they found anything, they were both sent to look.

"If you take the living room and I take the bedroom we might be able to finish this search quickly and get you back on your date," Max said.

"Sounds good," she said.

She followed Max out of the room where Will was working and went into the living room. It was dusty and cluttered, but as Amberley walked around the room she noticed a system. There was a pile of *Royal Gazettes* next to his recliner. The weekly newspaper was stacked up almost to the arm of the chair. She glanced down at the paper on top. It was the one from two weeks ago that had run the story of Will coming to town to help find and stop Maverick.

He'd underlined the word *Maverick*. That was interesting. It could be a clue or maybe Haskell was just ticked off that someone else was ruining the lives of Royal's citizens and taking over his role.

Amberley sorted through the top papers and noticed that he'd used his black pen to mark every story relating to the cyber menace. Was it a kind of trophy for him? Seeing the stories about himself in the paper? She set them in a neat stack on the seat of the chair to show to the officers who were in the house and then started looking through the mess on the side table. There were prescription pill bottles and a community college book on computer software that looked to be about three years old. She stuck that on her pile of stuff and kept moving.

She found some other things that were personal and she realized how odd it was to be going through someone else's house. Haskell always seemed like an old curmudgeon to her when she'd seen him in town but she found a picture of him on one of the bookshelves with a girl from when he'd been in his twenties. He'd been smiling at the camera and he had his arms wrapped around the woman. Amberley didn't recognize her but she wondered what had happened to her.

Was she the reason why Haskell hated the residents of Royal so much now?

"Find anything?" Max asked as he entered the room.

"Not the hard drive, but I did find these papers,

where he has underlined every mention of Maverick. Not really hard evidence but I saw on a crime show that serial criminals like to keep references to their crime as a sort of trophy. So this might mean something. And I found this old computer book on his table. Maybe he was brushing up his skills?" Amberley said. "There's a lot of junk and dust in this room."

"In this house," Max said. "I think the papers might be a lead. And the computer book, let me see that, please."

She handed it to Max. He opened the book and read some of Haskell's handwritten notes. "Let me see if Will can make anything of this."

She followed Max back into the area where Will was. Will turned when they entered.

"He was definitely using an external source," Will told them. "I think if we find that we might find the evidence we need. Did you two find anything?"

"We found this," Max said, handing it over to Will. "It was an MS training class. So not anything in here that would help him mask his online presence. So we're done here?"

"I think so," Will said.

"I'll let everyone know," Max said, leaving the room.

Will went back to the small home office and Amberley followed him, watching from the doorway as he pounded his fists on the desk.

Going in to check on Will hadn't seemed like a bad idea until she put her hands on his shoulders and he pulled her closer to him. He was frustrated—she could see that. He stood up and she looked into his eyes and she wanted to say something or do something to help him not feel so hampered by this investigation.

"Let's finish this up so we can get back to our date," Will said. "I'm not close to being finished with you."

She hoped she looked calmer than she felt because every part of her was on fire and she knew that she'd changed. That sharing the past with Will had freed her in a way she hadn't expected it to.

The secret that she'd always hid from the men she'd hooked up with had been a weight she hadn't even been aware of until now. Until she was free of it. She heard the cops talking and Max went in to talk to Will and she just stood there in the cluttered, dusty living room, knowing that her entire world had changed.

A new hope sprang to life inside her and she wondered if she'd found a man she could trust.

Eleven

"I should get you back home," Will told her as they walked out of Haskell's house.

"Okay," Amberley said, glancing at her watch. "I have to be up early for the horses."

"Wait a second," he said, turning and leaving her by his car to go over to where Max stood.

She watched as he spoke to Max, his business partner and friend, and remembered how Max had talked to her. She wasn't sure if he'd been warning her to be careful with his friend, or just warning her that Will might not be ready for whatever was happening between them.

She rubbed her hand along the back of her neck and shivered a bit. The night was chilly and she was outside without a coat on. But it wasn't too cold. She just suddenly felt very unsure.

And she didn't like it. It wasn't as if Max had said anything that she hadn't been aware of, she knew that Will hadn't dated since Lucy's death. She knew that she might be someone he cared for but she might also be the woman he was using to help him get over losing his wife. But hearing it from someone else's mouth was making her think that maybe she wasn't being smart.

Her heart didn't care and neither did her body. In fact, maybe her being his temporary woman was exactly the right thing for her. He was her first in many ways, too. The first guy she'd told about losing the baby. The first guy she'd really cared about since she was eighteen.

She'd thought she loved Sam. Well…at least cared about him. But this thing she felt for Will was so much stronger. She didn't know if it was real, either. And it was harder than she had anticipated to keep her cool. Not to let her emotions overwhelm her. But when Will came back over, shrugged out of his jacket and draped it over her shoulders, she felt like she was fighting a losing battle inside of herself.

"Max is going to text me if he hears anything," Will said. "Let's go home."

Home.

An image of her, Will and Faye popped into her mind and she didn't want to shove it out. She wanted it to be true. Watching Faye take her first steps today and feeling that punch of joy in her stomach had made her realize that she could have a family. She didn't have to give birth to love a child. And while a part of her realized that it was dangerous to think that way about Will and Faye, another part of her was already putting herself in the picture.

"Okay."

He held open the door for her and she slid into the passenger seat. She slipped her arms into the sleeves of Will's jacket. It smelled like his aftershave and after she fastened her seat belt she put her hands in the pockets and felt something…

She pulled it out. It was a photo. She glanced down at it and saw Lucy. He was carrying around a picture of his wife. The door opened and she shoved the photo back in her pocket, but it caught on the fabric and he noticed her hand as he slid behind the wheel.

"What's that?" he asked.

She felt like there was a weight in the pit of her stomach… "This."

She handed it to him.

He took it and as he did she noticed there was typed information on the back of the photo. And she realized what it was. She had a card like that with her mom's picture on it that she'd gotten at her funeral. It was Lucy's funeral card.

"I—I haven't worn that jacket since the day we buried her," Will said. "I didn't even realize it was in there."

He looked down at the picture and ran his thumb over her features and Amberley felt like she'd interrupted a very private moment. She shouldn't be in the car with him. Or wearing his jacket or even falling for him. She didn't know where Will was in his head but he wasn't with her. Would he ever fully be able to be with her?

That thought hurt more than she'd expected it to.

"She would have liked you," Will said.

"Would she?" Amberley asked.

Watching Will gently caress his late wife's picture gave Amberley an odd feeling. Like when she had cut herself with a knife cooking dinner and she knew she'd cut herself, but it didn't start bleeding right away or hurt for a few seconds. The wound was there. She was just in denial about how deep it went.

"Yes. It's not…I'm not holding on to the past," Will said. "This isn't like the other night."

"Please, you don't have to explain."

"But I want to. Lucy is gone and she's a part of my past," Will said. "She'll always be a part of my life because of Faye."

"I know that. Really I do. I'm not upset," she said. She was trying to make the words true by saying them with conviction but in her heart, she was sad. And she felt just a little bit sorry for herself.

"Amberley."

She looked over at him and she'd never seen him so intense before.

"I want you to know that I'm not dating you just to try to move on from Lucy's death. And I know that we haven't had much time together but I'm not fooling around with you and using you."

She wanted to believe him. He had said the words that she could have asked him to say but she wasn't too sure they were the truth.

Will dropped off Amberley at her place, where she shrugged out of his jacket and gave it back to him. "Thanks for a very interesting date."

"You're welcome," he said. He wanted to come in.

His gut said that he shouldn't just let her walk away, but he didn't know if pushing her now was the right thing to do. So he waited until she was safely inside her house and then drove back to his place.

But when he got there he just sat in the car holding Lucy's picture. Life with Lucy had been uncomplicated. They'd met in college and both of them had come from similar backgrounds. Everyone had said they were a match made in heaven. And while he loved her and cared for her, he knew they'd been growing apart in the months before Faye's birth.

Sometimes he suspected his guilt stemmed from that. That he'd been drifting out of their marriage when she'd died. He went home and the house was quiet with everyone sleeping. He checked in on Faye.

He had the funeral card that Amberley had found earlier and brought it into Faye's room with him. When he looked down at his sleeping daughter's face he could see the resemblance to Lucy. It was growing stronger every day and it made him miss his wife.

He felt a pang in his heart when he thought about raising their daughter alone. And there was a part of him that wondered if he'd ever really be able to bring another woman into their lives. He liked Amberley. He wanted her fiercely but he didn't know if he was right for her.

If she was just a good-time girl, then he wouldn't hesitate to get involved, but everything had changed tonight when she'd told him about the child she'd lost. There was a hidden vulnerability to her that he couldn't ignore now that he'd glimpsed it. And no matter how hot they might burn together he sensed that she was going to want more from him. And he knew she deserved more from him. He couldn't do it.

After a restless night he woke up early and went into the kitchen, where Erin was feeding Faye breakfast. He poured himself a cup of coffee and then sat down.

"How was your date?" Erin asked.

"It was okay. We did get a break in the Maverick case last night."

"That's good," Erin said. "So does that mean we won't be here much longer?"

"I'm not sure yet," Will said. "Why?"

"Just wondering if I should start packing up our stuff. I've got to run a few errands in town this morning," Erin said.

"We'll probably be here at least until the end of the month," he said.

"Okay," she said.

"I'll watch Faye while you go to town," Will said.

"Are you sure?" she asked.

"Yes. I missed spending time with her last night and you had to work overtime."

"You know I don't mind."

Will nodded at her. "I do know that. But I also know errands go quicker without Faye."

"True. Thanks, Will."

"No problem," he said. He moved around to take the spoon from Faye. "Go on. I've got breakfast."

Erin quickly left the room. He touched his daughter's face and she cooed and blinked up at him.

"Hello, angel," he said. "You're hungry this morning."

She kicked her legs and arms and smiled at him. "Dadada."

"That's right. Daddy's here," he said as he scooped her up into his arms.

He held her close and buried his face in the soft curls at the top of her head. He changed her diaper and then carried her into his office. "Ready to help Daddy work?"

"Dadadada," Faye said.

"I'll take that as a yes," he said, then grabbed his laptop and Faye's little toy computer and sat down in the big double chair in the corner. He put his laptop on his lap after he'd set down Faye and she reached for her toy and mimicked his motions.

Then she looked over at him and smiled.

He smiled back at her as she started pounding on the keys with her fingers. His little computer whiz.

He knew he should be looking up some of the information he had found on Haskell's computer, but Amberley was on his mind and he typed her name into the search bar instead. He saw the pictures of her in the rodeo and then did a deeper search and found an old newspaper article from when she was a junior in high school. It was a profile of her as the junior barrel-racing champ with her horse. She looked so young and innocent.

Only seeing that photo of her and comparing it with the woman he knew now showed how much life had changed her. He leaned back and Faye crawled over to him and climbed on his lap the way she did. He lifted her with one hand and shifted his computer out of her way with the other.

She looked at the picture on the screen.

He looked down at her.

"Dadada," she said. Then babbled a string of words that made no sense to him.

Had she recognized Amberley? They'd played together for an entire afternoon but would that be enough for her to recognize her?

And was he doing Faye a disservice by allowing her to get attached to Amberley when Will wasn't sure what was going to happen between them. Sure he'd told her he saw a future with her, but now he was having second thoughts. How could he promise her something like a future when he wasn't even sure where he was going to be in a month's time. He was pretty sure he wasn't going to stay in Royal. His entire family was in Bellevue. His parents and Faye's maternal grandparents. But Lucy's sisters didn't live in Bellevue; one of them was in Oregon and the other in San Francisco.

And after she'd seen that picture of Lucy in his pocket was she going to want to be with him? Did she think he was still hung up on his wife?

Hell.

There were no answers, only more confusion and a little bit of sadness because if there was ever a woman he wanted in his life it was Amberley. She suited him. She wasn't his twin, which was probably why he enjoyed her so much. She was blunt and funny and unafraid to admit when something confused her. She was sassy and spunky and he wanted her to have all the happiness that he saw on her face in that picture when she'd been sixteen.

He didn't want to be the man who'd completed

what the jerk from the dude ranch had started. The man who showed her that she couldn't trust.

But how could he do that for Amberley and not risk hurting himself. He'd promised himself that he would never fall in love again when he'd held Lucy's hand as she lay dying. He'd never felt that abandoned and alone before and he'd promised himself that he'd never feel that way again.

Amberley went about her business all morning, ignoring Will and anyone who wasn't four-legged. Cara arrived on Monday afternoon with the latest news about Adam Haskell. After he'd crashed his car and been captured, an ambulance had transported him to the hospital. Apparently his condition was still critical.

"Sheriff Battle impounded the car. I heard they had to medevac Mr. Haskell to the hospital after he crashed on the highway," Cara said.

"Sounds like it was nuts," Amberley said.

That meant that Will was probably going to be done here in Royal. Everyone seemed to agree that Haskell was Maverick and she was afraid that Will was going to leave now. It hardly mattered that she was still upset with him for the way their date had ended and angry at herself for letting pride make her send him away. But she was tired of trying to compete against a ghost for him.

But she couldn't change the past. She knew that better than anyone.

"Why do you think they were after Haskell? Maybe they finally got tired of his crappy online reviews."

Amberley glanced over at Cara, who was smiling and texting while she was talking to her. "What do you know about Haskell?" Amberley asked. Cara's family had lived in Royal for generations.

Cara looked up from her phone at Amberley. "Not much. He really didn't like high school kids. One time I tried to sell him a magazine subscription and he was a jerk."

"Why did you even bother?"

"Someone dared me," Cara said.

They worked in silence for twenty minutes until they were done with the horses, and Amberley wanted to pretend she'd found some inner peace about Will, but she hadn't.

"Amberley?"

"Yes."

"Will you watch me run the barrels? I need to gain a second or two and I can't figure out where," Cara said.

"Sure. The barrels are set up. I'll go and walk the path while you saddle up." Amberley walked out of the barn and over to the ring to double-check that everything was where it should be.

She noticed that Erin was walking toward the stables with Faye in her arms. The little girl was wearing a pair of denim overalls and a rust-colored long-sleeved shirt underneath it.

"Hi, Erin," Amberley said as the other woman came over to her. Faye held her hands out toward Amberley and she reached over to let her grab on to her finger as the baby babbled at her.

"Hiya," Erin said. "We were out for our afternoon

walk and I thought she might like to see some of the horses."

"Perfect. Cara is going to be out in a minute with her horse to practice. That will be fun to watch."

Amberley couldn't help thinking that Erin was here for something other than to watch the horses. And when Cara came out and noticed they had company, she gave Amberley a look.

"Warm up, Cara. Then let me know when you're ready to take your run," she said. She had a stopwatch on her phone that she'd use to time Cara after she warmed up.

"I didn't realize you were working," Erin said.

"It's okay. You haven't been over to the stables to ride. Do you like horses?" Amberley asked.

"I don't know. I mean, I read books with horses in them growing up but I've never been on one," Erin said.

"We can fix that. Do you want to go for a ride?" she asked.

"Yeah. Sort of. I'm not sure when, though," Erin said.

"Well, the best way to get to know horses is grooming them. And I think even little Miss Faye would like to be in the stables. When Cara is done with her run we could go and meet the horses," Amberley said.

"I'd like that," Erin said.

Faye squirmed around and reached for Amberley. Erin arched an eyebrow at her and held Faye out toward her. Amberley took the little girl in her arms and hugged her. She was going to miss Faye when she and Will left. And though she hadn't spent that much time with the baby she knew she'd become attached to her.

Not her smartest move.

But then everything about Will Brady rattled her.

Cara rode over to the fence and smiled down at Faye.

"Who is this little cutie?"

"Faye Brady. Will's daughter," Amberley said.

"She's adorable," Cara said.

Amberley agreed and she realized that she wanted this little girl to be hers. She wanted that image of the family that had popped into her head last night to be real and she knew it couldn't be. Finding Haskell meant Will would be leaving. Maverick was done terrorizing Royal and Will Brady was going to be leaving Texas and taking a piece of her heart with him.

She handed Faye back to Erin as Cara started doing her run. And Amberley tried to settle up with the fact that this was her life.

Twelve

Sheriff Battle, Will was told, had found a hard drive and some other incriminating evidence in Haskell's car. The police had brought it over to him this afternoon and Will was trying to break the security code to access the info within. The coding was different from anything he'd found on Haskell's home computer. It was more complex and nuanced than what he'd seen before.

Will was on the fence as to whether the same programmer could be responsible for both codes. Haskell had used a complex passcode on his computer, but the security on the hard drive was different. Will used all the skills he'd developed as a hacker back in his teenage days, before he'd settled down to working on the right side of the law.

He kept Max and the sheriff up-to-date on his

progress and after spending six hours working at a cramped desk, he got into the hard drive and found all of the files that Maverick had used to blackmail and scandalize Royal.

"This is it," Will said, calling over the sheriff. "All the files and the paths he used to upload the information are on here. This is pretty much your smoking gun."

"Just what I wanted to hear," Sheriff Battle said. He pulled his cell phone from his pocket. "I'm going to call the hospital and see if he's awake for questioning. Wonder if he has asked for a lawyer yet? Thanks for your help, Will."

"No problem, Sheriff," Will said.

The sheriff turned away and Will heard him ask for Dr. Lucas Wakefield. Will's own phone pinged and he saw that he had a text from Max, who was coming into the building. He went to meet him in the hallway.

"The hard drive had all the evidence the sheriff needs to charge Haskell. He's on the phone to the hospital right now to see if Haskell can be questioned. I'm a little concerned that the coding and some of the scripts on the hard drive were way too sophisticated compared to the home computer, but maybe he was just trying to cover his trail," Will said. "I'll put together some questions about that for the sheriff to ask when they interrogate Haskell."

"There won't be an interrogation," Sheriff Battle said as he came into the hallway. Will and Max turned to face him. "Haskell is dead."

The crash had involved Haskell's car flipping over when he hit a guard rail on the highway. They'd had to use the jaws of life to get him out of the car and then he'd been medevaced to the hospital.

"Well, hell," Will said. He didn't like the lack of closure on this case. He was used to catching hackers and seeing them brought to justice. The entire thing with Haskell was making the back of his neck itch. Something wasn't right. It had been too easy to find the hard drive in his vehicle. Though to be fair, Haskell probably hadn't expected to crash his car and die.

Max had some stronger expletives and the sheriff looked none too happy, either. Will didn't know about the other two but he was beyond ticked off. Hacking was one thing and unmasking cyberbullies was something that he was known for. It frustrated him that he was having such a difficult time unmasking Maverick. And it ticked him off even more to think that the man who'd had the messy house and seemed to have only taken a computer class at the community college had outsmarted everyone in Royal for months before he was fatally injured in a car crash.

Things weren't adding up as far as Will was concerned.

"What were you saying about maybe there being more than one person involved?" Sheriff Battle asked Will.

"It was just a theory. I can't confirm it without information from Haskell. He might have been smarter than everyone thought and used the town's perception of him as cover," Will said.

"Do you feel confident that I can tell the townspeople that Haskell was Maverick?" the sheriff asked him.

No. He didn't. And that wasn't like him. Had he let Amberley distract him from his job? Had he missed something obvious that he shouldn't have? He couldn't say and both men were looking at him for an answer. "The hard drive belonged to Maverick," Will said. "That is definite. But there is no real proof that it was Haskell's or that he programmed it."

"That's not good enough," the sheriff said.

"You could announce that Maverick's been caught and see what happens," Max suggested.

"I'm still running that program from the club's server and I can use the code on the hard drive to start a trace back…to see if I can tie the code to any known hackers on the dark web," Will said.

"Okay. Let's do it. I'm going to hold a press conference and say that we believe Haskell was Maverick. If there are no more attacks then… Hell, this isn't the way I like to do a job. It's half guesswork," Sheriff Battle said.

"I wish we had more to go on but without talking to Haskell there's just not enough on the drive or his personal computer to tie the two together," Will said.

He didn't like it. It felt to him like there was something more going on here.

"Well, I guess we're going to have to play the cards we've been dealt," the sheriff said.

"It could be a group effort," Will said. "In which case exposing Haskell might convince the other members or his partner to go underground."

The sheriff went out to make his announcement and Max took one look at Will and said, "Let's go get a drink."

The two of them went over to the Texas Cattleman's Club, and about thirty-five minutes later the television over the bar was carrying the press conference announcing that Maverick had been identified. A lot of people in the club were surprised but not overly so.

"He always had a beef with the townsfolk of Royal," someone remarked.

"Guess it was his way of getting back at all those supposed slights."

Max took a swallow of his scotch and Will did the same. He couldn't shake the feeling that something wasn't right. Chelsea Hunt joined them a few minutes later.

Will only had to glance at her to know she didn't believe that the trouble with Maverick was over, either. "Scotch?"

"Yes," Chelsea said as she sat down next to Max. "The sheriff brought me up to speed before he started his press conference."

"This isn't the way I expected this to end," Max said.

"Something tells me this isn't over," Will said. "It just doesn't feel like it."

And he was right.

He got a text three hours later when he was halfway back to the ranch that nude pictures of Chelsea Hunt had shown up on the website Skinterest.

The release of the photos seemed to be timed to embarrass the sheriff's department. Will pulled the car over to call Max; he didn't know Chelsea well enough to call her.

"St. Cloud," Max said.

"It's Will. I'm not back at my computer yet but I wanted to let you know that I can run a trace to see if the posting of the nude photos was time delayed or if they were put up after the sheriff's news conference."

"Good. This has gotten out of hand," Max said. "Chels is beyond ticked off. We need to know if it was Haskell."

"I'll do what I can. I'll be in touch soon," he said, hanging up.

The culprit had identified himself as Maverick and there was no doubt in anyone's mind that he was to blame since the way the photos were released was similar to the other scandals Maverick had caused. And after all, Chelsea was the one who'd been spearheading the effort to stop Maverick and she and Max were old buddies, which was how Will and Max had ended up in Royal.

Will remotely started the trace from the Skinterest site and then texted Max back that he should have something in a few hours. He was pissed. It felt like Maverick was thumbing his nose at them. He'd waited until after Sheriff Battle's press conference and, of course, the news that Adam Haskell had died in the hospital. It wasn't that the track was cold; they still had a few leads, but it was damn sure not as hot as it once had been.

Max told him to take the afternoon and evening off and they'd regroup tomorrow to figure out what to do next.

Next?

Will didn't bother to text Max back after that, he just got back on the road. He knew where he needed to be now and it wasn't the guest house he'd called home these last few weeks.

It didn't even matter to him that the way he'd left things with Amberley was less than ideal. He needed her. Needed to see her.

She was another loose end here in Royal and he was tired of running. Tired of feeling like he was losing. He needed to talk to her and…well, more. But he didn't dwell on these things as he pulled up in front of her house.

He sat in the car for a good ten minutes, debating between going up to her door and going somewhere else.

Maybe he would be better suited going to town and finding a rowdy bar and drinking and maybe getting into a fight to work out his frustration. But then her front door opened and she leaned there against the doorjamb wearing a pair of faded jeans and a top that hugged her curves. Her hair was pulled back in its customary braid.

She chewed her lower lip as their eyes met.

He turned off his car, shutting off the sound of screaming death metal that he'd put on because it suited his mood, and got out.

"We lost Maverick. It wasn't Haskell."

"I heard the news," she said. "Cara was texting with one of her friends in town when the Skinterest link popped up."

"I'm so…I don't know why I came here. I'm frustrated and edgy and I just couldn't go home and the only place I want to be is with you."

She nodded. "Then come on in."

He crossed her yard in angry steps and climbed

up the stairs. She stepped back to give him room to walk past her. But as soon as he stepped inside and smelled the fragrance of apples and cinnamon, his temper started to calm.

"I've got whiskey or beer, if you want to drink. I've got a deck of cards if you want to play poker. I would say we could go for a ride but I'm not a big fan of riding when you're upset. I think it puts the horse in danger," she said.

"I don't want to ride horses," he said.

"Good. So what's it going to be? Did I list anything that sounds good to you?" she asked.

"No," he said. "I want you. I can't think of anything except your mouth under mine and my body inside yours."

She flushed but didn't move from where she stood with her back against the cream-colored wall. Then, with a nudge of her toe, she pushed the front door. It closed with a thud and she stepped away from the wall.

"Where do you want me?" she asked.

"Are you sure?" he asked. Because even as he was walking toward her, his blood running heavy in his veins, he wanted to give her a chance to say no.

"Yes. Make that a 'hell, yes.' I have been aching for you, Will. Every night when I go to bed I'm flooded with fantasies of you and me together. That orgasm you gave me was nice but it only whetted my appetite and left me hungry for more."

"I'm hungry, too," he said.

Will walked forward until not even an inch of space separated them. He pulled her into his arms, kissing her slowly, thoroughly and very deeply. He caught her earlobe between his teeth and breathed into her ear, then said, "I'm not sure how long I can last."

She shivered delicately, her hands clutching his shoulders, before she stepped back half an inch.

"That's okay," she said, and it was. She had been dreaming of this moment—when he would forget about everything except her, when he needed her more than anything else. She wasn't about to let him slip away again without knowing what it was like to make love to him.

She tugged the hem of her thermal shirt higher, drawing it up her body, and he touched her stomach. His hands were big and warm, rubbing over her as she pulled the shirt up and over her head. She tossed it on the floor and he put his hands on her waist, turning her to face the mirror in the hallway.

He undid the button of her jeans and then slowly lowered the zipper. She stared at them in the hall mirror, concentrating on his hands moving over her body. Then, she glanced up to see he was watching her in the mirror, as well.

Their eyes met and he brought his mouth to her ear, and whispered directly into it, "I love the way you look in my arms."

He stepped back, tugged at her jeans and then slid them down her legs. She shimmied out of them, leaving her clad in only a pair of whisper-thin white cotton panties. Delicately she stepped out of the jeans pooled at her ankles, balancing herself by putting one hand on the table in front of her.

The movement thrust her breasts forward. He unclasped her bra, her breasts falling free into his waiting hands. She looked in the mirror as a pulse of pure desire went through her. He stood behind her, his erection nestled into the small of her back. His hands cupped her breasts, and his eyes never left her body as his fingers swirled around her nipples.

She turned in his arms, reaching up to pull his head down to hers. Her mouth opened under his and she wanted to take it slow but she couldn't. She was on fire for him. He was everything she ever wanted in a man and he was here in her arms.

He slid his hands down her back and grasped her buttocks, pulling her forward until he could rub the crown of his erection against her center. She felt the thick ridge of his shaft against her through the fabric of his pants. He reached between them to caress her between her legs.

He lowered his head, using his teeth to delicately hold her nipple while he flicked it with his tongue, and she moaned his name. She brought her hands up to his hair and held his head to her. He lifted his head and blew against her skin. Her nipples stood out. He ran the tip of one finger around her aroused flesh. She trembled in his arms.

Lowering his head, he took the other nipple in his mouth and suckled her. She held him to her with a strength that surprised her. She never wanted to let him go.

Her fingers drifted down his back and then slid around front to work on the buttons of his shirt. She pushed his shirt open. He growled deep in his throat when she leaned forward to brush kisses against his chest.

He pulled her to him and lifted her slightly so that her nipples brushed his chest. Holding her carefully, he rotated his shoulders and rubbed against her. Blood roared in her ears. She reached for his erection as he shoved her panties down her legs. He was so hard as she stroked him. She needed him inside her body.

He caressed her thighs. She moaned as he neared her center and then sighed when he brushed his fingertips across the entrance to her body.

He slipped one finger into her and hesitated for a second, looking down into her eyes. She didn't want his fingers in her, she wanted him. She bit down on her lower lip and with minute movements of her hips tried to move his touch where she needed it. But then she realized what she was doing and reached between them, tugging on his wrist.

"What?"

"I want you inside me," she said. Her words were raw and blunt and she felt the shudder that went through him.

He plunged two fingers into her humid body. She squirmed against him. "I will be."

"I need you now."

He set her on her feet and turned her to face the mirror.

"What are you doing?" she asked, looking over her shoulder at him.

"I want you to watch us as I make love to you. Bend forward slightly."

She did as he asked. Her eyes watched his in the mirror. "Take your shirt off, please. I want to see your chest."

He smiled at her as he finished taking off the shirt

she'd unbuttoned. His tie was tangled in the collar but he managed to get them both off. He leaned over her, covering her body with his larger one.

He bent his legs and rubbed himself at the entrance of her body. She pushed back against him but he didn't enter her. He was teasing her and she was about to burn up in his arms.

"Will."

"Just a second," he said. "Keep your eyes on mine in the mirror."

"Yes," she said, meeting his forest green gaze with her own.

He bit down on her shoulder and then he cupped both of her breasts in his hands, plucking at her aroused nipples. He slipped one hand down her body, parting her intimate flesh before he adjusted his stance. Bending his knees and positioning himself, he entered her with one long, hard stroke.

She moaned his name and her head fell forward, leaving the curve of her neck open and vulnerable to him. He bit softly at her neck and she felt the reaction all the way to her toes when she squirmed in his arms and thrust her hips back toward him, wanting to take him deeper.

He caressed her stomach and her breasts. Whispered erotic words of praise in her ears.

She moved more frantically in his arms, her climax so close and getting closer each time he drove deep. His breath brushed over her neck and shoulder as he started to move faster, more frantically, pounding deep into her.

He slid one hand down her abdomen, through the slick folds of her sex. Finding her center. He stroked the aroused flesh with an up-and-down movement that felt exquisite and drove her closer and closer to her climax.

He circled that aroused bit of flesh between her legs with his forefinger then scraped it very carefully with his nail. She screamed his name and tightened around his shaft. Will pulled one hand from her body and locked his fingers on hers on the hall table. Then penetrated her as deeply as he could. Biting down on the back of her neck, he came long and hard.

Their eyes met in the mirror and she knew that she wasn't falling for him. She'd fallen. She wanted this man with more than her body. She wanted him with her heart and with her soul.

Thirteen

Will lifted Amberley into his arms and carried her into the living room. She had deserved romance and a night to remember and he'd given her sex. He wanted it to be more. Because she was more than a hookup to him.

"Are you feeling relaxed now?" she asked with a grin.

"I'm definitely calmer than I was when I arrived," he said, pulling her onto his lap and holding her closer. "I'm sorry if I was too—"

"You were fine. We both needed that. For the first time I feel like you let your guard down around me," she said.

He had.

He shouldn't have because that meant he was letting her in and he wasn't sure there was room in the gray and gloomy parts of his soul. He had been too good at keeping everyone at arm's length. And now he was unsure what would come next.

"Want to talk about it?" she asked.

"No."

"Sorry. I thought maybe if you talked about what Maverick was doing I could help. Offer some insights."

Of course.

Maverick.

She hadn't read his mind and seen the tortured way he was trying to figure out how to hold on to her and not let go of Lucy. He had to get past that. This was the first time he'd made love to a woman since his wife's death. Maybe the second time like their second date would help him move forward.

"I hadn't thought of it that way," he said.

"I'm not sure why I offered to talk except that I'm nervous. I don't know what to do now."

"What do you usually do?" he asked.

She flushed. "I don't have a habit. I'm still new to this."

"Oh..." That was telling. She'd never trusted a man enough to have him in her house.

And here he was.

"Okay, well, do you want me to leave?" he asked.

"No. Will, you are the one guy that I really want to stay. I need you here."

She needed him.

Those words warmed his heart and made him feel invincible. Like he would do anything for her.

He knew that feeling.

He was falling in love with her.

His heart, which he'd thought was down for the count, was beating again and beating for this woman.

"How about if you go get a shower while I set up a little surprise for you in the bedroom."

"What kind of surprise? I thought you came here without thinking about it?"

"Enough with the questions, cowgirl, it's a yes or no, that's it."

"Yes."

"Stay in the bathroom until I come and get you," he said.

"I will."

She walked away and he watched her leave. He wanted to make sure he committed as much of Amberley to memory as he could. He stayed there on the couch for another minute then stood, fastened his jeans and put on his shirt.

He saw her jeans, shirt and underwear strewn in the hallway and remembered the animalistic passion that had taken over him.

Maybe that was what it had taken to break through the icy wall he'd put around his heart. But there was no going back now.

He folded her clothes and set them on the table by the door and then went out to his car and opened the trunk, where he had placed the box from their romantic dinner. The box he was supposed to have put to good use then. Well, now was definitely the right time.

He opened the box and took out the CD he'd made for her. She liked old-school stuff and he thought the music mix he'd burned onto it would be a nice surprise for her the next time she got in her truck.

He opened the door to the cab, which she never kept locked, pulled down the visor and grabbed the keys. He turned the key to the accessory position and ejected the CD she had in there. Garth Brooks.

He wasn't surprised. He pushed in the CD he'd made for her and then shut off the truck and got out after putting the keys back up in the visor.

He reentered the house and heard her singing in the shower and smiled to himself.

He wanted this night to be perfect. He wanted to give her a gift that was equal to what she'd given him when she'd welcomed him into her life and her body.

Luckily the flowers he'd had in the box were still somewhat preserved and he took his time placing rose petals in a path from the bathroom door leading to the bed. Then he strewed them on the bed. Next he took the candles out of the box and put them on different surfaces. They were fragrant lavender and he lit them before stepping back to admire his handiwork.

He heard the shower shut off. But he wasn't ready yet. He took one of the low wattage Wi-Fi stereo bulbs that he'd placed in the box and installed it in the lamp next to her bed.

Then he cued up his "Amberley" playlist and connected his iPhone wirelessly to the lightbulb. He hit Play and went to the bathroom door, realizing he was overdressed for this. He took off his clothes, neatly folding them on the comfy chair in the corner of the room.

"Will? Are you out there?"

"I am. Stay there," he ordered.

He walked over to the bathroom and opened the

door, quickly stepping inside so he wouldn't ruin the surprise that waited for her.

He washed up quickly at the sink while she combed her hair. "I need you to close your eyes."

"I'm still not—"

"Into the kinky stuff. I know," he said with a laugh.

She made him happy. And he hadn't realized what a gift joy was until he'd spent so long without it in his life.

"Can I open my eyes now?" she asked.

"Yes."

She wasn't sure what she'd been expecting but this was the perfect romantic fantasy. There were rose petals under her feet, candles burning around the room and soft, sensual music playing.

Will put his hands on her shoulders and guided her to the bed.

"Surprised?"

"Yes!"

She turned in his arms and he took her mouth in his, letting his hands wander over her body, still amazed that she was here in his arms.

She buried her red face against his chest. "I wasn't sure if I would see you again or if you were going to leave and go back to Bellevue without saying goodbye."

Her words hurt him but he couldn't argue with them. He hated that he'd done this to her. That his own grief and doubts had been transferred to her.

"I promise I would never leave without saying goodbye," he said. Then to distract her, he picked up a handful of the rose petals that littered the bed and, turning her onto her back, he dropped them over her breasts.

She shivered and her nipples tightened. He arranged the petals on each of her breasts so that her nipples were surrounded by the soft rose petals. "I'm not surprised. You're a noticing kind of guy."

He leaned down to lick each nipple until it tightened. Then he blew gently on the tips. She raked her nails down his back.

"Are you listening to me?" she demanded.

He made a murmuring sound, unable to tear his gaze from her body. He'd never get enough of looking at her or touching her—he was starting to fall for her and that felt like a betrayal. Something he wouldn't let himself think about tonight.

"I'm listening to your body," he said, gathering more rose petals. He shifted farther down her body and dropped some on her stomach.

Her hand covered his. She leaned up, displacing the petals on her breasts. She took the petals on her stomach and moved them around until they formed a circle around her belly button.

He did just that, taking his time to fix the petals and draw her nipples out by suckling them. He moved the petals on her stomach, nibbling at each inch of skin underneath before replacing the rose petals. Then he kneeled between her thighs and looked down at her.

He picked up another handful of petals and dropped them over the red hair between her legs. She swallowed, her hands shifting on the bed next to her hips.

"Open yourself for me," he said.

Her legs moved but he took her hands in his, bringing them to her mound. She hesitated but then she pulled those lower lips apart. The pink of her flesh looked so delicate and soft with the red rose petals around it.

"Hold still," he said.

He arranged the petals so that her delicate feminine flesh was the center. He leaned down, blowing lightly on her before tonguing that soft flesh. She lifted her hips toward his mouth.

He drew her flesh into his mouth, sucking carefully on her. He crushed more petals in both of his fists and drew them up her thighs, rubbing the petals into her skin, pushing her legs farther apart until he could reach her dewy core. He pushed his finger into her body and drew out some of her moisture, then lifted his head and looked up her body.

Her eyes were closed, her head tipped back, her shoulders arched, throwing her breasts forward with their berry hard tips, begging for more attention. Her entire body was a creamy delight accented by the bloodred petals.

He lowered his head again, hungry for more of her. He feasted on her body the way a starving man would. He brought her to the brink of climax but held her there, wanting to draw out the moment of completion until she was begging him for it.

Her hands left her body, grasped his head as she thrust her hips up toward his face. But he pulled back so that she didn't get the contact she craved.

"Will, please."

He scraped his teeth over her clitoris and she screamed as her orgasm rocked through her body.

He kept his mouth on her until her body stopped shuddering and then slid up her.

"Your turn," she said, pushing him over onto his back.

She took his erection in her hand and he felt a drop of pre-cum at the head. She leaned down to lick it off him. Then took a handful of the rose petals and rubbed them up and down his penis.

She followed her hand with her tongue, teasing him with quick licks and light touches. She massaged the petals against his sac and then pressed a few more even lower. Her mouth encircled the tip of him and she began to suck.

He arched on the bed, thrusting up into her before he realized what he was doing. He pulled her from his body, wanting to be inside her when he came. Not in her mouth.

He pulled her up his body until she straddled his hips. Then using his grip on her hips, he pulled her down while he pushed his erection into her body.

He thrust harder and harder, trying to get deeper. He pulled her legs forward, forcing them farther apart until she settled even closer to him.

He slid deeper into her. She arched her back, reaching up to entwine her arms around his shoulders. He thrust harder and felt every nerve in his body tensing. Reaching between their bodies, he touched her between her legs until he felt her body start to tighten around him.

He came in a rush, continuing to thrust into her until his body was drained. He then collapsed on the bed, laying his head between her breasts. He didn't want to let her go. But he wasn't sure he deserved to keep her.

* * *

I would never leave without saying goodbye.

The words suddenly popped into her head as Will got up to grab them both some water from the kitchen.

He'd said he wouldn't leave without saying goodbye.

But that meant he was still planning to leave.

She sat up, pulling the blanket with her to cover her nakedness.

He came back in with two bottles of water and a tray of cheese and crackers. "Thought you might want a snack."

"Thanks," she said.

He sat on the edge of the bed and she crossed her legs underneath her. Why had he done all of this? Created the kind of romantic fantasy that made her think…well, that he could love her. And he was only going to leave?

He handed her a bottle of water and she took it, putting it on the nightstand beside her bed.

"Will, can I ask you something?"

"Sure," he said.

"Did you say you won't leave without saying goodbye?"

"Yes. I wouldn't want you to wonder if I'd gone," he said.

"So you are still planning to leave?" she asked.

He twisted to face her.

"Yes. You know my life is back in Bellevue," he said. "I'm just here to do a job."

He was here to do a job.

She'd known that. From the beginning there had

been no-trespassing signs all over him and she'd tried to convince herself that she knew better.

But now she knew she hadn't.

"Then what the hell is all of this?"

He stood up and paced away from the bed over to the chair where his clothes were and pulled on his pants.

"It was romance. The proper ending to our date last night. I wanted to show you how much you mean to me."

She wasn't following the logic of that. "If I mean something to you then why are you planning to leave? Or did you think we'd try long-distance dating?"

"No, I didn't think that. Your life is here, Amberley, I know that. My world… Faye's world is in Bellevue."

"Don't you mean Lucy's world?" she asked. "Faye seems to like Royal pretty well and as she's not even a year old I think that she'd adjust. You said yourself Lucy's parents travel and your folks seem to have the funds to visit you wherever you are."

"It's my world, too," he said. "I care about you, Amberley, more than I expected to care about another woman again, but this…isn't what I expected. I made a promise to myself that I'd never let another woman into my life the way I did with Lucy. Losing her broke me. It was only Faye and friends like Max that kept me from disappearing. And I can't do that again."

She wasn't sure why not. "I'm willing to risk everything for you."

She watched his face. It was a kaleidoscope of emotions and, for a brief moment, as his mouth softened into that gentle smile of his, she thought she'd gotten through to him.

"I'm not. It's not just myself I have to think of. It's Faye, as well," he said. "And it's not fair to you to put you through that. You've lost enough."

"Lost enough? Will, I think…I think I love you. I don't want to lose you," she said. "If you asked me to go with you to Bellevue, I would." She knew she was leaving herself completely open but she had lost a lot in her young life. First her mom, then her innocence and then her baby. And she'd thought she'd stay locked away for the rest of her life but Will had brought her back to the land of the living.

If she didn't ride all out trying to win him over, then she would be living with regret for the rest of her life.

"You would?" he asked.

"Yes. That's what you do when you love someone."

Saying she loved him was getting easier. She got up from the bed and walked over to him. She put her hand on his chest and looked up into his eyes.

"I know your heart was broken and battered when Lucy died. I know that you are afraid to risk it again. But I think we can have a wonderful life together. I just need to know that you're the kind of man who will stand by my side and not turn tail and run."

He put his hand over hers and didn't say a word. He lowered his head and kissed her, slowly, deeply, and she felt like she'd gotten through to him. Like she'd finally broken the wall around his heart.

He lifted her in his arms and carried her back to the bed. "Will?"

Instead of answering he kissed her. The kiss was

long and deep and she felt like it was never going to end. And it didn't end until he'd made love to her again.

She wanted to talk. It felt like they needed to but he pulled her closer to him and she started to drift off to sleep in his arms. His hand was so soothing, rubbing up and down her back, and she wondered if words were really needed. She'd finally found the life she'd always wanted in the arms of the man she loved.

When she woke in the morning she sat up and realized she was alone in bed.

"Will?"

She got up and walked through the house but it was almost silent. She had always liked this time of the morning. She wondered if Will would like to take a morning ride. She wanted to show him the south pasture.

The clock echoed through the house and she realized it was very quiet.

Too quiet.

It was empty except for her.

He hadn't made love to her last night. It hadn't been the joining of two hearts that she'd thought it was. That had been his way of saying goodbye.

Tears burned her eyes and she sank down on the floor, pulling her knees to her chest and pressing her head against them. Why was she so unlovable? What was it about her that made men leave? And why couldn't she find a man who was as honorable as she believed him to be?

Fourteen

Amberley had thought she was ready for whatever happened with Will, but waking up alone… She should have expected it, but she hadn't and she was tired. She called Clay's house and asked for some time off. He wasn't too pleased to be down a person right around the big Halloween festival they were hosting this coming weekend and she promised she was just taking a quick trip home and she'd be back for that.

But there were times when a girl needed to be home. She wanted to see her brothers and sisters and just be Amberley, not the complicated mess she'd become since that city slicker had come into her life with his spiked hair and tight jeans. He'd looked at her with those hungry eyes and then left her wanting more.

Enough.

She wasn't going to find answers in her own head. She needed space and she needed to stop focusing on Will Brady. He had left. He'd said goodbye in a way she'd never really expected him to.

She got Montgomery into his horse trailer and then hit the road. She wasn't going to even glance at the guest house where Will and Faye were staying, but she couldn't help her eyes drifting that way as she pulled by his place. His car was in the drive, like that mattered. He wasn't in the right frame of mind to be her man. In a way she guessed he was still Lucy's.

She tried to tell herself she hadn't been a fool again but the truth was she felt like an idiot. What a way to be starting a long drive. She hit a button on the radio and the CD she had cued up wasn't one she'd put in there. She ejected it and read the Sharpie-written label.

Old-School Mix Tape For My Cowgirl.

She felt tears sting the backs of her eyes.

God, why did he do this? Something so sweet and simple that could make her believe that there was more between the two of them than she knew there was. She'd given him three chances and each time he'd wormed his way even deeper into her heart. And yet she was still sitting here by herself.

She couldn't resist it and finally put the CD back into the player and the first song that came on was "SexyBack."

She started to laugh and then it turned to tears.

He'd set the bar pretty high and it left both of them

room to fall. He'd made her expect things from him that she'd never thought she'd find with anyone else.

She hit the forward button and it jumped to the next track. That Jack Johnson song that he'd danced with her to. The one that had cured her broken heart and her battered inner woman who'd felt broken because she couldn't have her own child. He'd danced with her and made that all okay.

And maybe…

Maybe what?

"Hell, you're an idiot, Amberley. You used to be smart but now you are one big fat dummy. He's messed up."

But she knew that wasn't true or fair. He was broken, too. And she'd thought they were falling in love, that they would be able to cure each other, but instead…they were both even more battered than before. She should have known better.

Her and city guys didn't mix. Did she need some big-ass neon sign to spell it out?

She had no idea as the miles passed but the flat Texas landscape dotted with old oil derricks changed to the greener pastures of the hill country and she just kept driving. She'd expected the pain of leaving to lessen the farther she got from the Flying E ranch but it didn't. So when she stopped to let Montgomery out of the trailer and give him some water, she couldn't help herself. She wrapped her arms around her horse's neck and allowed herself to cry. Montgomery just neighed and rubbed his head against hers.

She put him back in the trailer, wiped her eyes and got back on the road again, pulling onto the dirt road that led to her family ranch just after sunset. She pulled over before she got to the house, putting her head on the steering wheel.

"God, please let me fall out of love with him," she said.

She put the truck back in gear and drove up to the old ranch house where she'd grown up, and the comfort she'd wanted to find there was waiting.

Her siblings all ran out to meet her. Her brothers took Montgomery to the stables while her sisters dragged her into the kitchen to help them finish baking cookies. They chatted around her and the ache in her heart grew. She knew she'd wanted this kind of family for herself and while it was true Will wasn't the last man on the planet, he'd touched her deep in her soul.

She'd started dreaming again about her future, had allowed herself to hope that she could have a family like this of her own, and now it was gone.

It was going to take a lot for her to trust a man enough to want to dream about sharing her life with him. And she was pretty damn sure she wasn't going to be able to love again.

He dad came in and didn't seem surprised to see her.

"Clay called and said you were heading this way. Everything okay?" he asked.

"Yes. Just missed seeing you all and we always carve pumpkins together," Amberley said.

"Yay. Dad said you might not make it home this year," her sister said. "But we knew you wouldn't disappoint us."

"That's right. Dad just knows how busy life is on

the ranch. I was lucky to get a few days off before the Halloween rodeo we're having on the Flying E."

Her dad nodded but she could tell that he knew she was here for more than a seasonal activity. Her siblings brought out the pumpkins and they all gathered around the table and worked on their masterpieces. She sang along to her dad's old "Monster Mash" album from K-Tel that he'd had as a boy growing up.

Tawny slipped her arms around Amberley as they were each picking a pumpkin to carve. "I'm glad you're home. I missed you."

"I missed you, too," Amberley said. "Daddy sent me a video of your barrel run last weekend. Looking good, little missy."

"Thank you. Randy said one day I might be as fast as you," Tawny said.

Amberley ruffled her fifteen-year-old sister's hair. "I'm guessing you're going to be faster than me one day soon."

"She might," Daddy said. "Randy's got himself a girl."

"Dad."

"Do you?" Amberley asked. "How come that's never come up when you call me?"

"A man's allowed to have some secrets."

"Unless Daddy knows them," Michael said.

"How did Daddy find out?" Randy asked.

"I might have told him that you were sweet on someone in town," Michael said.

Randy lunged toward Michael and the two of them started to scuffle the way they did and Amberley laughed as she went over and pulled Randy off his younger brother. "Want to talk about her?"

"No. Let's carve pumpkins," Randy said.

And they did. Each of them worked on their own gourd, talking and teasing each other. Amberley just absorbed it all. As much as she loved the quiet of her cottage she had missed the noise of family. She felt her heart break just a little bit more. When she was in Will's arms it was easy to tell herself that she could have had this with him. Could have had the family of her own that she'd always craved.

After everyone was done carving they took their jack-o'-lanterns to the front porch and put candles inside them. They then stood back to admire their handiwork. Her dad came over and draped his arm around Amberley's shoulder.

"You okay, girl?" he asked.

"I will be," she said.

"You need to talk?"

"Not yet, Daddy. I just needed some hugs and to remember what family felt like," she said.

Her father didn't say anything else, just drew her close for a big bear hug that made her acknowledge that she was going to be okay. She was a Holbrook and they didn't break…well, not for good.

Her heart was still bruised but being back with her family made her realize that the problem wasn't with her. It was with Will. He'd told her that he was in a world of firsts and she should have given him space, or at the very least tried to protect her heart a little more because he wasn't ready for love. And a part of her realized he might never be.

* * *

Will locked himself away in his office, telling Erin that he couldn't be disturbed. There were no leads on Maverick and that was fine with him. He wasn't in any state of mind to track down a kid who'd hacked his parents' Facebook accounts, much less a cyberbully who was too clever for his own good.

His door opened just as he was reaching for the bottle of scotch he kept in his desk. He was going to get drunk and then in a few days he was going to pack up and go back to Bellevue. But he didn't want to leave Amberley. He wished there was a way to talk to Lucy. To tell her he was sorry for their fighting and that he had never thought he'd find someone to love again. But that he had.

He loved Amberley. He knew that deep in his soul. But he had been too afraid to stay. He realized that losing her the way he'd lost Lucy would break him completely. That he'd never survive that. So instead of staying, he left.

"I said I'm busy."

Will saw his partner standing in the doorway with Chelsea. She looked tougher than the last time he'd seen her and he couldn't say he blamed her. "Come in. Sorry for being so rude a moment ago."

"That's fine," Chelsea said. "I've been biting everyone's heads off, as well. Did you find anything on the remote trace you did?"

Max followed her into his office and they both sat down on the couch against the wall. Will turned back to his computer.

"Yes. The coding was the same as what we recovered on the hard drive and I can tell you that it wasn't a time-delayed post. The person who put the photos up definitely has a Skinterest profile so I have been working on getting into that," Will said. "I should have an answer for you in a few days."

"Thank you," Chelsea said. "I am not above hacking the site if I have to. I'm done playing games with Maverick."

"I think we all are," Will said.

Chelsea's phone went off and she shook her head. "I have to get back to town. Thanks for your help on this project, Will."

"I wish I could have gotten to Haskell before he ran," Will said.

"Me, too," Max said. "Go on without me, Chels. I need to talk to my partner."

She nodded and then left. Max reached over, pushing the door shut.

"Give me everything you have so far," Max said.

"Why?"

"Because I think you have been working this too hard. You need a break."

"Uh, we're partners. I don't work for you," Will said.

"We are also friends. And you need a break," Max said. "I think you've been too busy. I think you should take a break."

Will turned in his chair to look at Max. He didn't want to do this. He needed time before he was going to be anything other than a douche to anyone who spoke to him.

"I can't."

"You can," Max said. "This isn't about Maverick."

"How do you know?"

"Because I saw the way the two of you were the other night," Max said.

"I don't know what you saw," Will said.

"Lying to me is one thing, I just hope you aren't lying to yourself," Max said.

His friend had always had a pretty good bullshit detector. "Hell."

Max laughed and then walked over to Will's desk, looked in the bottom drawer and took out the scotch. "Got any glasses?"

Will opened another drawer and took out two glasses. Max poured them both a generous amount and then went to sit on the chair in the corner where Will and Faye usually sat.

He took a swallow and Will did as well, realizing that Max was waiting for him to talk.

"I—I think I'm in love with her. And I don't know if I should be. What if I let her down? What if I can't be the man she needs me to be."

"Good. It's about time. Lucy wouldn't have wanted you to die when she did."

"But I did, Max. I lost some part of myself when she died that day. It was so unexpected."

"I know. I remember. But time has passed and she'd forgive you for moving on."

"I don't want to forget her," he said after a few minutes had passed. That was his fear along with the one that something would happen to Amberley now that he had let her into his heart, as well.

"You won't. Faye looks like Lucy and as she grows up, she'll remind you of her, I'm sure of that," Max said. "But if you are still punishing yourself you won't see it. All you will ever see is your grief."

Will knew Max was right. "I think I feel guilty that I have this new love in my life. You know Lucy and I were having some problems before…well, before everything. Just fighting about how to raise Faye and if Lucy should quit her job."

"You aren't responsible for her death," Max said. "You were fighting—all couples do that. It had nothing to do with what happened to Lucy."

"Logically I know that. But…" Will looked down in his drink. "It's hard to forgive myself."

"You're the only one who can do that," Max said, finishing his drink. "But I do know that you have to move forward. So that's why I'm going to do you a favor."

"You are?"

"Yup. You are on official leave from St. Cloud."

He leaned forward in his chair. "Are you serious?"

"Sort of. I'm not firing you but I think you need to take some time off. Don't worry about the investigation, we got this without you. You've been working nonstop and grieving and I think it's time you started living again."

"What if she won't take me back?" Will asked his friend.

"If she loves you, she will," Max said.

Max got up to leave a few minutes later and Will said goodbye to his friend, then walked him out. He realized that he'd been stuck in the past because of guilt, but also because of fear. And he wasn't afraid anymore. Amberley had said she loved him, and he'd made love to her and walked away rather than let her see how vulnerable that made him.

And he did love her.

He wanted to make his life with her. He scooped Faye up off the floor where she was playing and swung her around in his arms. His baby girl laughed and Will kissed her on the top of her head.

"Are you okay?" Erin asked.

"I'm better than okay," he said.

In fact he needed to get making plans. He needed to show a certain cowgirl that he wanted to be in her life and that he could fit into it.

He asked Erin to keep an eye on Faye while he went to find Clay Everett. He was going to need some serious lessons in being a Texas man if he was going to win over Amberley. He knew he'd hurt her and he hoped she could forgive him. Because he was determined to spend the rest of his life showing her how wrong he'd been and how much he loved her.

Amberley felt refreshed from her time with her family but she was glad to be back on the Flying E. The time away had given her some perspective. Will was in a tough spot and maybe he'd get past it and come back to her. But if he didn't…well, she knew that she wasn't the kind of woman to give her heart lightly. And she also wasn't the kind of woman to wallow in self-pity. She loved him and though living without him wasn't what she wanted, she'd give him time to realize what he was missing out on.

"Hi, Amberley," Clay called as she walked over to the area where the rodeo was set up on the Flying E. She saw Emily and Tom Knox, who had recently announced they were expecting a baby boy. Brandee Lawless was there taking a break from all the wedding planning she'd been doing and Natalie and Max were hanging together near the bleachers.

They had two rings set up and some bleachers for townsfolk. All of the kids from town were dressed up in their Halloween costumes.

"Hey, Clay. I just finished my shift at the dummy steer booth. The kids love roping those horns mounted in the hay bales. Where do you need me now?" she asked. She might have decided that she could give Will time, but she had discovered that it was easier to do that if she stayed busy.

"I'm glad to hear it," Clay said. "Why don't you take a break?"

She sighed. "I'd rather keep busy."

"I think you might want to check out the next contestant in the steer-roping competition," Clay said. "A certain city slicker is determined to prove he's got what it takes to be a cowboy."

"Will?"

Clay just shrugged.

"Are you crazy? He can ride. But roping a steer? That's dangerous," Amberley said.

"The man has something to prove," Clay said.

"Yeah, that he's lost his mind," Amberley said, taking off at a run toward the steer-roping ring. She pushed her way to the front of the crowd and saw Erin and Faye standing there. Erin just shook her head when Amberley walked up to her.

"Can you believe this? I always thought he was a smart guy," Erin said. "I'm afraid to watch this."

"Me, too. What is he thinking?"

"That he must prove something," Erin said. "Or

maybe he isn't. You know how guys and testosterone are."

She did. But Will had always seemed different. She leaned on the railing and looked across the way at the bay where the steer was waiting to be released and then saw Will waiting, as well.

"Will Brady!" she yelled.

He looked over to her.

"You're going to get yourself killed."

"Well, I love you, cowgirl and I need to prove that I'm worthy to be your man. So if I die at least I'll die happy."

What?

He loved her.

She didn't have a chance to respond as the steer was released and Will went into action. He roped the steer on his second try and in a few seconds he had it subdued. He'd had a good teacher and she suspected it had been Clay Everett. She ran around the ring to where Will was as he entered and threw herself into his arms.

He caught her.

"Did you mean it?" she asked.

"Yes. I love you."

"I love you, too."

He kissed her long and hard, and cheers and applause broke out. When he set her on her feet Erin brought Faye over to them. Will wrapped the two of them in his arms.

"Now my world is right. I have both of my girls back here in my arms."

He led them away from the crowd.

"I'm sorry I left the way I did. I was afraid of

letting you down and of not being the man you needed."

"It's okay. I kept forgetting that you were going through firsts and that I promised you time."

"I've had all the time I need."

"I'm glad."

Later that evening, after Faye had been bathed and put to bed, Will carried Amberley down the hall to the bedroom.

He put her on her feet next to the bed. "I can't believe you're really here, cowgirl."

"I can't believe you participated in a steer-roping competition for me," she said. He was everything she had always wanted in a man and never thought she'd find.

He was perfect for her.

He leaned down and kissed her so tenderly.

"Believe it, Amberley. There is nothing I won't do for you."

He undressed her slowly, caressing her skin and then following the path of his hands with his mouth. She couldn't think as he stood back up and lifted her onto the bed. He bent down to capture the tip of her breast in his mouth. He sucked her deep in his mouth, his teeth lightly scraping against her sensitive flesh. His other hand played at her other breast, arousing her, making her arch against him in need.

She reached between them and took his erection in her hand, bringing him closer to her. She spread her legs wider so that she was totally open to him. "I need you now."

He lifted his head; the tips of her breasts were

damp from his mouth and very tight. He rubbed his chest over them before sliding deep into her body.

She slid her hands down his back, cupping his butt as he thrust deeper into her. Their eyes met—staring deep into his eyes made her feel like their souls were meeting. She'd never believed in finding Mr. Right. Everything that had happened to her at eighteen had made it seem as if that wasn't in the cards for her. Everything that was until she met Will.

She felt her body start to tighten around him, catching her by surprise. She climaxed before him. He gripped her hips, holding her down and thrusting into her two more times before he came with a loud grunt of her name.

She slid her hands up his back and kissed him deeply. "You are so much wilder than that steer I tried to tame earlier."

His deep laughter washed over her and she felt like she'd found her place here in his arms. The family she'd always craved and never thought she'd have.

He held her afterward, pulling her into his arms and tucking her up against his side. She wrapped her arm around him and listened to the solid beating of his heart. She understood that Will was going to need her by his side, not because he didn't respect her need to be independent, but because of the way Lucy had been taken from him.

She understood him so much better now than she ever could have before. And because she had her own weaknesses, she didn't want him to feel that way with her. Will had given her back something she wasn't sure she could have found on her own.

"Are you sleeping?" he asked.

She felt the vibration of his words through his chest under her ear. She shifted in his embrace, tipping her head so she could see the underside of his jaw.

"No. Too much to think about." This had been at once the most terrifying and exciting day of her life. She felt like if she went to sleep she might wake up and find none of it had happened. "I'm not sure I can live in Bellevue. I mean, my life—"

"We're not going to live in Bellevue. I'm going to buy a ranch right here in Royal. Someplace where you can have as many horses as you want and we can raise Faye and maybe adopt some brothers and sisters for her."

"You'd do that?"

"Yes. Frankly, the thought of you being pregnant would have scared the crap out of me. I wouldn't have wanted to risk losing you and there are plenty of kids in the world who need parents," he said, rubbing his hand down her back. "Does a big family sound good to you?"

"It does," she said.

He rubbed his hand up and down her arm. "Perfect. So I guess you're going to have to marry me."

She propped herself up on his chest, looking down at him in the shadowy night. "Are you asking me?"

He laughed at that. "No. I'm telling you. You want to, but you might come up with a reason why we should wait and I'm not going to."

"Are you sure?"

He rolled over so that she was under him. Her legs parted and he settled against her. His arms braced on either side of her body, he caught her head in his hands and brought his mouth down hard on hers. When he came up for air, long minutes later, he said, "I promise I most definitely am."

She believed him. Will wasn't the kind of man to make promises lightly. When he gave his word, he kept it.

"Will?"

"Right here," he said, sinking back down next to her on the bed.

"I love you, city slicker."

"And I love you, cowgirl."

* * * * *

Don't miss a single instalment of the
TEXAS CATTLEMAN'S CLUB: BLACKMAIL
No secret—or heart—is safe in Royal, Texas...

THE TYCOON'S SECRET CHILD
by USA TODAY *bestselling author*
Maureen Child

TWO-WEEK TEXAS SEDUCTION
by Cat Schield

REUNITED WITH THE RANCHER
by USA TODAY *bestselling author*
Sara Orwig

EXPECTING THE BILLIONAIRE'S BABY
by Andrea Laurence.

TRIPLETS FOR THE TEXAN
by USA TODAY *bestselling author*
Janice Maynard

A TEXAS-SIZED SECRET
by USA TODAY *bestselling author*
Maureen Child

LONE STAR BABY SCANDAL
by Golden Heart winner
Lauren Canan

TEMPTED BY THE WRONG TWIN
by USA TODAY *bestselling author*
Rachel Bailey

TAKING HOME THE TYCOON
by USA TODAY bestselling author
Catherine Mann
BILLIONAIRE'S BABY BIND
by USA TODAY bestselling author
Katherine Garbera

and

November 2017:
THE TEXAN TAKES A WIFE
by USA TODAY *bestselling author*
Charlene Sands
December 2017:
BEST MAN UNDER THE MISTLETOE
by Jules Bennett

His voice came from right behind her.

At the open doorway, she turned and almost bumped into his chest.

"Oh, sorry." Wow, was his chest really that broad, or was she just so close it looked like he was taking up the whole world? Heat poured from his body, reaching for her, tingling her nerve endings. And he smelled so good, too.

Kelly shook her head and ignored the flutter of expectation awakening in the pit of her stomach. Deliberately, she fought for lighthearted, then tipped her head back and smiled up at him. "You know, I think I should get another point."

"For what?"

"For surprising you by not asking questions."

He studied her as if he were trying to figure out a puzzle. But after a second or two, he nodded. "You want to keep score? Then add this into the mix."

He pulled her in close and kissed her.

His voice came from right behind her.

At the [illegible] she turned, [illegible] [illegible].

"Dear [illegible]" [illegible] [illegible] [illegible] [illegible] [illegible] [illegible] [illegible] [illegible] [illegible] [illegible] [illegible] [illegible] [illegible] [illegible] [illegible] [illegible] [illegible]. And he smelled so good, too.

[illegible] [illegible].

"The [illegible]."

[illegible] [illegible] [illegible] [illegible] [illegible] [illegible]

He [illegible] [illegible] [illegible] [illegible] [illegible] [illegible] [illegible] [illegible] [illegible] [illegible] [illegible] [illegible] [illegible] [illegible] [illegible] [illegible] [illegible] [illegible] [illegible].

FIANCÉ IN NAME ONLY

BY

MAUREEN CHILD

First Published in Great Britain 2017
By Mills & Boon, an imprint of HarperCollins*Publishers*
1 London Bridge Street, London, SE1 9GF

ISBN: 978-0-263-92839-6

51-1017

Our policy is to use papers that are natural, renewable and recyclable products and made from wood grown in sustainable forests. The logging and manufacturing processes conform to the legal environmental regulations of the country of origin.

Printed and bound in Spain
by CPI, Barcelona

Maureen Child writes for the Mills & Boon Desire line and can't imagine a better job. A seven-time finalist for a prestigious Romance Writers of America RITA® Award, Maureen is an author of more than one hundred romance novels. Her books regularly appear on bestseller lists and have won several awards, including a Prism Award, a National Readers' Choice Award, a Colorado Romance Writers Award of Excellence and a Golden Quill Award. She is a native Californian but has recently moved to the mountains of Utah.

To my mom, Sallye Carberry,
and my aunt, Margie Fontenot,
for too many reasons to list.
They are the original Matriarchs.
Love you.

One

"Sorry about this," Micah Hunter said. "I really liked you a lot, but you had to die."

Leaning back in his desk chair, Micah's gaze scanned the last few lines of the scene he'd just finished writing. He gave a small sigh of satisfaction at the death of one of his more memorable characters, then closed the lid of the laptop.

He'd already been working for four hours and it was past time for a break. "Problem is," he muttered, standing up and walking to the window overlooking the front of the house, "there's nowhere to go."

Idly he pulled out his cell phone, hit speed dial, then listened to the phone ring for a second or two. Finally a man came on the other line.

"How did I let you talk me into coming here for six months?"

Sam Hellman laughed. "Good to talk to you, too, man."

"Yeah." Of course his best friend was amused. Hell, if Micah wasn't the one stranded here in small-town America, he might be amused, too. As it was, though, he didn't see a damn thing funny about it. Micah pushed one hand through his hair and stared out at the so-called view. The house he was currently renting was an actual Victorian mansion set back from a wide street that was lined by gigantic, probably ancient, trees, now gold and red as their leaves changed and died. The sky was a brilliant blue, the autumn sun peeking out from behind thick white clouds. It was quiet, he thought. So quiet it was damn near creepy.

And since the suspense/horror novels Micah was known for routinely hit number one on the *New York Times* bestseller list, he knew a thing or two about *creepy.*

"Seriously, Sam, I'm stuck here for another four months because you talked me into signing the lease."

Sam laughed. "You're stuck there because you never could turn down a challenge."

Harsh but true. Nobody knew that about Micah better than Sam. They'd met when they were both kids, serving on the same US Navy ship. Sam had run away from his wealthy family's expectations, and Micah had been running from a past filled with foster homes, lies and broken promises. The two of them had connected and then stayed in touch when their enlistments were up.

Sam had returned to New York and the literary agency his grandfather had founded—discovering, after being away for a while, that he actually *wanted* to be a part of the family business. Micah had taken any construction job he could find while he spent every other waking moment working on a novel.

Even as a kid, Micah had known he wanted to write books. And when he finally started writing, it seemed the words couldn't pour out of his mind fast enough. He typed long into the night, losing himself in the story developing on the screen. Finishing that first book, he'd felt like a champion runner—exhausted, satisfied and triumphant.

He'd sent that first novel to Sam, who'd had a few million suggestions to make it even better. Nobody liked being told to change something they thought was already great, but Micah had been so determined to reach his goal, he'd made most of the changes. And the book sold almost immediately for a modest advance that Micah was more proud of than anything he'd ever earned before.

That book was the precursor of things to come. With his second book, word-of-mouth advertising made it a viral sensation and had it rocketing up the bestseller lists. Before he knew it, Micah's dreams were a reality. Sam and Micah had worked together ever since and they'd made a hell of a team. But because they were such good friends, Sam had known exactly how to set Micah up.

"This is payback because I beat you at downhill snowboarding last winter, isn't it?"

"Would I do something that petty?" Sam asked, laughter in his voice.

"Yeah, you would." Micah shook his head.

"Okay...yeah, probably," Sam agreed. "*But*, you're the one who took the bet. Live in a small town for six months."

"True." *How bad could it be?* He remembered asking himself that before signing the lease with his landlady,

Kelly Flynn. Now, two months into his stay, Micah had the answer to that question.

"And, hey, research," Sam pointed out. "The book you're working on now is *set* in a small town. Good to know these things firsthand."

"Ever heard of Google?" Micah laughed. "And the book I set in Atlantis, how'd I research that one?"

"Not the point," Sam said. "The point is, Jenny and I loved that house you're in when we were there a couple years ago. And, okay, Banner's a small town, but they've got good pizza."

Micah would admit to that. He had Pizza Bowl on speed dial.

"Like I said, in another month or so, you'll feel differently," Sam said. "You'll be out enjoying all that fresh powder on the mountains and you won't mind it so much."

Micah wasn't so sure about that. But he had to admit it was a great house. He glanced around the second-floor room he'd claimed as a temporary office. The ceilings were high, the rooms were big and the view of the mountains was beautiful. The whole house had a lot of character, which he appreciated, but damned if he didn't feel like a phantom or something, wandering through the big place. He'd never had so much space all to himself and Micah could admit, at least to himself, that sometimes it creeped him out.

Hell, in the city—any city—there were lights. People. Noise. Here, the nights were darker than anything he'd ever known. Even in the navy, on board a ship, there were enough lights that the stars were muted in the night sky. But Banner, Utah, was listed on the International Dark-Sky roster because it lay just beyond a ridge that wiped out the haze of light reflection from Salt Lake City.

Here, at night, you could look up and see the Milky Way and an explosion of stars that was as beautiful as it was humbling. He'd never seen skies like these before, and he was willing to acknowledge that the beauty of it took some of the sting out of being marooned at the back end of beyond.

"How's the book coming?" Sam asked suddenly.

The change in subject threw him for a second, but Micah was grateful for the shift. "Good. Actually just killed the bakery guy."

"That's a shame. Love a good bakery guy." Sam laughed. "How'd he buy it?"

"Pretty grisly," Micah said, and began pacing the confines of his office. "The killer drowned him in the doughnut fryer vat of hot oil."

"Damn, man…that is gross." Sam took a breath and sighed it out. "You may have put me off doughnuts."

Good to know the murder he'd just written was going to hit home for people.

"Not for long, I'll bet," Micah mused.

"The copy editor will probably get sick, but your fans will love it," Sam assured him. "And speaking of fans, any of them show up in town yet?"

"Not yet, but it's only a matter of time." Frowning, he looked out the window and checked up and down the street, half expecting to see someone with a camera casing the house, hoping for a shot of him.

One of the reasons Micah never remained in one place too long was because his more devoted fans had a way of tracking him down. They would just show up at whatever hotel he was staying in, assuming he'd be happy to see them. Most were harmless, sure, but Micah knew "fan" could turn into "fanatic" in a flash.

He'd had a few talk their way into his hotel rooms, join him uninvited at dinner, acting as though they were either old friends or long-lost lovers. Thanks to social media, there was always someone reporting on where he had been seen last or where he was currently holed up. So he changed hotels after every book, always staying in big cities where he could get lost in the crowds and living in five-star hotels that promised security.

Until now, that is.

"No one's going to look for you in a tiny mountain town," Sam said.

"Yeah, that's what I thought when I was at the hotel in Switzerland," Micah reminded his friend. "Until that guy showed up determined to pummel me because his girlfriend was in love with me."

Sam laughed again and Micah just shook his head. Okay, it was funny now, but having some guy you didn't know ambush you in a hotel lobby wasn't something he wanted to repeat.

"This is probably the best thing you could have done," Sam said. "Staying in Banner and living in a house, not a hotel, will throw off the fans hunting for you."

"Yeah, well, it should. It's throwing me off, that's for sure." His scowl tightened. "It's too damn quiet here."

"Want me to send you a recording of Manhattan traffic? You could play it while you write."

"Funny," Micah said, and didn't even admit to himself that the idea wasn't half bad. "Why haven't I fired you?"

"Because I make us both a boatload of money, my friend."

Well, Sam had him there. "Right. Knew there was a reason."

"And because I'm charming, funny and about the only

person in the world who's willing to put up with the crappy attitude."

Micah laughed now. He had a point. Right from the beginning, when they'd met on the aircraft carrier they'd served on, Sam had offered friendship—something Micah had rarely known. Growing up in the foster care system, moving from home to home, Micah had never stayed anywhere long enough to make friends. Which was probably a good thing since he wouldn't have been able to *keep* a friend, what with relocating all the damn time.

So he appreciated having Sam in his life—even when the man bugged the hell out of him. "That's great, thanks."

"No problem. So what do you think of your landlady?"

Frowning, Micah silently acknowledged that he was trying to *not* think about Kelly Flynn. It wasn't working, but he kept trying.

For the last two months, he'd done everything he could to keep his distance because damned if he didn't want to get closer. But he didn't need an affair. He had to live here for another four months. If he started something with Kelly, it would make things…complicated.

If it was a one-night stand, she'd get pissy and he'd have to put up with it for four more months. If it was a long-running affair, then she'd be intruding on his writing time and spinning fantasies about a future that was never going to happen. He didn't need the drama. All he wanted was the time and space to write his book so he could get out of this tiny town and back to civilization.

"Hmm," Sam mused. "Silence. That tells me plenty."

"Tells you nothing," Micah argued, attempting to convince both himself *and* Sam. "Just like there's nothing going on."

"Are you sick?"

"What?"

"I mean, come on," Sam said, and Micah could imagine him leaning back in his desk chair, propping his feet up on the corner of his desk. He probably had his chair turned toward the windows so he could look out over Manhattan.

"Hell," Sam continued, "I'm married and I noticed her. She's gorgeous, and if you tell Jenny I said that I'll deny it."

Shaking his head, Micah looked down and watched Kelly work in the yard. The woman never relaxed. She was always moving, doing something. She had ten different jobs and today, apparently, still had the time to rake up fallen leaves and bag them. As he watched, she loaded up a wheelbarrow with several bags of leaves and headed for the curb.

Her long, reddish-gold hair was pulled into a ponytail at the back of her neck. She wore a dark green sweatshirt and worn blue jeans that cupped her behind and clung to her long legs. Black gloves covered her hands, and her black boots were scarred and scuffed from years of wear.

And though she had her back to the house, he knew her face. Soft, creamy skin, sprinkled with freckles across her nose and cheeks. Grass-green eyes that crinkled at the edges when she laughed and a wide, generous mouth that made Micah wonder what she would taste like.

Micah watched her unload the bags at the curb, then wave to a neighbor across the street. He knew she'd be smiling and his brain filled with her image. Deliberately, he turned his back on the window, shut the image of Kelly out of his mind and walked back to his chair. "Yeah, she's pretty."

Sam laughed. "Feel the enthusiasm."

Oh, there was plenty of enthusiasm, Micah thought. Too much. Which was the problem. "I'm not here looking for a woman, Sam. I'm here to work."

"That's just sad."

He had to agree. "Thanks. So why'd you call me again?"

"Damn, you need to take a break. You're the one who called me, remember?"

"Right." He pushed one hand through his hair. Maybe he did need a damn break. He'd been working pretty much nonstop for the last two months. No wonder this place was starting to feel claustrophobic in spite of its size. "That's a good idea. I'll take a drive. Clear my head."

"Invite the landlady along," Sam urged. "She could show you around since I'm guessing you've hardly left that big old house since you got there."

"Good guess. But not looking for a guide, either."

"What are you looking for?"

"I'll let you know when I find it," Micah said, and hung up.

"So how's our famous writer doing?"

Kelly grinned at her neighbor. Sally Hartsfield was the nosiest human being on the face of the planet. She and her sister, Margie, were both spinsters in their nineties, and spent most of their days looking out the windows to keep an eye on what was happening in the neighborhood.

"Busy, I guess," Kelly said, with a quick glance over her shoulder at the second-story window where she'd caught a glimpse of Micah earlier. He wasn't there anymore and she felt a small twist of disappointment as she turned back to Sally. "He told me when he moved in that he would be buried in work and didn't want to be disturbed."

"Hmm." Sally's gaze flicked briefly to that window, too. "You know, that last book of his gave me nightmares. Makes you wonder how he can stand being all alone like that when he's writing such dark, scary things…"

Kelly agreed. She'd only read one of Micah's seven books because it had scared her so badly she'd slept with a light on for two weeks. When she read a book, she wanted cheerful escape, not terror-inducing suspense. "I guess he likes it that way," she said.

"Well, everybody's different," Sally pointed out. "And I say thank goodness. Can you imagine how boring life would be if we were all the same?" She shook her head and her densely-sprayed curls never moved. "Why, there'd be nothing to talk about."

And that would be the real shame as far as Sally was concerned, Kelly knew. The woman could pry a nugget of information out of a rock.

"He is a good-looking man though, isn't he?" Sally asked, a speculative gleam in her eyes.

Good-looking? Oh, Micah Hunter was well beyond that. The picture on the back of his books showed him as dark and brooding, and that was probably done purposefully, considering what he wrote. But the man in person was so much more. His thick brown hair was perpetually rumpled, as if he'd just rolled out of bed. His eyes were the color of rich, dark coffee, and when he forgot to shave for a day or two, the stubble on his face gave him the air of a pirate.

His shoulders were broad, his hips were narrow and

he was tall enough that even Kelly's own five feet, eight inches felt diminutive alongside him. He was the kind of man who walked into a room and simply took it over whether he was trying to or not. Kelly imagined every woman who ever met him had done a little daydreaming about Micah. Even, it seemed, Sally Hartsfield, who had a grandson as old as Micah.

"He is nice looking," Kelly finally said when she noticed Sally staring at her.

The older woman sighed and fisted both hands on her hips. "Kelly Flynn, what is wrong with you? Your Sean's been gone four years. Why, if I was your age…"

Kelly stiffened at the mention of her late husband, automatically raising her defenses. Sally must have noticed her reaction because the woman stopped short, offered a smile and, thank heaven, a change of subject.

"Anyway, I hear you're showing the Polk place this afternoon to a couple coming in from California of all places."

Impressed as well as a little irked, Kelly stared at the older woman. Honestly, Kelly had only gotten this appointment to show a house the day before. "How did you know that?"

Sally waved a hand. "Oh, I have my ways."

Kelly had long suspected that her elderly neighbors had an army of spies stationed all over Banner, Utah, and this just cemented that idea. "Well, you're right, Sally, so I'd better get going. I still have to shower and change."

"Of course, dear, you go right ahead." She checked the window again and Kelly saw frustration on the woman's face when Micah didn't show up to be watched. "I've got things to do myself."

Kelly watched the woman hustle back across the street,

her bright pink sneakers practically glowing against all of the fallen leaves littering the ground. The ancient oaks that lined the street stretched out gnarly branches to almost make an arbor of gold-and-red leaves hanging over the wide road.

The houses were all different, everything from small stone cottages to the dignified Victorian where Kelly had grown up. They were all at least a hundred years old, but they were well cared for and the lawns were tidy. People in Banner stayed. They were born here, grew up here and eventually married, lived and died here.

That kind of continuity always comforted Kelly. She'd lived here since she was eight and her parents were killed in a car accident. She'd moved in with her grandparents and had become the center of their world. Now, her grandfather was dead and Gran had moved to Florida, leaving the big Victorian mansion and the caretaker's cottage at the back of the property to Kelly. Since living alone in that giant house would just be silly, Kelly rented it out and lived in the smaller cottage.

In the last three years, the Victorian had rarely been empty and when it wasn't rented out by vacationers, the house and grounds had become a favorite place for weddings, big parties and even, last year, a Girl Scout cookout in the huge backyard.

And, she thought, every Halloween, she turned the front of the Victorian into a haunted house.

"Have to get busy on that," she told herself. It was already the first of October and if she didn't get started, the whole month would slip past before she knew it.

Halfway up to the house, the front door opened and Micah stepped out. Kelly's heart gave a hard thump, and down low inside her she felt heat coil and tighten. Oh, boy. It had been four long years since her husband, Sean, had died, and since then she hadn't exactly done a lot of dating. That probably explained why she continued to have this over-the-top reaction to Micah.

Probably.

He wore a black leather jacket over a black T-shirt tucked into the black jeans he seemed to favor. Black boots finished off the look of Dangerous Male and as she admired the whole package, her heartbeat thundered loud enough to echo in her ears.

"Need some help?" he asked, jerking his head toward the wheelbarrow she was still holding on to.

"What? Oh. No." *Great, Kelly. Three. Separate. Words. Care to try for a sentence?* "I mean, it's empty, so not heavy. I'm just taking it around to the back."

"Okay." He came down the wide front steps to the brick walkway lined with chrysanthemums in bright, cheerful fall colors. "I'm taking a break. Thought I'd drive around. Get my bearings."

"After two months of being in Banner?" she asked, smiling. "Yeah, maybe it's time."

His mouth worked into a partial smile. "Any suggestions on the route I should take?"

She set the wheelbarrow down, flipped her ponytail over her shoulder and thought about it. "Just about any route you take is a pretty one. But if you're looking for a destination, you could drive through the canyon down to 89. There are a lot of produce stands there. You could pick me up a few pumpkins."

He tipped his head to one side and studied her, a flicker of what might have been amusement on his face. "Did I say I was going shopping?"

"No," she said, smiling. "But you could."

He blew out a breath, looked up and down the street, then shifted his gaze back to hers. "Or, you could ride with me and pick out your own pumpkins."

"Okay."

He nodded.

"No," she said. "Wait. Maybe not."

He frowned at her.

Having an audience while she argued with herself was a little embarrassing. She could tell from his expression that Micah didn't really want her along so, naturally, she really wanted to go. Even though she shouldn't. She already had plenty to do and maybe spending time with Micah Hunter wasn't the wisest choice, since he had the unerring ability to stir her up inside. But could she really resist the chance to make him as uncomfortable as he made her?

"I mean, sure," she said abruptly. "I'll go, but I'd have to be back in a couple of hours. I have a house to show this afternoon."

His eyebrows arched high on his forehead. "I can guarantee you I won't be spending two hours at a pumpkin stand." He tucked his hands into the pockets of his jacket. "So? Are you coming or not?"

Her eyes met his and in those dark brown depths, Kelly read the hope she would say *no*. So, of course, she said the only thing she could.

"I guess I am."

Two

"Why are you buying pumpkins when you're growing your own?"

They were already halfway down the twisting canyon road. The mountains rose up on either side of the narrow pass. Wide stands of pine trees stood as tall and straight as soldiers, while oaks, maples and birch trees that grew within those stands splashed the dark green with wild bursts of fall color.

"And," Micah continued, "isn't there somewhere closer you could buy the damn things?"

She turned her head to look at his profile. "Sure there is, but the produce stands have the big ones."

Kelly could have sworn she actually *heard* his eyes roll. But she didn't care. It was a gorgeous fall day, she was taking a ride in a really gorgeous car—even though it was going too fast for the pass—and she was sitting beside a gorgeous man who made her nervous.

And wasn't that a surprise? Four years since her husband Sean had died and Micah was the first man to make her stomach flutter with the kind of nerves that she had suspected were dead or atrophied. The problem was, she didn't know if she was glad of the appearance of those nerves or not.

Kelly rolled down the window and let the cold fall air slap at her in lieu of a cold shower. When she got a grip, she shifted in her seat to look at Micah. "Because I grow those to give away to the kids in the neighborhood."

"And you can't keep some for yourself?"

"I could, but where's the fun in that?"

"Fun?" he repeated. "I've seen you out there weeding, clipping and whatever else it is you do to those plants. That's fun?"

"For me it is." The wind whipped her ponytail across her face and she pushed it aside to look at him. "Besides, if I was going to take lessons on fun from somebody, it wouldn't be you."

He snorted. "If you did, I'd show you more than pumpkins."

Her stomach swirled a little at the implied promise in those words, but she swallowed hard and stilled it. He was probably used to making coded statements designed to turn women into slavering puddles. So she wouldn't accommodate him. Yet.

"I'm not convinced," she said with a shrug. "You've been in town two months and you've hardly left the house."

"That's work. No time for fun."

"Just a chatterbox," she mumbled. Every word pried out of him felt like a victory.

"What?"

"Nothing," she said. "So, what's your idea of fun then?"

He took a moment to think it through, and said, "I'd start with chartering a private jet—"

"Your own personal jet," she said, stunned.

He glanced at her and shrugged. "I don't like sharing."

She laughed shortly as she thought about the last time she'd taken a flight out of Salt Lake City airport. Crowded onto a full flight, she'd sat between a talkative woman complaining about her grandchildren and a businessman whose briefcase poked her in the thigh every time he shifted in his seat. Okay, she could see where a private jet would be nice. "Well sure. Okay, your jet. Then what?"

He steered the Range Rover down the mountain road, taking the tight curves like a race-car driver. If Kelly let herself worry about it, she'd be clinging to the edges of her seat. So she didn't think about it.

"Well, it's October, so I'd go to Germany for Oktoberfest."

"Oh." That was so far out of her normal orbit she hardly knew what to say. Apparently, though, once you got Micah talking about something that interested him, he would keep going.

"It's a good place to study people."

"I bet," she murmured.

He ignored that, and said, "Writers tend to observe. Tourists. Locals. How people are interacting. Gives me ideas for the work."

"Like who to murder?"

"Among other things. I once killed a hotel manager in one of my books." He shrugged. "The guy was a jackass so, on paper at least, I got rid of him."

She stared at him. "Any plans to kill off your current landlady?"

"Not yet."

"Comforting."

"Anyway," he continued, "after a long weekend there, I'd go to England," he mused, seriously considering her question. "There's a hotel in Oxford I like."

"Not London?"

"Fewer people to recognize me in Oxford."

"That's a problem for you?" she asked.

"It can be." He took another curve that had Kelly swerving into him. He didn't seem to notice. "Thanks to social media, my fans tend to track me down. It gets annoying."

She could understand that. The photo of Micah on the back of his books was mesmerizing. She'd spent a bit of time herself studying his eyes, the way his hair tumbled over his forehead, the strong set of his jaw.

"Maybe you should take your photo off your books."

"Believe me, I've suggested it," Micah said. "The publisher won't do it."

Kelly really didn't have anything to add to the conversation. She'd never been followed by strangers desperate to be close to her and the farthest she'd ever traveled was on her last flight—to Florida to visit her grandmother. England? Germany? Not really in her lifestyle. She'd love to go to Europe. Someday. But it wouldn't be on a private jet.

She glanced out the window at the familiar landscape as it whizzed past and felt herself settle. Micah's life was so far removed from her own it made Kelly's head spin just thinking about it.

"One of these days," she said suddenly, shifting her gaze back to his profile, "I'd like to go to Scotland. See Edinburgh Castle."

"It's worth seeing," he assured her.

Of course he'd been there. Heck, he'd probably been *everywhere.* No wonder he stuck close to the house. Why would he be interested in looking around Banner, Utah? After the places he'd been, her small hometown probably appeared too boring to bother with. Well, maybe it wasn't up to the standards of Edinburgh, or Oktoberfest in Germany, but she loved it.

"Good to know," she said. "But until then, I'll plant pumpkins for the kids." She smiled to herself and let go of a twinge of envy still squeezing her insides. "I like everything about gardening. Watching the seeds sprout, then the vines spread and the pumpkins get bigger and brighter orange." Smiling, she continued. "I like how the kids on the street come by all the time, picking out the pumpkins they want, helping water, pulling weeds. They get really possessive about *their* pumpkins."

"Yeah," he said wryly. "I hear them."

He never took his eyes off the road, she noted. Was it because he was a careful driver, or was he just trying to avoid looking at her? Probably the latter. In the two months he'd been living in her Victorian, Micah Hunter had made eluding her an art form.

Sure, he was a writer, and he'd told her when he first arrived in town that he needed time alone to work. He wasn't interested in making friends, having visitors or a guided tour of her tiny town. Friendly? Not so much. Intriguing? Oh, yeah.

Could she help it if tall, dark and crabby appealed to her? Odd though, since her late husband, Sean, had been blond and blue-eyed, with an easy smile. And *nothing* about Micah was easy.

"You don't like kids?"

Briefly he slanted a look at her. “Didn’t say that. Said I heard them. They’re loud.”

“Uh-huh,” she said with a half smile. “And didn’t you say last week that it was too quiet in Banner?”

His mouth tightened but, grudgingly, he nodded. “Point to you.”

“Good. I like winning.”

“One point doesn’t mean you’ve won anything.”

“How many points do I need then?”

A reluctant smile curved his mouth, then flashed away again. “At least eleven.”

Wow. That half smile had come and gone so quickly it was like it had never been. Yet, her stomach was swirling and her mouth had gone dry. Kelly took a breath and slowly let it out again. She had to focus on what they were talking about, *not* what he was doing to her.

“Like ping-pong,” she said, forcing a smile she didn’t feel.

“Okay.” He sounded amused.

“All right, good,” Kelly said, leaning over to pat his arm mostly because she needed to convince herself she could touch him without going up in flames. But her fingers tingled, so she pulled them back fast. “Then it’s one to nothing, my favor.”

He shook his head. “You’re actually going to keep score?”

“You started it. You gave me a point.”

“Right. I’ll make a note.”

“No need, I’ll keep track.” She looked ahead because it was safer than looking at him. Then she smiled to herself. She’d gotten him to talk and had completely held her own in the conversation—until her imagination and hormones had thrown her off.

As long as she could keep those tingles and nerves in check, she could handle Mr. Magnetic.

For the next few days, Kelly was too busy to spend much time thinking about Micah. And that was just as well, she told herself. Mainly because the minute they returned from their pumpkin-shopping expedition, Micah had disappeared and she'd gotten the message.

Clearly he wanted her to know that their brief outing had been an aberration. He'd slipped back into his cave and she hadn't caught a glimpse of him since. Probably for the best, she assured herself. Easier to keep her mind on her own life, her own responsibilities if the only time she saw Micah was in her dreams.

Of course, that didn't make for restful sleeping, but she'd been tired before. One thing she hadn't experienced before were the completely over-the-top, sexy-enough-to-melt-your-brain dreams. She hated waking up hot and needy. Hated having to admit that all she really wanted to do was go back to sleep and dream again.

"And don't start thinking about those dreams or you won't get any work done at all," Kelly told herself firmly.

It wasn't hard to push Micah into the back of her mind, since she juggled so many jobs that sometimes she just ran from one to the next. Thankfully, that gave her little opportunity to sit and wonder if sex with Micah in real life would be as good as it was in her dreams.

Although if it was, she might not survive the experience.

"Still," she mused, "not a bad way to go."

She shook her head, dipped a brush into the orange tempera paint, wiped off the excess, then painted the first of an orchard of pumpkins onto the Coffee Cave's front window. Of all her different jobs, this was her favorite. Kelly loved painting holiday decorations on storefronts.

But she was also a virtual assistant, she ran websites for several local businesses, and was a Realtor who had just sold a house to that family from California. She was a gardener and landscape designer, and now she was thinking seriously about running for mayor in Banner's next election, since she was just horrified by some of the current mayor's plans for downtown. As she laid the paint out on the glass, her mind wandered.

Kelly had a business degree from Utah State, but once she'd graduated, she hadn't wanted to tie herself down to one particular job. She liked variety, liked being her own boss. When she'd decided to go into several different businesses, a couple of her friends had called her crazy. But she remembered Sean encouraging her, telling her to do whatever made her happy.

That had her pausing as thoughts of Sean drifted through her mind like a warm breeze on a cool day. A small ache settled around her heart. She still missed him even though his features were blurred in her mind now—like a watercolor painting left out in the rain.

She hated that. It felt like a betrayal of sorts, letting Sean fade. But it would have been impossible to keep living while holding on to the pain, too. Time passed whether you wanted it to or not. And you either kept up or got run over.

On that happy notion, Kelly paused long enough to look up and down Main Street. Instantly, she felt better. Banner was a beautiful little town and had been a great place to grow up. Coming here as a heartbroken eight-year-old, she'd fallen in love with the town, the woods, the rivers, the waterfalls and the people here.

Okay, Banner wasn't Edinburgh or Oxford or wherever, but it was…cozy. The buildings were mostly more than a hundred years old with creaky floors and brick walls. The sidewalks were narrow but neatly swept, and every one of the old lampposts boasted a basket of fall flowers at its base. In another month or so, there would be Christmas signs up and lights strung across the streets, and when the snow came, it would all look like a holiday painting. So, yes, she'd like to travel, see the world, but she would always come home to Banner.

Nodding to herself, she turned back to the window and quickly laid out the rest of the pumpkin patch along the bottom edge of the window.

"Well, that looks terrific already."

Kelly turned to grin at her friend. Terry Baker owned the coffee shop and made the best cinnamon rolls in the state. With short black hair, bright blue eyes and standing at about five foot two, Terry looked like an elf. Which she didn't find the least bit amusing.

The two of them had been friends since the third grade and nothing had changed over the years. Terry had been there for Kelly when Sean died. Now that Terry's military husband had deployed for the third time in four years, it was Kelly's turn to support her friend.

"Thanks, but I've got a long way to go yet," Kelly said, taking a quick look at the window and seeing a spot she'd have to fill in with a few baby pumpkins.

"Hence the latte I have brewed just for you." She held out the go-cup she carried.

"Hence?" Kelly took the coffee, savored a sip, then sighed in appreciation. "Have you been reading British mysteries again?"

"Nope." Terry stuffed her hands into her jeans pockets. “With my sad love life, I’m home every night watching the British mysteries on TV.”

“Love lives can be overrated,” Kelly said.

“Right.” Terry nodded. “Who’re you trying to convince? Me? Or you?”

“Me, obviously, since you’re the only one of us with a man at the moment.”

Terry leaned one shoulder against the pale rose-colored brick of her building. “I don’t have one, either, trust me. It’s impossible to have phone sex on an iPad when half of Jimmy’s squad could walk in at any moment.”

Kelly laughed, grabbed another brush and laid down a twining green vine connecting all of the pumpkins. “Okay, that would be awkward.”

“Tell me about it. Remember when he called me as a surprise on my birthday and I jumped out of the shower to answer the call?” Terry shuddered dramatically. “I can still hear all the whistles from his friends who were there in the room.”

Still laughing, Kelly said, “Well, that’ll teach Jimmy to surprise you.”

“No kidding. Now we make phone appointments.” Terry grinned. “But enough about me. I hear you and the writer went for a long ride the other day.”

“How did you—” Kelly stopped, blew out a breath and nodded. “Right. Sally.”

“She and her sister came in for coffee yesterday and told me all about it,” Terry admitted, tipping her head to one side to study her friend. “The question is, if there was something to know, why didn’t I already know it?”

“Because it’s nothing,” Kelly said, focusing on her painting again. She added shadows and depth to the curling vines. “He took me to buy some pumpkins.”

"Uh-huh. Sally says you were gone almost two hours. Either you're really picky about your pumpkins or something else was going on."

Kelly sighed. "We went for a ride."

"Uh-huh."

"I showed him around a little."

"Uh-huh."

"Nothing happened."

"Why not?"

Kelly just blinked. A couple of kids on skateboards shot down the sidewalk with a roar that startled her. "What?"

"Honey," Terry said, stepping close enough to drop one arm around Kelly's shoulders. "Sean's been gone four years. You haven't been on a single date in all that time. Now you've got this amazing-looking guy living in the Victorian for six months and you're not going to do anything about it?"

Laughing a little, Kelly shook her head again. "What should I do? Tie him up and have my way with him?"

Terry's eyes went a little dreamy. "Hmm…"

"Oh, stop it." But even as she said it, a rush of heat filled Kelly. She only enjoyed it for a second or two before tamping it right down and mentally putting out the fire.

Honestly, she didn't want or need the attraction she felt for Micah. He clearly wasn't interested and Kelly had already loved and lost. She really had zero interest in a romance. Of any kind.

"Okay, fine," Terry said, laughing. "If you're determined to shut yourself up in a closet, wrapped in wool or something, there's nothing I can do about it. But I swear, if the CIA ever needs more spies, I'm going to recommend Sally and Margie. Those two have their fingers on the pulse of everything that happens in town."

And lucky Kelly lived right across the street from them. Sean used to laugh when he saw the older ladies, noses pressed to the windows. He would sweep Kelly into an elaborate dip and kiss her senseless, saying, *"The reason they're so nosy is no one's ever kissed them senseless. So let's give them something to talk about."*

That memory brought a sad smile that she just as quickly let slide away. Remembering Sean meant not only the good times, but the pain of losing him. She'd lost enough in her life, Kelly told herself firmly.

First her parents when she was just a kid, then her grandfather, then Sean. Enough already. And the only way to ensure she never went through that kind of pain again was to never let herself get that close with anyone again.

She had Terry. Her grandmother. A couple of good friends.

Who needed a man?

Micah's image rose up in her mind and she heard a tiny voice inside her whisper, *You do. He's only here temporarily, why not take advantage? There's no future there, so no risk.*

True, Micah would only be in Banner for four more months, so it wasn't as if—no.

Don't think about it.

Sure. That would work.

"You know," Terry said, interrupting Kelly's stream of consciousness, "there's a guy in Jimmy's squad I think you'd really like…"

"Oh, no." Kelly shook her head firmly. "Don't go there, Terry. No setups. You know those never go well."

"He's a nice guy," her friend argued.

"I'm sure he's a prince," Kelly said. "But he's not *my* prince. I'm not looking for another man."

"Well, you should be." Terry folded her arms over her chest.

"Didn't you just say there was nothing you could do about it if I wanted to lock myself in a closet?"

"I hate seeing you alone all the time."

"*You're* alone," Kelly reminded her.

"For now, but Jimmy will be home in another couple of months."

"And I'm happy for you." Deliberately, Kelly turned back to her paints. She picked up the yellow and a small brush, then laid in the eyes on the first pumpkin. With the bright yellow, it would look like the pumpkin was lit by a candle. "I had a husband, Terry. Don't want another one."

From the corner of her eye, Kelly saw her friend's shoulders slump in defeat. "I didn't say I wanted you married."

"But you do."

"Not the point," Terry said stubbornly. "Sweetie, I know losing Sean was terrible. But you're too young to live the rest of your life like a vestal virgin."

Kelly laughed. "The virgin ship sailed a long time ago."

"You know what I mean."

Of course she did. Terry had been saying pretty much the same thing for the last two years. She just didn't understand that Kelly was too determined to avoid pain to ever take the kind of risk she was talking about. Loving was great. Losing was devastating, and she'd already lost enough, thanks.

"Yeah, I do, and I appreciate the thought—"

"No, you don't," Terry said.

"You're right, I don't." Kelly glanced at her friend and smiled to take the sting out of her words. "Honestly, you're as bad as Gran."

"Oh, low blow," Terry muttered. "She's still worried?"

"Ever since Sean died and it's gotten worse in the last year or so." She focused on the paints even while she kept talking. "Gran's even started making noises about moving back here so I won't be lonely."

"Oh, man." Terry sighed. "I thought she loved living in Florida with her sister."

"She *does*." Kelly crouched down to paint in the faces of three other pumpkins. "The two of them go to bingo and take trips with their seniors club. She's having a great time, but then she starts worrying about me and—"

Her cell phone rang and Kelly stood up to drag it from her jeans pocket. Glancing at the caller ID, she sighed and looked at Terry. "Speak of the devil…"

"Gran? Really?" Terry's eyes went dramatically wide. "Boy, her hearing's better than ever if she could catch us talking about her all the way from Florida!"

Kelly laughed. With a wince of guilt, she sent the call to voice mail.

"Seriously?" Terry sounded surprised. "You're not going to talk to her?"

"Having *one* conversation about my lack of a love life is enough for today."

"Fine." Terry held up both hands in surrender. "I'll back off. For now."

"Thanks." She tucked her phone away and tried not to feel badly about ditching her grandmother's call.

"*But*," Terry added before she went back into the coffee shop, "just because you're not interested in a permanent man..."

Kelly looked at her.

"...doesn't mean you can't enjoy a temporary one. I'm just saying."

After she left, Kelly's brain was racing. *A temporary man.* When she went back to her painting, she was still thinking, and as an ephemeral plan began to build in her mind, a speculative smile curved her mouth.

Three

Micah hated cooking, but he'd learned a long time ago that man cannot live on takeout alone. Especially when you're in the back end of beyond and can't get anything but pizza delivered.

He took a swig of his beer and flipped cooked pasta into a skillet with some olive oil and garlic. Adding chopped tomatoes and sliced steak to the mix, he used a spatula to mix it all together. The scent was making him hungry. Most people would think it was way too early for dinner, but Micah didn't eat on a schedule.

He'd been wrapped up in his book for the last several hours, hardly noticing the time passing. As always happened, once the flow of words finally stopped, he came out of his cave like a grizzly after six months of hibernation.

"Hi."

Micah turned to look at the open back door. It was late afternoon and the cool air felt good. Of course, if he'd known he'd be invaded, Micah would have kept the door shut. Too late now, though, since there was a little boy standing there, staring at him. The kid couldn't have been more than three or four. He had light brown hair that stuck up in wild tufts all over his head. His brown eyes were wide and curious and there was mud on the knees of his jeans and the toes of his sneakers. "Who are you?"

"I'm Jacob. I live there." He waved one hand in the general direction of the house next door. "Can I go see my pumpkin?"

The sizzling skillet was the only sound in the room. Micah looked at the kid and realized that he was one of the crew who made so much noise in Kelly's garden. That still didn't explain why the kid was here, talking to Micah. "Why are you asking me?"

"Cuz Kelly's not here so I have to ask another grown-up and you're one."

Can't argue with that kind of logic. "Yeah. Sure. Go ahead."

"Okay. What're you doin'?" Jacob came closer.

"I'm cooking." Micah glanced at the boy, then, dismissing him, went back to his skillet. "Go look at your pumpkin."

"Are you hungry, too?" The boy gave him a hopeful look.

"Yeah, so you should go home," Micah told him. "Have lunch." What time was it? He looked out the window. The sky was darkening toward twilight. "Or dinner."

"I hafta see my pumpkin first and say good-night."

That was a new one for Micah. Telling a vegetable

good-night. But the boy looked so…earnest. And a little pitiful in his dirty jeans with his wide brown eyes. Micah didn't do kids. Never had. Not even when he *was* a kid.

He'd kept to himself back then, too. He'd never made friends because he wouldn't have been able to keep them. Moving from home to home to home kept a foster kid wary of relationships. So he'd buried his nose in whatever books he could find and waited to turn eighteen so he could get out of the system.

But now, staring into a pair of big brown eyes, Micah felt guilt tugging at him for trying to ignore the kid. The feeling was so unusual for him he almost didn't recognize it. He also couldn't ignore it. "Fine then. Go ahead. Say good-night to your pumpkin."

"You hafta open the gate for me cuz I'm too little."

Rolling his eyes, Micah remembered the gated white-picket fence Kelly kept around her garden patch. She'd told him once it was to discourage rabbits and deer. Even though the deer could jump the fence with no problem, she wanted to make vegetable stealing as hard as possible on them.

With a sigh, Micah turned the fire off under his skillet, and said goodbye to the meal he'd just made. "All right." Micah looked at the boy. "Let's go then."

A bright smile lit the kid's face. "Thanks!"

He hustled out of the kitchen, down the back steps and around to the side of the house.

Micah followed more slowly, and as he walked, he took a second to appreciate the view. All around him fall colors exploded in shades of gold and red. The dark green of the pines in the woods beyond the house made them look as if they were made of shadows, and he idly plotted another murder, deep in the forest.

"I could have some kid find the body," he mumbled, seeing the possible scene in his mind. "Freak him out, but would he be too scared to tell anyone? Would he run for help or run home and hide?"

"Who?"

Coming back to the moment at hand, Micah looked at the child staring up at him. "What?"

"Who's gonna run home? Are they scared? Is it a boy? Cuz my brothers say boys don't get scared, only girls do."

Micah snorted. "Your brothers are wrong."

"I think so, too." Jacob nodded so hard his hair flopped across his forehead. He pushed it back with a dirty hand. "Jonah gets scared sometimes and Joshua needs a light on when he sleeps."

"Uh-huh." Way too much information, Micah thought and wondered idly if the kid had an off switch.

"I like the dark and only get scared sometimes." Jacob shifted impatiently from foot to foot.

"That's good."

"Do you get scared?"

Frowning now, Micah watched the boy. For a second he was tempted to say no and let it drop. Then he thought better of it. "Everybody gets scared sometimes."

"Even dads?"

Micah had zero experience with fathers, but he suspected that the one thing that would terrify a man was worrying about his children. "Yeah," he said. "Even dads."

"Wow." Jacob nodded thoughtfully. "I have a rabbit I hold when I get scared. I don't think my dad has one."

"A rabbit?" Micah shook his head.

"Not a real one," Jacob assured him. "Real ones would be hard to hold."

"Sure, sure." Micah nodded sagely.

"And they poop a lot."

Micah hid the smile he felt building inside. The boy was so serious he probably wouldn't appreciate being laughed at. Did all kids talk like this? And whatever happened to not talking to strangers? Didn't people tell their kids that anymore?

"There it is," Jacob said suddenly, and pointed to the garden as he hurried to the gate and waited for Micah to open it. Once he had, Jacob raced across the uneven ground to one of the dozen or more pumpkins.

Micah followed, hands in his jeans pockets, watching the kid because he couldn't very well leave him out here alone, could he? "Which one?"

"This one." Jacob bent down to pat the saddest pumpkin Micah had ever seen.

It was smaller than the others, but that wasn't its only issue. It was also shaped like a lumpy football. It was more a pale yellow than orange, and it had what looked like a tumor growing out of one side at the top. If it had been at a store, it would have been overlooked, but here a little boy was patting it tenderly.

"Why that one?" Micah asked, actually curious about what would have made the kid pick the damn thing.

Jacob pulled a weed, then looked up at Micah. "Cuz it's the littlest one, like me." He looked at the vines and all of the other round, perfect orange blobs. "And it's all by itself over here, so it's probably lonely."

"A lonely pumpkin." He wasn't sure why that statement touched him, but he couldn't deny the kid was getting to him.

"Uh-huh." Smiling again, Jacob said, "None of the other kids liked him, but I do. I'm gonna help my mom draw a happy face on him for Halloween and then he'll feel good."

The kid was worried about a pumpkin's self-esteem. Micah didn't even know what to say to that. When *he* was a kid, he'd never done Halloween. There'd been no costumes, no trick-or-treating, no carving pumpkins with his mom.

Micah had one fuzzy memory of his mother and it drifted through his mind like fog on a winter night. She was pretty—at least, he told himself that because the mental picture of her was too blurred to really tell. She had brown hair and brown eyes like his and she was kneeling on the sidewalk in front of him, smiling, though tears glittered in her eyes. Micah was about six, he guessed, a little older than Jacob. They were in New York and the street was busy with cars and people. He was hungry and cold and his mother smoothed his hair back from his forehead and whispered to him.

"You have to stay here without me, Micah."

Fear spurted inside him as he looked up at the dirty gray building behind him. The dark windows looked like blank eyes staring down at him. Worried and chewing his bottom lip, he looked back at his mother. "But I don't want to. I want to go with you."

"It's just for a little while, baby. You'll stay here where you'll be safe and I'll be back for you as soon as I can."

"I don't want to be safe, Mommy," he whispered, his voice catching, breaking as panic nearly choked him and he felt tears streaking down his face. "I want to go with you."

"You can't come with me, Micah." She kissed his forehead, then stood up, looking down at him. She took a step

back from him. "This is how it has to be and I expect you to be a good boy."

"I will be good if I can go with you," he promised. He reached for her hand, his small fingers curling around hers and holding tight, as if he could keep her there. With him.

But she only walked him up the steps, knocked on the door and gave Micah's fingers one last squeeze before pulling free. Fear nibbled at him, his tears coming faster, and he wiped them away with his jacket sleeve. "Don't leave..."

"You wait right here until they open the door, understand?"

He nodded, but he didn't understand. Not any of it. Why were they here? Why was she leaving? Why didn't she want him to be with her?

"I'll be back, Micah," she said. "Soon. I promise." Then she turned and left him.

He watched her go, hurrying down the steps, then along the sidewalk, until she was lost in the crowd. Behind him, the door opened and a lady he didn't know took Micah's hand and led him inside.

His mother never came back.

Micah shook off the memory of his first encounter with child services. It had been a long, confusing, terrifying day for him. He was sure he wouldn't be there long. His mother had said so. For the first year, he'd actually looked for her every day. After that, hope was more fragile and, finally, the hope faded completely. His mother's lies stuck with him, of course.

Hell, they still lived in a tiny, dark corner of his mind and constantly served as a reminder not to trust anyone.

But here, in Banner, those warnings were more silent

than they'd ever been for him. Watching as Jacob carefully brushed dirt off his pumpkin, Micah realized that this place was like stepping into a Norman Rockwell painting. A place where kids worried about pumpkins and talked to strangers like they were best friends. It had nothing at all to do with the world that Micah knew.

And maybe that's why he felt so out of step here.

That's how Kelly found them. The boy, kneeling in the dirt, and the man standing beside him, a trapped look on his face—as if he were trying to figure out how he'd gotten there. Smiling to herself, Kelly climbed out of her truck and walked toward the garden at the side of the house. Micah spotted her first and his brown eyes locked with hers.

She felt a jolt of something hot that made her knees feel like rubber, but she kept moving. She had to admit it surprised her, seeing Micah here with Jacob. She hadn't pictured him as the kind of guy to take the time for a child. He was so closed off, so private, that seeing him now, walking through a fenced garden while a little boy talked his ears off gave her a warm feeling she couldn't quite describe.

"What're you guys up to?" she asked as she walked closer.

"I showed Micah my pumpkin," Jacob announced. "He likes mine best, he said so."

"Well, of course he did," she agreed. "Yours is terrific."

The little boy flashed Micah a wide grin. Micah, on the other hand, looked embarrassed to have been caught being nice. Interesting reaction.

"It's okay I came over, right?" Jacob asked, looking

a little worried. "Micah was cooking, but he opened the gate for me and stuff."

"Sure it's okay," Kelly told him.

"Okay, I gotta go now," Jacob said suddenly, giving his pumpkin one last pat. "Bye!"

He bolted through the gate and tore across the backyard toward the house next door.

Micah watched him go. "That was fast."

Kelly laughed a little, then looked over at Micah. "You were cooking?"

He shrugged. "I was hungry."

She glanced at the lavender sky. "Early for dinner."

"Or late for lunch," he said with a shrug. "It's all about perspective."

What did it say about her that she enjoyed the sharp, nearly bitten off words he called a conversation? Kelly wondered if he'd been any easier with Jacob, but somehow she doubted it. The man might be a whiz when typing words and dialogue, but actually speaking in real life appeared to be one of his least favorite things.

"So, why keep the fence when you told me it doesn't stop the deer?

She looked around at the tall, white pickets, then walked toward the still-open gate. Micah followed her. Once through, she latched the gate after them and said, "Makes me feel better to try. Sometimes, I could swear I hear the deer laughing at my pitiful attempts to foil them."

He looked toward the woods that ran along the back of the neighborhood and stretched out for at least five miles to the base of the mountains. "I haven't seen a single deer since I've been here."

"You have to actually be outside," she pointed out.

"Right." He nodded and tucked his hands into his jeans pockets.

"There's a lot of them and they're sneaky," Kelly said, shooting a dark look at the forest. "Of course, some of them aren't. They just walk right into the garden and sneer at you."

He laughed and she looked at him, surprised. "Deer can sneer?"

"They can and do." She tipped her head to one side to stare at him. "You should laugh more often."

He frowned at that and the moment was gone, so Kelly let it go and went back to his first question. "The fence doesn't even slow them down, really. They just jump right over it." Shaking her head, she added, "They look like ballet dancers, really. Graceful, you know?"

"So why bother with the fence?"

"Because otherwise it's like I'm saying, *It's okay with me guys. Come on in and eat the vegetables.*"

"So, you're at war with deer."

"Basically, yeah." She frowned and looked to the woods. "And, so far, they're winning."

"You've got orange paint on your cheek."

"What? Oh." She reached up and scrubbed at her face.

"And white paint on your fingers."

Kelly held her hands out to see for herself, then laughed. "Yeah, I just came from a painting job and—"

"You paint, too?"

"Oh, just a little. Window decorations and stuff. I'm not an artist or anything, but—"

"Realtor, painter, website manager..." He just looked at her. "What else?"

"Oh, a few other things," she said. "I design gardens, and in the winter I plow driveways. I like variety."

His eyes flared at her admission and her stomach jumped in response. Not the kind of variety she'd meant, but now that the thought was in her brain, thank you very much, there were lots of other very interesting thoughts, too. Her skin felt heated and she was grateful for the cold breeze that swept past them.

Kelly took a deep breath, swallowed hard and said, "I should probably get home and clean up."

"How about a glass of wine first?"

Curious, she looked up at him. "Is that an invitation?"

"If it is?"

"Then I accept."

"Good." He nodded. "Come on then. We can eat, too."

"A man who cooks *and* serves wine?" She started for the back door, walking alongside Micah. "You're a rare man, Micah Hunter."

"Yeah," he murmured. "Rare."

Naturally, she was perfectly at home in the Victorian. She'd grown up there, after all. She'd done her homework at the round pedestal table while eating Gran's cookies fresh out of the oven. She'd learned to cook on the old stove and had helped Gran pick out the shiny, stainless steel French door refrigerator when the last one had finally coughed and died.

She'd painted the walls a soft gold so that even in winter it would feel warm and cozy in here, and she'd chosen the amber-streaked granite counters to complement the walls. This house was comfort. Love.

At the farmhouse sink, Kelly looked out the window at the yard, the woods and the deepening sky as she washed her hands, scrubbing every bit of the paint from her skin. Then she splashed water on her face and wiped that away, too. "Did I get it all?"

He glanced at her and nodded. "Yeah."

"Good. I like painting, but I prefer the paint on the windows rather than on me."

Kelly got the wine out of the fridge while Micah heated the pasta in the skillet. She took two glasses from a cabinet and poured wine for each of them before sitting at the round oak table watching him.

What was it, she wondered, about a man cooking that was just so sexy? Sean hadn't known how to turn the stove on, but Micah seemed confident and comfortable with a spatula in his hand. Which only made her think about what other talents he might have. Oh, boy, it had been a long time since she'd felt this heat swamping her. If Terry knew what Kelly was thinking right this minute, she would send up balloons and throw a small but tasteful party. That thought made her smile. "Smells good."

He glanced over his shoulder at her. "Pasta's easy. A few herbs, some garlic, olive oil and cheese and you're done. Plus, some sliced steak because you've gotta have meat."

"Agreed," Kelly said, taking a sip of her wine.

"Glad to hear you're not one of those *I'll just have a salad, dressing on the side* types."

"Hey, nothing wrong with a nice salad."

"As long as there's meat in it," he said, concentrating on the task at hand.

"So what made you take up cooking?"

"Self-preservation. Live alone, you learn how to cook."

Whether he knew it or not, that was an opening for questions. She didn't waste it. "Live alone, huh?"

One eyebrow lifted as he turned to look at her. "Did you notice anyone else here with me the last couple of months?"

"No," she admitted with a smile, "but you do write mysteries. You could have killed your girlfriend."

"Could have," he agreed easily. "Didn't. The only place I commit crimes is on a computer screen."

"Glad to hear it," she said, smiling. Also glad to hear he could take some teasing and give it back. But on to the real question. "So, no girlfriend or wife?"

He used the spatula to stir the pasta, then gave her a quick look. "That's a purely female question."

"Well, then, since I am definitely female, that makes sense." She propped her chin in her hand. "And it was very male of you to answer the question by not answering. Want to give it another try?"

"No."

"No you won't answer or no *is* the answer?"

Reluctantly, it seemed, his mouth curved briefly into a half smile. "I should know better than to get into a battle of words with a woman. Even being a writer, I don't stand a chance."

"Isn't that the nicest thing to say?" But she stared at him, clearly waiting for his answer. Finally he gave her the one she was looking for.

He snorted. "No is the answer. No wife. No girlfriend. No interest."

"So you're gay," she said sagely. Oh, she knew he wasn't because the two of them had that whole hot-buzz thing going between them. But it was fun to watch his expression.

"I'm not gay."

"Are you sure?"

"Reasonably," he said wryly.

"Good to know," she said, and took a sip of wine, hiding her smile behind the rim of her glass. "I'm not, either, just so we're clear."

His gaze bored into hers and flames licked at her insides. “Also good to know.”

Her throat dried up so she had another sip of wine to ease it. “How long have you been a writer?”

“A writer or a published writer?” he asked.

“There’s a difference?”

He shrugged as he plated the pasta and carried them to the table. Sitting down opposite her, he took a long drink of his wine before speaking again. “I wrote stories for years that no one will ever see.”

“Intriguing,” she said, and wondered what those old stories would say about Micah Hunter. Would she learn more about the closed-off, secretive man by discovering who he had been years ago?

“Not very.” He took a bite of pasta, “Anyway, I’ve been published about ten years.”

“I don’t read your books.”

One eyebrow lifted and he smirked. “Thanks.”

She grinned. “That came out wrong. Sorry. I mean, I read one of your books a few years ago and it scared me to death. So I haven’t read another one.”

“Then, thank you.” He lifted his glass in a kind of salute to her. “Best compliment you could give me. Which book was it?”

“I don’t remember the title,” she said, tasting the pasta. “But it was about a woman looking for her missing sister and she finds the sister’s killer, instead.”

He nodded. “*Relative Danger*. That was my third book.”

“First and last for me,” she assured him. “I slept with the light on for two weeks.”

“Thanks.” He studied her. “Did you read the whole book? Or did you stop because it scared you?”

“Who stops in the middle of a book?” she demanded,

outraged at the idea. "No, I read the whole thing and, terror aside, it ended well."

"Thanks again."

"You're welcome. You know, this is really good," she said, taking another bite. "Your mom teach you how to cook?"

His face went hard and tight. He lowered his gaze to his plate and muttered, "No. Learned by trial and error."

Sore spot, she told herself and changed the subject. She had secret, painful corners in her own soul, so she wouldn't poke at his. "How's your book coming? The one you're working on now, I mean."

He frowned before answering. "Slower than I'd like."

"Why?"

"You ask a lot of questions."

"The only way to get answers."

"True." He took a sip of wine. "Because the book's set in a small town and I don't know small towns."

"Hello?" Laughing, she said, "You're *in* one."

"Yeah. That's why I came here in the first place. My agent suggested it. He stayed here a couple of years ago for the skiing and thought the town would work for my research."

"*Here*, here?" she asked. "I mean, did he stay at the Victorian?"

"Yeah."

"What's his name?"

"Sam Hellman. He and his wife, Jenny, were here for a week."

"I remember them. She's very pretty and sweet and he's funny."

"That's them," Micah agreed.

Kelly took a drink of her wine. "Well, first, I'm glad

your agent had a good time here. Word of mouth? Best advertising."

"For books, too," he agreed.

"But if you want to use the town for its setting and ambience, it might help if you left the house and explored a little. Get to know the place."

He ate for a couple of minutes, then finally said, "Getting out doesn't get the typing done."

Kelly shrugged and set down her glass. "But you can't get to know the town by looking through a window, either. And, if you don't know what it's like here, you've got nothing to type anyway, right?"

"I don't much like that you've got a point."

Kelly grinned. "Well, that makes two points for me, doesn't it? I'm still winning."

Unexpectedly, he laughed and the rich, warm sound seemed to ripple along her spine.

"Competitive, aren't you?"

"You have no idea," Kelly admitted. "I used to drive my grandparents crazy. I was always trying to be first in my class, or the fastest runner or—"

"Your grandparents still live here?"

"No." She picked up her wineglass and watched the light play on the golden wine. "My grandfather died six years ago and my grandmother moved to Florida to live with her sister a year later." Kelly took a sip, let the cold liquid ease her suddenly tight throat. "When my husband died four years ago, Gran came home for a few weeks to stay with me."

"You were married?" He spoke quietly, as if unsure exactly what to say.

No surprise there, Kelly thought. Most people just immediately said, *I'm sorry.* She didn't know why. Social convention? Or was it just the panic of not being able to think of anything else?

She lifted her gaze to his. “Sean died in a skiing accident.”

“Must’ve been hard.”

“Yeah,” she said, nodding. “It was. And thanks for not saying you’re sorry. People do, even though they have nothing to be sorry about, you know? Then I feel like I have to make them feel better, and it’s just a weird situation all the way around.”

“Yeah. I get that.”

The expression on his face was sympathetic and that was okay. Telling someone your husband was dead was a conversation killer. “It’s okay. I mean, no one ever really knows what to say, so don’t worry about it.” Another sip of wine to wash down the knot in her throat. “Anyway, it wasn’t easy to get Gran to go back to her new life—she thought she was abandoning me. And I love that she loves me, you know? But I don’t want to be a worry or a burden or a duty—not really a duty, but that little nudge of worry. I don’t want to be that, either.” She took a breath and smiled. “Whoa. Rambling. Anyway, Gran’s still worried, and unless I can convince her I’m just fine, she’s going to move back here to keep me company.”

“And that’s a bad thing?”

She looked at him. “Yes. It’s bad. She’s having a blast in Florida. She deserves to enjoy herself, not to feel like she has to move back to take care of an adult granddaughter.”

Nodding, Micah leaned back in the chair, never taking his gaze from hers. “All right. I can see that. So you know what you want. How’re you going to manage it?”

Good question. There was a ridiculous idea worming its way through her mind, but it was so far out there she felt weird even entertaining the idea while Micah was here.

"I don't know yet." She smiled, had another sip of wine and said, "But, hey, as fascinating as my whirlwind life can be, enough already. I've given you my story. What's yours?"

He stiffened. "What do you mean?"

"Well, for starters," Kelly said, "have you ever been married?"

Micah shook his head. "No."

Kelly just stared at him, waiting. There had to be more than just a no.

Finally, he scowled and added, "Fine. I was engaged once."

"Engaged but not married. So what happened?"

"It didn't take." His features were tight, like the doors of a house locked against intruders.

Okay, that was obviously a dead-end subject. "You know, for a writer—someone supposedly good with words—you're not particularly chatty."

He snorted and the tension left him. "Writers *write*. Besides, men aren't 'chatty.'"

"But they do talk."

"I'm talking."

"Not saying much," she pointed out.

"Maybe there's not much to say."

"Oh, I don't believe that," Kelly told him. "There's more, you're just stingy about sharing."

He started to speak—no doubt protest, Kelly told herself, but she stopped him with another question.

"Let's try this. You're a writer and you travel all over the world, I know. But where's home?"

"Here." He studiously avoided her gaze and concentrated on the pasta.

"Yeah," she said. "For now. But before this. Where are you from?"

"Originally," he answered, "New York."

Honestly, it would probably be easier if she asked him to *write* the information and let her read it. "Okay, that's originally. How about now—and not this house."

"Everywhere," he said. "I move around."

She hadn't expected that. Everyone was from *somewhere.* "What about your family?"

"Don't have any." He stood up, took his plate to the sink, then came back for his wineglass. Lifting it for a drink, he looked at her. "And I don't talk about it, either."

Message was clear, Kelly thought. He'd put up his mental No Trespassing signs. His eyes were shuttered and his jaw was tight.

Whatever bit of closeness had opened up between them was over now. Funny that while they were talking about *her*, he was all chatty, but the minute the conversation shifted to him, he clammed up so tightly it would take a crowbar to pry words from his mouth.

It surprised her how disappointed she was about that. Since Sean died, she hadn't been as interested in a man as she was in Micah. And for a while, as they sat together sharing a meal, she'd felt that buzz humming between them like an arc of electricity. And now it was fizzling out. The expression on his face told her he was waiting for her to pry. To ask more questions. And since she hated being predictable, Kelly said simply, "Okay."

Suspicion gleamed in his eyes. "Just like that."

"Everybody's got secrets, Micah," she told him with

a shrug. “You’re entitled to yours.” Tipping her head to one side, she asked, “Why so surprised?”

“Because most women would be hammering me with questions right now.”

“Well, then, it’s your lucky day, because I’m not like most women.” Besides, hammering him wouldn’t work.

“Got that right,” he muttered.

She heard that and smiled to herself as she carried her dishes to the sink, then turned for the back door. Kelly didn’t want to leave, but she knew she should. Otherwise, she might be tempted to be like every other woman in the world and try to get him to open up some more—which would be pointless and exactly what he expected.

“So, thanks for lunch or dinner or whatever. And the wine.”

Micah was right behind her. “You’re welcome.”

His voice came from right behind her. At the open doorway, she turned and almost bumped into his chest.

“Oh, sorry.” Wow, was his chest really that broad, or was she just so close it *looked* like he was taking up the whole world? Heat poured from his body, reaching for her, tingling her nerve endings. And he smelled so good, too.

Kelly shook her head, and ignored the flutter of expectation awakening in the pit of her stomach. Deliberately, she fought for lighthearted, then tipped her head back and smiled up at him. “You know, I think I should get another point.”

“For what?”

“For surprising you by not asking questions.” She held up three fingers and gave him a teasing smile. “So that makes it three to nothing my favor and don’t you forget it.”

"Not a chance in hell you would *let* me forget, is there?"

"Nope." Kelly grinned. "And how nice that you know me so well already."

"That's what I thought." He studied her as if he were trying to figure out a puzzle. But after a second or two, he nodded. "You want to keep score? Then add this into the mix."

He pulled her in close and kissed her.

Four

Everything inside Kelly lit up like a sparkler, showering her head to toe in red-hot flickers of heat and light. Instinctively, her eyes closed and her body swayed closer to him. His mouth covered hers and his arms came around her, molding her to him, and she lifted both arms to hook them around his neck.

It had been so long since she'd been kissed she was dizzy with the sensations pouring through her. God, she'd forgotten how sensations poured through her system in a kiss, the tangle of feelings that erupted. She couldn't think. Couldn't have spoken even if she had wanted to pry her mouth from his. His tongue stroked hers and the groans lifting from her throat twisted with Micah's, the soft sounds whispering into the twilight.

Breathing was becoming an issue, but she didn't care. She wanted to revel in the feeling of her body awakening as if from a coma. Fires quickened down low inside her and a tingling ache settled at her core. Need clawed at her and she moved in even closer to him. She might have stood there all night, taking what he offered, feeling her own desires tearing at her. But, as suddenly as he'd kissed her, he ended it.

Tearing his mouth from hers, he lifted his head to look down at her. From Kelly's perspective, his features were blurry. She swayed unsteadily until she slapped one hand to the door frame just for balance. As her mind defogged, her vision cleared and her heart rate dropped from racing to just really fast.

He still held her waist in a tight grip, and when he looked down into her eyes, Kelly saw that *his* eyes were a molten brown now, shot through with the fires that were burning her from the inside out.

"I think that makes it three to one now, doesn't it?" His voice was low, a deep rumble that was almost like thunder.

Points? Oh, yeah. Kelly's brain was just not working well enough at the moment to count points. But since her body was still smoldering, she had to say, "Oh, yeah. Point to you."

He gave her a slow, satisfied smile.

Reluctantly, her mouth curved, too. "You're enjoying this, aren't you?"

"I'd be a fool not to," he admitted.

"Yeah. Well." She lifted one hand to touch her fingers to her lips. "Let's not forget, I've still got three points to your one."

His smile faded and his eyes flashed as he let her go. "But the game's not over yet, is it?"

"Not even close to finished," she said, then turned

and started the short walk home. She felt him watching her as she walked away and that gave her a warm rush, too. Kelly had the feeling that this game was just getting started.

She couldn't wait for round two.

Micah watched her go for ten agonizing seconds, then he shut the door firmly to keep himself from chasing after her. God, he felt like some girl-crazed teenager and that just wasn't acceptable. He was a man who demanded control. He didn't do spontaneous. Didn't veer from the plan he had for his life. And that plan did *not* include a small-town widow who tasted like a glimpse of heaven.

He wanted another taste. Wanted to feel her body pressed to his, the race of her heart, the warmth of her arms around his neck.

"Damn it." He took a deep breath to steady himself, but her scent was still clinging to him and it invaded his lungs, making itself a part of him.

His own heartbeat was a little crazed and his jeans felt like an iron cage around his hard body. Micah didn't know what had made him grab her like that. But the urge to taste her, hold her, had been too big to ignore. If he'd been thinking clearly, he never would have done it. The problem was, every time he was around Kelly, thinking was an impossible task.

"Maybe Sam's right," he told himself. "Maybe an affair is the answer." Something had to give, he thought. Because if he spent the next four months as tied up in knots as he was at the moment, he'd never get any writing done.

Something to think about.

* * *

Kelly walked home across the wide front lawn, mind racing, nerves sizzling from that unexpected but amazing kiss. She stopped halfway to the carriage house, turned around and looked at the big Victorian.

In the deepening twilight, the house looked as it had to her when she was a child—like a fairy tale. The house was painted a deep brick red with snow-white trim that seemed to define every little detail. Three chimneys jutted up from the shake roof, indicating the tiled fireplaces—in the living room, the master bedroom and the kitchen. The wide, wraparound porch was dotted with swings, chairs and tables, inviting anyone to sit, enjoy the view and visit for a while. Double front doors were hand-carved mahogany with inset panes of etched glass. The last of the sunset glanced off the second-story windows, making them glow gold, and downstairs a lamp in the living room flashed on, telling Kelly exactly where Micah was in the house.

She lifted one hand to her mouth as she looked at that light, imagining him striding through that front door, marching across the yard to her and kissing her again. God, one kiss and all she could think was she wanted more.

"Oh, man, this could be bad..." Deliberately then, as if to prove to herself she *could*, she turned away and continued to the cottage.

It was a smaller version of the big house. Same colors, same intricate trim, made by a long-dead craftsman more than a hundred years ago. Just one bedroom, bathroom, living room and kitchen, the cottage was perfect for one person and normally, when Kelly stepped inside, it felt like a refuge.

She'd moved out of the Victorian not long after Sean's death because she simply couldn't bear the empty rooms and the echo of her own footsteps. Here, in this cottage, it was cozy and safe and, right now, almost suffocating. But that was probably because she still felt like there was a tight band around her chest.

Kelly dropped into the nearest chair and snuggled into the deep cushions. The comfort and familiarity of the cottage didn't relax her as it usually did. Shaking her head, she sighed a little and told herself to get a grip. But it wasn't easy since Micah Hunter had a real gift when it came to kissing. So, naturally, she had to wonder how gifted he was in…related areas. Oh, boy. She was in deep trouble.

The worst part was that she wanted to be in even deeper.

When her cell phone rang, she dug it out of her pocket, grateful for the distraction. Until she saw the caller ID. Guilt rose up and took another healthy bite out of Kelly's heart. She'd forgotten all about returning her grandmother's call. Seeing Micah, sharing a meal with him, had thrown her off, and then that kiss had completely sealed the deal on her mind, shutting down any thought beyond *oh, boy*!

Taking a breath, she forced a smile into her voice and answered. "Hi, Gran! I'm sorry, I just didn't have a chance to call you back before."

"That's okay, honey," her grandmother said. "I hope you were out having fun…"

Kelly sighed a little and leaned her head back against the cushioned chair. She could hear the worry in her grandmother's voice and wished she couldn't. Ever since Sean died, Gran had been worried and it didn't seem to be easing. If anything, it was getting worse. As if the older Gran got, the more she was concerned about eventually leaving Kelly on her own.

Kelly had been trying for months to convince Gran that she was fine. Happy. But nothing worked because the only thing Gran would accept was Kelly in love and married again. She wanted her settled with a family and no matter how many times Kelly told her that she didn't need a husband, Gran remained ever hopeful.

Even knowing that Kelly had just been kissed until her brain melted wouldn't be enough to satisfy Gran. Not unless she and Micah were married or—

Suddenly, the idea she'd played with earlier came back to her. Maybe it was the kiss. Maybe it was sitting across that table from Micah, talking, laughing, sharing dinner. Whatever the reason, Kelly made a decision that she really hoped she didn't come to regret. "Actually, Gran," she said, before the still-rational corner of her brain could stop her, "I was with my fiancé."

"*What?* Oh, my goodness, that's wonderful!"

The joy in her grandmother's voice made Kelly smile and wince at the same time. Okay, yes, technically she was lying to her grandmother. But, really, she was just trying to give the older woman some peace. The chance to enjoy her life without constant worries about Kelly. That wasn't a bad thing, was it? It's not like she was pretending to be engaged for her own sake. This was completely altruistic.

"Tell me everything," Gran insisted. "Who is he? What does he do? Is he handsome?"

"It's Micah Hunter, Gran," she said, hoping a lightning bolt didn't streak out of the sky and turn her into a cinder. "The writer who's renting the Victorian for six months."

"Oh, my, a writer!"

Kelly's eyes closed tightly on another wince, but that didn't help because Micah's image rose up in her mind and gave her a hard look. She ignored it.

"He's very handsome and very sweet." Oh, it was a wonder her tongue didn't simply rot and fall out of her mouth. *Sweet?* Micah Hunter? Sexy, yes. Prickly, oh, yeah. But she'd seen no evidence of sweet. Still, it was something her grandmother would want to hear. And as long as Kelly was lying through her teeth to the woman who had raised her, she was determined to make it a *good* lie.

"When did this happen?" Gran asked. "When did he propose? What does your ring look like?"

Before Kelly could answer, Gran covered the receiver and shouted, "Linda, you won't believe it! Our girl is engaged to a writer!"

Gran's sister squealed in the background and Kelly sighed.

"I'm putting you on speaker, sweetie. Linda wants to hear the story, too."

Great. A command performance. Boy, it was a good thing they didn't do video chatting.

"It just happened tonight," Kelly blurted. Her grandmother's friends in Banner no doubt gave her updates on Kelly, so she would know that nothing had happened between her and Micah any sooner.

"How exciting!" Linda exclaimed, and Gran shushed her.

"Tell us everything, honey," Gran urged. "I want details."

"He cooked dinner tonight," Kelly continued, and consoled herself that at least that part of the story wasn't a lie. "He proposed while we were sitting out on the porch."

"Oh, that's lovely." Gran gave a heavy sigh and Kelly felt terrible.

She was already regretting this, but she was in so deep now there was no way to back out without admitting she had lied. Nope. Couldn't do it.

"Yeah, it was lovely." Kelly nodded and kept going, making it as romantic as she could for her grandmother's sake. The woman loved watching Hallmark movies and had been known to cry at particularly touching commercials, so Kelly knew Gran would expect romance in this story.

Thinking fast, she said, "He had flowers on the porch and those little white twinkle lights hung from the ceiling. Music was playing, too," she added, telling herself to remember all of these details. "He brought out a bottle of champagne and went down on one knee and when I said yes, he kissed me."

Kissed her brainless, apparently, because otherwise why would she be inventing all of this? Oh, God, just remembering that kiss had her blood humming and heat spiraling through her body. One kiss and she was making up an engagement.

What was she doing?

"Well, good, I'm so glad to hear he gave you romance, sweetheart. I'm so happy for you." Her grandmother sniffled a little and her sister said, "Oh, Bella, stop now. The girl's happy. You should be too."

"These are happy tears, Linda, can't you tell?"

"They're still tears, so stop it."

Kelly grimaced. Could you actually be *devoured* by guilt?

"Pay no attention to my sister," Gran said softly. "You know, honey, since you lost Sean, I've been so worried."

"I know." Kelly told herself she was doing the right thing. She was easing an old woman's heart. Making her happy. It wasn't hurting anyone. Not even Micah, really. He was only here temporarily. Heck, he didn't even have to meet her grandmother. And, when he left in four months, Kelly would simply tell Gran that they'd broken up. Maybe the very fact that Kelly had been engaged, however briefly, would be enough to assure Gran that she didn't have to worry so much.

"Will you take a picture of your ring and send it to me?"

Oops. She looked at her naked ring finger and sighed.

"Um, I don't have a ring yet," Kelly said.

"The man thought of twinkle lights but didn't bother with a ring?" Linda asked.

The two women together were really hard to stand against. "Micah wants to wait until we go to New York so we can pick one out together."

"New York?" Linda's tone changed. "How exciting!"

"Hush, Linda," Gran told her sister. "When are you going to New York, sweetie? Can you send me pictures? I'd love to show the girls at bingo."

"Sure I can, Gran." *Oh, my God, stop talking, Kelly.*

But the lies kept piling on top of each other until any second now, she'd be buried beneath a mountain of them. There was no way to stop now. She'd started all of this and she had to follow through because admitting a lie to her grandmother was simply impossible.

"I don't know when we're going to New York though…" That was true, at least. "He's busy with work and I've got Halloween coming up and—"

Gran clucked her tongue and Kelly muffled a groan.

"Well, you both just have to take the time for each other," Gran told her firmly. "Work will always be there, but this is a special time for you two."

Oh, it was special, all right. And wait until she told Micah about all of this. That scene promised to be extra special.

"Why a New York ring?" Linda demanded. "They don't sell rings in Utah?"

"Well," Kelly said, making it up as she went along, "when I told Micah I'd never been to New York, he insisted on flying me out there in a private jet so he could show me around. So, we really want to wait on the ring until then."

"Oh, my goodness," Gran whispered. "Linda, can you imagine? Private jets."

"He must be rich," Linda said thoughtfully.

"Course he is," Gran told her. "Haven't we seen his books just everywhere? Don't tell him we don't read his books because they're too scary, though, all right dear?"

"Sure, I won't tell him," Kelly promised.

"You know," Aunt Linda said, "I saw a documentary on those private jets not long ago. They've got *bedrooms* on those jets. You could live on them, I swear."

Kelly couldn't sit still anymore. She lunged out of the chair, walked to her tiny, serviceable kitchen and threw open the fridge. Grabbing the bottle of chardonnay, she pulled out the cork and took a swig straight from the bottle. Oh, if Gran could see her at that moment. Sighing a little, Kelly got a wineglass from a cabinet and poured herself what looked like eight ounces. It might not be enough.

"Well," Gran continued to argue with her sister.

"They're not looking to live on the plane, for heaven's sake, and you just keep your mind out of bedrooms."

"Nothing wrong with a good romp," Linda told her sister. "It would do you good to try one."

Kelly took a big gulp of wine. She didn't want to know about her grandmother's sex life. Or her aunt's, for that matter. Actually, she didn't want to know they *had* sex lives.

"What's that supposed to mean?" Gran sounded outraged. "Just because you don't have standards..."

"I have standards," Linda countered, "but they don't get in the way of a good time."

This argument could go on all night, Kelly knew. The two women loved nothing better than arguing with each other. Drinking her wine, Kelly told herself that while they were arguing about their men friends, they weren't interrogating Kelly about *her* love life. That was something, anyway.

Halfheartedly listening to the two of them, Kelly had enough of a break from her lie fest that she had the time to start worrying about breaking all of this to Micah. How was she supposed to explain it to him when she could hardly figure out herself why she'd started all of this?

She stared out the kitchen window at the yard and the stately Victorian where the man she was using shamelessly was currently living, unaware that he'd just gotten engaged. Oh, boy.

"When's the wedding?" Linda asked suddenly.

"She's *my* granddaughter," Gran said tightly. "I'll ask the questions here. When Debbie gets engaged, then it'll be your turn. Kelly, when's the wedding, honey?"

Kelly's cousin Debbie had already insisted that she and her girlfriend were *never* getting married because the two grans would drive her insane. Kelly could understand that. After all, she'd already lived through one wedding where Gran had made and changed plans every day. If she ever really did get married again one day, she'd elope. Vegas sounded good.

But, for now, Gran was waiting for an answer and since Kelly couldn't tell the truth, she told another lie. It seemed she was on a roll.

"Oh, the wedding won't be for a while yet," she hedged, and had another drink of wine. At this rate, she was going to pass out in another few minutes. "I mean, Micah's got this book he's working on and then he has to do other writing stuff—" Oh, God, that sounded weak, even to her. What did writers have to *do*? "Um, book tours and research trips for the next book, so we probably won't be able to get married for at least another six months, maybe even a year. It all depends on Micah's work." There. That was reasonable, right?

"Wonderful," Gran said, and Kelly released a breath she hadn't realized she'd been holding. "That gives us plenty of time to *plan*. You'll have the wedding at the Victorian, of course…"

"Oh, of course," Kelly agreed, rolling her eyes so hard she heard them rattle.

"Or," Linda argued. "You could get married on the beach right here in Florida. Next summer, maybe?"

"I don't know, Aunt Linda…"

"Why would you want to get married on a beach?" Gran snorted. "All that sand in your shoes and the wind ruining your hair and seagulls pooping all over the place."

"It's romantic," Linda insisted.

"It's dirty," Gran countered.

"Oh, God," Kelly murmured, so quietly that the other two women on the line didn't hear her.

Completely wrapped up in their argument, the ladies didn't notice when Kelly went quiet and that was good. Carrying her wine back to the living room, Kelly dropped into a chair again and listened with only half an ear to her grandmother and aunt.

She didn't have to pay attention now. Kelly knew that she'd be hearing nothing but plans for the next four months—until Micah left and she could break this imaginary engagement. Supposing, of course, that she could talk Micah into going along with this in the first place. If she couldn't, then what? She'd have to claim insanity. That would be the only excuse accepted by her family.

Guilt was becoming such a familiar companion she hardly noticed when it dropped into the pit of her stomach and sat there like a ball of ice. Wine wouldn't melt it, either, though she gave it her best shot.

Her grandmother was talking about white dresses while Linda insisted that white was outdated and Kelly wasn't a virgin, anyway.

A snort of laughter escaped her throat and Kelly was half-afraid it would turn into hysteria. Shaking her head, she tried to figure out the best way to approach Micah about the story she'd created. Once she hung up the phone, Gran would be calling all of her friends in Banner to share the happy news, so Micah had to be prepared for questions. And for behaving like a man in love so she could keep her grandmother blissfully unaware for four short months.

Oh, boy. Lying got out of hand so quickly Kelly could only sit and stare blankly at the wall opposite her. Really, even when a lie seemed like the best idea, it wasn't. No one ever looked far ahead as to what that lie was going to look like once other people picked it up and ran with it. But it wasn't as if she'd had a whole lot of options. She wasn't dating anyone, so she'd had to name Micah. She couldn't let her grandmother give up her new life and sacrifice herself on the altar of Sad Lonely Granddaughter.

But, even though she knew she was doing the right thing, the hole she'd dug for herself was beginning to feel like a bottomless chasm.

At least, she *hoped* it was bottomless. Otherwise, the crash landing she was going to make would be spectacular.

Micah woke up irritated. Not surprising since what little sleep he had gotten had been haunted by images of Kelly Flynn.

"Your own damn fault," he muttered. "If you hadn't kissed her…"

The taste of her was still with him. The feel of her body, warm and pliant against his. Her eager response had fired his blood to the point that it had taken everything he had just to let her go and back off.

Hell, the woman had been making him nuts for the last two months. Sexy, smart and a wiseass, Kelly was enough to bring any man to his knees.

"But damned if I will," he muttered darkly, and got out of bed. Disgusted with himself *and* her, he stalked to the bathroom, turned the water on to heat up, then stood under the shower. He let the hot water slam into his head, hoping it might wash away the last of the dreams that had tormented him and had had him waking up hard as iron.

Naturally it didn't work. It was like her features were imprinted on his brain. Her wide green eyes, the way she had lifted one hand to her lips when their kiss ended. Her smile, her ridiculous insistence on keeping track of "points" scored.

Shaking his head, he saw her in the stupid pumpkin patch talking about her war with deer, of all things. Micah had never *seen* a deer. He closed his eyes and reminded himself that he didn't want or need a woman. But maybe that was wrong, too. If he was fantasizing this much about the landlady, it had clearly been too long since he'd been with a woman.

"Gotta be it," he murmured, shutting off the water and stepping out of the tiled, glassed-in shower. "That's the reason I can't stop thinking about a woman who doesn't even know when she has orange paint on her face."

He dried off, then walked into the bedroom, not bothering to shave. Hell, he'd gotten so little sleep he'd probably slit his own throat if he attempted it.

"What I need to do is put this out of my head and get to work." Losing himself in a grisly murder was just the thing to take his mind off finding Kelly and dragging her here to his bed.

He pulled on a pair of black jeans, then tugged a forest green T-shirt over his head. Micah didn't bother with shoes. It might be gray and cold outside, but inside the old house was toasty. All he wanted was some coffee and then some quiet so he could create another murder.

As soon as he opened the bedroom door, the unmistakable scent of fresh coffee hit him hard. But it wasn't just coffee. It was bacon, too. And toast. "What kind of burglar breaks into a house to make breakfast?"

He started down the long staircase, his bare feet silent on the sapphire-blue carpet runner. Two months here and he still felt like a stranger in this big old house with its creaky doors and polished, old-world style.

He couldn't complain about anything. The house had been updated over the years and boasted comfortable furniture, every amenity and a view from every window that really was beautiful. But it was a lot more space than he was used to. A lot more quiet than he was happy with. Being solitary was part of being a writer. After all, the bottom line was sitting by yourself at a computer. If you needed people with you every damn minute, then writing was not the job for you.

But even solitary creatures needed sensory input from time to time. And being on your own in a house built for a family of a couple dozen could be a little unsettling. Hell, as a mystery/horror writer, Micah could use this house, the solitude and the woods behind the property as the perfect setting for a book.

As that thought took root in his mind, he stopped at the bottom of the stairs, considered it and muttered, "Of course I should be using this house. Why the hell aren't I?"

He continued on through to the kitchen, his senses focused on the tantalizing scents dragging him closer even while his mind figured out how big a rewrite he was looking at. To move his heroine from a small apartment in town to this big house, he'd have to change a million little things. But, he told himself, the atmosphere alone would be worth it.

A cold winter night, the heroine closed up in her bedroom, a fire burning as the wind shrieked and sleet pelted the windows. Then over that noise, she hears something else. Someone moving downstairs—when she's alone in the house.

"Oh, yeah," he told himself, nodding, "that's good. I like it."

He hit the swinging door into the kitchen, stepped inside and stopped dead. Kelly stood at the stove, stirring scrambled eggs in a skillet. Morning sunlight danced in her hair, making the red and gold shine like a new penny. Her black yoga pants clung to her behind and hugged her legs before disappearing into the tops of the black boots on her feet. She half turned toward him when he came in. Her pale green long-sleeved shirt had the top two buttons undone, giving Micah just a peek at what looked like a lacy pink bra.

Instantly his body went hard as stone again. He swallowed the groan that rose in his throat. Wasn't it enough that she'd tormented him all damn night? Why was she here first thing in the morning? Cooking? God, he needed coffee.

And the only way to get it was to deal with the woman smiling at him.

Five

"What're you doing?"

"Cooking." She smiled at him and Micah felt every drop of blood drain from his brain and head south.

After turning the fire down under the pan, she walked to the coffeemaker, poured him a cup and carried it to him.

"I made breakfast." She sounded bright, cheerful, but her eyes told a different story. There was worry there and a hesitation that put Micah on edge.

Whatever was going on, though, would be handled best *after* coffee. He took his first sip of the morning and felt every cell in his body wake up and dance. How did people survive without coffee?

After another sip or two, he felt strong enough to ask, "Why?"

"Why what?"

One eyebrow lifted. "Why are you here? Why are you cooking?"

"Just being neighborly," she said, and he didn't believe a word of it.

"Yeah." He walked to the table, sat down and had another sip. "I've been here two months. This is the first time you've been 'neighborly.'"

"Well, then, shame on me." She stirred the eggs in the pan and neatly avoided meeting his gaze. Not, Micah told himself, a good sign.

"You're not really good at prevarication."

Her eyes widened. "Oh. Good word."

"And," Micah added wryly, "not very good at stalling, either."

She sighed heavily. "Okay, yes, there is something I need to talk to you about, but after breakfast, okay?"

He grabbed a slice of bacon, took a bite and chewed. When he'd swallowed, he sent her a hard look. "There. I ate. What's going on?"

Taking a deep breath, she turned the fire off under the eggs before facing him. "I need a husband."

Not enough coffee, he told himself. Not nearly enough. But he said only, "Good luck with that."

"No," she corrected quickly. "Not a husband, really. I just need a fiancé."

"Again. Happy hunting." He got up to refill his coffee and thought seriously about just chugging it straight from the pot.

"Micah, I need you to pretend to be my fiancé." After she blurted out that sentence, she grabbed her own cup and took a drink of coffee.

He leaned back against the granite counter, feeling the cold of the stone seep through his T-shirt and into his bones. He crossed his bare feet at the ankles, kept a tight grip on his coffee mug and looked at her. "That seems like an overreaction to one kiss."

"What?" She flushed, flipped her hair behind her shoulders and said, "For heaven's sake, this isn't about the kiss. Though, I admit, it gave me the idea..."

More confused than ever, he could only say, "What?"

"Oh, man, this is harder than I thought it would be." She dropped into a chair at the table, grabbed a slice of bacon and took a bite. "I don't even know how to say all of this without sounding crazy."

"I'll give you a clue," he said softly. "Just say it. Don't lie to me, either, trying to soften whatever it is that's going on. Just say it."

"I wasn't going to lie to you."

"Good. Let's keep it that way."

"Okay." She nodded, took another breath that lifted her breasts until he got another peek at that lacy bra, then started talking. "When I went home last night, my gran called and she started in on moving back again because I'm so alone, and before I knew what I was saying, I told her that she didn't have to worry about me being lonely anymore because I'm engaged. To *you*."

Well, he'd wanted the truth. Micah shook his head, walked to the table, sat down opposite her and waited. Objectively, as a writer, he couldn't wait to hear the rest of this story, because it promised to be a good one. As a man with zero interest in marrying *anyone*, he felt itchy enough that he snatched another piece of bacon and bit into it.

Her green eyes were flashing and her chin was up defiantly, but she chewed at her bottom lip, and that told him she was nervous. That didn't bode well.

"You have to understand, Micah. Gran's my only family and she was so sad after my grandfather passed away." She folded both hands around her coffee mug. "Then she moved to Florida with her sister, my aunt Linda, and she was happy again. Then Sean died and she came home to be with me and she started worrying and the sorrow crept back into her eyes, her voice, everything. It was like she was being *swallowed*, you know?"

No, he didn't know. He didn't have family. Didn't have the kind of deep connections she had, so he couldn't be sure if he'd have reacted the same way she did or not. But just looking at Kelly told him that she was emotionally torn in a couple of different directions.

"I finally convinced her to go back to her life by telling her I needed time alone—which wasn't a lie," she added. "And being away from here, the memories of Grandpa and Sean, helped her and she was happy again. Micah, she's determined to come back here and protect me. To sacrifice her own happiness on the altar of what she thinks of as my misery."

"*Are* you miserable?" he asked, interrupting the stream of words pouring from her.

"Of course not." She took a sip of coffee. "I mean, sure, I get lonely sometimes, but everybody does, right?"

He didn't say anything because what *could* he say? She was right. Even Micah experienced those occasional bouts when he wished there was someone there to talk to. To hold. But those moments passed, and he realized that his life was just as he wanted it.

"But when I told her I was engaged to you…" Kelly sighed helplessly. "She was so happy, Micah, that from there, I just grabbed the proverbial ball and ran with it."

"Meaning?"

"Oh." She put her head in her hands briefly, then looked up at him again. "I told her how romantic your proposal was—"

"What did I do?" Now he was just curious. He couldn't help it. This was all so far out there that it didn't even seem real. It was like watching a movie or reading a book about someone else.

Still worrying her bottom lip, she said, "You set up a candlelit dinner on the porch around back and you had roses everywhere and music playing and little twinkle lights strung over the ceiling…"

He could *see* it and thought she'd done a nice job of scene setting. "Well, I'm pretty good."

She gave a heavy sigh. "You're laughing at me."

"Trust me," he said. "Not laughing."

"Right." She nodded, swallowed hard and said, "Anyway, then you went down on one knee and asked me. But you didn't have a ring because you want to take me to New York to pick one out."

"That's thoughtful of me."

"Oh, stop." She tossed her slice of bacon onto her plate. "I feel terrible about all of this, but I was so worried that Gran was going to hop on the first plane out of Florida…" She plopped both elbows on the table and cupped her face in her palms again, making her voice sound weirdly muffled when she added, "Everything's just a mess now and if I call her back and tell her it never happened, she'll think I lied—"

"You *did* lie."

She looked up at him. "It was just a little lie."

"So now size *does* matter?" He shook his head.

"Oh, God. How can you even make jokes about this?"

"What should I do? Rant and rave? Won't change what

you told your grandmother. But I never understood," Micah said, watching her as misery crossed her face, "how people could convince themselves that *little* lies don't matter. Lies are never the answer."

"Oh." She smirked at him and Micah was pleased to see the snap and sizzle of her attitude come back. "Mr. Perfect never lies?"

"Not perfect," he told her tightly. "But, no, I don't."

"You've never had to tell a lie to protect someone you care about?"

Since he had only a handful of people he gave a flying damn about, the answer was an emphatic no. Micah didn't do lies. Hell, his mother's lie—*I'll come back for you. Soon...*—still rang in his ears. He would never do to someone what she had done to him with that one lie designed, no doubt, to make him feel better about being abandoned.

He scrubbed one hand across his face. It was too damn early to be hit with all of this and maybe that's why Micah wasn't really angry. Confused, sure. Irritated? Always. But not furious. A part of him realized he should be mad. He was used to people trying to use him to get what they wanted. It was practically expected when you were rich and famous. And those people he had no trouble getting rid of.

But Kelly was different. He looked across the table at her and noted the worry in her eyes. Why was he so reluctant to disappoint her? Why was he willing to give her the benefit of the doubt when he never did that for anyone else? She was *lying* to her grandmother. That wasn't exactly a recommendation for trustworthiness. And yet...

"Why me?" he asked abruptly. He got up, walked to the coffeepot and carried it back to the table. He filled both of their cups, then set the pot down on a folded towel. Staring at her from across the table, he said, "There have to be some local guys you could choose from. Pick someone you know. Someone who knows your grandmother and might want to help you out with this."

She took a gulp of coffee like it was medicinal brandy and she was swilling it for courage. "Why you? Who else could I tap for this? Gran knows everyone in town. She'd never believe a sudden engagement to Sam at the hardware store. Or Kevin at the diner. If anything romantic had been going on between me and someone in town, her friends would have told her about it already."

Irritating to realize she had a point.

"But you're a mystery," she continued, leaning toward him. "She knows I have a famous writer living here, but no one in town could have told her anything about you. You hardly ever leave the house, so, for all anyone knows, we could have been carrying on some torrid affair right here in the house for the last two months."

Torrid affair? Who even talked like that anymore? But as archaic as the words sounded, they were enough to make breathing a little more difficult and Micah's jeans a little tighter. Still, he shifted his mind away from what his body was feeling and forced it to focus on what she'd said.

Kelly wasn't doing this because he was rich. Or for the thrill of claiming a famous fiancé. He was her choice because no one in town knew him. Because her grandmother would believe her lie. So it wasn't *him* so much that she wanted. Probably any single renter would have done. That made him feel both better and worse.

"That's why I picked you. You're perfect."

Perfect, he thought wryly. *And handy.*

"Why should I go along with this?" Not that he was

considering it, he assured himself. But he was curious what she'd come up with.

"As a favor?" she asked, throwing both hands high. "I don't know—because you're a fabulous human being and I'm flawed and you feel sorry for me?"

He snorted.

She sighed and scowled at him. "Micah, I know it's a lot. But this is really important to me. Gran's happy in Florida. She has friends, a nice life with her sister. She's enjoying herself and I don't want her to give it all up for *me*."

He heard the sincerity in her voice, read it in her eyes and knew she meant every word. And he wondered what it would be like to love someone so much you were willing to do whatever it took to make them happy? But since he avoided all closeness with everyone, he'd never know.

Hell, he'd broken off his own real engagement because, bottom line, he couldn't bring himself to trust the woman he'd proposed to. He didn't believe she loved him—because she hadn't known the *real* him. He hadn't allowed her to peek behind that curtain, so he couldn't trust that she would still care for him if she ever found out that he was a man whose past haunted every minute of his present. So he'd ended it. Walked away and vowed he'd never do that again.

Yet here he was, actually considering another engagement? This one based on a lie?

"Micah, I don't want anything from you."

He laughed shortly. "Except an engagement to fool an old woman, the lies to keep the pretense going, and a trip to New York to pick out a ring..."

"Oh, God." She flushed and shook her head. "Okay, yes, I do want you to pretend to love me. But you won't have to lie to Gran—"

"Just everyone else you know."

"Okay, yes—" She winced a little as she admitted that. "But there won't be a trip to New York and there won't be a ring, either. I can keep postponing our *trip* when I talk to Gran and—"

"More lies."

"Not more lies, just a bit more emphasis on the original lie," she argued. Frowning, she met his gaze squarely and said, "If you think I *want* to be dishonest with my grandmother, you're wrong. I love her. I'm only doing this because it's the best thing for *her*."

He drank his coffee and felt her steady gaze focus on him. As if she could will him to do this just by staring at him. And, hell, maybe it was working. He was still here and listening, right?

She must have sensed that he was weakening because she leaned toward him, elbows on the table. Did she know that the vee of her blouse gaped open wider, giving him a clear and beautiful view of the tops of her breasts?

"I'll sign anything you want, Micah," she said. "I know you probably have lots of people trying to get things from you—"

Surprised that she seemed to have picked that thought right out of his mind, he watched her carefully.

"But I'm not. Really. If you're worried I'll sue you or something, you don't have to. I don't want anything from you. Really. Just this fake engagement."

In his experience, everyone wanted something. But Micah was intrigued now. "And when I leave town? What then?"

"Then," she said, heaving a sigh as if she already dreaded it, "I'll tell Gran we broke up. She'll be upset, but this *engagement* will buy me some time. Gran will be able to stay in Florida without worrying and…" She took a breath, then lifted her coffee cup for another sip. "Maybe I'll think of a way to convince her to stay there even if I'm not engaged."

He didn't like it, but Micah couldn't see where this ploy was going to cost him anything, either. He'd only be in town four more months, and then he'd be gone and this would all be a memory. Including the fake engagement. And, he had to admit, the longer he looked at Kelly, seeing the worry in her eyes, hearing it in her voice, the more he wanted to ease it. He didn't explore the reasons he was wanting to help her out because he wasn't sure he'd like the answers.

"All right," he said, before he could think better of it.

"Whoop!" Kelly jumped out of her chair, delighted. She came around the table, bent to him and gave him a hard, quick hug. Then she stood up and smiled in relief. "That's so great. Thanks, Micah. Seriously."

That hug had sent heat shooting straight through him, so he needed a little space between him and Kelly. Fast.

"Yeah," he said, rising to put the coffeepot back on its burner. He turned around to face her. "So what do I have to do?"

"Nothing much," she assured him, and joined him at the counter, closing the distance he'd just managed to find. "Just, when we're around people in town you have to act like you're nuts about me."

"Oh." Well, he thought, that would be easy enough. Not that he was in love with her or anything. Sure, he liked her. But what he felt for her was more about extreme *lust.* So, he could sure as hell act like he *wanted* her, because he did. Now more than ever.

What he didn't want was a wife. Or a fiancée. But he'd

never wanted *anything* in his life more than he wanted Kelly in bed.

She looked insulted as she stared up at him. "Oh, come on," she said. "You don't have to look so horrified about pretending to love me. It won't be that hard to do."

Hard? Not a word Micah should be thinking about at the moment. Staring into her green eyes was almost hypnotic, so Micah shifted his gaze slightly. "Yeah," he said with just a hint of sarcasm, "I think I can handle it."

She laid one hand on his arm, and once again a flash of heat shot through him. "I really appreciate this, Micah. I know it's weird, but—"

"It's okay, I get it." He didn't. Not really. How the hell could he understand real family? He'd lost whatever family he had when he was six years old. But, as a writer, he did what he always did. He put himself in someone else's point of view. Tried to look at a situation through their eyes. Over the years, he'd been in the minds of killers and victims. Children and parents.

Yet, he was coming up blank when he tried to figure out what Kelly was thinking, feeling. In fact, she was the one woman he'd ever known who was as damn mysterious as the stories he created. Ironic, he told himself, since he made his living inventing mysteries—and now he was faced with an enigma he couldn't unravel.

It wasn't just Kelly confusing him. It was what being near her did to him that had him baffled.

And he didn't like the feeling.

A couple of hours later, Kelly was at Terry's house, wishing she was anywhere else.

"I tell you to have a steamy affair and you say no," Terry mused thoughtfully as she tapped one finger against her chin. "But you *do* get engaged. Sure that makes sense."

Kelly hung her head briefly, then lifted it to look at her best friend. Terry's place was just a block or two off Main Street. It was a small old brick house with a great backyard and what Terry called *tons of potential.* She and Jimmy were completely rehabbing the old place that Kelly had found for them, a little at a time. The living room was cozy, the kitchen was fabulous, the bathroom was gorgeous—and the rest of the house still needed work.

Sitting on her friend's couch sipping tea and eating cookies was pure comfort. Which Kelly really needed at the moment. In fact, it almost took the sting out of what Terry was saying.

"It's crazy," Kelly agreed. "I know that."

"Good for you," Terry said, injecting false cheer into her voice. "Always best to recognize when you've completely lost your mind."

"You're not helping."

"Of course I'm not helping." Terry shook her head, sending the silver hoops at her ears swinging. "For Pete's sake, Kelly, what were you thinking? You're setting yourself up for God knows what, and now there's no way out."

Kelly knew all of that, but hearing it made her feel worse somehow. Honestly, she still wasn't sure what had made her come up with this idea in the first place. And she sure didn't know why Micah had agreed.

Actually, when she'd first started talking to him that morning, she was positive he'd give her an emphatic no and tell her to get out. But the longer she talked, the more she saw him change, his features changing from irritated to sympathetic to amusement and finally acceptance.

Kelly still could hardly believe he'd agreed to this, but she was super grateful he had. Yes, it was a mess, but at least for the short term, her grandmother was happy and wasn't trying to give up her own happiness for Kelly.

"You should have heard Gran though, Terry," Kelly said softly, remembering. "She was so happy when I told her Micah and I were engaged."

Terry's concerned frown only deepened. "Sure, until you 'break up.'"

Okay, yes, that conversation with her grandmother wasn't one Kelly was looking forward to. But she'd find a way to soften the disappointment. "Yeah, but until then, I've got time to think of a way to keep her from worrying."

"Well, I hope your next plan is as entertaining as this one."

Scowling, Kelly picked up a lemon cookie drizzled with thin caramel stripes and took a bite. Seriously, nobody made better cookies than Terry. People clogged up her tiny coffee shop just to buy the baked goods. And they weren't wrong to do so.

"You're my best friend," Kelly said. "You're supposed to be on my side."

"And if you wanted to rob a bank or drive off a cliff, I should just pick up my pom-poms and cheer you on?"

"That's hardly the same thing as—"

Terry held up one hand. "I'm sorry. You refused a blind date, then got engaged, instead."

"Fake engaged."

"I stand corrected." Terry finished off her tea and set the cup on the coffee table in front of them. "Really, though, I'm on your side, Kelly. I'm just not sure what your side *is*."

"If it makes you feel any better, neither am I." It had all seemed so reasonable when she'd thought of it the night before. But facing Micah with it a couple of hours ago had shaken her a little. Still, Kelly knew this was the best thing to do. The *only* thing, as far as she could tell. Gran was happy, and Kelly didn't have to worry about the older woman giving up her new life.

Micah was fine with it—okay, maybe *fine* wasn't exactly right. *Resigned* might be better. Either way, though, Kelly was getting what she wanted: a reprieve for her worried grandmother.

As far as pretending feelings for the town's benefit, she could pretend to be in love with Micah. She would just have to keep reminding herself that it wasn't real.

Because, honestly, one kiss from that man had melted away every reservation she'd had. Every vow she'd ever made to *not* get involved with another man had simply melted under the incredible rush of heat enveloping her during that kiss. God, even remembering it could set her on fire.

So, okay, this pretense would be a little risky for Kelly. Micah Hunter was the kind of man who could slip past a woman's defenses if she wasn't careful. Even defenses as strong as hers. So Kelly would be *very* careful.

She popped the last of the cookie into her mouth, then said, "Okay, enough 'torture Kelly' time."

"Oh, I'm not nearly finished," Terry told her.

"Fine. We'll pick it up again later, but, for now, are you going to help me with the load of plywood I need to pick up or not?"

"Sure." Terry shrugged and pushed off the couch. "Get engaged, then build a haunted house. What could be more normal?"

Kelly reached for another cookie as Terry picked up the plate and cups to take back to the kitchen. Sighing, Terry said, “And I bet you want to take some cookies home with you.”

“That’d be great,” Kelly said. “Thank you, very-best-friend-in-the-world-who-is-always-on-my-side-and-only-wants-what’s-best-for-me.”

Laughing, Terry shook her head and said, “I’ll put some in a bag for you.”

Kelly grinned as she tugged on her sweatshirt. “Thanks. And to respond to your earlier statement… *normal* is way overrated.”

But, while she waited for Terry, Kelly’s smile faded and her brain raced. Images of Micah rose up in her mind, and instantly a curl of something dangerous spun in the pit of her stomach.

Yeah. Maybe this fake engagement wasn’t such a great idea, after all.

Six

Micah came out of the house as soon as he saw the two women struggling to pull sheets of plywood out of the back of Kelly's truck.

"So much for getting any work done," he muttered, and made a mental note to tell Sam that if this book went in late, it would be *his* fault. How the hell was Micah supposed to get work done when Kelly was always interrupting? Even when she wasn't there, thoughts of her plagued him, interfering with his concentration and leaving him staring into space as he willed his body into submission.

Hell, how did *any* writer work when they had people coming in and out of their lives? There was just no way to concentrate on your fictional world when the *real* world kept intruding.

As he approached, he noticed for the first time that Kelly's truck had definitely seen better days. It had once been red, but now was an oxidized sickly pink. There were rust spots along the bottom of the body, no doubt caused by all the salt used on winter roads to prevent skidding. There was an old dent in the back right fender, and he had a feeling the inside of the damn thing was no prettier than the outside.

Frowning, he remembered that Kelly had said she plowed driveways and roads during the winter. Did she use this truck? Of course she did, and it probably hadn't even occurred to her that it looked as if it was on its last legs. He didn't like the idea of her out in some snowstorm in a broken-down truck, freezing to death in the cab while she waited for someone to dig her out of a snowdrift—and, yeah, sometimes being a writer was a bad thing. His mind was all too willing to make up the worst-possible scenario of any given situation just to torture him. He shook off the vague ideas and focused on the now.

He was down the front steps and headed across the lawn before either woman noticed him. Kelly had her back to him, but the tiny woman with dark hair and wide silver hoops at her ears spotted him.

Tipping her head back, she stared at the gray sky and shouted to whoever might be listening, "Thank you!"

Looking back at Micah, she grinned. "Well, hi, gorgeous. You must be the new fiancé. I'm the best friend, Terry."

"Good to meet you." It was impossible to *not* smile back at a woman who looked like a seductive elf. "I'm Micah."

Kelly jolted upright from where she was bent over trying to lift one end of the boards. Seductive elf or not, the only woman Micah could see was Kelly. Her hair was back in a ponytail, her gray sweatshirt was paint stained, and her worn denim jeans were ripped high on her right thigh. She must have changed into work clothes after she'd left him that morning. And even in what she was wearing right now, she looked amazing.

She dropped the plywood sheets she was trying to maneuver, and they clattered when they hit the truck bed. Straightening up, she smiled a little nervously. "Um, hi, Micah. This is Terry."

"Yeah, we met." He walked closer, looked into the truck bed, then up at Kelly. "What's all this for?"

She pushed one stray windblown lock of hair out of her face. "Every year I build a haunted house for the kids."

That didn't even surprise him. "Of course you do."

Kelly kept talking. "Last year Terry's husband, Jimmy, helped me out, but he's deployed this year."

Terry sat on the edge of the truck. "I think Kelly misses him almost as much as I do."

"Today I do," Kelly agreed. Her heart flipped over as Micah's gaze was fixed on her with the wariness of a man waiting to see if a suspicious package will explode. And of course she *had* to look absolutely hideous. "So, Micah, can you help carry these boards to the front of the house?"

"I can." He dropped both hands onto the side of the truck. "Does it get me a point?"

"A what?" Terry asked.

"No," Kelly said, smiling because he was acting as he always had around her. Things weren't awkward and she'd worried about that. Oh, she knew he was as good as his word and that he'd act like her lover in public. But she'd been afraid that asking him to do this for her might make things weird between them in private. "This is a favor. Not a point earner."

"What points are we talking about?" Terry looked from one to the other of them.

"Hmm," he mused, "seems to me I already did you a favor earlier. If I do this one, as well, that's two in one day. Is there any kind of payoff for a favor?"

"What'd you have in mind?" Kelly's stomach did a fast spin and roll. Honestly, the man's eyes were so dark that when they were fastened on her, as they were now, she could feel the earth beneath her feet slide and shift.

"Another kiss," he said.

All of her breath left her in a rush.

"Okay," Terry murmured. "This is getting interesting. Wait a minute. Did he say *another* kiss?"

Kelly paid no attention to Terry because she couldn't see anything but Micah. It took everything in Kelly not to vault over the side of the truck and lock her mouth onto his. Just the thought of being held close to him again made her want it more than anything. But she had a question first. "Why?"

He shrugged and his broad chest sort of rippled beneath his black T-shirt. "You said we needed to put on a show in front of people, right?"

"Yeah..." she said, "but Terry doesn't count."

"Thanks very much," Terry said, "however, since Jimmy's gone, I wouldn't mind seeing a red-hot kiss. A little vicarious living would do me worlds of good."

"Pay no attention to her," Kelly advised.

"I wasn't talking about Terry," Micah said, his gaze flicking briefly to a point over Kelly's shoulder. "I was talking about the two old women watching from their window."

"Oh, God…" Kelly murmured. She'd forgotten all about her neighbors, but the two sisters probably had their noses pressed to the glass.

"Hi!" Terry shouted as she turned to wave at Sally and Margie.

The curtains dropped instantly, blocking the women from view. But Kelly knew they were still there. Watching. Hoping to see something worth gossiping about.

"So? Is it a deal?" Micah asked.

Kelly sighed. This had been all her idea, after all. "Deal."

She moved to the side of the truck and Micah reached up to grab her at the waist. His hands were big and strong and hot enough to sear her skin right through the fabric of her shirt. He lifted her out of the truck bed as if she weighed nothing and then let her slide slowly along his body until she was standing on her own two feet again.

By the time her feet hit the ground, Kelly's insides were sizzling and her brain was fogging over. Her hands at his shoulders, she stared up into his brown eyes and read a wild mix of desire and amusement there. She couldn't have said why that particular combination appealed to her, but it did. "Well," she asked after a long minute of simply staring into each other's eyes, "are you going to kiss me?"

"Nope."

Surprised, she tried to pull away, but his hands only tightened on her waist. "Fine. But I thought you wanted a kiss for a favor."

"Yeah," he said, his gaze sliding over her face before meeting hers again, "but this time, *you* kiss *me.*"

Another swirl of hot nerves inside, but she had to admit it was only fair. He'd surprised her with their first kiss, and now she wanted to surprise him with just how hot a kiss could be if she knew it was coming. Giving him a faint smile, Kelly went up on her toes and slanted her mouth over his.

He held on to her but didn't take the lead. This show was all Kelly's. She parted his lips with her tongue, slid into his mouth and felt his breath catch in his throat. She explored his mouth, tasting, plundering. Spearing her fingers through his hair, she turned her head slightly to one side and groaned as he finally surrendered to the fire building between them. He clutched her tightly to him and tangled his tongue with hers until Kelly's mind splintered and floated out of her head to blow away in the cold breeze.

"Niiiiccceee..." Terry's voice was no more than a buzz that Kelly barely registered.

Kelly's heart banged against her ribs. She held on to Micah because if she didn't, she'd have keeled over from the rush of sensations pouring through her. His hands fisted at her back and held her so tightly to him she felt the hard length of him pressing into her belly. She rubbed against him, torturing them both. Knowing he felt what she felt, wanted what she wanted, only made her own feelings that much deeper. More intense.

God, she wanted to feel his skin beneath hers. She wanted to feel his heavy weight on top of her. Feel his hard body sliding into hers...

"Um, guys?" Terry's voice came again, hesitant but insistent. Then she got louder, demanding they hear her. "*Guys!* You realize you're about to get way out of control right in the front yard?"

In a daze, feeling a little drunk, Kelly pulled her head back and turned to look blearily at her friend. "What?"

"Damn." Terry fanned herself with both hands. "I think that's enough of a show for now or you'll kill Sally and Margie."

"What?" Kelly asked again, and then realization slammed into her, and she turned to Micah and dropped her forehead on his chest. She could hardly believe what had just happened. If Terry hadn't spoken up, who knows what might have happened? "Oh, God."

"Yeah," Micah said tightly as he struggled to even out his ragged breathing. "I think Terry's right. I'll just get those boards for you now. Where do you want them?"

"Okay, that's good. Um, right in front of the porch," she whispered, and he let her go. Amazing how *alone* she felt without the strength of his arms wrapped around her middle.

Still a little shaky, she leaned against the truck and watched while Micah lifted a few of the huge plywood sheets and, balancing them on his shoulder, carried them to the front of the Victorian. His muscles stretched and shifted beneath his shirt. His black jeans hugged his behind and his long legs, and her mouth went dry just watching him.

"Honest to God," Terry murmured in her ear, "if you don't jump that man immediately, you're not the brave, intrepid Kelly I know."

"It's not that easy," Kelly said, gaze locked on him.

"Why the hell not?" Terry gave Kelly's shoulder a nudge. "You want him. He clearly wants you. I almost went up in flames just watching, and I can tell you that after seeing that kiss, when I get home, I'm video chatting Jimmy and hoping he's alone."

"That's different," Kelly grumbled. "You're married."

"And you're *engaged*," Terry reminded her. "For God's sake, take advantage of it."

But that hadn't been part of their deal, Kelly told herself. Was it fair to try to alter their agreement now? Then she remembered the grinding pressure of his mouth on hers and knew that he'd be okay with changing the rules. The question was, could she keep her emotions separate from the physical desire engulfing her? And could she live with herself if she *didn't* act on what she was feeling?

Micah walked back across the yard for the next load and Kelly's gaze fixed on him. Black jeans. Black boots. Black T-shirt. Dark brown hair ruffling in the cold breeze. Brown eyes that met hers for one long, blistering moment.

And she knew that, complicated or not, deal or not, she had to have him.

Micah ignored the noise from the front of the house for the next two hours. He heard the constant hammering, the arguing between Kelly and Terry and told himself it had nothing to do with him. What did he care about haunted houses? Besides, he had work to do. If thoughts of Kelly and that kiss ever left him the hell alone.

Scowling, he glared at the computer screen, rereading what he'd just written. His heroine was in deep trouble and getting in deeper every second. She was wandering the woods, looking for a lost child, and had no idea there was a killer right behind her.

Grimly he kept typing, in spite of the fact that his jeans were so tight he felt he was going to be permanently injured. He kept tasting Kelly on his lips and told himself that it didn't matter. It had been for show. To impress the neighbors and show them that Kelly's fiancé was crazy about her. The fact that it had impacted *him* so much wasn't the point.

Points. Kelly and her points. What was it now, three to one with her in the lead? Hell, if she'd brought it up at the time, he'd have awarded her five more points for that kiss today. He felt like her mouth was permanently imprinted on his. If he lived to be a hundred, he'd still be able to bring back the taste of her and the feel of her in his arms while the cold wind danced around them.

"This isn't getting any work done," he muttered, and stood up from the desk. It wasn't until that moment that Micah realized how quiet it was. The hammering had stopped, and there was no more good-natured shouting from Kelly and Terry.

He walked to the window and looked out. At that angle, all he could see were the tops of plywood panels the two women were fixing together and standing in front of the porch. But it seemed that work on the haunted house was over for the day. Good. No noise meant not being reminded of Kelly. With no thoughts of Kelly, maybe he'd get some pages written.

"Where did she go?" he muttered an instant later, drumming his fingers on the window frame. "And why do you care?"

He didn't, of course. Curiosity didn't translate into *caring.*

Shaking his head, Micah walked to the desk and it felt like the computer screen was glaring at him, mocking him for stopping in the middle of a damn sentence. Well, he didn't have to be insulted by his own tools. He slammed the laptop shut and stalked out of the office. Work wasn't happening. Relaxing wasn't happening. So he'd try a beer, the game on TV and a chance to shut off his mind. Micah took the stairs, then turned and headed for the kitchen.

He never made it.

Kelly stepped through the swinging door from the kitchen into the dining room and stopped dead when she saw him. Everything in Micah tensed and eased at the same time.

Her hair tumbled wild and wavy around her face and down over her shoulders. Her eyes were bright and locked on him like laser beams. Micah's breath caught in his chest as a tight fist of need closed around his throat.

"Surprised to see me?" she whispered.

"Yeah." He nodded. "A little. But then you seem to be full of surprises."

"I'll take that as a compliment," she said, and moved a couple steps closer to him.

"You should." Micah walked toward her, too, one slow step at a time. "I never know from one minute to the next what you're going to do." He didn't admit how much he liked that about her. Didn't mention that he saw her *everywhere.* That images of her were dancing through his brain 24/7. Hell, he didn't even like admitting that to himself, let alone her.

Kelly's eyes flashed and his insides burned.

"Like being here now for instance," Micah said quietly. "What're you doing, Kelly?"

"I came to ask you a question."

He blew out a breath. "What is it?"

"Pretty simple, really," Kelly said, moving still closer.

He could have reached out and touched her, but Micah curled his hands into fists to keep from doing exactly that. After that kiss this afternoon, he was sure that if he held on to her now, he might not let her go again.

"There's a lot of…tension between us, Micah."

He snorted. "Yeah, you could say that."

She kept talking as if he hadn't spoken at all. "I mean, that kiss today? I thought the top of my head was going to blow off."

Micah reached up and rubbed the back of his neck. "I felt the same."

"Good," she said, nodding. "That's good."

"Kelly…" He was at the ragged edge of his near-legendary control. Her scent was reaching for him, and the look in her spring-green eyes was tempting him to just let go. "What're you getting at?"

"Well, we're both grown-ups, Micah," she said, tipping her head back to look at him.

"Yeah," he said tightly. "That might be part of the problem."

She laughed shortly. "True."

Her hair fell in a red-gold curtain behind her, and a light floral scent that clung to her skin seemed to surround him. "But, since we *are* adults, there's a simple way to take care of that tension." She took a breath and held it. When she spoke again, the words tumbled from her in a rush. "I think we should just go to bed together. Once we do that, we'll both be able to relax and—"

Control snapped at the suggestion he'd been hoping for. Micah grabbed her, speared his fingers through her hair and held her head still for his kiss. He poured everything he felt into it. The unbearable frustration that had tortured him for two months. The wild, frantic need that disrupted his sleep every night. The desire that pulsed inside him like an extra heartbeat.

She groaned, fueling the fire enveloping him, and kissed him back with the same fierce hunger that was clawing at him. Her hands moved up and down his back, up into his hair, then clutched at his shoulders.

Micah's brain simply shattered. He didn't need it anyway. The only thing either of them needed now was their own willing bodies. When Micah tore his mouth free of hers and gasped for air, Kelly grinned at him. "I guess that's a yes?"

Surprise after surprise.

"No, it's a *hell yes*," he corrected, then picked her up and slung her over one shoulder in a fireman's carry.

"Hey!" Hands against his back, she pushed up and swung her hair back in an attempt to see him. "What're you doing?"

He glanced back at her and rubbed one hand over her behind until she shifted in his grasp.

"This is faster. No time to waste," he told her, and headed for the stairs again.

"Right." She rubbed her own palms over his back, then down to his butt. "Hurry."

He took the stairs two at a time, his long legs making short work of the distance separating them from the nearest bed. He covered the hallway in a few long steps, walked into his bedroom and tossed her onto the mattress.

"Whoop!" She laughed as she bounced, then her gaze met his and all amusement fled. "Oh, I'm so glad you didn't say *thanks, but no thanks*."

"Not a chance of that," Micah assured her, and yanked his T-shirt off over his head.

Kelly smiled, licked her lips and toed off her shoes before immediately tugging at the button and zipper of her jeans. She squirmed out of them, making Micah's mouth water at his first peek at the tiny triangle of pink lace panties she had on under those jeans.

She kept her gaze locked on his as she worked on the buttons of her long-sleeved shirt and slowly let it slide down off her arms. The pink lace bra matched the panties and displayed more of her breasts than it hid.

He couldn't look away from her. Every breath came loud and harsh in the room. Micah felt like he was straining against a leash that had held him in place for two long months. Now that it was ready to snap, he didn't know what to do first. Where to touch. Where to kiss. Where to lick. He wanted it all. When she took off the bra and panties then tossed them over her head to the floor, the leash finally snapped.

She lay there, her pale skin luminous against the forest-green duvet. Her hair spilled out around her head like a red-gold halo of silk. Her breasts were fuller than he'd imagined, but delicate, too, her dark rose nipples rigid with the desire pumping through her.

His mind simply went blank. Like a starving man suddenly faced with a gourmet feast, Micah froze, helpless to look away from the woman laid out in front of him like a dream.

"Micah…you're wearing too many clothes," she murmured, licking her lips.

"Right. I am." He peeled out of his clothes, and in seconds he was naked and covering her body with his. Her hands slid up and down his back, across his shoulders to his chest and then up to cup his face. When Micah kissed her again, their bodies moved against each other as if they both were looking for that skin-to-skin contact. To revel in the heat. To drown in it. As if to assure each other that they were finally going to ease the raging desperation that had chased them both through torturous days and long, sleepless nights.

He swept one hand down the length of her as he shifted, dragging his mouth from hers to trail kisses along the line of her jaw, the slim column of her throat. She sighed, gasped and arched up into him. Her legs tangled with his, smooth to rough, adding new sensations to those already crashing down on them.

He slid his hand across her abdomen, down her belly to the center of her. To the heat he needed to claim, to bury himself in. She jerked helplessly. To drive her higher, faster, Micah took one hard nipple into his mouth.

Instantly, Kelly writhed in his arms as if trying to escape even while she held his head to her breast to keep him from stopping. "Micah… Micah, this is too much."

"No," he whispered, "not nearly enough." He covered her damp, hot core with his hand and slid first one, then two fingers inside her. She arched into him and his mind splintered at the feel of her generous, oh-so-eager body shaking and twisting in his arms.

His lips, teeth and tongue worked her nipple as his fingers continued to push her toward a release they both needed so badly.

"Stop, Micah," she whispered brokenly.

He lifted his head, questions in his eyes. "You want me to stop?"

Shaking her head, she choked out a short laugh. "Not on your life. I just want more than your hand on me." She was breathless, eyes a little wild, and she'd never looked more beautiful. "If you keep touching me like that, I'm going to climax and I don't want to. Not without you inside me."

Relief flooded him. He'd have had to back away if she'd changed her mind, and Micah knew without a doubt that stopping would have killed him. Knowing that she was simply trying to hold back an orgasm gave him the freedom to push her beyond the ability to fight it.

"One now," he said, stroking that one sensitive nub at her core with his thumb. "More later."

"Oh…my…goodness…" Her fingers dug into his shoulders. Her hips rocked frantically into his hand. She planted her feet and lifted herself higher, higher. He watched as Kelly's eyes glazed. "Micah—I… What are you doing to me? I've never…"

Micah had never been with anyone like her before. What she felt echoed inside him. The taste of her filled him, the scent of her swamped him, and the shattered, hungry look in her eyes fed the fires inside him like nothing he'd ever experienced before.

He hadn't been prepared for this, he thought, frantic himself as he watched her body bow and twist. He'd thought it would be a simple matter of bodies meeting, doing what came naturally. Feeling that sweet flash of release and moving the hell on. But no woman had ever affected him like this. No woman had slipped beneath his defenses, made him crave *her* release as much as his own. He didn't know what any of it meant, and now wasn't the time for trying to figure it out.

Micah felt the first shudder take her, body rippling with too much sensation all at once. She fought for breath, grasping at his shoulders, digging her head back into the mattress, struggling for air as she screamed his name like a prayer to an indifferent god.

His own breath caught in his chest. Mouth dry, heart hammering, body as tight as a bowstring, Micah set her down on the bed and shifted, reaching for the drawer of the nightstand. He pulled it open, grabbed a condom and ripped the foil packet. He had to have her. Now.

"Micah, that was—" She shook her head, at a loss for words. The smile that curved her lips shone in her eyes, as well. "I've never…" She stretched like a happy cat and damn near purred. Then she opened her eyes at the sound of foil tearing.

"Wow. You went out and bought condoms just in case?"

He shook his head. "Nope, had them with me."

"You *travel* with condoms?" she asked, surprise in her voice.

He glanced at her. "Doesn't everyone?"

"Hoping to get lucky, were you?"

"Babe," he admitted as he sheathed himself, "I'm a *guy*. I'm always hoping to get lucky."

Her grin spread as she held out her arms to him. "Well, since I think we're both pretty lucky at the moment, I can't really complain, can I?"

He returned her grin, and as he shifted to part her thighs and kneel before her, he quipped, "So, having a condom handy means a point for me, huh?"

"Oh," she teased, "I don't know about that. I mean *points* are serious business and—"

He slid into her heat, and she went instantly quiet as she shifted a little to accommodate him. Then she groaned and tipped her head back into the mattress.

"Yes," she said. "If you can keep making me feel like—*oh!*—this, definitely a point for you."

"I love a challenge," he whispered. Still smiling, he covered her mouth with his and tangled their tongues in a dance that mimicked the movements of their bodies. She gave as much as she took, Micah thought, and realized that for the first time he was with a woman who was completely herself. There was no pretense with Kelly.

Whatever she felt, she let him know. Her soft cries

and whimpered moans told him exactly what she liked. She was a little wild and he liked it. His mouth moved on hers as his hips rocked, slipping into a rhythm that had her kissing him hungrily, sliding her hands up and down his back, dragging her nails across his skin.

When he was strangling for air, he lifted his head to watch her expressive face as he claimed her completely. Her body held his in a tight, hot embrace, and he gritted his teeth to keep from giving in to the urge to let go. He wanted this to last. Wanted to make her crazy before he finally gave them both what they needed most.

Outside, twilight stained the sky a deep violet. Inside, the only light was in her eyes as she stared up at him, a look of wonder in her gaze. Their hands met, fingers linked, and he felt it when her climax slammed into her. Her body arched, her heels dug into his lower back. She screamed his name, and Micah watched the inner explosions ripple across her face and felt more satisfaction himself than he could ever remember. His heart raced, and his body continued to move in hers, and only when the last of the tremors coursed through her did he let himself go, finally giving up control and diving into the maelstrom, willingly letting it take him.

Seven

Kelly didn't know how much time had passed. And truthfully, she couldn't have cared less. Her whole body was humming as if her finger was somehow stuck in a light socket and electricity was pouring through her.

Finally, though, when she thought she could speak again, she said simply, "Wow."

"Agreed." Micah's voice was muffled because his face was buried in the curve of her shoulder.

She smiled to herself and stared blankly up at the ceiling. Good to know that he was as shattered as she felt. Micah's body pressed her into the bed and she knew she should ask him to move, but it was so lovely to feel the heavy press of a man's body on hers after so long on her own.

At that thought, Kelly felt a pang of sorrow that peaked and ebbed inside her in seconds. *Sean.* She closed her eyes briefly, as if thinking about him now was a breach of trust, somehow. Which was just stupid and she knew it. But, until today, Sean was the only man she'd ever been with. Hardly surprising that thoughts of her late husband would rise up.

Sean and Micah were so very different in so many ways. Micah's body was stronger, bigger—in every way, she thought with a tiny stab of guilt for the comparison. But it wasn't just their physical differences that set them apart.

With Micah there was laughter along with the sex. Kelly smiled, remembering the teasing about points and traveling condoms. With Sean, lovemaking had been a serious business. Instead of romance and fun, she'd always felt as if Sean had had a mental checklist. *Turn lights off, check. Kiss Kelly, check. Tongue, check. Touch breasts, check.* Their times in bed together had been almost clinical, more of a task to be accomplished.

God, she couldn't believe she was even having these disloyal thoughts. Kelly had never told anyone how unsatisfied she'd been in her marriage. Not even Terry. Though she had loved Sean, until now Kelly had believed that she simply wasn't capable of the kind of orgasms that Terry described—*blinding, mind-shattering, earthshaking*. Because in her husband's arms, Kelly had never felt more than a tiny blip of pleasure. Before today, sex had been just a sense of closeness.

She'd had absolutely no idea that there was a tsunami of sensations she'd never experienced.

Kelly opened her eyes and looked at the man she still held cradled to her. In the first few moments with Micah, Kelly had discovered more, *felt* more than she ever had with her husband. And maybe, Kelly thought for the first time, that was the reason she hadn't been interested in going on dates, finding another man. Because being with Sean hadn't been all that great.

She'd long blamed herself for the lack of spark between her and Sean, assuming that she just wasn't experienced enough to really make things heated between them. Now she had to admit that maybe the truth was that she and Sean had been friends too long to make the adjustment to lovers.

"I can hear you thinking," Micah murmured. "Keep it down."

Kelly grinned, grateful he'd interrupted her thoughts. Silently she let go of the past and returned to this amazing moment and the man she'd shared it all with. "Are you sleeping?"

"Yes," he muttered.

She laughed and the motion had his body, still locked inside her, creating brand-new ripples of expectation. Stunned, she couldn't believe she was ready to go again after what had been the most staggering orgasm of her life. Kelly slid her hands up and down his broad back and lifted her hips slightly to recreate that feeling. Instantly she was rewarded with another tiny current of electricity.

He hissed in a breath, lifted his head and looked down at her, one eyebrow arched high. "You keep moving like that and we're going to need a new condom."

Naturally she wriggled again, deliberately awakening a wave of fresh need. Reaching up, Kelly cupped his face in her palms and asked, "How many condoms do you have?"

He rocked his hips against her and she gasped.

One corner of his mouth lifted. "I'm thinking not nearly enough."

Was it bad that her heart did a slow roll and flip at

the sight of his smile? Was it dangerous that she wanted nothing more than to stay here, like this, with Micah smiling down at her, forever? Her heart pounded painfully in her chest and her whole body trembled as he sat back onto his heels, drawing her with him, keeping their bodies locked together.

"Oh, boy." She said it on a sigh as she settled onto Micah's lap. Face-to-face, their mouths only a kiss apart, Kelly was lost in the rich brown of his eyes. His body went deep. She *felt* him growing, thickening inside her, and she swiveled her hips, grinding her core against him to feel even more.

He bent his head to take her nipples, one after the other, into his mouth. Kelly looked blindly around the familiar room, trying to distract herself so she wouldn't climax as quickly this time. She wanted to draw this moment out as long as she could. So she looked at the forest-green walls, the white crown molding, the now-cold white-tiled fireplace and the chairs drawn up before it.

She'd lived here most of her life and knew every corner of the old Victorian; yet, she'd never been more alive than she was at that moment. Never been so in tune with her surroundings, with her own body and with the man currently setting her on fire with a desire sharper, richer than she'd known ever before.

He suckled at her as if trying to draw everything she was within him. Kelly surrendered to the moment, concentrating not on where she was but what was happening. His big hands scooped up her spine and into her hair, fingers dragging along her scalp. Kelly watched him at her breasts while that delicious tugging sensation shot through her body.

Another first. She'd never made love like this—sitting

atop a man so that every stroke of his body into hers was like a match struck. Kelly went up on her knees and slid down slowly, taking him as deep as she possibly could.

When Micah groaned and lifted his head, staring into her eyes, she felt stronger than she ever had. She moved on him again, picking up a rhythm that tormented both of them, and every time she rocked on him, she swore she could feel him touch her heart.

Her breath came in sharp, short puffs as she rode that crest of building pleasure again. How could she have not known all there was to *feel*? To *experience*?

Micah's jaw was tight as he fought for control. He looked into her eyes and dropped his hands to her hips to guide her into a faster rhythm. Bracing her hands on his broad shoulders, Kelly bit her bottom lip, tossed her hair back and stared deeply into Micah's steady gaze. She couldn't look away. Couldn't stop the growing wave of sensation inside her. Sliding her hands from his shoulders, she ran the flat of her palms across the sharply defined muscles of his chest. She ran her thumbnails across his nipples and watched him shudder and grind his teeth in response and she felt…powerful. Knowing what she was doing to this strong man made her feel sexy. Desired.

On his knees, he pushed into her and she twisted on his lap, grinding her pelvis against his, torturing them both, hurrying them along the path to a climax that would, she knew, completely shatter her. She wanted it. More than anything. She raced blindly toward it.

"Micah," she whispered, still scraping her nails across his nipples, still looking into his eyes. "Go faster. Go harder."

"You're killing me," he ground out, then flipped her

over onto her back. Still locked inside her, he drove himself into her, again and again, harder, higher, faster until neither of them could breathe easily. He lifted her legs, draped them across his shoulders and continued his relentless claiming of her.

Kelly shouted and fisted her hands in the duvet beneath her. The world was rocking wildly. He was so deep inside her she thought he might always be there. And she wanted that, too.

Again and again, they moved in a frantic dance designed to end in a splintering of souls, until the world shrank down to the bed alone and nothing outside the two of them mattered. He took her hard and fast and deep and she went with him eagerly.

Kelly called his name over and over again until it became a chant. Lifting her hands, she held on to his upper arms as he braced himself over her and dug her nails into his skin.

"It's coming. Come with me," she said brokenly, voice tearing like wisps of fog in a heavy wind. The tension inside her heightened unbearably. She moved into it, trying to throw herself at the pleasure waiting for her. "Now, Micah. Please, *now.*"

"Come then," he ground out, staring into her eyes. "Let me see your eyes when I take you."

Her release slammed into her like a freight train. She forced her eyes to stay open. She wanted him to see what he was doing to her. What only he had ever done. She quaked and shivered and finally screamed his name in desperation.

And, before the last of the tremors shuddered through her, he called out her name and stiffened as his body joined hers. Kelly held him as he took from her as much as he had given. Then he collapsed, bonelessly atop her, and, shattered, Kelly cradled him in her arms.

It was dark when Kelly woke up. She was a little stiff. A little sore. And a lot desperate for air. Micah was sound asleep on top of her. Couldn't really blame him for being wiped out, but as good as he felt on top of her, Kelly really needed to breathe easier. Shaking her head, she said, "Micah! Micah, roll over."

"What?" Groggy, he lifted his head and opened his eyes. Understanding instantly, he rolled to one side, keeping an arm locked around her middle. "I fell asleep."

"We both did." Taking a deep breath, she curled into his side and just managed to swallow a sigh of satisfaction. "What time is it, anyway?"

"Who cares?" He threw one arm across his eyes.

"Good point."

"Hey," he said. "Another point for me."

"That wasn't a point. That was just a figure of speech. So it's still three to two, my favor."

He smiled. "So I *did* get a point for all of this."

Kelly sighed. By rights she should have given him ten, twenty, even thirty points for everything he'd made her feel. "Oh, boy, howdy."

"I can live with that."

She laughed. "Okay, so, are you hungry? I'm hungry."

He opened one eye. "You're kidding."

"I never kid about food." She went up on one elbow and looked down at him. Oh, my, he was great looking when he was dressed, but *naked*? The man was drool-worthy. Kelly shook her head. If she kept going down that path, she would start something that wouldn't get her fed.

And if she didn't eat soon, she wouldn't have the strength for everything else she wanted to do with Micah. Now that was motivation. "Come on, you've got to be hungry, too."

"Not enough to move anytime soon."

"Really?" Kelly sat up and stretched, feeling looser and more limber than she had in years. "I'm not tired at all. In fact, I feel energized. We should have done this a long time ago."

He stared up at her and frowned.

"What?"

"Seriously?" He studied her as if she were on a slide under a microscope. "You feel great and you're hungry. That's all you have to say?"

Confused, Kelly laughed. "What were you expecting?"

Propping himself up on both elbows, Micah tipped his head to one side. "So you're not going to say that you've been doing some thinking and that we should talk?"

"About what?"

"About your feelings," he said. "And how sex changes things between us and we should figure out where our *relationship* goes from here."

She would have laughed again, but he looked so serious she just couldn't do it. Shaking her head, Kelly held up one hand. "Wait. Is that what most women do? Have sex with you and then ruin it with…*talk*?"

He frowned. "Well, generally, yeah."

She didn't know whether to be insulted that he'd expected her to be like every other woman he'd met in his life—or to feel bad that he had to protect himself against wily women looking to hook him into a relationship he didn't want. So she did neither.

Kelly smiled, bent down and planted a quick, hard kiss on his mouth. "Well, then, I'm happy to surprise you again. I came to you, remember? All of this was *my* idea—"

"Well," he said, "in my defense, I'd had the same idea—I just hadn't approached you with it yet."

"Even if you had, it wouldn't matter." She shrugged. "We're two adults, Micah. We can have sex—really *good* sex—without it meaning hearts and flowers, right?"

Confusion shone in his eyes. "Well, yeah, it's just—"

"What's wrong now?" Hadn't she eased his mind yet?

"Nothing," he said, a scowl tugging at his lips. "It's just, I'm the one who usually gives that little speech. It's weird being on the receiving end."

"Another first." Kelly took a deep breath then blew it out. "Well, I'm done talking. But I could really go for a sandwich."

She scooted off the bed, picked up his discarded T-shirt and pulled it over her head. God, she felt good. "You want one?"

"Sure," he said slowly, thoughtfully. "I could eat."

"Great. I'll see you in the kitchen." Kelly left the room and didn't stop walking until she was downstairs. Then she paused and looked back up toward the room where she'd left him.

She'd told him she didn't want to talk and that was true. What she didn't tell him was that she was starting to feel a lot more for him than she'd planned on. Maybe it was the way he was so hesitant about letting people in. Maybe it was the half smile that curved his mouth so unexpectedly. She didn't know exactly what it was that was growing inside her, but Kelly was pretty sure that she was headed for trouble.

* * *

For the next few days, Micah and Kelly developed a routine that worked for both of them.

Micah spent the mornings working, building his novel page by page while Kelly raced from one job to the next. In the afternoons, they worked together on her Halloween project.

And every night they were together at the Victorian in Micah's bed.

Micah glanced over at Kelly now as she showed three kids how to roll black paint onto the plywood sheets. A reddish-gold ponytail hung down between her shoulder blades and swung like a metronome with her every movement. She wore her favorite worn jeans with the rip on the right thigh, black work boots and a faded red sweatshirt with the slogan Women Do It Better scrawled across the front. There was black paint on her cheek and a smile on her face as she listened to some long, involved story one of the kids told her.

A sharp stab of desire hit Micah so hard, so fast he nearly lost his breath. Hell, the skies were gray and there was an icy wind sliding through the nearby canyon, and Micah felt like his insides were blazing.

He and Kelly had thought to ease the sexual tension between them by sleeping together. Instead, they'd poured gasoline on a smoldering fire and started an inferno. Micah wanted Kelly all the time now. She was constantly on his mind. Her image, her scent, the harsh cries she made when he was inside her, pushing her over the edge.

This had never happened to him before. He should have known, he told himself, that Kelly would be unlike any woman he'd ever met. That had to be why he found her so intriguing. It was the newness factor. Her unpredictable nature. Her ability to keep him guessing, always on his toes. Hell, she *still* hadn't started that whole *we should talk* conversation he kept expecting. And a part of him was waiting for that shoe to drop.

There was no one else in his life who could have gotten him to stand out in the cold putting up plywood walls for a neighborhood Halloween maze. Shaking his head, he didn't know whether to be impressed by her or ashamed of himself.

He emptied his mind and took a good look at what they were building. It wasn't really a haunted house, but more of a passageway kids would have to go through to collect candy on Halloween night. Black walls, fake spiderwebs, a recording of scary sounds and voices, there were also going to be black lights to cast weird shadows and a few ghoulish mannequins to finish it all off.

If anyone had told him a year ago that he'd be in a small town in Utah building scary Halloween stuff, he would have called them crazy. Yet, here he stood.

"How the hell did this happen?" he muttered.

"You said a bad word," Jacob said, frowning up at him.

He looked down at the little boy and sighed. For some reason, this one particular kid had adopted Micah. Apparently, since Micah had taken the kid to visit his pumpkin, that had forged a bond. At least in Jacob's mind.

"What?"

"A bad word," the boy said. "You said *hell*."

"Oh." He rolled his eyes. Really had to watch that, he supposed. But then he wasn't exactly accustomed to dealing with children, was he? Even when he was at Sam and Jenny's place, Micah didn't spend much time with their two kids. In his defense, Isaac was a baby, so the kid didn't have much to say. And Annie, he realized suddenly, was Jacob's age.

Funny. He'd always told himself that he didn't pay attention to Sam's kids because he had no idea how to act with them. But he and Jacob got along so well that the boy had unofficially adopted him. That made him wonder if maybe he should have tried harder to get to know Sam's daughter, Annie.

But at the same time, Micah remembered that he didn't *like* kids. He didn't ask Jacob to hang around all the time, did he? Micah didn't want to get close to anyone. Had, in fact, spent most of his life avoiding any kind of connection.

And how has that worked out for you?

He glanced at the little boy kneeling beside him and gave an inner sigh. Now he had to remember to watch his language because a child had decided the two of them were best friends.

"Yeah, well," Micah said finally. "I shouldn't have said the bad word. And don't you say it."

Jacob's eyes went wide. "Oh, I won't cuz once Jonah said *damn* and Mommy made him go sit in his room and he *cried*."

And the ten-year-old probably wouldn't appreciate his little brother sharing that bit of news. Still, nodding sagely, Micah said, "Learn from your brother's mistakes then. Now," he added, "hold the hammer in both hands and hit the nail."

Micah yanked his fingers out of the way just in time, as Jacob's aim was pretty bad. But the grin on the kid's face was infectious. He was clearly proud of himself and loved being thought of as big enough to help like the other kids. Micah smiled at the kid and wondered again just how this had happened to him.

"Can I do another one?" Jacob asked, turning his face up to Micah's.

"Sure," he said, glancing at the bent, smashed nail. Micah would fix them later. For now, let the kid feel important. Memories of his own childhood swept through Micah's mind in an instant. Ignored by adults, he'd taken advantage of their disinterest and learned how to become invisible. He didn't cause trouble. Didn't stand out for good or bad reasons. And because he'd spent every minute trying to not be seen, not once had he *ever* felt important. To anyone.

Micah held out another nail and watched Jacob situate it just right. "Be careful. If you smash your fingers Kelly will get mad."

Jacob laughed delightedly. "No, she won't. But I can be careful."

When his cell phone rang, Micah grabbed it from his back pocket and looked at the screen. "Can you be careful on your own?"

"I can do it. I'm not a baby."

"Right. I forgot." The phone rang again and Micah stood up. "I'll be right back," he told Jacob, then answered the phone as he stepped away from all the hammering and kids' high-pitched voices. "Hey, Sam."

"Hey, yourself," his agent countered. "You haven't called to whine in a few days so I figured you were dead."

Reluctantly Micah laughed. "That's not bad. Giving up the agent life to hit the stand-up circuit?"

"I could," Sam said. "Annie thinks I'm funny."

"Your daughter is three." Micah kept walking until he was ten feet from the small crowd gathered in front of the Victorian. The breeze was stronger out here, without the big house giving any shelter. "She thinks your evil cat is funny."

"Sheba's a perfectly nice cat," Sam pointed out. "With excellent judgment. She likes everyone but you."

"She knows I'm a dog person," Micah said, then frowned. Hell, he didn't know if he was a dog person. He'd never had a pet. Not that he cared. It was just odd to suddenly realize that. But he was always traveling. How was he supposed to take care of an animal if he didn't have a home?

"Great, I'll get you a puppy."

"Do it and die," Micah told him, though it surprised him to realize that a puppy didn't sound like such a bad idea. He scrubbed one hand over his face as if he could wipe away thoughts that had no business in his mind. "If you're calling about the book, it's still coming slowly."

Mostly because instead of just imagining what it might be like to have sex with Kelly, he was spending most of his free time remembering what they'd done together the night before. Hell, it was a wonder he got *any* work done.

"Yeah, this isn't about the book," Sam said. "I'm flying out to California in a couple days. I've got a Friday meeting with an indie publishing house."

Thanks to the internet, independent publishers were springing up all over the place. Most started and disappeared within a span of a few months—just long enough to fulfill and then crush would-be writers' dreams. But a few started small and built a strong list of writers and grew into houses with good reputations and steady sales.

Micah's gaze shifted to Kelly. She was bent over, helping Jacob's older brothers and a girl from down the street apply layers of black paint to plywood. The curve of her behind drew his gaze unerringly, and Micah had to look away for his own sanity.

He started paying attention again just in time.

"So," Sam was saying, "I thought you might want to fly out for the weekend. Take a break from small-town life and visit with an old friend."

It sounded like a great idea to Micah. He'd been here in Banner for more than two months and he could do with a good dose of city life. Plush hotel, room service, noise, people…

"Sold," he said abruptly, then looked at Kelly again. She tossed her ponytail and laughed as Jacob's big brothers started painting each other. Looking at her wide smile, he could only think about getting her away from her home ground. Into some plush, luxurious life where he could seduce her nonstop. "But I won't be coming alone."

"Yeah?" He actually heard the intrigued smile in Sam's voice.

"Thought I'd bring my fiancée with me." He grinned, anticipating Sam's reaction. He wasn't disappointed.

A couple of long seconds filled with stunned silence ticked past before Sam sputtered, "Your *what*?"

"Can't get into it right now. I'll explain when I see you," Micah said, and had to admit he was enjoying leaving Sam hanging on the information front. "Where do you want to meet?"

"I'm staying at the Monarch Beach Resort in Dana Point, and who is this fiancée and when did this happen?"

"Got it," Micah said, ignoring the questions. "When's your meeting?"

"I'm flying in early Friday for a meeting that afternoon. But I'll be staying until Sunday."

"Okay." Micah did some fast figuring. It was Tuesday now—he had plenty of time to arrange for a suite at the hotel and a private jet to get him and Kelly to Orange County. All he had to do was convince her to leave town for a few days. He had confidence in his ability there. "I'll see you then."

"You are *not* going to leave me hanging with no information," Sam complained. "Do you know what'll happen if I go home with this news and no details? Jenny will hound me."

Micah laughed. "Sounds perfect."

"You're gonna pay for this—"

Micah hung up and enjoyed it. Sure, Sam would find a way to get revenge, he told himself. But that's what good friends were for, right?

His gaze locked on Kelly. She must have felt him staring, and something inside him turned when she met his gaze and smiled at him. Her eyes were shining, the curve of her delicious mouth was tempting and when she turned back to the kids and bent down, his gaze locked on her behind again. The woman really had a world-class butt.

His body went tight and hard in an instant. Yeah. A few days away from here. No work interfering for either of them. Just relaxing and enjoying each other. What could be better?

Going online, Micah went to the hotel's website and reserved the Presidential Ocean Suite. He stayed there whenever he was in Southern California and he knew that Kelly would love it. The hotel was top-of-the-line, and this room in particular was damn impressive, with a private balcony that offered sweeping views of the Pacific. Micah smiled to himself as he imagined her on that terrace, the wind in her hair, moonlight making her bare breasts seem to glow. Naked with only the sky, the stars and the sea as witnesses. That's how he wanted her.

All he had to do now was find a way to convince her to take a break from her many responsibilities.

Kelly was flabbergasted.

One of her grandmother's favorite words, it was the *only* one that fit this situation, Kelly told herself. In fact, she was so stunned she couldn't think of a thing to say. And that was so unusual for her, she couldn't remember the last time it had happened.

Micah's invitation had come out of the blue and she'd instantly agreed. True, she had to rearrange the jobs she had lined up, but the chance to get away with Micah was one she didn't want to miss. Being with him was so important to her she was already worrying about what it would be like when he eventually left. But, until then, she wanted to be with him every minute she could be.

She and Terry had made an emergency shopping run to Salt Lake City. It had taken them hours, since Terry had insisted on hitting every single boutique and dress shop in the city, but it had been worth the trip. In her suitcase now, Kelly had clothes suited to a five-star resort.

As soon as Micah told her about the Monarch Bay Resort, Kelly had looked it up online so she'd have some idea of where she'd be staying. The hotel was lovely, elegant. And completely intimidating.

First there had been the limo ride to the airport, then they had been ushered to a private concourse and escorted onto the jet Micah had chartered. Kelly had felt like a queen, lounging in the supple blue leather chairs set into conversation areas. *So* much better than flying like a sardine in an overcrowded can.

She and Micah had sipped champagne and nibbled on strawberries during the short flight. The limo ride to the hotel hadn't flustered her and she'd idly wondered if she was already getting accustomed to being spoiled. But walking into this hotel, where the staff called Micah by name and rushed to do his bidding, and then this spectacular suite… Kelly was simply overwhelmed.

The Presidential Ocean Suite was breathtaking. There was a fireplace, several overstuffed couches and chairs in soft pastels. The carpet was thick and the color of sand. There were vases filled with fresh yellow roses, and there were French doors leading to the private terrace.

The bedroom was huge, with its own fireplace and another set of French doors leading to the balcony they shared with no one. There were crystal chandeliers over the dining table and the bathroom was bigger than her whole cottage back home, with a tub wide and deep enough to swim in and a shower built for a cozy party of five or six, with built-in benches that made Kelly think of any number of things she and Micah could do on them.

And *when* had she become so interested in sex?

Answer, of course—the first time Micah kissed her. He'd created a monster. Smiling to herself, Kelly said simply, "Micah, this is just…amazing. The whole day has been—" She broke off, at a loss for words for the first time in forever. "I wouldn't have missed this for anything."

She walked toward the open terrace doors and caught the shimmer of sunlight on the deep blue of the ocean as it stretched out into eternity. A soft sea breeze danced into the room, ruffling the sheer white curtains.

"I'm glad you came," he said.

"So am I."

Kelly turned to him. He wore black slacks, a dark red dress shirt with the collar open and a black sports coat. He looked comfortable in his surroundings and she realized that *this* was how he lived all the time. He'd told her that he moved from hotel to hotel when he was working, but somehow, even knowing he was rich and famous, she hadn't considered that the hotels he was talking about were really more like palaces.

Kelly tried to imagine living in a place like this and just couldn't do it. The thought of trying to fit into this kind of lifestyle on a daily basis was exhausting. For Kelly, this was an aberration. A step outside her own reality. Okay, more than a step. A *leap*. But the reality was this: as gorgeous as this place was, as glad as she was that she'd come away with Micah, Kelly felt like an interloper here. But, for the next few days, she was going to pretend that she *did* belong, because there was nowhere else she'd rather be.

His gaze locked on her. "Did I tell you before we left that you look beautiful today?"

Kelly flushed, relishing the heat that always raced through her when Micah was near. And now she was doubly glad she and Terry had done so much shopping. Her new black slacks, white silk blouse and deep green brocade vest looked good on her, she knew. And she didn't want to *look* as out of place here as she felt. "You did tell me. Thank you."

He walked across the room to her, took her hand and then led her to the French doors. Stepping onto the terrace, she took a quick look around at the earth-toned tile floor, the table and chairs in one corner and the pair of lounge chairs complete with deep blue cushions and red pillows.

"It just keeps getting better and better," she murmured, and, letting go of his hand, walked to the iron railing and looked out at the sea. The ocean was a deep blue with gold glints of sunlight shining on its surface. Boats with jewel-toned sails skimmed along the waves while surfers closer to shore rode their boards with a grace she envied.

A soft breeze tossed her hair across her eyes. She plucked it free and sighed. "It's like a fairy tale."

"I've pictured you here," he said, and when she turned to look at him, she found his gaze locked on her. "Standing just there, the wind in your hair, a smile on that incredible mouth."

Her heartbeat skittered. "And is the reality as good?"

"Almost," he said, moving in close.

"Only almost?" Her eyebrows lifted and she laughed softly.

"Well, when I pictured you standing there, I was seeing you naked in the moonlight," he admitted, pulling her up against him.

A curl of damp heat settled at her core, and Kelly lifted her head to meet his gaze. Hunger shone in his eyes as he slid his hands down to cup her bottom and hold her tight to his erection. What was it about this man that turned her into a puddle of desires she'd never known before? Why was it he could touch her and send her up in flames? How could one smile from him turn her heart upside down?

She was very much afraid she knew the answers to all of those questions. But now wasn't the time to explore it. The next few days were just for them. To be together. To revel in each other. She didn't want to waste a minute of it.

"Well," she said, when she could breathe past the knot

in her throat, "it's important to make dreams come true. So tonight…"

He hissed in a breath through gritted teeth and held her even tighter to him. "That's a date," he promised, then deliberately took a step back, groaning. "But if I want to show you anything of California, we'd better get going. How about we go down, pick up the car I've got waiting and drive up the coast?"

At that moment, she would have gone with him anywhere.

Eight

Micah took her up the coast to Laguna where they parked the car and walked along Pacific Coast Highway. They popped into art galleries, bought ice cream from a vendor and swayed in time to a street performer's smooth, slow saxophone performance.

Early October in California meant it was still warm, and with the sun shining down on them, the day couldn't have been more perfect. Then he spotted something in a shop window.

"Come with me," he said, taking Kelly's hand and pulling her into the cool quiet of the jewelry shop. The interior of the shop was cool and dimly lit so that the jewels in the glass display cases could shine like stars in the night beneath lights fixed to the underside of the cabinets. There was a dark red rug on the wood-plank floor, and a grandfather clock ticked loudly into the hushed quiet.

"Micah, what're you doing?"

"I saw something I want to get." He signaled an older man behind the gleaming glass cases filled with diamonds and gemstones.

"May I help you?" He wore round, wire-rimmed glasses. His gray hair was expertly trimmed, and his pin-striped suit complete with vest made him look as though he'd stepped out of the nineteen forties.

"Yeah." Micah glanced at Kelly as she wandered down the glass cases, admiring everything within. Turning back to the man in front of him, he said, "The emerald necklace in the window."

The man brightened. His eyes sparkled and a tiny smile curved his mouth. "One of our finest pieces, sir. One moment."

Kelly wandered back to Micah and leaned into him. "What're you buying?"

"A gift for someone," he said, leaving it at that as the man came back, laid the emerald necklace out on a black velvet tray and waited for their admiration.

"Oh, my, that's gorgeous," Kelly whispered, as if she were in church.

"It is, isn't it?" Micah liked the look of it himself, but he was more glad that Kelly approved of it, too. Square cut, the emerald was as big as his first thumb joint. The setting was simple, with platinum wire at the gemstone's corners and twin diamonds on either side of it, the stone hung on a delicate platinum chain. And the emerald itself, he thought, was exactly the color of Kelly's eyes. That's what had caught his attention in the first place. "Okay, I'll take it."

The older man's eyebrows lifted but, otherwise, he

remained cool and polite. "Of course. Would you like it gift wrapped?

"Not necessary," Micah said, reaching for his wallet and then his credit card. He didn't bother to ask the price. It didn't matter, anyway.

"I'll take care of it straight away," the man said, then looked at Kelly. "I hope you enjoy it." Then he scurried away to ring up the sale, clearly wanting the business done before Kelly talked Micah out of the purchase.

"Oh," she said to the man's back as he left, "it's not for me..."

Her voice trailed off as Micah lifted the necklace from the black velvet and turned to her.

Eyes wide, Kelly looked horrified as she took a step back. "Micah, no."

Again, she surprised him. She hadn't even considered the possibility that the necklace was for her. "You said you liked it."

"Well," she said, "I'd have to be blind *and* stupid to not like it. That's not the point."

"You're right," he said, pushing past her reservations. "The point is, I want you to have it." He stepped behind her, laid the jewel at the base of her neck and ordered, "Lift your hair."

She did, but all the while she was shaking her head. "You can't just buy me something like this out of the blue—"

"Well," he said, voice low and teasing, "you did tell your grandmother that we were going to New York for a ring, so..."

"Micah." She turned her head to look at him, and he smiled at her to ease the worried look in her eyes.

When the necklace was secured around her neck, he

moved to stand in front of her. The emerald shone like green fire on her skin and he felt a swift tug of satisfaction seeing her wearing it. "It looks perfect."

"It would look perfect on a three-legged troll," Kelly argued, but her fingers reached up to touch the stone and her gaze slipped to a mirror on the counter to admire it. "It's beautiful, Micah. Seriously. But you don't have to do this. Buy me things, I mean."

No, she wouldn't expect that from him and he found that…refreshing. Most of the women he'd ever been with had anticipated trinkets like this. They'd oohed and aahed over jewelry-store windows or even, on occasion, dragged him inside to let him know in no uncertain terms which piece they'd most like to have. But Kelly didn't want anything from him. Didn't demand anything. She was happy just being with him, and that had never happened before.

And maybe that was why Micah had felt compelled to buy her that damn necklace. He wanted her to have something to remember him by. In a few months, he'd be gone from her life, but every time she looked at that necklace, she'd remember today and she'd…what? *Miss him?* Had anyone, anywhere ever missed him? Had he ever wanted them to? Questions for another time, another place, he told himself.

"I wanted you to have it," he said simply. "It's the same color as your eyes."

"Oh, Micah…" Those big beautiful green eyes filled with tears and, just for a second, he panicked. But Kelly blinked the moisture back and lifted her chin. "You don't want to make me cry. I look hideous when I cry. I'm a sobber. I don't do delicate weeping."

Of course she wouldn't cry. He chuckled—how could

he not? Kelly was one in a million at everything. "Good to know. I'll make a note. No making Kelly cry."

A wry smile curved her mouth briefly, then her shoulders slumped and a defeated sigh escaped her. "I can't stop you from doing this, can I?" she asked, still touching the cold, green stone.

"Already done, so no."

Nodding, she took a breath, let it out again and said, "Fine. Am I allowed to thank you?"

"Only briefly," he told her warily.

"Thank you, Micah," she said, going up on her toes to lay a soft, slow kiss on his mouth. "I've never owned anything more lovely. Whenever I wear it, I'll think of you."

His heart jolted. It was just what he'd wanted, yet hearing her say it he could almost hear the "goodbye" in her voice. He hadn't thought it would bother him, but it did. For the first time in his adult life, he wasn't looking forward to moving on. Frowning, he told himself he would. He had to. Eventually. But Micah didn't want to think about endings today.

Looking at her, the pleasure in her eyes, an emerald at her throat and a smile on that fabulous mouth of hers, all he could say was, "I'll think of you, too."

And he knew he'd never meant anything more.

Later that night, Kelly did a quick spin in place on her three-inch heels, sending the skirt of her new black dress flying. Then she stopped and looked up at Micah. "Today was so lovely. Thank you, Micah."

He shrugged. "It was fun."

It was a revelation, she thought but didn't say. She'd seen Micah in a whole new light. He was famous. Rich. Important. Everywhere they went, people scrambled to please him. Fans—mostly women—had stopped him on the street to coo over him, completely ignoring Kelly's presence. And she'd seen his reaction to all of the notoriety. It all made him uncomfortable. Sure, he was polite to everyone, but there was a cool detachment in everything he did that told Kelly he'd much prefer going unnoticed.

Micah lived a life that was so far removed from Kelly's they might as well have been on different planets. But, for now anyway, they were together. And maybe that was all she should think about.

She strolled across the terrace to the railing and lifted her face into the sea breeze that was soft and cool. Turning her head to him, she said, "I thought the maître d' at dinner was going to cry when you signed his book for him."

Micah poured them each a glass of champagne and carried them to her. Handing her one, he had a sip of his own. "I couldn't believe he had it with him at work."

She laughed and took a drink of the really fabulous wine. Shaking her hair back from her face, she sighed. "I can't believe I'm here. Not just California," she amended. "But here… Here. In this beautiful hotel. With you."

"I'm glad you are," he admitted, then frowned slightly as if he'd like to call the words back.

But it was too late, because Kelly heard them and held them close in her heart. He might not want to care about her, but he did. For now, that was enough for her. Neither of them had gone into this expecting anything but a release of sexual tension. And if she was feeling… more, then she'd just keep that piece of info to herself. He wouldn't want to hear it and she wasn't ready to admit it, anyway.

Pushing those thoughts out of her mind, Kelly turned from the railing, walked to the table and set her champagne flute down. When she turned back to Micah, she smiled and reached behind her back for the zipper. "I think we made a date for this terrace tonight, didn't we?"

She saw his grip on the fragile stem of the flute tighten. "Yeah. We did, didn't we?"

The zipper slid down with a whisper and she lifted both hands to hold the deeply scooped bodice of the dress against her. "And you're sure no one can see us?"

He took a drink and speared her with a look that was so hot, so barely contained, his brown eyes burned with it. "Private terrace. No neighbors. Empty ocean."

"Okay then." Kelly took a breath and let the dress drop to pool at her feet. She'd never done anything like this, and she felt both excited and exposed. But Micah's gaze on her heated her through, and she forgot about feeling self-conscious and instead enjoyed what she was doing to him.

On that shopping trip with Terry, Kelly had indulged in some new lingerie, as well. His expression was all she'd hoped for.

Micah's gaze moved up and down her body before settling on her eyes again. "You're killing me."

"You like?" He more than liked and she knew it.

"Yeah," he ground out. "You could say so. One point for the black lace."

Kelly grinned. "Nice! That makes it four to two, my favor."

"You keep dressing like that, I'll give you all the points you want."

She shook her head slowly and said, "But didn't you say that in your dream I was naked?"

"So you *are* trying to kill me."

"No," she assured him. "Just torture you a little." Slowly she peeled out of the black lace bra, dropping it onto the nearest chair. And, leaving her high heels on, she slipped out of the matching scrap of her panties and stood there with the ocean breeze drifting across her skin like a lover's hands.

"Well," she asked softly, "as good as the dream?"

"Better," he told her, and bent to take a kiss while his hands cupped her breasts, rolling her nipples between his thumbs and forefingers.

Kelly groaned and leaned into him, loving the feel of his hands on her skin. The taste of his mouth on hers. She felt completely wicked and absolutely wonderful.

He dropped one hand to her core and she parted her thighs for his touch. Micah had shown her more about herself, what her body was capable of, than she'd ever have believed possible. And now she wanted him all the time. Craved what happened between them when they were together. He stroked her, explored her, and she whimpered with need as an oh-so-familiar tension crept through her.

His thumb moved over that one sensitive spot and she gasped, moving her hips, trying to feel more, faster. He pushed one finger, then two, inside her and Kelly groaned again, clutching his shoulders, holding on while her body went on another wild ride courtesy of Micah Hunter.

The cold air brushed against her while his warm hands stoked fires inside her. Over and over, he touched, caressed, until she was just on the brink of a shattering climax. Then he stopped and she nearly shrieked.

"Micah—don't—"

"Wait." He lifted her, plopped her onto the table then, as she watched, he parted her thighs and knelt in front of her.

"What're you— Oh, Micah…"

Beneath her, the heavy metal table was cold against her behind, but she didn't feel cold. She felt as if she were on fire. Then Micah covered her center with his mouth and Kelly cried out in surprised pleasure. His lips, tongue and teeth drove her crazy. She threaded her fingers through his hair and held him to her as he continued his delicious torment.

He licked and suckled at the very heart of her, and the sensations rising inside her were powerful. Overwhelming. She had to hold on to him or she was sure she would have simply fallen off the face of the earth. She rocked helplessly in place as he pushed her so high there was no higher to go. Then the crash came and Kelly cried his name in a broken voice and let the sound drift away into the night wind.

Still trembling, she locked her eyes on his as he stood up and looked down at her. "Point to you," she whispered. "That was—"

"Four to three then," he said, scooping her off the table to cradle her close. "I'm catching up."

She smiled because she felt so darn good, but Kelly looked up at him through glazed eyes as she admitted in a whisper, "I've never— I mean no one…"

"I know what you meant," he said softly, his gaze locked with hers. "And if you're interested, there are a lot more firsts headed your way."

"I love to learn," she said, reaching up to briefly cup his face in the palm of her hand. Kelly laid her head on his chest as he carried her through the spacious living area into their bedroom.

Whatever he had in mind, Kelly was ready for it.

The following night, Micah and Kelly had dinner with Sam and Jenny Hellman, then the four of them took a walk around the hotel property. Both women were strolling slowly ahead of the men, and Micah could only guess they were still bonding over their favorite romance author.

Since Sam and Jenny had arrived, the four of them had spent a lot of time together, and Micah was pleased at how well Jenny and Kelly were getting along. Though why it mattered, he told himself, he couldn't have said. It wasn't as if they were all going on vacation together. And unless Sam and Jenny rented the Victorian for ski season again, they wouldn't be seeing each other after this weekend. Once Micah had moved on, none of the others would have any reason to meet. So why did it matter to him that the people he was closest to were becoming friends?

Hell, he didn't know. But that was typical. Since meeting Kelly, Micah had felt off his game. Off balance. And she was doing it to him. Micah's gaze locked on Kelly. She wore a bright yellow dress that made her look like a lost sunbeam in the night. Her hair was long and loose and the wind kept lifting it, as if teasing her. Something inside him stirred and warmth spread through his chest.

"You're sleeping with her, aren't you?"

"None of your business," Micah said tightly, and he knew that was as good as saying *yes*.

"Ah, touchy." Sam nodded thoughtfully. "That's interesting."

"What're you talking about?" Micah kept his gaze straight ahead because looking at Kelly was more fun than looking at Sam.

"Just that you've never minded talking about your women before..."

Micah ground his teeth together. "She's not one of my women," he said. "She's Kelly."

"Also interesting." Sam smiled to himself. "Getting attached, huh?"

"No." He was definitely not getting attached. Of course he cared about her. But there was nothing more than that because he wouldn't allow it. "Leave it alone, Sam."

"Not gonna happen." His old friend punched him in the shoulder and said, "For the first time, you've brought a girl home."

Micah snorted. "Are you crazy?"

"Come on. We both know Jenny and I are as close to family as you've got, and here we are, the four of us, bonding nicely. So I think that says something."

"And I think you should stick to being an agent," Micah told him. "Because the fiction you dream up sucks."

Sam laughed and waved one hand at his wife when Jenny turned around to look at them. "Why not just admit that you and Kelly have something good together?"

Micah sighed and fixed his gaze on Kelly again. The way her hair fell around her shoulders. Her long legs, the way that yellow dress clung to her curvy body. Everything about her appealed to him. And that was enough to make him wary. She was the only woman he'd ever met who had tempted him to look deeper. That made her dangerous.

"Because what we have is temporary." Saying it aloud reinforced what he knew was pure truth. There was no future here.

"Well, I like her."

"Yeah," Micah said grimly. "So do I."

"Well, you don't sound too happy about it."

Micah scowled and wasn't sure if he was directing the expression at his friend or himself. "Why should I be? You know as well as I do I'll be leaving in a few more months."

Although, as he said it, Micah realized that moving on didn't sound as good as it usually did. Strange. Normally, after three months in one place, Micah was already getting restless. Making plans for where he would go next. Polishing up one book and already plotting the next. That was his life. Had been for years. And it worked for him, so why would he even consider changing it?

"And your point is…?"

"Don't say *point*."

"What?"

"Never mind." Micah shook his head. He'd never be able to hear that word again without thinking of Kelly. What were they now? Four to three. He remembered how he'd been awarded that last point and his body went hard as stone.

"This is *temporary*," he said again, emphasizing that last word, more for his own sake than for Sam's.

Sam stared at him as if he had three heads. "It doesn't have to be, that's what I'm saying. Hell, Micah, you're already engaged to her."

And this engagement would end just like the last one, he told himself. Sighing, Micah stuffed his hands into his slacks pockets. “We explained the whole thing to you. It’s just a lie for Kelly’s grandmother’s sake.”

“Lies can become truths.”

Micah snorted. “No, they can’t.”

Sam shrugged. “Hey, look at it from my perspective. You guys get married, and Jenny, me and the kids have a place to stay every ski season.”

“That’s very thoughtful,” Micah said wryly.

Sam smiled as he watched his wife stumble, catch herself and keep walking. “Jenny could trip over air, I swear.” Sighing in exasperation, he said, “You and Kelly are good together, Micah. Why be in such a damn hurry to throw it away?”

Because he didn’t know what to do with it.

“You don’t buy gigantic emeralds for a woman you don’t give a damn about—and thanks for that, by the way. Jenny’s already reminded me that her favorite stone is a sapphire.”

Micah laughed a little and it felt good to ease the tightness in his chest. “That’s your problem. As for the emerald, I just wanted Kelly to have it. That’s all.”

They were walking through the hotel gardens and past the pool where a couple dozen people splashed in the aquamarine water. The sky was clear, the air was warm and the ocean breeze was cool and damp.

“Why?” Sam asked. “Why’d you want her to have it?”

“Because,” Micah said in exasperation. “Just...because.”

Sam laughed and Jenny turned around to look at him. He waved her off again and said, “Damn, Micah. No wonder I can get you so much money for your books. You’ve got a real way with words.”

“Drop it, Sam.”

Sam stopped. He was a couple inches shorter than Micah, a little heavier and a lot more patient. "Just admit it, man, she's got you. You care about her."

"Of course I care. What am I—a monster?" Micah stared out at the black ocean. "She's a nice woman." *Lame*, he thought. "We have a good time together." *They had a hell of a lot together.* "I like her." *Like. Care.* Hell, even he didn't believe him.

"Must be love."

Micah's head snapped around and his gaze burned into Sam's. "Nobody said anything about love."

Shaking his head, Sam mused, "Damn, you react to that word like a vampire does to a cross."

"I've got my reasons," Micah reminded him.

"Yeah, you do," Sam agreed. He leaned back against the railing behind him, folded his arms over his chest and said, "I'm the first to agree you had a crap time of it as a kid. So I get why you've closed yourself off up until now."

"I hear a 'but' coming," Micah mused.

Sam slapped his shoulder. "That's because you're a very smart man. So here it is. *But*, how long are you going to use that excuse?"

Micah shot him a look that would have had most people backing up with their hands in the air. Not Sam, though.

He gave Micah a bored smile. "Please. Don't bother giving me the Death Stare. It's never worked on me."

Micah rolled his eyes. True. "Fine. But my past is not an excuse, Sam. It's a damn *reason*."

"Because you had a miserable childhood you can't love anyone? That's just stupid." Shaking his head, Sam said, "It's like saying you never had a burger when you were a kid so now you can't have a Big Mac."

Micah scowled.

"Basically, buddy," Sam continued, "you're letting a crappy past mess with your present and future."

Micah ground his teeth together so hard it was a wonder they didn't turn into a mouthful of powder. Having his past reduced to a stupid analogy didn't help the situation any, and Micah felt compelled to defend his decisions on how he chose to run his life. If he wanted to be a footloose wanderer with no connections to anyone, that was his call, wasn't it? If it sounded lonely all of a sudden, that shouldn't be anyone's business but Micah's. And it had *never* mattered to him before, so he'd get over it. He liked being alone. Liked the freedom. Liked being able to pick up and move and have no one miss him. Right?

He frowned to himself over that last thought. Would Kelly miss him when he left? Would she think about him? Because he damn sure knew he would be thinking about her. *Just another reason to leave.*

"Wow," he said finally, "thanks for the analysis. How much do I owe you?"

"This one's on the house," Sam said, ignoring the sarcasm. "At some point," he paused. "Sorry. Used the word 'point' again, and someday you'll have to explain why we're not using it anymore."

Micah choked out a harsh laugh, but Sam wasn't finished.

"You have to decide if you want a life—or if you'd just rather be somebody else's victim for-freaking-ever."

"I'm not a damn victim," Micah muttered, insulted at the idea.

"Glad to hear it," Sam countered. "Now, what do you say we catch up with our women and go get a drink?"

"God, yes."

Sam hustled on ahead to catch up with Jenny and Kelly. Micah smiled in spite of everything as his friend offered each of them an arm and then led them off toward the hotel bar. Kelly turned her head to smile at him, and even at a distance Micah's heart gave a hard jolt.

He hadn't planned on any of this. All he'd wanted was a quiet place to work for six months. He hadn't asked to have Kelly come into his life. And now that she was there, he didn't know what to do about it. Sam meant well, but he couldn't understand what drove Micah. How the hell could he?

When you lived a life in the moment, tomorrows just never came into play. So, like always, Micah wouldn't look to the future—he'd just make the best of today.

Luxury hotels, limos and five-star restaurants made for a wonderful holiday, but after two weeks back at home, it all seemed like a pretty dream to Kelly.

As soon as they'd got home, she had stepped right back into her routine as if she'd never left, and that's how Kelly liked it. Her time away with Micah had been wonderful, but being here in her small town with him was perfect. She never took off the emerald necklace he'd given her so that, even when she was busy with her different jobs and Micah was shut away in the Victorian working on his book, it was like she had him with her everywhere she went.

Micah.

"You're doing it again."

Kelly jumped guiltily and grinned at Terry. "Sorry, sorry."

"Where were you?" Terry held up a hand. "Nope. Never mind. I know that look. I have it on my face constantly when Jimmy's home."

Kelly sighed a little, took a sip of her latte and scooted closer to where Terry was rolling out dough for the next batch of cookies for her shop. The kitchen smelled like heaven and, like Terry, was organized down to the last cookie sheet stacked carefully on its rack.

Kelly kept her voice down so the girls running the counter out front couldn't hear her. "Terry, I've never—I mean, I had no idea that— Why didn't you tell me how amazing sex is?"

Terry laughed and shook her head. She picked out a cookie cutter and quickly, efficiently, stamped out a dozen shapes in the dough. Then she carefully lifted each of them to put on a cookie sheet for baking. "Honey, you were married, I thought you knew."

Feeling disloyal again, Kelly said, "It was never like this with Sean. I didn't know feelings could be so *big*. I mean," she said, sighed heavily and closed her eyes briefly to bring back the magic of Micah's hands on her skin. "What he does to me, it's..." She couldn't even find the words to explain and maybe that was best. "I just never want him to stop touching me."

Terry took a moment to fan herself with her hands. "Good thing Jimmy's calling me tonight because I'm dying of jealousy here." Then she took another long look at Kelly and said, "You're feeling guilty, too, aren't you? About Sean, I mean."

"A little." A lot. She didn't mean to compare the two men, but it was inevitable when what she felt with Micah was so much more than anything she'd ever known.

"You don't have to." Terry patted her hand. "Sean was

a sweetie, but it's not like you two were legendary lovers or anything."

"I loved him," Kelly said softly.

"Of course you did," Terry agreed. "In a nice, comfortable, safe kind of way."

Was that what her marriage had been, Kelly wondered? Had she simply married Sean because he'd made her feel safe and settled? If Sean had lived, would they have stayed together? Would they have been happy? Kelly sighed again. There were no answers, and even if there were, they wouldn't change anything.

"He loved you, too," Terry said. "Enough, I think, to want you to be happy, Kelly. So, if Micah makes you happy, then yay him!"

Kelly picked up a finished cookie and took a bite, thinking about what Terry said. "He really does, you know? Every day, it just gets better between us. He's funny and crabby and kind and, God, the man has magic hands. In California, we were together all the time and… look." Leaning in, Kelly reached beneath the collar of her T-shirt and pulled out the emerald.

"Holy Mother of Cinnamon!" Terry all but leaped over the marble counter to lift the emerald with the tips of her fingers. She looked from the stone to Kelly and back again. "Is it real? Of course it's real. Rich guys don't buy junk. I didn't know emeralds *got* that big, for heaven's sake. And those are diamonds…

"Oh my God, I can't believe it took you two weeks to show me!"

Kelly laughed at her friend's reaction. "I just—it's kind of embarrassing. I mean, I told him not to buy it—"

"Of course you did." Terry sighed. "Why are you embarrassed to show me?"

"Because it sort of felt like bragging, I guess."

"Why wouldn't you want to brag about it?" Terry lifted the emerald and turned it back and forth so that the light caught and flashed off it. "That is amazing. If it was mine, I'd wear it stapled to my forehead so everyone would see it."

Laughing, Kelly realized she should have shown it to Terry as soon as she got home. But hiding the necklace wasn't just about not wanting to show off.

It was about the unshakable feeling she had that the emerald had been Micah's way of saying goodbye. Of letting her know that he would be leaving but he wanted her to have something to remember him by. Being Micah, it just had to be an emerald-and-diamond necklace, but the point was, she worried that he was already pulling away.

She'd noticed it more after Sam and Jenny had shown up. It was as if having his friends there had somehow made Micah shut down, go into self-defense mode. Jenny had told her that she'd never seen Micah happier than he was with Kelly. But since their weekend away, he'd drawn more into himself. It was nothing overt, but she *felt* the distance he was slamming down between them, and she had no idea how to get past it.

Yes, this had all started as a lie to make her grandmother feel better, but it had become so much more for Kelly. And maybe, she told herself, this was Karma's way of punishing her for the lie. Make her feel. Make her want. Then deny her. But even if it was, she told herself, she still had three months with Micah and she wouldn't let him leave her emotionally before he actually left.

Ruefully, Kelly admitted, "I can't bring myself to take the necklace off. It's like as long as I wear it, Micah's mine."

"Oh, sweetie, you've got it bad, don't you?"

"I love him." Her eyes went wide and she gasped a little before saying, "Oh, God. I love Micah." Kelly slapped both hands to her stomach as if she were going to be sick. "How could I do this?"

"Are you kidding?" Terry demanded. "Have you *looked* at him lately? It's a wonder it took you this long to fall for him. And that's not even counting the jewelry and the great sex."

Kelly laughed, but it sounded a little hysterical, even to her. She hadn't meant to fall in love, and she knew all too well that Micah would be horrified if she confessed what she felt for him. Heck, he'd probably be nothing more than a blur on his way out the door if he thought she was in love with him.

This had just slipped up on her. She hadn't meant to love him. And it wasn't the luxury vacations. Or the necklace. Or the sex—okay, maybe the sex was part of it. But she'd fallen in love with the *man*.

The man who could look so surprised when she didn't react the way he expected. The man who helped her with her haunted maze. The man who stood with a little boy so he could say good-night to his pumpkin.

"Oh, God," she whispered again. "This isn't good."

"Honey," Terry reached for her hand and squeezed it. "Maybe he loves you, too."

"Even if he did, he probably wouldn't tell me." Kelly shook her head. He'd been pretty clear, hadn't he? One engagement in his past and no desire for another. She could still hear him… *No wife. No girlfriend. No interest.* She closed her eyes and took a breath to try to steady herself. It didn't work.

"This wasn't supposed to be about love, Terry," she

said, and was talking to herself as much as her friend. “This was just…”

“An affair?” Terry shook her head. “You’re just not the affair kind of person, sweetie. This was *always* going to end up with you in love.”

“You might have warned me,” Kelly said miserably.

“You wouldn’t have listened,” Terry assured her and carried the cookie sheet to the oven. She slid it inside, set the timer and came back again. “You might be upset over nothing. I’ve seen you guys together and he does feel something for you, Kelly. If it’s not love, it’s close. So, maybe he won’t leave when his time here is done.”

“I want to think that, but I can’t.” Kelly shook her head firmly. She’d already set herself up to have her heart broken. She wouldn’t make it harder by holding on to the hope that things would change. “If I believe he’ll stay, when he does eventually leave it’ll only be worse on me.”

“You could *try* to keep him here.”

“No.” Kelly had some pride, after all. She took another breath, squared her shoulders and lifted her chin. “If I had to *make* him stay then it wouldn’t be worth it, would it?”

Terry sighed. “I hate when you’re rational.”

Kelly laughed sadly. “Thanks. Me, too.” She finished off her latte. “He’s going to leave, and I’ll have to deal with that when it happens. For right now though, he’s here. And I’ve got to go. Micah went to the university library today to do some research—”

“He’s never heard of the internet?” Terry asked.

“He’s a writer,” Kelly said, with a sad smile. “He likes books. Anyway, I want to beat him home because I’m making dinner.”

“I thought you said you loved him,” Terry quipped.

“I’m not that bad,” Kelly argued, though she could

admit that she wasn't the best cook in the world, no one had died from eating what she made.

"Right." Terry turned and headed to the cooling racks. "Why don't I send some cookies home with you and then at least you'll have dessert."

"You're the best."

"So I keep telling Jimmy," Terry said with a wink.

The drive home only took a few minutes, but even at that, her faithful truck wheezed and coughed like an old man forced to run when all he wanted was a nap. Kelly sighed a little, knowing she'd be buying a new one soon.

Micah's car wasn't in the driveway, so Kelly took that as a good sign. She wasn't completely ready to face him yet. The whole *I'm in love* revelation had hit her hard and she needed a bit more time to deal with it.

Grabbing the grocery bags from the passenger seat, she headed into the kitchen through the back door. She had steaks, potatoes for baking, a salad and now the world's best cookies. After she put everything away, she opened a bottle of wine so it could breathe. Because, boy, she needed a glass of wine. Or two. Maybe it would help her settle.

She'd been married, been in love and, yet, this feeling she had for Micah was so huge it felt as if she might drown in it. And she couldn't tell him. Kelly had absolutely no desire to hand him her heart only to have him hand it right back.

She looked around the familiar kitchen as if she were lost and looking for a signpost to guide her home. Micah had stormed into her life with the promise to leave again in six months. Now she was halfway through that timeline and Kelly knew that nothing in her life would be the same without him in it.

"Oh, stop it," she told herself, slapping both hands onto the cold granite counter. "You're feeling sorry for yourself. You're missing him even though he's not even gone yet. So cut it out already." Nodding, she reacted to the personal pep talk by tucking her feelings away. There'd be plenty of time to explore them all later. But for now… "Grab a shower, and put on something easy to take off."

Wow. She was thinking about sex. Again. And had been since… "Micah came into your life, that's when."

Her stomach swirled again as she headed for the stairs. Nerves? Anticipation? Worry? She frowned a little. "Please don't be getting sick, that's all. There's enough going on without that. Besides, it's almost Halloween and there's way too much to do."

Kelly climbed the stairs, walked down the hall, turned into the big bedroom and stopped dead. "Who are you?"

The completely naked stranger propped up against Kelly's pillows stared at her. "I'm Misty. Who're you? Where's Micah?"

Nine

"Micah?" Kelly stared blankly at the woman. Why was she naked? Why was she here? In *their* bed? And mostly Kelly's brain screamed, *Why are you just standing there talking to her? Why aren't you calling the police?* All very good questions. And still, Kelly started with, "How did you get in?"

"The doors weren't locked." Misty sat up higher in the big bed, clutching the duvet to her bare breasts. Thick black hair fell in tousled waves around her shoulders. She had too much makeup on her wide blue eyes and her lips had been slicked a bright red. As for the rest of her, Kelly didn't want to know.

"You need to get dressed and get out of my house." Kelly folded her arms across her chest and tapped the toe of her boot against the rug. She was hoping to look intimidating. If that didn't work, the sheriff was next.

"*Your* house?" The woman sniffed and settled back more comfortably against the bank of pillows. "Micah Hunter lives here and I don't know what you're trying to pull, but he won't be happy when he comes home to find you."

God, Micah would be home any minute, too. Good thing? Bad? Who could tell?

"How do you know Micah?" Kelly had to wonder at the woman's complete confidence. Was she a girlfriend Micah hadn't told Kelly about? An ex, maybe?

"He's my soul mate," Misty declared dramatically. "I knew it the first time I read his books. His words speak to my *heart.* He's been waiting for me to find him and he won't appreciate *you* being here and spoiling our reunion."

Kelly shook her head. "Reunion?"

"We've lived lifetimes together," Naked Misty intoned with another touch of drama. "In each incarnation, we struggle to find each other again. At last now, we can be together as we were meant."

Baffled, Kelly could only stare at the woman. She was clearly delusional and that might make her dangerous. And she was *naked.* What was going—and that's when the truth hit her.

Naked Misty had to be one of the crazed fans Micah had told her about. He'd said they tracked him down and sneaked into hotel rooms. Sneaking into an unlocked Victorian had to have been a snap. Kelly was now alone with a crazy person who might at any moment decide that Kelly was her competition. She had to get Misty out of the house and she wanted backup for that plan. Finally, she pulled her cell phone from her back pocket.

"I'm calling the police if you're not out of this house in the next minute."

"You can't make me leave." Misty pouted prettily. She probably practiced the look in a mirror. "I'm not going anywhere until I see Micah. He'll *want* to see me," she said, letting the duvet slip a little to display the tops of a pair of very large breasts.

Irritated, Kelly realized she was going to have to burn the sheets, the duvet…maybe the bed. First, however, she had to get rid of Naked Misty.

"Kelly?" Micah's voice came in a shout from downstairs. "Are you here?"

"Well, backup's arrived. It seems you're about to get your wish," Kelly told the woman who was still pouting and using one hand to further tousle her hair to make the best possible impression. Without taking her eyes off the woman, Kelly shouted, "I'm upstairs, Micah. Could you come up?"

The tone of her voice must have clued him in that something was wrong. Kelly heard him come upstairs at a dead run, and when he swung around the corner into the room, he stopped right behind her.

"What the hell?"

"Micah," Naked Misty cried, then sat up straight, threw her arms wide in welcome and let the duvet drop, displaying what had to be man-made breasts of monumental proportions.

Kelly slapped one hand across her eyes. "Oh, I didn't need to see those."

"Me, neither," Micah muttered.

"Who's *she*?" Naked Misty demanded with a finger point of accusation at Kelly.

Micah gritted his teeth, then gave Kelly an apologetic

look before saying, "Kelly's my fiancée. Who the hell are you? No," he corrected. "Never mind. Doesn't matter."

"You're *engaged*?" Misty sputtered and still managed to sound outraged. Betrayed.

"Yeah," Kelly said, then pointedly used Misty's own words in retaliation. "His words speak to my heart."

"How can you be engaged to *her*?"

Insulted, Kelly countered, "Hey, at least *my* breasts are real."

Honestly, she might have laughed at this mess, but the situation was just too weird.

"That's it," Micah ordered, stepping past Kelly to stride to the bed. "Get up whoever you are—"

"Misty."

"Of course you are." He huffed out a breath. "Well, Misty, get out of my bed, get dressed and get out."

"But I *love* you."

"Oh, boy," Kelly murmured. She didn't know whether to feel sorry for Misty or Micah or all three of them.

"No, you don't love me." Micah glared down at the woman until Misty seemed to shrink into the covers.

Kelly's stomach churned. Yes, Misty was crazy and an intruder, but she'd told Micah she loved him and he'd brushed it off coldly. And she knew that he probably wouldn't accept her declaration any better.

His features were cold, tight, as he stalked across the bedroom, scooping up the woman's discarded clothes. He tossed them at her and Naked Misty's pout deepened.

"You're mean."

"Damn straight." He stood beside the bed, legs braced, arms folded across his broad chest, and gave Misty a look that singed even as it iced. "If you're not out of this house in two minutes flat, I'll have you arrested."

"But—"

"If you ever come back," he added, "I'll have you arrested."

Naked Misty was pulling on a shirt as quickly as she could, thankfully tucking away those humongous breasts. "I only wanted to tell you how I feel. I do *love* you."

Kelly was watching now and saw the miserable resignation on Micah's face, and she didn't know how to help. She felt sorry for Misty, but she felt sorrier for herself. Loving Micah was hard. Knowing he wouldn't want her to was even harder.

"You don't even know me." He moved out of the woman's way when she leaped out of the bed and dragged her jeans on. Once she was dressed, Micah gave her enough time to scoop up her shoes and grab her purse from a chair. Then he took her by the arm and steered her out of the room.

Kelly heard them taking the stairs, but she didn't wait for Micah to come back. The only way to get a handle on the strangest situation she'd ever been in was to return things to normal. She immediately began stripping the bed. When Micah returned, he helped her take the sheets and duvet off and put on fresh sheets. Through it all he was silent, but the expression on his face told Kelly he wasn't happy.

"Did Misty get away all right?"

"Yeah." He huffed out a breath. "What the hell kind of name is Misty?" He smoothed the sheet, still avoiding her gaze. Well, Kelly wanted things back to normal between them, too.

"This wasn't your fault, Micah." She pulled the top sheet taut and folded the top back.

"She only came here because of me," he said, reaching for a replacement duvet, this one brick red, and flipping it out to cover the mattress.

"Still doesn't make it your fault." Kelly stacked pillows in fresh cases against the headboard. "How did she even find you?"

"Easy enough." Scowling, he too tossed a few pillows onto the bed. "Like I told you. Social media is everywhere. Someone in Banner probably put it out on Facebook or Twitter that I was here. That's enough to get every nut in the world moving." Shaking his head, he smoothed wrinkles that weren't there. "She shows up in town, talks to a few people, finds out where I am and bingo. Naked in my bed."

That was just beyond creepy. Living your life knowing there were thousands of would-be stalkers out there, ready to hunt you down and barge into your life? Kelly shuddered. "I don't know how you deal with this stuff all the time."

"It's why I don't stay anywhere for very long," he said, walking around the end of the bed to come to her side. "And now that one has found me, others will be coming too. I can't stay, Kelly."

Panic blossomed in the center of her chest and sent out tendrils of ice that wrapped around her heart and squeezed. This was what she'd been feeling since their holiday in California. If Naked Misty hadn't shown up, it would have been something else. For whatever reason, Micah wanted to get away from Banner. From Kelly. "But…you haven't finished your book yet."

"I'm close though," he said. "I can finish it somewhere else."

She was losing him. Standing right in front of him and

he was slipping away. "Why should you have to move out because of a crazy person?"

He sighed, dropped both hands onto her shoulders and met her eyes squarely. "It's not just her. Things have gotten…complicated between us, and I think it'd be easier if I left early."

"Easier? On who?"

"On both of us," he said, and stepped back. "Better to stop this before things get more tangled up."

But she wanted those three months. She wanted Micah here for the first snow, for Christmas. For New Year's Eve. She wanted him here *always.*

"Micah—" She broke off because anything she said now would sound like begging him to stay and she couldn't bring herself to do it. Couldn't make herself say *I love you*, either. He wouldn't believe her any more than he had Misty. Or, worse, he *would* believe her and feel sorry for her, and she refused to put herself in the position of having to accept either reaction.

"It's the best way, Kelly." His gaze locked with hers, and though she tried to read what he was feeling, thinking, it was as if he'd erected a barrier across his eyes to keep her out.

"Halloween's in a few days," he said. "I'll stay for that, okay? I'd like to see the kids go through that maze after spending so much time building the damn thing…"

A few days. That was all she had with him. So she'd take it and never let him know what it cost her to stay quiet. To let him go without asking him to stay.

"I'd like that, too," she said, and forced a smile that felt brittle and cold. "Where will you go?"

"I don't know," he admitted, stuffing his hands into his

jeans pockets. "There's a hotel in Hawaii I like. Maybe I'll go there for a few months."

"Hawaii." Well, that couldn't be farther from Utah, could it? He was so anxious to be apart from her, he was sticking an ocean between them. Couldn't be clearer than that. "Okay, then."

He reached for her again but let his hand fall before he touched her, and that, Kelly thought, was so sad it nearly broke her heart.

"It's best this way, Kelly."

"Probably," she said, agreeing with him if only to see a flicker of surprise flash across his face. "Don't worry about me, Micah. I was good before you got here and I'll be fine when you leave." She wondered idly if her tongue would simply rot and fall out of her head on the strength of those lies. She picked up the dirty sheets and the duvet and held them to her like a shield. "I'll just go start the washing."

Kelly felt his gaze on her as she left the room, so she didn't look back. There was only so much she was willing to put herself through.

The morning of Halloween, Kelly had the black lights up and ready, the CD of haunted house noises—growls, moans, chains rattling and a great witch's cackle—loaded up and a mountain of candy for all of the trick-or-treaters.

She also had the same unhappy stomach she'd been dealing with for days. She wasn't worse, but she wasn't getting better, either. Which was why she'd made a quick trip to the drugstore. Not being a complete idiot, she didn't go to the mom-and-pop shop in Banner, instead driving down to Ogden to shop anonymously. One thing Kelly didn't need was the gossips in town speculating on if she was pregnant or not before she knew herself. At that thought, her stomach did another quick spin.

Micah was in his office typing away—pretty much where he'd been since Naked Misty had crashed into their lives uninvited, precipitating his announcement that he was leaving early.

The only time Kelly saw him lately was at night in bed. And though he might be trying to keep distance between them during the day, in the darkness Micah turned to her. Sex was just as staggering, but shadowed now with a thread of sorrow that neither of them wanted to talk about.

Kelly wanted to be with him as much as she could, but at the same time, whenever they came together, another tiny piece of her heart broke off and shattered at her feet. Seconds, minutes, hours were ticking away. All of her life she'd loved Halloween, and now for the first time, she hated it. Because he'd be leaving in the morning and Kelly was already dreading it.

She looked into the mirror over the bathroom sink and saw the misery in her own eyes. Her face was paler than usual, her freckles standing out like gold dust on vanilla ice cream. Kelly lifted her fingers to touch the cold surface of Micah's emerald as it shone brightly in the overhead light.

The tick of her kitchen timer sounded like a tiny heartbeat in the bathroom. *Tiny heartbeat.* Was it possible? Was she pregnant? And if she was, what then? When the buzzer sounded, letting her know the three minutes were up, Kelly shut down the timer, picked up the early-pregnancy-test stick and held her breath, still unsure what she was hoping for.

"A plus sign." She released that breath and giddily took

another one. "Plus sign means *pregnant.*" She laughed and suddenly she knew exactly how she felt about this. Kelly grinned at her reflection. All of her doubts and worries disappeared, washed away by a wave of pure joy. "You don't have the flu. You have a *baby. Micah's baby.*"

She couldn't stop smiling. The woman in the mirror looked like a fool, standing there with that wide grin on her face, but Kelly didn't mind. This was…amazing. The most amazing thing that had ever happened to her. When Sean died, Kelly had never intended to remarry, so she'd had to accept that she'd never have children. And that was painful.

Then along came Micah, who swept her off her feet and into a tangle of emotions that had left her reeling right from the first time he'd kissed her. The misery of the last few days, pretending she was all right with him leaving just slid off her shoulders. He was leaving, but he had also given her a gift. A wonderful gift. When Micah was gone, she'd still have a part of him with her. Always. She wouldn't be alone. She'd have her child and the memories of the man who'd given that child to her.

"I have to tell him," she said aloud, and looked down at the pregnancy test stick again as if to reassure herself that this was really happening. *It was.* Even though Micah was leaving, he had a right to know about his child. Her feelings were her own, but this baby, they shared.

Still smiling, she laid one hand over her belly in a protective gesture. "We'll be okay, you know. Just you and me, we'll be good."

Steeling herself, she nodded at her reflection, feeling new strength and determination fill her. When Micah left, her heart would be crushed. But she would have her baby to look after now and that was enough to keep her strong. "I'll tell him tonight. When Halloween's over. I'll tell him. And then I'll let him go."

Halloween was a rush of noise, laughter, shrieks and a seemingly never-ending stream of children. Micah had never done Halloween as a foster kid. And as an adult, he'd kept his distance from kids on general principle, so this holiday had never made much of an impact on him. Until celebrating it with Kelly.

Up and down the block, porch lights were on and pumpkins glowed. Even the two nosy sisters, Margie and Sally, were across the street sitting on their front porch. They were bundled up against the cold and sipping tea, but they clearly wanted to watch all the kids.

The pumpkins Micah had taken Kelly to buy on their first ride together were carved into faces and shining with glow sticks inside them. Orange lights were stretched out along the porch railing. Black crepe paper fluttered from the gingerbread trim on the house and twisted in the wind. Polyester spiderwebs were strung out everywhere, and ghosts were suspended from the big oak tree out front.

Kelly was dressed up, of course, as her idea of a farmer, in overalls, a long-sleeved plaid shirt and work boots. Her hair was in pigtails and the emerald peeked out from behind the collar of her shirt. From the porch Micah handed out candy to those who made it through the haunted maze. Kelly had stationed herself in front of the maze to walk the little kids through personally so they wouldn't be scared. Cries of "Trick or treat!" rang out up and down the block. Parents kept stopping to congratulate him on his engagement, and Micah had to go along with the lies because he'd promised.

He wondered, though, what all of these people would think of him tomorrow when he left town, supposedly walking out on Kelly? He frowned. Good thing he didn't care.

Passing out candy like it was about to be banned, Micah glanced around the yard and knew he was right to leave early. This wasn't his home. The sooner he got to a nice anonymous hotel the better. For everyone. Hell, he was handing out *candy.* He was carving pumpkins, for God's sake. Too much was changing and he didn't like it.

Even the tone of the book he'd been working on had changed. As if Kelly and what he'd found here with her had invaded even his fictional world. His heroine was now stronger, sexier, funnier than before. She stood up for herself and drove the hero as crazy as Kelly made Micah. Life was definitely imitating art. Or more the other way around.

"Micah!" A small hand tugged at the hem of Micah's coat, splintering his thoughts, which was just as well, since he had at least three hundred pounds of candy to give out.

Jacob, dressed like a lion, stared up at him. His lion's mane was yellow yarn and his nose had been colored black to match the whiskers drawn across his cheeks. "Are you scared cuz I'm a lion?"

"You bet." No point in dampening the excitement in the boy's eyes just because Micah was in a crap mood. "You make a good one."

"I can roar."

"I believe you."

"And you can come see my pumpkin all lit up, can't you? I put a happy face on it, but Daddy cut it cuz I'm too little to hold the knife."

"I will later," Micah said, wondering how he and this little boy had become friends. "Don't you have to go with your brothers to get more candy?"

"Yeah, and I can have lots my dad says even though Mommy says no cuz daddies are the boss when Mom's not looking my dad says and Mommy laughed at him but said okay."

Micah blinked. That was a lot of words for one sentence. He wondered what the kid would be like next year. Or the year after. The kid would grow up in this town, play football, fall in love, get married and start the whole cycle over again. But Micah wouldn't be there to see any of it. Soon Jacob would forget all about a friend named Micah. And wasn't that irritating? "No, it's not."

"What?"

He looked down at the tiny lion. "Nothing, Jacob. Go on. Find your brothers. Have fun."

"Okay!"

As he ran off, Micah looked around and realized that he didn't belong there. He wasn't a part of this town. He could pretend to be. But the truth was he didn't belong anywhere and that's how he liked it. Who the hell else could just pick up and take off for Hawaii at a moment's notice? He was damn lucky living just the way he wanted to, answering to no one. He liked his life just fine and it was time to get back to it.

Several minutes later, he saw Jacob's parents rush up to Kelly, talking fast, looking all around frantically. Something was wrong. Micah left the candy bowl on the porch and took the steps down through the crowd. "What's going on?"

Kelly looked at him, worry etched into her features. "Jacob's missing."

He snorted. “No, he’s not. He was just here a few minutes ago.”

Jacob’s mother, Nora, shook her head. “Jonas saw Jacob run into the woods. He was following a deer and Jonas ran to get us instead of going in after him.”

“It was the right thing to do,” her husband said. “Or they’d both be lost. You stay here, Nora, in case he finds his way out on his own. I’ve got my cell. Call me if you see him.” Then he looked at Kelly, Micah and a few of the other adults. “If we split up, we should be able to find him fast.”

Kelly pulled her cell phone out of her overalls, hit the flashlight app and looked up at Micah. “He’s only three.”

Micah was already headed to the woods, fighting a hard, cold knot that had settled in his gut. “We’ll find him.”

The woods were thick and dark and filled with the kind of shadows that lived in Micah’s imagination. It was the perfect setting for murder. Wisps of fog, moonlight trickling through bare branches of trees, the rustle of dead leaves on the ground and the quick, scuttling noise of something rushing through them. It was as if he’d written the scene himself. But it wasn’t so good for a lost little boy. They moved as quickly as they could, their flashlights bobbing and dancing in the darkness. Roots jutted from the ground and Kelly tripped more than once as they hurried through the trees.

Kelly called for Jacob over and over, but there was no answer. The flashlight beams looked eerie, shining past the skeletons of trees to get lost in the pines. *Where the hell was he? He hadn’t had enough time to go far.* Micah fought down his own sense of frustration and worry, but they came rushing back up. Anything could happen to a kid that size. His writer's mind listed every possibility and each was worse than the last.

He shouldn't have let the kid wander off to find his brothers alone.

"God," Kelly murmured, turning in a slow circle. "Where is he?"

"Hiding? Chasing the deer?" Micah strained his eyes, looking from right to left. "Who the hell knows?"

From a distance came the calls of the others searching for the little boy, and their flashlights looked like ghosts moving through the shadows. Micah had to wonder why Jacob wasn't answering. Was he hurt? God. Unconscious? In the next instant, Micah thought he heard something so he pulled Kelly to a stop.

"Listen. There it is again." He whipped his head around. "Over there."

"Jacob?" Micah shouted and this time he was sure he heard the little boy yell, "I'm lost."

"Thank God." Kelly ran right behind him and in seconds they'd found him. Jacob was scared and cold and his sneaker was caught under a tree root.

"The deer ran away," he said as if that explained everything.

Micah's heart squeezed painfully. "The deer doesn't matter. You okay, buddy? Are you hurt?"

"No," he said, "I'm stuck. And I'm cold. And I spilled my candy."

Kelly's flashlight caught his overturned pumpkin basket with the candy bars scattered around it. She quickly scooped them all up.

"See? Kelly's got your stuff and we can fix the rest," Micah said. "Kelly, call Jacob's dad. Tell him he's okay."

"Already on it," she said, and he heard her talking.

"Am I in trouble?" Jacob rubbed his eyes, smearing his whiskers.

Once he freed the boy's foot, Micah picked him up. "I don't think so. Your parents are probably going to be too happy to see you to be mad."

"Okay, good. I still need to get more candy." Jacob wrapped his arms around Micah's neck. "When we get back you wanna see my pumpkin?"

Kelly laughed. Micah caught her eye and grinned. Kids were damn resilient. More so than the adults they scared the life out of. He took a breath and slowly released it. With the boy's arms around his shoulders and Kelly smiling at him, Micah knew he'd become too attached. Not just to Kelly, but to this place. Even this little boy.

And as they left the shadows and stepped into the light again, Micah knew he'd stayed too long. He had to leave. While he still could.

A part of Kelly wanted to do just what he was sure she would. Cry, ask him to stay. But none of that would help. Just as she'd told Terry, if she had to force him to be with her, then what they had wasn't worth having.

She wouldn't tell him she loved him. He should know that already from the way they were together—and if he didn't, it was because he didn't *want* to know. So Kelly would keep her feelings to herself and remain perfectly rational.

Too bad it did nothing for the hole opening up in the center of her chest.

"I called for the jet," Micah said, stuffing his folded clothes into a huge black duffel. His suits were already in a garment bag laid out on the bed. Their bed.

"So you'll be in Hawaii late tonight."

"Or early in the morning, yeah." He zipped the bag closed, straightened up and faced her. His features were unreadable, his eyes shadowed. "Look, I know I said I was leaving tomorrow, but there's no reason to wait and I thought it would be easier this way."

Nothing about this was easy, but Kelly smiled. She would get through this. "Did you get everything?"

He glanced around the room, "Yeah. I did. Kelly..."

God, she didn't want him to say he was sorry. Didn't want to see sympathy in his eyes or hear it in his voice. She cut him off with the one sure way she knew to make him stop talking. "Before you go, I've got something you need to see."

His eyes narrowed on her suspiciously. "What is it?"

Kelly took a breath, pulled the test stick from her pocket and handed it to him. Still confused, he stared at her for another second or two, then his gaze dropped to the stick. "Is this—" He looked into her eyes. "You're pregnant?"

"I am. Thought I was getting sick, but no."

"We used protection."

"Apparently latex just isn't what it used to be." It was hard to smile, but she did it. Hard to keep her spirits up, but she was determined. Kelly took a step toward him. "Micah, I just thought you had a right to know about the baby. I—"

"How long have you known?"

"Since this morning."

"And you waited until I'm all packed and ready to go before you drop it on me?"

"Well," she said, her temper beginning to rise, "I didn't know you were leaving tonight, did I? Sprung that one on me."

"What's that supposed to mean?"

"Oh, come on, Micah." Her vow to remain rational was slowly unraveling. But then, she told herself, temper wasn't pitiful. "You know exactly what I mean. You wanted to catch me off guard so I wouldn't have time to plead with you not to go."

He stiffened. "That's not—"

"Relax. I'm not asking you to stay, Micah. Go ahead. Leave. I know you have to, or at least that you think you have to, which pretty much amounts to the same thing anyway. So go. I'm fine."

"You're pregnant," he reminded her.

Kelly laid both hands on her belly and for the first time that night gave him a real smile. "And will be, whether you're here or not. I'm *happy* about the baby. This is a gift, Micah. The best one you could have given me."

"A gift." He shook his head and paced the room, occasionally glancing down at the stick he still held. "Happy. My God, you and this place..."

"What're you talking about?" Now it was her turn to be confused, but she didn't like the cornered anger snapping in his eyes.

He shoved one hand through his hair. "You don't even see it, do you?" Muttering now, he said, "I told myself earlier that I didn't belong here and I know why. But you just don't get it."

"I don't appreciate being talked down to," Kelly snapped. "So if you've got something to say, just say it."

"You're pregnant and you're *happy* about it, even though I'm walking out and leaving you alone to deal with it."

"That's a bad thing? Micah—"

"You live in a land of kids and dogs." He choked out

a short laugh and shook his head as if even he couldn't believe all of this. "You paint pictures on windows, carve pumpkins." He threw up his hands. "You have nosy neighbors, deer in your garden and ghosts hanging from your tree, and none of that has anything to do with the real world. With the world I live in."

He was simmering. She could see frustration and anger rippling off him in waves and Kelly responded to it. If he was leaving, let them at least have truth between them when he did.

"Which world is that, Micah?" When he didn't speak, she prompted, "Go ahead. You're clearly on a roll. Tell me all about how little I know about reality."

He laughed, but there was no humor in the sound. Tossing the test stick onto the bed, he stalked to her side. "You want reality?" He looked down into her eyes and said, "I grew up in foster homes. My mother walked out when I was six and I never saw her again. I didn't have a damn friend until I met Sam in the navy, because I never stayed anywhere long enough to make one." His gaze bored into hers. "My world is hard and cruel. I don't have the slightest clue how to live in a land where everything is rosy all the damn time."

He was breathing fast, his eyes flashing, but he had nothing on Kelly. She could feel her temper building inside her like a cresting wave, and like a surfer at the beach, she jumped on board and rode it.

"Rosy?" Insult stained her tone as she poked him in the chest with her index finger. "You think my world is some cozy little space? That my life is perfect? My parents died when I was little and I came here to live when I was twelve. Then my grandfather died. My *husband* died. And my best friend's husband is in danger every day he's deployed."

He swiped one hand across his face. "God, Kelly..."

"Not finished," she said, tipping her head back to glare at him. "Life happens, Micah. Even in *rosy* little towns. People die. Three-year-olds get lost in the woods. And men who don't know any better walk away."

His jaw was tight and turmoil churned in his eyes. "Damn it, Kelly, I wasn't thinking."

She heard the contrition in his voice, but she couldn't let go of her anger. If she did, the pain would slide in and that might just finish her off. Thank God she hadn't told him she loved him—that would have been the capper to this whole mess.

"You're the one who doesn't get it, Micah," she said. "Bad things happen. You just have to keep going."

"Or you stop," he countered. "And back away." Micah shook his head. "I don't know how to do this, Kelly. You. This town. A *baby*, for God's sake. Trust me when I say I'm not the guy you think I am."

"No, Micah," she said, feeling sorrow swallow the anger. "You're not the guy *you* think you are."

He snorted and shook his head. "Still surprising me." He walked to the bed, picked up his bags and stood there, staring at her. "Anything you need, call me. You or the baby. You've got my cell number."

"I do," she said, lifting her chin and meeting his gaze steadily. "But I won't need anything, Micah. I don't want anything from you." All she wanted was *him*. But she realized now she couldn't have him. Her heart was breaking and that empty place in her heart was spreading, opening like a black hole, devouring everything in its path.

She felt hollowed out, and looking at him now only made that worse. He was close enough to touch and so far away she couldn't reach him.

"Goodbye, Kelly," he said, and, carrying his bags, he walked past her.

She heard him on the stairs. Heard the front door open and then close, and he was gone.

Dropping to the end of the bed, Kelly looked around the empty room and listened to the silence.

Ten

By the following afternoon, Kelly had most of the Halloween decorations down and stacked to be put away. This chore used to depress her, since the anticipation and fun of the holiday was over for another year. But today she already felt as low as she could go.

"I still can't believe he left, knowing you're pregnant."

Kelly sighed. She'd told her best friend the whole story and somehow felt better the more outraged Terry became. But it had been an hour and she was still furious. "Terry, he was always going to leave, remember?"

"Yeah, but *pregnant* changes things."

"No, it doesn't."

"Plus," Terry added, "I can't believe you're pregnant before me. Jimmy's got his work cut out for him when he gets home."

Kelly laughed as Terry had meant her to. What did

people without best friends do when the world exploded? Her mind wandered as she rolled up the orange twinkle lights from the porch and carefully stored them in a bag marked for Halloween.

She'd done a lot of thinking the night before—since God knows she hadn't gotten any sleep—and had come to the conclusion that she'd done the right thing. Kelly didn't want Micah to stay because of the baby. She wanted him to stay for *her*.

"If he had stayed because I'm pregnant," she told Terry, "sooner or later, he'd resent us both and *then* he'd leave." Shaking her head firmly, she said, "This way is better. Not great, but better."

"Okay, I get that, and I hate it when you're mature and I'm not," Terry said. "But I'd still feel better if Jimmy were here and I could tell him to go beat Micah up."

Kelly laughed, hugged her best friend and said, "It's the thought that counts."

Her cell phone rang and she cringed at the caller ID. Looking at Terry, she said, "It's Gran."

"Oh, boy." Shaking her head, Terry said, "Let's go inside. You can sit down and I'll make some tea."

As the phone continued to ring, Kelly mused, "It's a shame I can't have wine because, boy, after this conversation, I'm going to need some."

Kelly wasn't looking forward to breaking this news to her grandmother, but she might as well get it over with. She followed Terry into the house and answered the phone. "Hi, Gran."

"Sweetie, I found the prettiest wedding dress—it would be perfect on you. I'm going to send you the picture, okay, and I don't want to interfere, but—"

Kelly sat down at the table and winced at Terry, already moving around the kitchen. Bracing herself, she interrupted her grandmother's flow. "Gran, wait. I've got something to tell you."

"What is it, dear? Oh, hold on. Linda's here, I'm putting you on speaker."

Great. Kelly sighed and winced again. "Well, the good news is, I'm pregnant!"

Terry frowned at her and mouthed, *Chicken*, as she wandered the kitchen making tea. Kelly set the phone on the table, hit speaker and her grandmother's and Aunt Linda's voices spilled into the room.

"Oh, a baby!"

"That's so wonderful," Linda cooed. "You know my Debbie keeps telling me she's going to one of those sperm banks, but she hasn't done it yet. You should talk to her, Kelly."

Terry laughed and once again, Kelly felt bad for her cousin Debbie. First an engagement and now a baby. She was putting a lot of pressure on Debbie and Tara.

"Oh, Micah must be so excited," Gran said.

"Yeah," Terry threw in. "He's thrilled."

Kelly scowled at her. *Not helping.*

"That's the thing, Gran," Kelly said quickly. "The bad news is that Micah and I broke up."

"What?" Twin shrieks carried all the way from Florida, and Kelly had the distinct feeling she might have heard the two women without the phone.

Terry set out some cookies and brewed tea while Kelly went through the whole thing for the second time that day. A half hour later, Gran and Aunt Linda were both fuming.

"I'll get Big Eddie to go out there and give that boy a punch in the nose."

"Oh, for heaven's sake, Linda," Gran said. "Big Eddie's seventy-five years old."

"He's tough, though," Linda insisted. "Spry, too and I have reason to know."

"Spry or not, you can't ask the man to fly somewhere just to punch someone, no matter how badly he deserves it," Gran snapped.

Terry set cups of tea on the table, then gave two thumbs-ups in approval.

"No one needs to beat anybody up," Kelly said, sipping her fresh cup of tea. "I had no idea my family was so violent. Terry already offered to have Jimmy do the honors."

"Terry's a good girl, I always said so."

"Thanks, Gran," Terry called out.

"What are you going to do about all of this, Kelly?" Gran asked.

"I'm gonna have a baby," she said, then added quickly, "and I'm going to be fine, Gran. I don't want you rushing home to take care of me."

"She's got me right here," Terry said.

"This just doesn't seem right, though," Gran mumbled. "You shouldn't be alone."

Kelly ate a cookie and thought about another one.

"Get a clue, Bella," Linda told her. "The girl doesn't want you there hovering. She's got things to do, to think about, isn't that right, Kelly?"

If she'd been closer, Kelly would have kissed her aunt. "Thanks, Aunt Linda. Honest, Gran, I'm fine. Micah's doing what he has to do and so am I."

"I don't like it," her grandmother said, then sighed. "But you're a grown woman, Kelly, and I'll respect your decisions."

Terry's eyes went wide in surprise and Kelly stared at the phone, stunned. "Really?"

"You'll figure it out, honey," Gran said.

"You will," Linda added. "And if you need us for anything, you call and say so. A great-grandchild's something to celebrate, like I keep telling Debbie."

"This one's mine," Gran pointed out.

"Oh, you can share," Linda said. "I'll share when Debbie finally comes through."

Terry was laughing and Kelly almost cried. She'd been hit by a couple of huge emotional jolts in the last twenty-four hours, but the bottom line was that she had her family. She wasn't alone. She just didn't have Micah.

And that was going to hurt for a long time.

For a solid week, Micah holed up in his penthouse suite. He couldn't work. Couldn't sleep. Had no interest in eating. He lived on coffee and sandwiches from room service he forced down. A deep, simmering fury was his only companion and even at that, he knew it was useless. Hell, *he* was the one who left. Why was he so damn mad?

The second week gone was no better, though anger shifted to worry and that made him furious, too. He hadn't wanted any of this. Hadn't asked to care. Didn't want to wonder if Kelly was all right. If the baby was okay. And it was November and that meant snow for her, and he started thinking about her broken-down truck and her riding around in it, and that drove him even crazier.

Micah wasn't used to this. Once he moved on from a place, he wiped it from his mind as if it didn't even exist anymore. He was always about the next place. He didn't do the past. He moved around on his own and liked it.

He didn't *miss* people, so why the hell did he wake up every morning reaching for Kelly in that big empty bed?

"You Kelly Flynn?"

The burly man in a blue work shirt and khaki slacks held a clipboard and looked at her through a pair of black-framed glasses.

"Yes, I am. Who're you?"

"I'm Joe Hackett. I'm here to deliver your truck?"

"My what?" Kelly stepped onto the porch of the cottage and looked out at the driveway. Parked behind her old faithful truck was a brand-new one. November sunlight made the chrome sparkle against the deep glossy red paint. It was bigger than her old one, with a shorter bed but a longer cab with a back seat bench. It was shiny. And new. And beautiful. Kelly loved it. But it couldn't be hers. "There must be some mistake."

"No mistake, lady," Joe said. "Sign here and she's all yours. Paid for free and clear including tax and license."

She looked from the truck to the clipboard and saw her name and address on the delivery sheet. So not a mistake. Which could mean only one thing. Micah had sent it.

He'd been gone two weeks. The longest two weeks of her life. And, suddenly, here he was. Okay, not *him*, but his presence, definitely. Tears filled her eyes and she had to blink frantically to clear her vision. What was she supposed to think about this? He leaves but buys her a new truck? Why would he do it?

"Lady? Um, just sign here so we can get going?" He was giving her the nervous look most men wore around crying women.

"Right. Okay." She scrawled her name on the bottom line and took the keys Joe handed over. As he and another guy left in a compact car, Kelly walked to her new truck. She ran her hand across the gleaming paint, then opened the driver's-side door and got in. The interior sparkled just as brightly as the outside. Leather seats. Seat warmers. Backup camera. Four-wheel drive. She laughed sadly. The truck had so many extras it could probably drive itself.

"Micah, why?" She sat back and stared through the windshield at the Victorian. Her fingers traced across the surface of the emerald she still wore, and she wondered where he was now and if he missed her as much as she missed him.

Micah hated the hotel. He felt like a rat in a box.

The penthouse suite was huge, and still he felt claustrophobic. He couldn't just step outside and feel a cold fall breeze. No, he'd have to take an elevator down thirty floors and cross a lobby just to get to the damn parking lot.

He didn't keep the doors to the terrace open because they let in the muffled roar of the city far below. He'd gotten so used to the quiet at Kelly's place that the noise seemed intrusive rather than comforting.

Three weeks now since he'd left Kelly, and the anger, the worry, the outrage had all boiled down into a knot of guilt, which made him mad all over again.

What the hell did he have to feel guilty about? She'd known going in that he wasn't going to stay. And if she'd wanted him to stay why didn't she say so?

No. Not Kelly. *I'm fine. I have the baby. We don't need anything from you.*

"Perfect. She doesn't need me. I don't need her. Then we're both happy. *Right?*" Was she driving that new truck? Had it snowed yet? Had she gotten the plow blade attached to the new truck? Was she out plowing people's roads and drives? Was she doing it alone?

God, he hated this room.

Pregnant.

She was carrying *his* kid, and what the hell was he supposed to do about that? If she'd wanted his help, she would have said so. But she didn't beg him not to leave. Hell, she hadn't even watched him go. What the hell was that about? Did she just not give a damn?

Irritation spiking, he grabbed his cell phone, hit the speed dial and waited for Sam to answer.

"Hi, Micah. What's up?"

What *wasn't* up? Micah hadn't talked to Sam since leaving Utah mainly because he just hadn't wanted to talk to anyone, really. Now he'd been alone with his own thoughts for too long and needed…something. He pushed one hand through his hair, walked to the open terrace doors and stared out at the ocean. The last time he'd had an ocean view, he'd been on a different terrace. With Kelly. And *that* memory would kill him if he started thinking about it. So he didn't.

"Kelly's pregnant." He hadn't meant to just say it, but it was as if the words had been waiting for a chance to jump out.

"That's great. Congratulations, man."

He scowled. "Yeah, thanks I guess. Kelly told me about the baby the night I left."

"You left? Where the hell are you?"

"Hawaii." Paradise, his ass. There was too much sunshine here. People were too damn cheerful.

"Why?"

"Because it was time to go." Micah scrubbed one hand

across his jaw and remembered he hadn't shaved in a couple weeks. "I couldn't stay. Things were getting too—"

"Real?" Sam asked.

He frowned at the phone. "What's that supposed to mean?"

"It means that you've never lived an ordinary life, Micah. You went from your crap childhood to the navy to posh hotels."

Micah scowled into the wide mirror over the gas fireplace as he listened.

"You've never had a real woman, either. All those models and actresses? They weren't looking for anything more than you were—one night at a time." Sam paused. "Trust me when I say that has nothing to do with the real world."

God, hadn't he thrown practically the same accusation at Kelly that last night with her?

"What's your point?" God. *Points.* He rubbed his eyes tiredly. They felt like marbles in a bucket of sand.

"My point is—Kelly is *real.* What you had there mattered, Micah, whether you admit it or not, and I think it scared the crap out of you."

"I wasn't scared." He remembered telling little Jacob that everybody got scared sometimes. That included him, didn't it?

The realization was humbling.

"Sure you were," Sam said jovially. "Every guy is scared out of his mind when he meets the one woman who matters more than anything."

"I never said anything like that—"

"You didn't have to, Micah." He chuckled, which was damn irritating. "I've known you long enough to figure things out for myself. For example. When's the last time you left a hotel in the middle of a book?"

He blew out a breath. "Well…"

"Never, that's when," Sam told him. "You stay six months at every place you go. This time you bolt after three? Come on, Micah."

The man in the mirror looked confused. Worried. Was that it? Had he run from Kelly because she mattered? Because he was afraid? He turned away from the damn mirror because he couldn't stand to see the questions in his own eyes. "Look, I didn't call for advice. I just wanted you to know where I am."

"Great, but you get the advice anyway," Sam said. "Do yourself a favor and go back to Kelly. Throw yourself on her mercy and maybe she'll take your sorry ass back."

Micah glared at the room because it wasn't the Victorian. Because Kelly wasn't here with him. Because he was hundreds of miles away from her and he didn't know what she was doing. How she was feeling. "How the hell can I do that? What do I know about being somebody's father, for God's sake?"

"If nothing else," Sam said, "you know what *not* to do. And that's stay away from your own kid. You grew up without a father. That's what you want for your baby, too?"

Putting it like that gave Micah something to think about. He'd done to his kid exactly what his mother had done to him. "I'm no good at this stuff, Sam."

"Nobody is, Micah. We just figure it out as we go along."

"Well, that's comforting."

"Figure it out, Micah. Don't be an ass."

On that friendly piece of advice, Sam hung up, leaving Micah with too much to think about.

The first snow hit two days later, but it was a mild storm after warm days, so the snow wasn't sticking. Which meant Kelly didn't have to go out and clear any drives or private roads. Instead, she was cozy in the Victorian, enjoying the snap and hiss of the fireplace. She'd been staying in the cottage because she didn't want to torture herself with memories of Micah in the Victorian. But, with winter here, she wanted the fireplace, so she convinced herself that the only way to get past the pain of missing Micah was by facing it.

With a cup of tea, a book and the fire, the setting would have been perfect. If Micah were there.

The front door opened suddenly and Kelly's heart jolted. She jumped up, ran to the hall, and all of the air left her lungs as she stood there in shock staring at Micah. Snow dusted his shoulders and his hair. He dropped his duffel bag, slammed the front door and flipped the dead bolt. When he turned around and saw her, he scowled.

"Lock the damn door, Kelly. *Anybody* could just walk into the house."

She laughed shortly and seriously considered racing down the hall and throwing herself into his arms. It was only pride that kept her in place. "Anybody did."

"Very funny." Still scowling fiercely, he walked down the hall, took her arm and steered her into the living room.

"What're you doing, Micah?" She pulled her arm from his grip even though she wanted nothing more than to hold on to him. And she desperately wished she wasn't wearing her new flannel pajamas decorated with dancing pandas. "Why are you here?"

His gaze moved over her as if he were etching her image into his brain. Then he stepped back and stalked to the fireplace. Turning around to face her from a safe distance, he said, "You know, I thought I was doing the right thing."

"By leaving?"

"Yeah." He sighed heavily. Shaking his head, Micah stared down at the fire for a long minute before lifting his gaze to hers. "Kelly, I have no idea how to do *this*." He waved one hand to encompass the house, her, the baby and everything else that was so far out of his experience. "You know how I told you I was engaged once before? I said it didn't take?"

"Yes." She'd wondered about that woman in his past.

"I ended it because I didn't care enough. I figured I was incapable of caring enough," he ground out, and she could see that the words were costing him. "Then I met you."

Heat began to melt the ice that had been around her heart for weeks. Hope rose up in her chest, and Kelly clung to it but kept quiet, wanting him to go on. To say it all.

He threw his hands high, then snorted. "Hell, I've never known anyone like you. You made me nuts. Made me feel things I never have. Want things I never wanted."

"Thanks."

Micah laughed and shook his head. "See? Like that. You surprise me all the damn time, Kelly. I never know where I'm standing with you and, turns out, I like it."

"You do?"

"Gotta have it," he admitted, and swallowed hard. He

took a step toward her, then stopped. "The last three weeks I've been so bored I thought I was losing my mind. I was at a hotel I'd been in before and this time, I hated it. Hated that it was small and there was no damn yard with deer and kids running through it. Hated that it was so damn noisy—but the wrong kind of noise, you know?"

"No," she admitted, smiling. "What are you saying, Micah?"

"I'm saying—all I could think about was you. And the baby. And this place. But mostly *you.*"

Tears were coming and she couldn't stop them this time. Didn't even try. They rolled unheeded down her cheeks as Kelly kept her gaze fixed on the only man in the world for her.

"You love me," he said, pointing a finger at her.

"Do I?" she said, and her smile widened.

"Damn right you do." Micah started walking—well, *stalking* the perimeter of the room. "A woman like you… love shows. Not just the sex, though that was great, for sure."

"It was."

"But you were there. Every day. You laughed with me. You cooked with me." He glared at her. "Yet, when I tell you I'm leaving, you just say, have a nice trip and by the way I'm pregnant."

Kelly flushed. "Well, that's not exactly—"

"Basically," he snapped. "That was it. And I finally started wondering why you hadn't told me that you love me. Why didn't you use the baby as a lever to keep me here? Why didn't you beg me to stay?"

She stiffened and tried to look as dignified as possible in her panda pj's. "I don't beg."

"No," he said thoughtfully, his gaze locked with hers.

"You wouldn't. Just like you wouldn't coerce me to stay. You were way sneakier than that."

"Me?" Now Kelly laughed. "I am *not* sneaky."

"This time you were," he said, and walked across the room to her. "You let me go, knowing I'd be miserable without you. You didn't say you loved me because you knew I'd wonder about that. And you didn't tell me I loved you because you wanted me to figure it out for myself. You wanted me to be away long enough to realize I was being a damn fool."

"That was clever of me." Or would have been if she'd actually planned it. She swayed, bit her bottom lip and held her breath. "And did you? Figure it all out?"

"I'm here, aren't I?" He blew out a breath, grabbed her and pulled her in close to him. Wrapping his arms around her, he rested his chin on top of her head and whispered, "You feel so good. This—*us*—is so good. I love you, Kelly. Didn't know I *could* love. But maybe I was only waiting to find you."

"Oh, Micah..." She held on to him, nestled her head against his chest and listened to the steady beat of his heart. It was as if every one of her dreams was coming true. The last three weeks had been so painful. Now there was so much joy she felt as if she were overflowing. "I love you, too."

"I know."

She laughed and tipped her head back to stare at him. "Sure of yourself, are you?"

"I am now," he admitted. "And I'm sure about this, too. You're going to have to marry me for real. It's the only answer. I have to be here in this big old house with you. I need to be with you at Christmas. I have to help you run for mayor. And next year, Jacob and I will help you plant the pumpkin patch. I want to meet Jimmy—I think he and I can be friends when we bond over our crazy women."

Kelly's heart was flying. "I'll have to give you a point for that crazy proposal."

He grinned. "Not a proposal. Just an acceptance of your earlier proposal. Remember?"

"You're right. So, no points."

"No more points at all," he said softly. "Say yes and we *both* win."

Kelly laughed, delighted with him, with everything. "Of course, yes."

"Good." He nodded as if checking things off a mental list. "That's settled. I've got to ride with you when you start plowing and—" He stopped. "Did you like the truck?"

She laughed again, a little wildly, but she didn't care. "I love it, you crazy man."

"Huh. You plow snow, but I'm crazy." He shook his head and stared down at her with hope and relief and *love* shining in his eyes.

"I never should have left, Kelly," he whispered, "but in a way I guess I had to, because I never learned how to *stay.* But I want to stay now, Kelly. With you. With our kids…"

"Kids?" she asked hopefully. "Plural?"

He grinned. "It's a big house. We should do our best to fill it."

God, this was everything Kelly had ever wanted, and more. The firelight threw dancing shadows across Micah's face, making his eyes shine with hope and promise and love. "I love you so much, Micah. I'm so glad you came home."

He cupped her face in his palms and kissed her tenderly. "The only home I ever want is wherever you are. For the first and last time in my life, I'm in love. And I never want to lose it."

"You won't," she promised. "*We* won't."

He blew out a breath and said, "Damn straight we won't. Now. For part two of my brilliant plan."

"You had a plan?"

"Still do and I think you'll like it," he said, sweeping her up in his arms, surprising a laugh out of her. He sat down in one of the overstuffed chairs and held her on his lap. He frowned at her pajamas. "What are those? Dogs?"

"Pandas."

"Sure. Why not?" Shaking his head, he said, "I'm thinking we hire a jet and fly to Florida tomorrow—"

"Tomorrow?"

"—pick up your grandmother and your aunt, and then all of us go to New York for a week. Maybe the Ritz-Carlton. I think they'd like that place."

"What?"

He shrugged. "I've never had a family before. I'd like to get to know them. Have them meet Sam and Jenny and the kids, because they're as close to family as I've ever known. And while we're there, your grandmother can help you pick out that ring we talked about."

"Oh, Micah!" Many more surprises and her head would simply spin right off her shoulders. She threw her arms around his neck and kissed him hard and fast. Then something occurred to her. "We'd better call first, though."

"Why?"

"I told Gran and Aunt Linda that we broke up and

they were arranging for one of the seniors to fly out and punch you in the nose."

"More surprises," Micah said, grinning. "I'll risk it if you will."

"Absolutely," she said.

"I love you, Kelly Flynn."

"I love you, Micah Hunter," she said, melting against him. As he bent his head to claim another kiss, Kelly whispered, "Welcome home."

* * * * *

If you loved this sexy, emotion-filled romance from USA TODAY *bestselling author Maureen Child, pick up these other titles!*

THE TEMPORARY MRS. KING
HER RETURN TO KING'S BED
DOUBLE THE TROUBLE
THE COWBOY'S PRIDE AND JOY
THE BABY INHERITANCE

Available now from Mills & Boon Desire!

1017/51